# THE DUTCHMAN TRILOGY BOOK ONE

# THE DUTCH CENTURY

## Control of the Mediterranean Sea, and the Atlantic Ocean

I0646393

### BY
### CARL DOUGLASS
Neurosurgeon Turned Author Writes With Gripping Realism

PUBLICATION
CONSULTANTS
We Believe In The Power Of Authors

PO Box 221974 Anchorage, Alaska 99522-1974
books@publicationconsultants.com, www.publicationconsultants.com

ISBN Number: 978-1-63747-004-6
eBook ISBN Number: 978-1-63747-005-3

Manufactured in the United States of America

# FICTION

*Last Phoenix-A Novel of Betrayal and Revenge, A Story of the CIA's Phoenix Program*
*Saga of a Neurosurgeon Series,* **Six Books**

- *Young Coyote-Book One: Garven Wilsonhulme's Way to Success-No Quarter Asked and None Given*
- *Anything Goes-Book Two*
- *Heaven and Hell-Book Three: Garven Wilsonhulme Takes on All Comers in the Jungle of Modern Competition*
- *Long Climb-Book Four: Young M.D., Garven Wilsonhulme, Engaged in a Social Poker Game of Winner Takes All*
- *Academia: The Law of the Jungle-Book Five: Surgeon in Training, Garven Wilsonhulme, Fang-and-Claw Competition for Glory*
- *The Vulture and the Phoenix-Book Six: Neurosurgeon, Garven Wilsonhulme, the Final Great Fight*

*All in Jest-Renowned Neurosurgeon in the Fight of Her Life*
*Gog and Magog—Yawm al-Qiyamah, Yawm al-Din, The Day of Judgment*
*Finders Keepers, Losers Weep-A Novel of Innocence Betrayed and the Search for Restitution*
*Sheep Dog and The Wolf-A Story of Terrorism and Response, and the Sheep Dogs Who Protect*

*Trojan Horse in the Belly of the Beast, Three Books*

- *Though They Come From the Ends of the Earth-Book One*
- *Dancing with the Devil-Book Two*
- *Trojan Horse in the Belly of the Beast-Book Three*

*The Mysterious Alexandra Tarasova-Yusupov: A Novel of a Woman Who Was, as Churchill said, "a riddle, wrapped in a mystery, inside an enigma…"*

*The Rise and Fall of the Fifteenth Caliphate: The CIA giveth, and the CIA taketh away…*

*The Charlemagne Murders: The Murder of Six World War II Generals Leads to the Greatest Manhunt in History*

*The Dutchman Trilogy*

- *A Life of Adventure, Book One*

# NOVELLAS

## The Sybil Norcroft Series

- 1st Novella-*The End of the Beginning*

- 2nd Novella-*Uncharted Country, Uncertain Future*

- 3rd Novella-*Secrets*

- 4th Novella-*Secrets and Scandals*

- 5th Novella-*Decisions*

- 6th Novella-*Running with the Big Dogs*

## The McGee Series

- 1st Novella-*Friends at Homeland Security: McGee Meets Federal Resistance*

- 2nd Novella-*Crossing the Cult: McGee Confronts a Murderous Cult*

- 3rd Novella-*Wednesday's Child: McGee's Case of Orphanage Girls Taken by Traffickers*

- 4th Novella-*Death on a Pale Horse: McGee Investigates Murders on a Reservation*

- 5th Novella-*The Boss's Daughters: McGee Works for a Mob Boss*

- 6th Novella—*Another Whistle Blower: McGee and Big Pharma Criminals*

- 7th Novella-*Sybil Norcroft Meets the Devil-Sybil's Public Battle with Beelzebub the Magnificent*
- 8th Novella-*To Be or not to Be*
- 9th Novella-*The Oath*
- 10th Novella-*The Struggle*
- 11th Novella-*Rumors of Wars, Secession, and Trouble*
- 12th Novella-*War and the Endgame*

# NONFICTION

*On Evolution:* The Origin of Selection, Order,
Progression, and Diversity–out of print
*Something About Religion*—out of print

# DISCLAIMER

This book is fiction; the characters are the products of the author's imagination and are not persons who ever lived. Any resemblance to the characters and actual people, or of the story to actual events would be purely coincidental and unintentional.

# Author's Comment and Disclaimer:

This is historical fiction, with an emphasis on fiction. The historical background is as accurate as my research could produce with world events in the 17th century being generally accurate as to dates and actions. There are a few events described that occurred on different dates, but the author changed in order to keep the flow of the story in sync. It was a most remarkable era, and this novel could not begin to do justice to what went on in toto or even with its limitation to the exploits of the Netherlands, its expansions, commercial ventures, and its wars.

The main character is wholly a product of the author's imagination and is not intended to depict any person who ever lived, nor even a composite of real people. Nonetheless, every effort has been expended to make him a product of his era, its thinking, its avarice, and its great explorations and colorizations. The intent is for you, the reader, to enjoy a glimpse of the dynamic past and to gain an appreciation for the underpinnings of western civilization that took place in the seventeenth century. More than that, I hope you enjoy reading the book as much as I did writing it.

# AUTHOR'S NOTE ABOUT THE ORGANIZATION OF THE TRILOGY

There is a rough division of the novel into a first part covering the protagonist's early life, voyages, and adventures, a second part about his life of commerce and conflict in the Scent Islands, and the third part covering the man's life as a great white hunter in the southern African bush and his encounters with dangerous beasts and remarkable indigenous people. Because the amount of historical research, difficulties with languages, cultures, and the complex nomenclature of ships and maritime commerce in the Golden Age of the Netherlands, there will be a brief nonfiction presentation between most chapters to bring everyone up to speed and to allow the novel-in-chief to flow unhampered by short translations or explanations. This inclusion of historical explanations will be particularly useful in the third—African—segment of the story when people come together from the ends of the earth and have to find a way to communicate, to hunt, and to trade with each other—no mean feat. Finally–throughout the book–there are, of necessity, many foreign words and phrases. Again, to avoid an impediment to flow, some italicized foreignisms will be included in the post chapter explanatory note as needed.

# TABLE OF CONTENTS

# CHAPTER ONE

# THE NETHERLANDS
# AT THE BEGINNING OF THE 1600S

IN THE YEAR OF OUR LORD, 1621, THE MONTH OF MAY

Piet Corneliuszoon Van Brakel entered the world and the prominent Van Brakel merchant family on the twenty-first day of May. The tulips were beginning to fill the family's fields in a splendorous rainbow of colors that stretched for 247 *akkos* [100 acres] over some of the best ground in the lowlands. Piet was a large, robust child—the seventh in chronology—weighing nearly 8.2 *Amsterdams ponds* [*waaggewicht*] and measuring 0.5 *Amsterdams ells* from his crown to his heels. Fortunately for him, Greta Corneliuszen, his mother, could boast of being a fine producer of milk—enough to feed her three younger children, newborn Piet, and to serve as a wet-nurse for two less fortunately endowed young women in the parish.

Little new Piet was fortunate in the timing of his birth in terms of Dutch history and the family's rise in Amsterdam society as well. The Netherlands were becoming well established in their evolving Golden Age, and the Van Brakel family was advancing apace in the first quarter of the century. Father Cornelius Van Brakel and Mother Greta Van Brakel came from northern farmer stock with little to look forward to as the new century dawned. They married in 1599; and–in starting their own family–they decided on a considerably more adventurous course for their life. They moved from Leeuwarden in the north to Amsterdam in the south where commerce, trading, and maritime enterprises, were beginning to flourish.

The couple made a fateful decision a decade before Piet was born to sell their fairly comfortable business interests in favor of entering the rapidly growing, but still speculative, tulip growing and exporting industry. Now—ten years later—they were vindicated for their choice by their ascension of several rungs of the societal ladder and by the accumulating size of the numbers in their bank account.

The Low Countries were situated in a most favorable position among the countries of Europe, a favorability that fostered the tulip trade. The position lay perfectly at the east-west and north-south intersection for the bi-directional trade routes. The Van Brakels cautiously invested in the crossing of trade. The merchant marine—in which the Van Brakels and their partners in the Northern Provinces established a major position in the North Sea and Baltic, carrying rye and timber from East Germany and Poland which was shipped via Danzig; furs, wax, honey, pitch, tar, and timber, from Russia via Narva and Riga; copper, iron ore, weapons, and salt herring, from Sweden; salted cod, and timber, from Bergen in Norway.

In return they carried re—exports of English woolen textiles, salt (for preserving fish and meat) and re—exports of wine from France, Portugal, and Italy. Apart from these merchanting activities, they acted as carriers, e.g. between Danzig and Riga, when opportunities arose. wine from France, Portugal, and Italy, moving to the Baltics. In the opposite direction, the Van Brakels and their compatriot Dutch traders moved grain from the Baltics to the countries bordering on the Mediterranean and the Hanseatic League. Many of their friends were beginning to think about trading with the new American country. Trade with New Amsterdam was showing promise, but the jealous English were putting up impediments. Necessity led Cornelius to begin building his own fleet of ships when the established builders became overwhelmed with orders.

Tulips were quite new throughout the world, and for the burgeoning economies building without seriously destructive wars, such luxury items were becoming ever more profitable. The cost of growing and transporting them diminished rapidly due to Dutch efficiency. As Piet grew, his father took pride in being able to get his boy to work hard. He set the five-year-old and his older brothers to planting, weeding, irrigating, and picking, them at just the right moment for export. Piet was quicker and cleverer than his brothers. He also balked less than they did against the demands of their hard task-master of a father. Even at such a young age, Piet was able to rationalize that his efforts made a real contribution to the income that made the life of his family so comfortable. He was a curious boy and liked to learn.

During the next ten years—from 1626 to 1636 tulips rapidly became a coveted luxury item, and a profusion of varieties followed, each more desired than its predecessors and were consequently more expensive and profitable. Greta and the girls–Hillegont, Femma, Vrouwtje, Hilletje (also called Hilda), Ytje, and Geertje–became adept packers, publicists, and communicators, with actual and potential customers. That necessitated that everyone in the family become a fairly accomplished polyglot. Each year the list of faithful customers grew, and it appeared that the family had found the goose that laid the golden egg. There was every reason to presume that the tulip business would continue to improve with each passing year.

Greta, Ytje, and Geertje traveled as often as possible to discover hardier, faster growing, and more exotic, tulips from everywhere in the Low Countries, and later to England and France. Father Cornelius balked at the cost of the travel, at the girls' exposure to foreign temptations, and because of his innate fear of overreaching and of losing everything. He was a born worrier.

Greta was a short, stout, golden haired, Saxon of a woman. She was almost moon-faced with red cheeks, naturally full pink lips, and was more buxom than any other woman they knew in Amsterdam—probably owing (at least in part) to her generous gift as a wet-nurse. She had strong round arms and legs, short fingers with carefully cut short nails. She habitually chose as her daily mode of dress rather conservative clothing made in Holland rather than in France, England, or Russia as the fashions were beginning to dictate.

From the early years of her marriage, Greta was strongly religious. She held to the older fashion of bodices with very high necklines. Other women in her social set were beginning to appear in public in the shockingly low, rounded necklines with short wings at the shoulders. Like her friends, Greta usually wore separate cartwheel ruffs with a standing collar. The collar was something of a bother since it required support by a small *supportasse* for casual wear, which was most of Greta's needs. She did give in to hiring a series of servant girls from some of the country farms to make dressing more efficient.

She continued to wear long sleeves with deep cuffs matching the ruff for several years after they went out of style. The cartwheel ruff disappeared among the fashionables in London around 1613, but Greta held on for another five years. She finally gave in and discarded her ruffs in favor of the newer wired *rebatos*.

"Well, my Pumpkin," Cornelius greeted his wife with a big smile when she returned from a buying trip to Belgium in 1628, "what new and expensive tulips that I won't like, have you bought this time?"

She smiled indulgently at Cornelius's crude attempt at humor, knowing that he was unaware of the little hurts he was inflicting.

"Let me explain, my dear. I have separated the purchases—all bulbs, identifiable and separable only by drawings. There are single-hued tulips of red, yellow, or white—*Couleren*; multicolored *Rosen* which have white streaks on a red or pink background; and *Violetten* which you see from the drawings have white streaks on a purple or lighter lilac background. Aren't they beautiful?"

"And these four boxes, what secrets do they hold, my dear Greta?"

"Oh," she said almost dismissively, "some called *Bizarden* or *Bizarre*."

"And?" he asked, detecting a tell from his wife's tightened lips that she was withholding something from him.

Greta Van Brakel was not a capable *Klaverjassen* player at all. Her face betrayed her.

She fidgeted a moment before answering. Cornelius knew his wife too well. He raised a quizzical eyebrow.

"Oh, all right. I have some very rare, very valuable, quite fragile, bulbs. *Bizarden* are exotic, truly lovely. They have yellow or white streaks on a red, brown, or purple, background. The multicolor effects of intricate lines and flame-like streaks on the petals are vivid and spectacular, and highly sought after."

She reached into one of the *Bizarden* boxes and extracted a dried plant with attached bulb from among the separated bulbs that produced the exotic-looking plants.

"The tulip flowers are very popular among the wealthy and the aristocracy. This is partly because of the appearance of the bulbs themselves. People now really seek the exotic and are trying to understand the tulip industry and how to get involved."

"Are you sure these paintings are entirely accurate, Greta. The petals look…different…like they were somehow broken, even artificial."

"No, Dear Husband, I have seen the blossoms in full bloom. The growers found a very special set of flowers, saved the bulbs, and got them to grow successfully, in Belgium. The growers told me that they seem to have a flaw that causes the sharp break in color. I told them to avoid letting others know of the origin of these bulbs and to establish exclusive trade with us. I had to guarantee that they would be highly compensated."

"And you think these will sell at a price worth all the bother and secrecy?"

"I do. My growers have circulated some plants at a four hundred percent profit."

Cornelius's eyebrow went up again, but this time, Greta did not display her tell.

## The History:
## 1585–1622

The period from the mid-16th century into the first quarter of the 17th century constituted the evolution of what became the Golden Age of the Netherlands. For multiple reasons—most significantly, the nature of the Dutch people—the country saw a rapid and remarkable accumulation of trade capital. Not only were the Netherlands situated in an ideal crossroads geographically, but the nation's and the people's policy of tolerance was most inviting. The early capital for the great degree of expansion came in with displaced Antwerp merchants, other European merchants, and New Christians who were displaced from the Iberia by religious persecution that were quickly attracted by the new opportunities in Amsterdam. After 1491, the entire Iberian peninsula was controlled by highly intolerant Christian rulers motivated in large part by a desire for revenge. The conquest [*Reconquista*] generated the Alhambra Decree of 1492 mandating the expulsion from Spain Jews who would not convert to Christianity then a series of edicts from 1499–1526) which forced the conversions of all Muslims in Spain with the only alternative being death. Despite their apparent conversions, later a most of them were expelled from the Iberian Peninsula.

Many of the people who were expelled were the best educated and most industrious members of peninsular society, among them skilled and experienced merchants. These merchants entered the Netherlands determined to protect themselves by accumulating wealth which increased the Netherlands tax base dramatically. This merchants often invested in high-risk ventures like pioneering expeditions to the Mughal Empire with which they had deep ties to engage in the spice trade. These ventures soon led to the creation of the Dutch East India Company [VOC-*Vereenigde Oost-Indische Compagnie*]. Other mercantile adventurers turned their skills towards trade with Russia and the Levant. The new Netherlanders were enthusiastic citizens and plowed their profits back into financing new trade, which led to an exponential growth for their welcoming new country.

From 1400 to 1700, Dutch per capita income growth was the fastest in Europe; and from 1600 to the 1820s its level was the highest. The Dutch and their newly acquired dynamic citizens from around Europe and the Iberian peninsula, developed an essentially new entity: merchant capitalism. The emerging capitalistic device was based on trading, shipping, and finance, rather than the limited and limiting manufacturing or agriculture and preceded the transition of the Dutch economy to the new stage and its Golden Age for the Netherlands. Capital in this early period accumulated in enormous amounts. That in turn generated demand for productive investment opportunities beside the immediate reinvestment in their own businesses. It also necessitated innovative institutional arrangements to bring demand and supply of investment funds together. The Amsterdam Stock Exchange, the *Amsterdamsche*

*Wisselbank*, innovations in marine insurance, the creation of legal structures–firms like the joint stock company–blossomed. These innovations helped manage risk and made the Netherlands not only extremely profitable but also safe. For example, ships were financed by shares, with each of sixteen merchants usually holding a 1/16 share. This minimized risk and maximized opportunity for windfall gains.

Information and foreign words from Chapter One:
Dutch unit of weight: For the Van Brakels, the unit used was *Amsterdams ponds* [*waaggewicht*]–494.09 grams.
Dutch unit of length: *Amsterdams ells*, the distance of the inside of the arm (i.e. the distance from the armpit to the tip of the fingers). The Dutch "*ell*" varied from town to town–55–75 cm—about 1 *ell*=42 inches.
Dutch National Game: *Klaverjassen*. The Dutch national card game is played with a 32 card pack (A-H-V-B-10-9-8-7) of each suit.
Dutch Women's Clothing:
> *Supportasse*–standing collar, supported by a small wire frame.
> *Rebatos*—newer, wired neck ruff.
Dutch naming in the early 1600s:
- Use of foreign names. This class is much larger for the names of women than for the names of men. Many were borrowed from Hebrew. For example: From the wives of Abraham, Isaac and Jacob, and even of Assuerus, including Sara, Rebecca, Rachel, Hester, and Deborah. From the New Testament–the Hebrew names of Anna, Elizabeth, and Magdalena. From the Greek names of saints–Catharina, Agatha, Margaretha, Sophia, Helena, and Apollonia. From Latin names came–Maria Cornelia, Agneta, Christina, Celia, Caneva, Emerentia, and Ursula.
- Derivatives of foreign names. For example: Anna®Annetje and Anneke, Elizabeth, and Betje, Magdalena®Magdaleentje, Helena®Leentje.
- Patronymics. Earlier, and persisting, the old patronymic system was very much in use among the Dutch even until 1686, so that such forms existed as Abrahams, Andries, etc. were seen. Later consensus resulted in a Dutch patronymic being a *man's* name with its genitive ending, much later in history added as a surname, to the given name of a person who stands under his *patria potestate* [who belong to his household]—wife, son, daughter, wife, or his grandchild. There were different types: Frankish, which ends in "-en", and Saxon, which end in "sen", "zen,", "soon", or "zoon," meaning son. For example, Corneliuszoon. Only men used Hebrew patronymics, e.g. Abrahams or Jans. Surnames as such began to appear in the 17th century but did not become commonplace until ~1680.

# CHAPTER TWO

# THE TULIP BOOM

IN THE YEAR OF OUR LORD, 1636, THE MONTH OF APRIL

Piet was something of a prodigy when it came to the two national pastimes—tulip floriculture and trade. Under the tutelage of his father, mother, and older brothers, he became an expert at managing the family's most important and lucrative venture—growing *Bizarden* tulips. By age twelve, Piet was left in sole charge of that portion of the family's floriculture, even to the point of hiring and firing nonfamily help. By age sixteen, he managed the entire commerce of the important product. The boy was a quick learner, much more so than any of his brothers. In fact, his older brothers– Willemt, Metten, Bart, and Hendrick, willingly accepted their younger brother's dominance with regards to the *Bizarden* since Father Cornelius assigned them additional responsibilities where they were of importance.

Of necessity–and as a result of his growing experience–Piet became fluent in the languages of trade extant in that period and place. His native languages were Dutch [both Flemish and Hollandic dialects]. In addition, he became fluent enough with the *linga francas* of trade–Middle Low German and Danish for trade in Northern and Northeastern Europe. He picked up some French and Italian which were widely used in diplomacy and in finance in western Europe beginning in the 1300s, but the northern tongues dominated trading ports.

Cornelius was not keen on his children attending school and was adamantly against his daughters doing so. He relented with the boys by permitting the older boys to attend part time until they had the rudiments of an eighth-grade education. At the strong insistence of his wife, Greta, Cornelius gave in to allow Piet to attend regular school so long as it did not interfere with his work on the family business. That decision paid serious dividends. Piet picked up mathematics and bookkeeping so rapidly and well that he was able take over management of the family finances related to trade and commerce. Greta was happy to be rid of a task usually assigned to women that she was not at all suited to manage.

Among the things Piet learned—and his parents did not know about—was how to fight. For all the myriad rules of the strict Dutch education, boys found times and places to settle their differences with their fists. Piet was a big boy, and he intimidated some would-be opponents, and regularly defeated others. There were three boys who had moved into Amsterdam from the East Indies where their fathers were in the diplomatic corps or the military. They had had to learn to fight to protect life and limb and purse. They each learned no-holds-barred, hands, feet, and heads tactics from masters of oriental arts of self-defense which made them a class unto themselves among the more genteel boys of the Netherlands. Piet struck up friendships and proved himself teachable; so, the three friends with the secret skills fully shared with him.

By the time he finished his education in the other fields required of him, Piet could use most of his body to vanquish an opponent; and he could also use an assortment of knives, swords, and even flintlock pistols, with some facility. He developed an air of self-assurance which—along with his size—made it seem to most boys and men who might consider disrespecting or attacking Piet Van Brakel to be a less than intelligent idea.

When he turned sixteen, Piet had achieved his full adult stature and was three inches taller that his father and an inch taller than the tallest of his brothers. He stood six feet tall; his father never exceeded 5'9½". Related to his steady activity of hard work and sparse eating habits, he weighed a lean 185 pounds. His father had a rich man's protuberant abdomen from a lifetime of dietary excess, something he loved even though he feared getting gout as did many of his business associates. At sixteen, Piet had a full head of curly blond hair, and his father had a monk's tonsure of grey-brown hair. Cornelius had long since given up trying to create comb-overs from either or both sides.

Piet never learned to consume alcohol other than an occasional stein of Belgian Pilsner. His father, on the other hand, was a prodigious drinker of distilled liquors and local beers. He had the gut to prove it. From the end of the sixteenth century, distilled drinks existed throughout the West but did not constitute a large enough market for Cornelius to get involved. However, improved transportation meant that beer could be shipped to as far as the New World. It was a lucrative business, and Cornelius pushed his way into it as much as he could. He used to laugh with his friends by retelling the story of the Puritans. They reputedly loaded more beer than water onto their ship, the *Mayflower,* before casting off for the New World.

The Pilgrims landed at Plymouth in the colony of Massachusetts in 1620 aboard the *Mayflower.* With the long voyage, beer was extremely short supply on board, and the seamen forced the passengers ashore. This was to ensure that they would have enough beer for their return trip to England," Cornelius told his drinking mates, and they all had another alcohol fueled laugh at an old joke.

Piet was handsome; his father was not when he became obese; but then, he never was. It was unclear where Piet's Nordic good lucks came from, but neither parent could claim the honor with a straight face. Piet had a mildly cleft chin, high cheek bones, deep dimples in his cheeks, and eyes as blue as the Aegean Sea. His teeth were big, straight, and strong. Cornelius had very poor dentition owing to his fondness for very sweet rum, which also contributed to his soft pudgy figure.

Cornelius developed a fondness for fancy clothes and stayed fully in the current style of the day. Piet was content to dress comfortably in sturdy working clothing. Western European clothing began to replace the Flemish dress of his youth. The waistlines of his trousers rose through the period as they did for both men and women; and Cornelius struggled to get pants large enough, full enough, and a belt broad enough, to hold his pants above his impressive girth. He succumbed to vanity and wore a large white wig long before it was truly fashionable and an overly showy dress sword. He adopted the manly affectation of showing his obese and hirsute chest.

Piet generally contented himself to wearing sober styles with sadd colors favored by Puritans and exported to the early settlements of New England. He preferred—when not working—to wear dark colors, open collars, unbuttoned robes or doublets, and a mildly disheveled appearance. He wore high soft leather knee-high boots with buckles on the toes and a wide fold-over at the knees. When occasion required, Piet could fit in with the swells; he never wore a periwig or dress sword—too foppish for him.

Piet and Cornelius communicated fully and regularly about business as they never did about current events, fashions, religion, or changes in buying activities, unless the subject related to their frenetically increasing business enterprises.

They were sitting on the broad porch that surrounded the Van Brakel home. It was a rare day with no pressing obligations. The sisters carried steaming platters of Greta's best dishes from the hot kitchen to the cool and breezy porch. The effect was charming enough to inspire Piet to stand, bow to all the girls and to give them a fond embrace. Cornelius was considerably more reserved by habit, but even he stood and bowed then leaned over and kissed his daughters' fingers in a courtly gesture. They blushed and giggled as good girls are supposed to do and returned smiles that required no words. They bustled about to serve a sumptuous brunch which in the preceding two centuries would have been only available to the aristocracy. In fact, only the wealthy, like the Van Brakels could expect to see such variety.

There were plates of sliced bread with toppings: appelstroop, Edam kaas, cold meats, jam, honey, some with hazelnut-chocolate spread and others with sweet sprinkles–*hagelslag*, ordinarily reserved for cake and for more formal gathering. Greta had outdone herself with the *hagelslag*; the spreads included chocolate, aniseed, and fruit flavors. The younger girls served round rusk *beschuit* with strawberries, buttered *ontbijtkoek,* brined herring, and currant buns with cheese imported from Denmark. Vrouwtje and Hilletje—the two older girls–had tried their hands on *Stamppot* with locally made *rookworst*, old family favorite Dutch fare.

"*Eet smakelijk*," Vrouwtje said shyly.

They waited, hearts on their sleeves, for any sign of approval, which came quickly with slurping noises, burps of pleasure, and broad smiles.

Neither breakfast nor brunch would be complete without servings of granola and muesli, accompanied by fresh fruit. It was not the time of year for citrus fruits to be available, but the two men washed down their kingly meals with choices of Arabic *koffie*, Chinese tea, Dutch *jenever* apperitifs, and Swedish *Åkerö* apple juice.

After the special meal, Cornelius had to stand up and walk around to ease his back, to let his stomach settle, and to fret secretly a bit about the possibility of developing gout.

Piet remained seated and opened the conversation, "Father, some of my trading partners have expressed fears that the tulip trade has become heated out of all proportion, especially that involving our precious *Bizarden*. They are beginning to talk about moving their interests and funds away from tulips and into moving more grains farther to the west and south. I have considerable investment in the *Bizarden*, and a serious downturn in the market would be very bad for me, maybe even put me into the work farm.

"I need your advice."

"Balderdash!" Cornelius said with finality and certainty. "You could have said the same thing about Dutch shipping twenty years ago or even forty years ago. Or about Dutch banking. The markets and good Dutch hard work and planning ahead have resulted in nothing more or less than increasing success year after year. The high prices of tulips, and our treasures, the *Bizarden*, are defying the odds and the naysayers all over the world by becoming even more popular as more and more women discover them in such obscure places as New Amsterdam in the Americas. That country will grow, as will England; and as they grow, so will the tulip demand.

"Be happy about a good thing, my boy. This is the goose that laid the golden egg. As long as we tend the goose, we will reap a harvest of golden eggs for as long as we can imagine into the future. Have some more *jenever*, Son, and rest your mind. God's in his heaven, and all's right with the world. I know whereof I speak. I was peddling tulips while you and your young friends were still in knee pants. Trust my long experience."

# The History:
## 1622-1636

The Netherlands remained in a bull market status as it passed through the middle quarter of the 17th century.

Staples market

The staples market (*stapelmarkt*) served to manage the risk of price fluctuations. Dutch financial masters provided trade credit to suppliers in order to secure favored access to raw materials. Dutch merchants routinely bought up grain harvests in the Baltic area and grape harvests in France–important in the wine trade–before they were harvested, looking forward to market control and increase for decades to come and to maintain funding to ease market downturns. Bankers were creative. They developed the financing of commodity trade with bills of exchange. That resulted in binding customers to the merchants.

The Dutch system was geared to export and to reexport commodities, and it also serviced a large domestic market. This was accomplished by binding Dutchman to the economy either as final consumers or as intermediate users of raw materials and intermediate products for processing to finished products. The Dutch were not only creative about ideas, but they were also very adept at copying fabricating methods of other peoples. As small as the Dutch Republic was, its urban population around in 1622-to as far into the future as 1650, was larger than that of the British Isles and Scandinavia *combined*. Of considerable benefit to the Dutch was the fact that it was able to remain larger than that of all German lands combined, which were devastated by the Thirty Years' War and not yet rebuilt. This gave the Dutch a sizable domestic market helped the Amsterdam to perform a price-stabilizing function beneficial to itself and to the rest of Europe.

There was nothing idle about the Dutch. While they were experiencing an explosive growth in accumulation of capital, the Dutch did not allow their money to sit idle as did other Europeans. The increase in capital led directly to an equally steep growth in investment in fixed capital for industries related to trade. That drove the Dutch to seek technological innovations like the wind-driven sawmill–invented by Cornelis Corneliszoon–which significantly increased productivity in ship building and offered even more opportunities for profitable investment. The textile industries did the same thing. They capitalized on the competition they faced and their highly motivated and skilled work force that came up with mechanized fulling and a quicker, better, and cheaper, way to make new draperies. Like other industries they made use of mechanization which afforded the previously unharnessed wind power to ease work loads of men and animals. Again, Corneliszoon made the crucial discovery and patented it in the late 16th century. He made a crankshaft that converted the continuous rotational movement of the wind from windmills and also to convert the energy of rivers by a water wheel into a reciprocating one.

During the period, the Dutch built up by far the largest merchant fleet in the world. In the North Sea and Baltic there was little risk of piracy during those crucial years and trips shuttled between markets quickly and safely. Where the risk of piracy or shipwreck was high, Dutch ships traveled in convoys with a light guard. This became the underpinnings of an increasingly stronger defensive and offensive navy, merchant marine, and army.

A major technological advance came with the design of a new Dutch merchant ship known as the *fluyt*. Taking advantage of the peaceful oceanic trade routes, the *fluyt* was designed for rapid, efficient sea trade, not for possible conversion in wartime to a warship unlike the ships of rival nations. It was cheaper to build, carried twice the cargo, and could be handled by a smaller crew. Construction by specialized ship-yards using new tools made it half the cost of rival ships. These salutary factors combined to lower the cost of transportation for Dutch merchants sharply, giving them a major competitive advantage; they could move larger cargoes, farther, faster, and with decreased turnaround time.

The ship building district of Zaan, near Amsterdam, became the first industrialized area in the world, By the end of the 17th century there were about nine hundred large industrial windmills in and around Amsterdam, a number that dwarfed the industrial capacity of the rest of Europe. In addition, the Netherlands developed smaller scale industrialized towns and cities. Throughout the country, growth was fostered for papermaking, sugar refining, printing, the linen industry—with lucrative spin-offs in vegetable oils, like flax and rape oil. The industrious and creative Dutch developed industries during this period that capitalized on the use of cheap peat fuel—including brewing and ceramics. Around the nation, brickworks, pottery and clay-pipe making, flourished and enriched the republic.

As a result of the above described innovations and advances, there was a truly explosive growth of textiles industries in several specialized Dutch cities. Cities like Enschede for woolen cloth, Haarlem for linen, and Amsterdam for silk, grew exponentially and demonstrated a dynamism unheard of elsewhere in Europe. That booming economy was mainly facilitated by the influx of skilled workers and capital from the Southern Netherlands in the final decades of the 16th century, when Calvinist (Protestant) entrepreneurs and workers were forced to leave the Spanish (Catholic dominated areas) there and in other European countries. Entire industries migrated lock, stock, and barrel, to the welcoming Northern Netherlands, reinvigorating the northern textile industry, that had been moribund before the Revolt.

This rate of industrialization was accompanied by rapid growth of the nonagricultural labor force. Labor supply and demand resulted in unusual benefits to the republic and its citizenry. There was a significant and growing increase in real wages during the same time. Between 1570 and 1620 the labor supply increased three percent per year, a truly phenomenal growth in comparison to the previous history in the Netherlands and low countries and other European nations. Almost irrationally, wages repeatedly increased, outstripping price increases. Real wages for unskilled laborers were sixty-two percent higher in 1615–1619 than in 1575–1579.

Another important growth sector were the fisheries, especially the important herring fishery–known as the "Great Fishery". Technology played a role in this sector as well. There was a Flemish invention of gibbing–which made better preservation possible. The herring fishery experienced a further tremendous growth due to the development of a specialized ship type, the Herring Buss. This was a highly efficient and successful factory ship. Dutch herring fishermen–unlike their competitors–became able to follow herring to the shoals of the Dogger Bank and other places far from the Dutch shores, and stay at sea working for months at a time.

Actually, linked to the fishery itself was an important onshore processing industry that prepared the salted herring for export across Europe. It also attracted its own supporting industries, like salt refining and the salt trade; fishing net manufacture; and specialized shipbuilding. The fisheries were not particularly profitable in themselves (they were already a mature industry by 1600), but organizational innovations (vertical integration of production, processing, and trade) enabled an efficient business model, in which the traders used the revenues of fishing to buy up grain in Baltic ports during the winter months (when otherwise the fishing boats would have been idle), which they transported to Western Europe when the ice floes thawed in Spring. The revenues of this incidental trade were invested in unrefined salt or new boats. The industry was also supported by the Dutch government by market regulation (under the tutelage of an industry body, the Commissioners of the Great Fishery), and naval protection of the fishing fleet against privateers and the Royal Navy (because the English looked askance at Dutch fishing in waters they claimed). The combination of these factors secured a *de facto* monopoly for Dutch soused herring in the two centuries between 1500 and 1700.

Information and Foreign Words and Phrases from Chapter Two
- *Åkerö*—Swedish: Apple juice, originated in 1570
- *Beschuit*—Dutch: round rusk cookies/biscuits
- *Bizarden* tulips—A uniquely beautiful Belgian/Dutch tulip with clearly split) demarcated colors. This effect is due to the bulbs being infected with a type of tulip-specific mosaic virus, known as the "tulip breaking virus", so called because it "breaks" the one petal color into two or more.
- *Eet smakelijk*—Dutch: enjoy your meal
- *Hagelslag*—Dutch: bread spread with hazelnut or sweet sprinkles–ordinarily reserved for cake and for more formal gatherings. Spreads may include chocolate, aniseed, and fruit flavors
- *Jenever*–Dutch gin
- *Kaas*—Dutch: cheese
- *Nieuwe haring*—Dutch (Hollandse): for "new herring", indicating the first catch of the season.

The Dutch are passionate about herring–a fatty, oily fish, full of flavor and omega-3 vitamins. Some sea-hardened men ate whole "raw" herrings—actually slightly brined) on the streets of Amsterdam, of which part is not quite true, i.e. the "raw" part since the fish were slightly brined. Herring fishing has been inseparable part of the Amsterdam history from its very beginning, largely responsible, together with the beer trade, for its fast-growing wealth, especially after the Dutch came up with the idea of curing the fish, thoroughly gutted beforehand, to make it last longer. The herring season commences in May.

- *Ontbijtkoek*—Dutch spiced bread—best when slathered with butter
- *Rookworst*—Dutch: locally made smoked sausage
- *Sadd* colors—Plain colors favored by country people and strict religionists like the Puritans: "liver" color, de Boys, tawney, russet, purple, French green, ginger, lyne, deer color, orange
- *Stamppot*–mashed potatoes combined with *boerenkool* [kale], *hutspot* [onions and carrots], *andrauweandijvie* (endive). or *zuurkool* [sauerkraut]

# CHAPTER THREE

# DUTCH FINANCIAL BUBBLE

IN THE YEAR OF OUR LORD, 1638, THE MONTH OF NOVEMBER

ornelius traveled the sixty-five and a half kilometers from Amsterdam to *Die Haghe* for an emergency gathering of the Great Council of Merchants of the Netherlands to discuss the impending collapse of the nation's economy. It was too far for the family's light and rather flimsy carriages; so, Cornelius was forced to endure a stagecoach ride—something his back and sitting muscles dreaded. He boarded the lumbering Hague-Leiden-Haarlem-Amsterdam stagecoach in front of Amsterdam Barbizon Palace Hotel on Prins Hendrikkade Street.

Nine of the more prosperous passengers—including Cornelius Claes Van Brakel–were packed inside; at least they were spared some of the elements. There were no glass windows in stagecoaches of the time to protect the faces of the passengers from the wind, dust, and blown pebbles. That change would come twenty years hence. Second-class seats were available in a large open basket attached to the back. It was uncomfortable and unsafe; but, at least, where was some semblance of a seat. The least privileged travelers were jammed onto every square foot of the roof accompanying the luggage They had to rely on a thin iron handrail to prevent themselves from being thrown off as the coach jounced over the rocks and ruts of the primitive dirt road. This immensely unwieldly vehicle–drawn by six horses–lurched along the irregular and often muddy roads at an average speed of about four miles an hour. The stagecoach had no form of springs. Finally–to add tension to the otherwise nearly intolerable physical endurance test–danger from highwaymen was an ever-present inconvenience of the journey.

The national commercial situation was severe enough that the conclave was scheduled to take place in the Binnenhof, the center of the Dutch government. Every member of The Hague Stock Exchange, the officers of the *Amsterdamsche Wisselbank*, the Foreign Exchange Trading Guild officers, Directors and members of Brokers Guild of The *Wisselbanken,* and the Electors of the Guilds at Large—like Cornelius Van Brakel–were expected to be there. Bank of Amsterdam officers and the *entrepreneurs*—who rounded up potential clients and steered them to the available offerings on any other regular business day—now more assertedly pushed them into the Binnenhof.

The grand ball room was huge and packed with sober, sweating, rich men, as befitted the gravity of the reason for calling the meeting. Conversation was hushed and solemn, like the elegant room. The men were dressed very much the same as befitted the august assembly—large and long periwigs, kaolin clay pipes emitting a thick cloud of blue smoke, the disappearance of the ruff in favor of broad lace or linen collars, high waistlines full, voluminous slashed sleeves, and tall and broad hats with wide brims. Hose had disappeared in favor of breeches. Black was the only color for suits on the occasion. On the serious occasion.

The meeting, chaired by the Prince William II of Orange, acknowledged Stadtholder of The *Staten-Generaal*, was brought to order.

"Gentlemen, burgers, stadtholders, and directors, in the name of the Republic, I declare this meeting to be in session. We will not waste time on pleasantries because we are here to stave off a severe recession which all of us can see looming and to be threatening to our futures personally and collectively as a nation.

"I will leave to the experts the details of the economy, its history, and the most accurate predictions for its future. Let me declare on record for the government that this is a problem for the republic, for the provinces, for the territories of Holland, and the Low Countries in toto. It is a time to unite for the common good. We will accomplish nothing by exercising personal greed, or by reacting to panic, or by caving-in to the nay-sayers. We will overcome this pending crisis as our great Netherlands has done in the past and will almost certainly have to do in the future.

"Our first speaker will be Governor-General of the *Vereenigde Oost-Indische Compagnie*, Andries Laurens, on subjects related to our foreign trade and how it impacts the domestic scene. He will be followed by our foremost grower and exporter of tulips, Cornelius Claes Van Brakel. I will announce the remainder of the agenda after the remarks of these two outstanding experts of our economy have enlightened us. General Laurens,"

"Thank you, my Prince. It is an honor and an obligation to give you my insights into the current growing crisis. The VOC, perhaps better known to the citizens of the republic as the Dutch East Indies Company, has been overwhelmingly successful in its conduct of the import-export business of the nation and our investors. The costs have been high and necessary, but the profits have—thus far—been worth every hour of effort and every penning and guilder expended. On the near horizon, we see difficulties coming at us from the British, the French, the Indonesians, and the Moluccans. All of them seem to be sensing a chink in our armor and that soon, it will be time to strike. Our informers tell us of planned riots, strikes, attacks on our men and properties, and of the potential for an organized military strike against us here, in the Indies, in the Baltics, and along the west coast of Africa. The company and the citizens of the Netherlands must unite to strike pre-emptory blows against the plotters.

"Supply and demand principles operate as a law unto themselves. There is a finite amount of demand that can be for need or for luxury. When we exceed our supply because we are efficient or because we are industrious, we see a concomitant drop in prices in order to keep interest in our product. What we have to fear most is for our oversupply to make our product so plentiful and readily available that our buyers find the product no longer to be interesting, exciting, or hard to obtain. The product becomes commonplace, then cheap, then ignored. Our textiles are getting into a rut. They are fine, well-made products which once were difficult for our far-flung customers to obtain. Now, we can bring years' supplies in one *fluyt* load. We may get our price then, but not the next time. I believe the next several ships will have to settle for less per item or even come back home with the cargo holds still half full. The worst situation is developing in the tulip industry. Our Cornelius Van Brakel can enlighten and maybe frighten us."

He nodded to the corpulent merchant, who put his hands on his knees to help himself to stand erect then stepped to the center of the dais.

"Gentlemen, partners, friends, and countrymen, I fear for tulips, for our unique industry. In the past several decades, my sons and I have taken great care to find and to cultivate the most exciting and most beautiful tulips in our fields. In the early years, tulips were a luxury item. Our markets were all around the globe. Once people in those far distant places discovered our tulips, they had to plant them in their own gardens. They were ever more demanding of what was new, different, hardy, and better, than what their neighbors had. The sky was the limit in terms of demand and our ability to supply those demands. In the past several years, we have been making 400, 500, even 600, percent profits for our mercantile voyages. Our *Bizarden* are beautiful and exotic beyond measure. They are also profitable beyond our wildest imaginations.

"But... we are beginning to see a fall off of demand in those areas where we first introduced the *Bizarden*. Our specialists are seeing a slow-down of commerce in all areas of supply and of the ability of large houses and of simple folk to continue to pay our prices for what are more and more coming to look like luxury items to them. That certainly pertains to tulips.

"We Dutch were able to gain control of much of the trade with the nascent English colonies in North America; and again after the end of war with Spain in 1648. Even our trade with Spain has flourished. Amsterdam merchants are at the center of the lucrative East Indies trade. We have marketed and publicized well and have proved to be reliable providers. As a result, tulips rapidly became a coveted luxury item, and a profusion of varieties followed—each new variety more in demand than the last.

"By 1634–in part as a result of demand from the French–speculators began to enter the market. I cannot emphasize too strongly the impact of speculators–especially organized speculators–on the once entirely reliable market. The contract price of rare bulbs continued to rise throughout the first half of this year, 1636; but by November, the price of common–as we call unbroken–bulbs also began to increase. By May any tulip bulb could fetch hundreds of guilders. We enterprising and excellent business minds, the Dutch, created a formal futures market where *contracts* to buy bulbs at the end of the season were bought and sold. Traders—as they called themselves–met in so called colleges in what were really just taverns. Buyers… the so so hungry buyers…were found to be not only available everywhere, but they did not balk when required to pay a 2.5 percent upfront fee—like the "wine money" fee exacted in that overheated market. These excited buyers have been–until the present day–willing to pay up to a maximum of three guilders *per trade*—which at times could be a single tulip.

"Dutch law prohibits either party from paying on the margin, or a mark-to-market margin. But, all contracts were between one individual and another; and they have been able to avoid working with the limitations and controls of the Exchange. We men in the business for decades and who have done our true work describe such tulip contract trading as *windhandel* because no bulbs were actually changing hands. The entire business was accomplished on the margins of Dutch economic life, not in the Exchange itself. By late 1636, the tulip bulb has become the fourth leading export product of the Netherlands, after gin, herrings, and cheese. The price of tulips is skyrocketing because of speculation in tulip futures among people who never even see the bulbs. We are seeing many men make or lose fortunes overnight. Gentlemen, we must so something before it is too late!"

The response at the Binnenhof was polite; but with the twin specters of war and of struggles to maintain ownership in the profitable properties of the East Indies raising their grim visages, a tempest over tulips fell on largely deaf ears. Cornelius made the uncomfortable ride home in a state coach in a blue funk.

Piet sought out his father to find out what the grand men of the Dutch East Indies Company, the VOC, and Prince William II and his minions in the *Staten-Generaal* had to offer.

"Father, what are these august leaders with all the power, expertise, and wisdom proffering as solutions for the tulip boom and the similar over-inflationary actions in many of the other Dutch industries? What are they? and what are we going to do?"

"My educated son, you ask very hard questions. Sometimes, I wish you were neither so intelligent nor so well informed; and we could go about enjoying the golden haze of our Dutch Golden Age as do our neighbors. However, I am convinced that what you fear, what you express fear about, what you agitate about, is true. And, I agree that we must do something. We must do it now."

"What?"

"You will not want to hear this, but this is the only solution I can think of. First, we must sell our entire stock of tulips, even the *Bizarden*, at whatever prices we can get. We must get out of the market first, or we will left holding a bag of bulbs like all the rest of the fools when the crash takes place.

"Painful as it is, Son, it must be done. You are the expert; so, you must do it. We will need to sell our stockpiles of raw textile cloth with the same ruthlessness, because, when the walls created by the tulip bulbs begin to cave in, the textiles will join soon thereafter."

Piet thought he might cry. He felt all the more so, as he actually began divesting the family of the beautiful tulip bulbs. However, as fast as he could sell them, the priced dropped even faster. He ended up feeling lucky when he could trade tulips for garden vegetable seeds which his family needed for sustenance.

Tulip mania reached its peak during the winter of 1636 and 1637. In some taverns, certain bulbs were changing hands ten times in a day with profits on paper ever increasing with accounting and control managed by *participanten*. No deliveries were ever made to fulfil any of those contracts—which were based on tulips that existed only on paper anyway–because in February 1637, tulip bulb contract prices collapsed abruptly and completely; and the trade of tulips ground to a total halt. The collapse began in Haarlem. Buyers finally refused to show up at a routine bulb auction. As it happened, Haarlem was then suffering from an outbreak of bubonic plague; and every person in the area was in a hide-at-home panic. That auction failed and created a domino effect whether the cause was accurate or not.

People had been purchasing bulbs at higher and higher prices, presuming that they could always re-sell them for a profit. Most could not even imagine the day when the balloon would burst. Such an empty bubble could not last unless more people were ultimately willing to pay ever increasing high prices without having to take physical possession of the bulbs and to transmit them to the next buyers. By the end of February, 1637, speculating tulip traders could no longer find new buyers willing to pay increasingly inflated prices for their bulbs. The bottom fell out of the tulip market, then the economy of the Netherlands, and finally of the holdings of the wealthy Van Brakel clan.

## THE HISTORY:
## 1634-1637

The entire seventeenth century was the Golden Age of the Netherlands. Everything went the way the industrious and progressive Dutch planned and worked for, with the exception of a few short periods such as the Great Tulip Crash in 1637. By then, the entire economy was overheated and difficult to manage and a genuine correction was in order. The brilliant concepts of mercantile capitalism brought in over the previous two centuries fostered the seagoing trade, the commerce in spice, the agriculture that provided the raw materials, the factories that produced finished goods, the shipping that moved products all over the world, and finally the Tulip Craze, then the Tulip Crash that ended it all for a time.

Robert Burns in *Ode to a Mouse* told of "the best laid schemes o' mice an' men gang aft agley." Dutch plans were developed slowly, carefully, and with foresight. The wise men of the Netherlands recognized that they had at their beck and call the elements of prolonged success and riches. They also recognized that innovative institutional arrangements were necessitated to bring demand and supply of investment funds together. They created careful legal structures, the Amsterdam Stock Exchange, the *Amsterdamsche Wisselbank,* joint stock companies, and the concept of sharing profits wherein ships were financed by shares, with each of sixteen merchants holding a 1/16 share. There were also innovations in marine insurance. All these innovations were designed to minimize risk and maximize opportunity for windfall gains. Even the groups of the wisest of men could not have envisioned the impact of profit on people—the human factor in the economy. "But, Mousie, thou art no thy lane, In proving foresight may be vain." The people gave into vanity and overspent. They were seduced by success they saw as never ending. But the commerce in tulips brought about a bubble and its collapse.

Dutch traders commanded the shipping of wine from France and Portugal to the Baltics. They returned with enough grain for countries around the Mediterranean Sea to be able to determine prices. By the late decades of the 17th century nearly 1000 Dutch ships entered the Baltic Sea each year to trade with markets of the fading Hanseatic League. They finally took over those lucrative marketing routes. The Dutch were able to gain control of much of the trade with the English colonies in North America. After the end of war with Spain with a decided Dutch victory, Dutch trade with Spain returned and quickly flourished. Then there was the hard won vastly profitable East Indies Trade controlled by Amsterdam merchants who saw profits soar into several hundred percentiles. No one could have anticipated that a market that was small and relatively unimportant could eventually almost unhinge all the rest of that carefully planned power and prosperity.

The efficiency and success of the Dutch manufacturers and shippers created products that reached all around the known world and were surprisingly inexpensive. Tulips were different; they were beautiful; and they were by 1620 available around the globe. As a result, tulips rapidly became a coveted luxury item, and a profusion of varieties followed thereby enhancing the demand. Dutch tulip growers industriously kept up with the demand and prices gradually inclined. By the late 1630s, those prices climbed precipitously. The growers and shippers made valiant efforts to keep up, and they became imprudently greedy, finally killing the goose that laid the golden eggs (tulip bulbs).

The death knell was sounded by 1634, when unprincipled speculators entered the market and employed the amazing financial tools to further their profits gained without labor. Contracts–rather than actual bulbs–became the medium of exchange. Ordinary bulb prices—on paper—increased out of proportion to their actual value. The contract price of rare bulbs continued to rise at a much greater rate from 1634. The prices reflected a nearly insane hyperinflation after November. The price of bulbs soared to the point that any tulip bulb could fetch hundreds of guilders—nearly the equivalent, gram for gram of gold. In 1637, the Dutch created a type of formal futures markets where *contracts* to buy bulbs at the end of the season were bought and sold for a handling fee even though actual bulbs never changed hands. The men who created the stable Dutch economy derisively called tulip contract trading as *windhandel* because no bulbs were actually changing hands. The entire trading business was conducted well outside the confines and constraints of the well-controlled Dutch Exchange. By mid-1636, the tulip bulb—in fact, the on-paper bulb–became the fourth leading export product of the Netherlands, after gin, herrings, and cheese. Speculation in tulip *futures* caught the fancy of people who never saw the bulbs. Finally, many men made fortunes overnight, then discovered that when the bill came due, they did not have the money to pay their debt. Also, overnight fortunes disappeared; and their families suffered the impact. The amazing Dutch Golden Age economy ground to a crawl, necessitating a great many changes in land ownership, wealth, overlordship, bankruptcies, and inheritance. It was a manmade disaster.

Information and Foreign Words and Phrases from Chapter Three
- *Commissionairs*: Dutch for intermediaries who acted on behalf of other merchants for a commission.
- Foreign Exchange Traders: Commercial agents who were the middle-men who kept trade moving to and from the Netherlands for a percentage fee.
- *Participanten*: Dutch for investors. In the tulip trade and many others many such investors formed groups and hired agents to manage accounts and to control risks.
- *Staten-Generaal*: Dutch for The States-General. From 1588 until 1795, the States-General were the assembly of the Seven United Provinces constituting the Dutch Republic–Gelderland, Holland, Zeeland, Utrecht, Friesland, Overijssel, and Groningen–. During this period, the States-General acted as the de facto federal government of the Dutch Republic. It is to be noted that not all

the Netherlands fell under this governmental authority, especially the lands of Holland.

- VOC [*Vereenigde Oost-Indische Compagnie*]: Dutch for the Dutch East India Company, a publicly traded private company which largely acted as an entity unto itself—collecting taxes, maintaining a large army and navy, conducting trade and wars, governing colonialized people, and doing extensive exploration
- *Windhandel*: Dutch, literally "wind trade" [a derogative term. Uncollateralized paper-controlled business.]
- *Wisselbrief* [*wissel* for short]: Dutch, for a bill of exchange–an early innovation which obviated the need to transport coins in payment. The practice gave rise to the *Wisselbanken*.

# CHAPTER FOUR
# DUTCH TULIP COLLAPSE

IN THE YEAR OF OUR LORD, 1639, THE MONTH OF DECEMBER

In the two years following the Great Tulip Crash, life for the Van Brakel family and its many employees had gone from bad to worse. All liquid cash vanished as the honest father tried his best to pay the family debts. The family assets vanished along with the worthless paper contracts ostensibly representing actual tulip bulbs—which did not exist, except on paper. Mother Greta—who had a spine and will made of the best steel—decided that the family must shed itself of its acquired luxuries and to revert back to a genuine–albeit Spartan–life as farmers. She and the girls held auctions, advertised with estate brokers in Amsterdam, and communicated with old friends and neighbors to sell off what were once precious heirlooms of the family at bargain basement prices.

Father Cornelius and Piet Corneliuszoon, spent their days divesting themselves of what were once productive fields, flourishing businesses, and bulging bank accounts. Piet resigned from school, a bitter disappointment for him. Every Van Brakel child was withdrawn from school. The younger brothers and sisters, Witt de, Egbert Meeuwszoon, Hillegont, and Femma were sent to distant cities as indentured servants with well-known Dutch families which had somehow escaped the economic collapse. They communicated as often as work permitted and made valiant efforts not to describe their conditions in too much detail.

Willemt and Metten—the two boys just older than Piet–stayed with Father Cornelius to run what was left of the farm properties. Bart and

Hendrick—the two oldest boys—had already been placed on family mercantile ships as junior officers, with little choice as to different careers. They were quite happy with the choices made for them by Cornelius and Greta, and saw their futures as bright, but rather slow in coming.

January, 1639 was the worst of the worst—a month that all but destroyed Mother Greta. An epidemic of measles struck Amsterdam and infected four of the children, three of whom made slow and difficult, but complete recoveries. Poor little Geertje developed a brain fever which the doctors at the university called measles encephalitis, for which there was no cure. She died in her mother's arms on the last day of the month, and Greta was never the same after that. Willemt was spending a month in the city while the snows prevented any real farm work. In the crowded and dirty conditions where he lived, a cholera epidemic exploded and killed Willemt and thirty-two other youngsters. Cornelius was stricken, and Greta was inconsolable and became mute in her grief for most of the rest of the year.

There was a pall on the land. Dances and parties were cancelled. Festivals were postponed until better times—hoped for better times—came. Like many other Dutch families, the Van Brakels had been indifferent followers of the national religion—The Dutch Reformed Church. They attended services on Christmas and Easter or when an important pastor came to speak. Cornelius faithfully gave monetary support when times were good; and now that times were bad, he had to accept assistance from the Poor Fund to put food on the table. It broke his spirit to return to the hard days of his youth as a poor farm boy; but now, he was worse than poor; he was a pauper. He could not hold his head up in public or look his neighbors and fellow parishioners in the eye.

Being reduced to near destitution caused a serious change of hearts and minds of the Van Brakels. Greta was the first to come out of her torpor around Christmas time and to make rational suggestions.

"Cornelius, we are Dutch even though we are seeing bad times. We must get back to our roots, get back to work, and to start over. I ask that you call a family council and ask our remaining children and our other relatives to follow us back into the fold of our religion."

"I think you to be right, my Good *Vrouw*," he responded and followed up by making it happen.

Having a useful project slowly began to bring Cornelius out of his self-imposed slump. He gathered up church literature, approved Bibles, and discussions of right religious actions from the church elders.

On the day of the council, everyone dressed up, as if attending a solemn church assembly. There was genuine agreement that their church held the answer to bringing back peace and prosperity to the believers.

17th century Dutch dress for women had been the time when women in their finery were at their most glorious. On this day, a nearly bygone era was resurrected. Because black is a more expensive color to reproduce in clothing, and because it is emblematic of solemnity, black over garments prevailed. Below the rich black cloth, there was an abundance of rich and expensive fabrics, jewels, lace, and accessories. In a statement rejecting Spain, the elaborate colors and flamboyant patterns had given way to a lighter style of patterning with nuanced scrolling floral motifs, woven or embroidered, but subtle.

Needle-lace was now popular all over the European world, and the women of the family were not to be out done, even in those days of sparsity. By dint of their own needle work, the women appeared with geometric reticella created from their cutwork that had evolved into true *punto in aria,* which was the equal of the popular scrolling floral designs found in European courts.

The huge, stiff, and intricate ruffs which were the height of fashion in the glorious 1620s had been replaced by the flat 'falling' collar. The proper outfit of the late 1630s had to include a *vlieger*–a large floor length sleeveless gown—all studies of beauty in black.

Greta's older and richer sister Caroline wore a *stomacher* which had an eye-catching edging of black-on-black cut-out floral motifs. The two sisters wore black silk sleeves that matched their *vlieger* mantles. In Greta's case, the black silk came from a small bolt she had saved as a last vestige of the grand old times for use on just such an important occasion. Cornelia's were plain, but her more affluent sister's were decorated with interwoven stripes and embroidery made of black silk and black-dyed wool. Greta's entire hoard of silk was used up to complete her skirt.

Caroline's large skirt made the *stomacher* stand out proudly and to show it off even more—enough to draw disapproving glances from the more conservative members of the Reformed Dutch congregation that dominated the religious scene that day. There was little to criticize since all the Dutch fashions and were as modest as the burkas worn by the heathen women of the east.

Unlike the avian world, Dutch and most other European men had markedly less opulent dress. Fashion in the period 1600–1640 in Western European clothing, including the Netherlands was characterized by the grateful disappearance of the uncomfortable ruff in favor of broad lace or linen collars. The men's shirts were bright white voluminous sleeves; shoe buckles were large and either silver or gold; suits were black, as fitted both the times and the occasion of the day.

The times seemed to require a more austere religion, and Pastor Seurt was the man to promulgate it. His unsmiling demeanor, harshly cut blond beard, thatch of plastered down blond hair, prominent hook nose and thrusting chin, and his silvery blue penetrating eyes would have made him appear formidable by themselves. His stature, lanky and unusually tall—well over six feet—set him off more as a likely opponent than a benevolent minister. No one would mistake his clothing for that of a bon vivant or a rustic. He wore a starched white shirt that was in good company with his stiff facial expression and his ramrod stiff posture. He wore no rings, ruffs, or flourishes. His suit fit perfectly making him look something like a black beanpole. No color, buckle, or button, altered the starkness of his religious black garb.

Seurt wasted neither time nor syllables as he approached his task of bringing back into the only true religion these people he regarded as rich dilettantes who had strayed into worldly ways. He made it clear that it was his sworn duty to correct back-sliders and to restore the proper decorum, practices, beliefs, and practices of his beloved church.

"Ladies and gentlemen. Thank you for inviting me here. It seems providential that I have been asked to speak on this auspicious occasion about a subject that has no equal in importance."

He paused to look each person directly in his or her eyes with an uncannily piercing gaze, it seemed to them.

"It is time you came back to the true church. Past time. Our *Nederlandse Hervormde Kerk* is God's abode on an earth infested with heathens, pagans, papists, and false prophets. The NHK has been the largest Christian denomination in the Netherlands from the onset of the Protestant Reformation. Our first Synod in the Dutch Republic was held in Dordrecht in 1578. Aside from making clear that we would no longer bend to the Romanist's pagan dogmas and rituals, we established a core principle of tolerance. Large groups of Marranos settled in Emden and converted to our blessed Christianity. Even many Jewish groups escaping from the clutches of the Spanish devils converted here to Christianity and were rewarded by a religious tolerance theretofore unknown by them. They have prospered in God's true church since and are a core entity of strength to this day. Originally, we were called the *Nederduitsche* or *Niederdeutsche* church but now more properly as the Dutch Reformed Church.

"As you return to the fold and begin once again to practice our only true Christian church, we will take the necessary time to learn again the doctrines and nuances of our belief as expostulated by our learned church scholars, free of papist influence. Today, we will touch only on right religious actions. Like children who cannot eat meat before they can drink milk, we will begin on simpler stuff—the pablum, the pap—before we delve into the intricacies and difficult intellectual and faith challenging doctrines. We will speak of what we do in the churches."

Even that limited focus created a sermon that lasted more than two hours. Men, women, and children, made a valiant effort not to squirm or to roll their eyes. Seurt was the answer to their crying need, and not a single person in the congregation gathered that day doubted the need to make the changes that the pastor was going to offer. It was a moral imperative upon which the foundation of the new and powerful Dutch Republic was to be anchored.

## THE HISTORY:
## RELIGION

The economy, wars, and religion, of the Netherlands were strongly interlinked. Protestants chafed under the domination of the Spanish Roman Catholics. It took wars to rid the low countries of the Catholic overlordship. When the Protestants prevailed, a new world of opportunity presented itself which led to the "Dutch Miracle" or "Golden Age of the Dutch". Protestants were especially well-represented among the skilled craftsmen and rich merchants of the port cities of Bruges, Ghent, and Antwerp. More moved to the north towards Amsterdam between 1585 and 1630 than Catholics moved in the other direction, although there were also many of these. Many of those moving north settled in Amsterdam, transforming what was a small port into one of the most important ports and commercial centers in the world by 1630.

There is good reason to attribute an important part of the Dutch ascendancy to its Protestant work ethic based on Calvinism, which promoted industry, thrift, and education. In the Netherlands in the 17th century, social status was largely determined by income. The rich, then the aristocrats, then lower status which was attributed to farmers, craft and tradesmen, shopkeepers, and government bureaucrats, constituted the upper and middle classes. Below them were positioned skilled laborers, maids, servants, sailors, and other persons employed in the service industry. At the bottom of the pyramid were the poor and "paupers"–impoverished peasants, many of whom tried their luck in a city as beggars or day laborers. The church made serious efforts to help and to encourage workers to achieve their best success.

The Dutch were relatively tolerant toward competing religious ideas during the 17th century, when their economic dominance expanded. The acceptance of Catholics and Jews, however, did not play a major role in the rich Asian and American trades. After the revolt from Catholic Spain, the Dutch created a quasi-official church that was initially based on a more liberal form of Calvinism, but many cities in the Netherlands allowed other religions to worship in private. Voyages in the rich trades were also able to take investments from Catholics and Jews as well since Amsterdam did not persecute or prosecute them. These investors worked on a much more limited scale than came from the Dutch Reformed Church members.

In Holland during the 17th century, there were no Catholics among the elite and successful merchants. Some Jews were able to invest, but in limited numbers and monetary amounts. Only two Jewish investors were recorded in the VOC, indicative that toleration of different religions was not essential to the financial growth of the Netherlands. Tolerance–at least of Jews–resulted in benefit to the Dutch Republic. They contributed some financial resources, and Jewish refugees from Portugal and Spain had valuable skills to offer the Dutch, especially in terms of navigational knowledge and experience. This contribution aided in the rapid Dutch expansion into the East and West Indies. The northern Netherlands obtained the necessary knowledge of far off regions without the help of Iberian Catholics. Hollanders had been participating in the rich Asian trades with their Iberian overlords. For example, an important member of the state Protestant church and government worker who also worked for Iberian overlords, traveled to Portuguese Goa in India and wrote an important book. He detailed trade routes and important information about Asia. The book contributed significantly to Holland's early seafaring knowledge.

Along with religious and ethnic tolerance, a bourgeoisie society was created which contributed to the economic success of the Republic. In the Netherlands, the beneficiaries of the atmosphere of religious tolerance became the bourgeoisie who made the greatest investments and reinvestments of their wealth. The old and continuing landed aristocracy—mostly found in the more northern areas of the Netherlands—were far more inclined to invest and reinvest their wealth into land and then collect their rent earnings without contributing to the new ventures that created the Golden Age. Many of the original aristocracy were hidebound Catholics and not inclined to join with the Protestants to further the interests of the Republic. This diminution of general economic activity carried on the traditions and failures of Spain. There, many merchants who succeeded in business, then left business to buy land and titles with their wealth rather than reinvest in new ventures. While this advanced their individual and family status, it did not create industry or employment. Changes in The Netherlands—including the important religious tolerance—resulted in a decidedly weaker aristocracy and considerably larger and more successful middle class, which caught the vision of reinvesting in business.

The Dutch Reformed Church was created during a European religious upheaval, the Protestant Reformation. Catholicism dominated Dutch religion until the early 16th century as it did in the vast majority of the Christian world. In the 16th century and well into the 17th, it was dangerous to profess Protestant beliefs outwardly in most of Europe, including the Netherlands. In Catholic countries of Europe, Protestants were ruthlessly prosecuted, and not rarely, killed. During the 1500s and 1600s, numerous people, church congregations, and some countries, were spurred on by ideas that broke with the established powers of the Catholic Church. Many of the main grievances levied against the Catholic Church were its corruption, with the sale of indulgences, and the incredible amounts of secular power that Catholic rulers controlled across Europe. Prosecution forced dissenting church leaders to flee first to Germany–a relative safe haven for Protestants at the time. In Germany the Reformed Church gained its early support and was able to adopt a new ideology. After a few years in exile, church leaders eventually returned to the Netherlands to spread these ideas to their own people. The third wave of the Reformation–Calvinism–arrived in the Netherlands in the 1540s, converting both parts of the elite and the common population, especially in Flanders.

As the Protestant Reformation progressed, Lutheranism did not gain much support among the Dutch; but Calvinism–introduced two decades later–did. In reaction to Spanish Catholic persecution, the Calvinists rebelled. Once ignited, the movement quickly spread among all Dutch regions and finally resulted in what would become the Dutch revolt. In 1566, the *Beeldenstorm* erupted, which involved the destruction of religious depictions in churches. In the same year, William the Silent, Prince of Orange–a convert to Calvinism–started the Eighty Years' War–1568-1648. Elizabeth I of England–for political reasons—lent assistance to the solidarity provided from the Protestant Dutch Reformed Church in opposition to Catholic Spain. This eventually resulted in the Netherlands winning the Eighty Years' War and achieving independence. The central role of the church in this drawn-out and historically significant conflict solidified its position as the de facto state Church of the Netherlands. The number of Catholics dwindled due outmigration and to the lack of priests.

Civil war broke out in the 1610s between strict and liberal Calvinists. The liberal States of Holland left the conservative Protestant Republic. The strict Calvinist side under Prince Maurice of Orange and the other provinces won and the previous official head of state of the County of Holland, Johan van Oldebarnevelt, was executed. Calvinism became the de facto state religion.

Soon after the effective expulsion of the Republic's Catholics, the Dutch Reformed Church garnered the status of being the "public" or "privileged" church. It was never *formally* adopted as the state religion, but it was that in all but statute. Dutch law required that every public official be a communicant member. Consequently, the church had hand-in-glove relations with the Dutch government. Only Dutch Reformed Church members could have their businesses open on Sundays. All others had to comply with the rules that considered Sunday to be a religious day and not one allowed for conducting business.

The relationship with the civil government allowed the church to grow rapidly in size, wealth, and power. Explorers, seafarers, and colonizers, from the Dutch Republic carried Dutch Reformed doctrines over much of the world. Settlers and missionaries proselytized their church's doctrines and practices all over the world, most notably in South Africa and in America.

Information and Foreign Words and Phrases from Chapter Four
- *Beeldenstorm* in Dutch [lit. statue/image storm], term for outbreaks of destruction of religious images by Protestants that occurred in Europe in the 16th century. Known in English as the Great Iconoclasm or Iconoclastic Fury.
- *NHK, Nederlandse Hervormde Kerk*: Netherlands Reformed Dutch Church. Earlier known as *Nederduitsche* [North Dutch or *Niederdeutsche* [North German] Church
- *Punto in aria*: Italian for needle-lace, point-lace in England. Literally, "stitch in air."
- *Stomacher*: Dutch for a richly ornamented garment covering the stomach and chest, worn by both sexes in the 15th and 16th centuries, and later worn under a bodice by women
- *Vlieger*: Dutch for a large floor length sleeveless gown
- *Vrouw*: Dutch for wife

# CHAPTER FIVE

## DOWN TO THE SEA IN SHIPS

IN THE YEAR OF OUR LORD, 1640, THE MONTH OF MAY

Piet Van Brakel's world as he had known it was gone, and he was only nineteen years old. His parents and sisters immersed themselves in the church and scarcely talked of anything else. His friends were gone from Amsterdam to foreign or at least far away schools or places of menial labor for subsistence. The family farm was eking out a meager living for the ones still at home, but there was not enough to feed a large, vigorous, young, man. It was time for Piet to find a new world.

"Father," he asked, "what do you think about the idea of me emigrating to England and starting in business there?"

"No good. When we Dutch gained supremacy on the seas, we trampled on the British in such a way that they will never forget or forgive. You would have to change your name, get rid of your accent, and fake a whole past. I don't think you can accomplish that in time to have a life there."

"So, go into the merchant marine like Bart and Hendrick? What do I know about being a sailor? Would I be a cabin boy or a swabbie?"

"You have asked the right question to the right man, my Son. It happens that I do still have connections which would let you start as a junior officer. What you accomplish in that position would determine your success or failure in the future. I have full confidence in you, Piet. There is nothing left here; but on the ships, merit is almost everything. You have a first step up, and then the rest will be up to you. What do you think?"

"What kind of connection do you have hidden in that clever brain of yours, Father?"

"Thanks for the compliment. Here is what I have. The Van Brakels still have majority ownership in two large *fluyts* and a fairly dominant position in the Flanders Genoese alum shipping industry. One of the captains contacted me asking if I knew a capable man who can learn sailing or is already a sailor and who has a good head for business. I told him that I might just know the right man. What do you say?"

"I have given thought to almost everything else. This is the best sounding offer I have had. I should say that I'll think about it, but there don't seem to be any other viable options. I'll do it. What do I have to do?"

"I have already written a letter of introduction and recommendation to the captain of the good ship *Z-Louisa Hendrika*. It is a 45-gun East Indiaman, refitted on loan by the VOC to the Admiralty of Zeeland to serve as combat ready freighter and warship. You take the letter with you and go by fast coach tomorrow morning to the Province of Zeeland. The shipping office and the ship itself are located in Brugge in the low country. When you get to the wharf area ask anyone for Captain Fookenzoon Corren and his ship the *Z-Louisa Hendrika*. You'll have no trouble getting directions. Everyone in shipping—and certainly everyone on the Brugge wharves–knows Corren or about him. He is something of a legend."

Change seemed to be the general rule of life for young Piet Van Brakel. He accepted his fate with some regret, thinking that it was unjust and unfair; but it was the best available to him. He vowed to make the best of the situation. Piet spent the day packing his meager collection of belongings, mostly books. At the break of dawn, he stepped into the fast coach headed for Zeeland and his new life, whatever that might be.

He was sweaty, dirty, tired, and hungry, when he finally stepped out of the coach and onto the Port of Bruges-Zeebrugge wharf. His first order of business was to get food. There were inns, restaurants, and vendors, aplenty along the wharf. Piet observed that the entire wharf—indeed, the entire city—had seen better days. Store fronts needed paint; wooden plank sidewalks needed repair; and the harbor itself seemed to have shrunk from years of silting of the delta of the Zwin River. The canal-laced city was one of Belgium's most important ports, and for a time during its history, Bruges had been known as the world's chief commercial city.

He chose the most prosperous looking of the seaside restaurants–the Old Flandrensis–walked in and found a seat at a table for four. A not-very-clean waitress with bad teeth in a frankly dirty dress and apron asked,

"What's yer pleasure, Laddie?"

"A menu, if you please,"

"Menu's in me 'ead. Printin's costs too much in these hard days. I can recite it fer ye, if ye wants."

"What's your best seafood, please?"

"Now, that's a geed cherse, Boy. Somma our best meals come frum the *frutas del mar.* Oysters is geed and geed fer ye, if ye gets me meanin'. Also, they're fresh caught this mornin'. With some ale and a hunk of strong German bread, ye have yerself a meal."

"Sounds good to me. Please bring plenty of fresh butter, too."

"Parta the fare. We got the best."

The plate, eating utensils, and the pewter tumbler were not nearly as clean as his mother provided…but then, his mother was not there and likely would never be. He shrugged and dug in. The fare—especially the hard, dark bread–was filling and tasted good. The ale was strong and dark, flavored with the Old Flandrensis' own herbal mixture called *gruit.* The restaurant's brewers purchased their mixture from the *gruithuis* in nearby Bruges then added an extra measure of hops and some brown sugar plus their own secret recipe for acidification to help preserve it. The recipe led to the development of red-brown beers. The resulting ale was the best Piet had ever tasted.

Near the end of his meal, an old sailor plunked himself in one of the chairs at Piet's table.

"Mind if Aye joins ye?" the gnarled old salt asked.

"Glad for the company. And I have a question for you, if you don't mind. Could you direct me to the Z-*Louisa Hendrika* and her captain, Mr. Corren?"

"Geed thing fer ye that eye took me seat at yer table. Aye happen ta be the first mate on said ship. Aye'll get me vittles and youse an' me can go right down and go aboard without no rigmarole."

"I'd be obliged," Piet said, recognizing good luck when he saw it.

"Aye'm Ephraim Van der Antwerpen. Where do youse hale frum?"

"Amsterdam."

"Ah, ha, come here lookin' fer work, I'd guess. Amsterdam is in the doldrums, I understand, of late."

"It is. That's a fact Ephraim. My name is Piet, by the way."

"The old man's lookin' fer a junior mate. Last one took off and stole somma the crew's holdin's. He's a dead mensch if any o' them catches up."

"That's why I'm here."

He produced the letter from his father.

"Sorry, Laddie, Aye'm not sa geed at the readin'; could ye tell me what it says?"

Piet summarized it, omitting the fact that it came from his father. The putative author became "a businessman of some importance".

Ephraim was definitely pleased.

"Cap'n'll be glad ta have ye aboard. 'Specially since ye kin read and write and all. Ye any geed wi' yer sums?"

"I am."

"All the better. I think ye'll work out right well, Laddie. Let me fill me pouch, and we'll git back to the ship. Aye think this'll be a geed day fer us all."

Ephraim had two large helpings of waffles smothered in thick salted butter and brown sugar syrup and a rafter of thick cut bacon and quaffed a pint and a half of Gersten [barley] lager made from the restaurant's special mash.

He wiped his whiskers with the back of his sleeve, and said, "Let's be one our way, then."

The walk was slow. The first mate had a peg leg and an exaggerated limp. He was older than Piet presumed most seagoing officers would be—probably as much as fifty. They climbed the gangplank of the good ship Z-*Louisa Hendrika* which was more of a combat ready gunboat that the commercial ship he had been expecting. Ephraim limped his way past the officers' staterooms and aft to the captain's cabin and knocked softly.

"Who knocks?" came the husky voice of Captain Jans Fokkenzoon Corren.

"I be Ephraim Van der Antwerpen, First Mate, Captain, Sir. I seek entry with a good prospect to fill the empty second mate post, Sir."

Piet posed a question with his face.

"He's a stickler for protocol, titles, and spit-and-polish. Best to learn that right off, Piet. Yuh'll get on a good deal better, if you do."

The door opened, and Capt. Corren gestured for the two men seeking entry to come in.

"First Mate," the captain greeted the older officer. "And I presume this is young Piet Corneliuszoon Van Bakel, son of Cornelius and Greta?"

"Yes, Sir," Piet said. "Beggin' your pardon, Sir, but the surname is Van Brakel," Piet enunciated.

"Oh, Aye. It's been a while since I had the pleasure of your mother's home cookin'. I got a bit rusty on the name. Pardon me. I have never been too good with land lubbers' names. Come in and have a seat."

Capt. Corren pointed to the two straight backed, very Italian looking chairs facing a modest sized wood desk covered with papers and charts.

The captain occupied what the officers, crew, and any passengers called the "great cabin". Capt. Corren's quarters spanned the entire width of the stern with large windows on each side and aft with a view of the ship's wake. Besides being a cargo vessel, the *Z-Louisa Hendrika* was fitted out as a 45-gun warship. The cabin was be separated from the rest of the ship, and further subdivided into day and night cabins with movable panels that could be removed in time of battle to leave the deck clear the whole length of the ship.

"That is very handsome wood in those chairs and the desk, Sir. Philippine mahogany?" Piet asked rubbing his hand over the shiny and waxed smooth brown wood.

"Nay, but you're close. Got it on a voyage some years ago in a stopover in Malaysia—Kuala Lumpur, the capital. Have you heard of that strange and exotic heathen place, Piet?"

"I have read of the country, Malaysia, but I am not acquainted with Kuala Lumpur, I'm afraid."

"Hardly any decent Christians are, My Boy; but if you sign on for a full hitch, I see you get there and to a good many other excitin' places. How does that sound?"

"Just like I had hoped for, Captain."

"Good answer, Son. I think we'll get along just fine. I have a few questions for you: Are you a good worker, loyal, and obedient to your superiors? How are you at your sums, readin' and writin'?"

"I think I measure up well in all categories, Sir."

"Then, Emanuel will get you off to the land sharks to board and fit you out. You'll need some trainin' to be able to be an officer and not to throw up every time we hit a bump. So, let's meet again in my cabin three days hence at second bell of the mornin' watch."

"Yes, Sir. I will be here on the correct day and at the right time, ready to learn or to sail or both, whatever is required of me."

"Good lad."

Capt. Corren turned his attention back to his charts and began making light marks with a compass and triangle. Piet divined that it was time to exit without being prodded.

In the passageway, Piet asked Emanuel, "Sorry to be ignorant, but what time on the clock is the second bell of the morning watch?"

"That'd be 0600, Piet. You'll get onto it quick enough. Won't be long before you won't say the hour anymore, just how many bells it is."

"Can I stow my gear on board, Emanuel, I don't have any other place to stay?"

"I'm gonna be presumptuous here, Piet, and take you to the second mate's stateroom. It'll be yours unless the captain demotes you between now and Friday."

The stateroom was neat, clean… shipshape; but it was small, smaller than the servant's rooms back at his boyhood home. With a moment's scrutiny, he decided it would do just fine. He set down his sea bag and ran a hand over the well-made bed. The blanket was so tight that he could have bounced a guilder coin on it with more than one bounce. He was going to have to learn how to make a bed like that, he decided; and he would have to do it very soon.

On the *Z-Louisa Hendrika*–as on most large sailing ships–the officers and paying passengers had an individual or shared cabin, whereas, the crew shared a large open sleeping area below decks with stacked cargo. They had a hammock each, which hung from a hook on the bulkhead.

"There'll be five passengers this voyage. A family'a three—one a little girl, and three daughters of one of the Dukes of Brugge –that's the Dutch way a sayin' it–who live in Cranenburg House—that's the Count of Flanders' palace. They're the hoity toity; so be very careful a those lasses. That's a word to the wise. Anyway, the passengers take up two staterooms, and I have the other. If we had more passengers, you would probably have the hut up by the head—a fate as bad as death."

"What's our cargo, Emanuel?"

"Somethin' of a hodgepodge—a little a this and a little a that. Mosta the crew deck has Flanders linen. But, the main thing is alum. We got crates and crates of that valuable stuff. We picked it up in Genoa, and we'll be haulin' it ta London—that's in England, as ya probably know."

"Beggin' your pardon for my ignorance, Emanuel; but I don't know what alum is."

"Oh, the long name's "aluminium". It's real valuable stuff. We've got ourselves a good fightin' ship and might well need it to keep off the thievin" Venetian pirates and even English sea bandits afore we get into port in London.

"It's used to make very expensive paper for the rich. The Jews use it for dyein' cloth; they have to have it to be able to dye their cloth before colorin'it. Makes the color stay fast. The Jews make the best and longest lastin' wholesale cloth in the world, ya know. In London, they use it to soften and tan leather. Sometimes we go to Morocco where they do the same thing. Very interestin' place, that Morocco."

"I am interested…in alum, I mean," said Piet, "I want to learn all about it. Are there any books aboard the *Z-Louisa Hendrika*?"

"Capt'n's got a fine library in his cabin. You'll have to get right chummy with him to use though. Those books're precious. Might not be real useful to the likes of men like us: fulla big words, small print, and scientific-like stuff. No penning novels or nuthin' like that, no, Sir."

"I'll give it a go once we're at sea, and I have a chance to prove myself."

"There's the spirit, Lad. Now, we need to do as the capt'un says and get you to the land sharks before closin' time."

Emanuel and Piet made three stops on their shopping trip. The first was at the Sailors' Emporium on Bruges Avenue. With Emanuel's guidance, Piet bought three sets of canvas pullover shirts and pantaloons, three pairs of deck shoes, and five pairs of under linens and stockings. He got two hooded slickers and oiled whale skin pants for the expected bad weather, and three good oily raw wool sweaters. At the Gentleman's Place, on Counts Street, he bought two navy blue uniforms with second mate's stripes and an officer's cap, white shirts, and dark ties. At The Outfitters—further down the street—Emanuel made him get two dirks, a short sea going saber with blood grooves, and a gold handled dress sword. Of necessity, he had to purchase a sea trunk to store his wares in.

When it came time to pay at the Sailor's Emporium, Piet was embarrassed to find that he did not have enough money, not by half.

He opened his mouth to say so, but Emanuel stopped him.

"Mr. Goldstein, this man is the new second officer of the Z-*Louisa Hendrika*. Cap'n Corren vouches for him, as do I. Let's just put it on the tab, if you please."

"But of course, First Mate Van der Antwerpen. We've a long and successful history with the captain and his crew. We wish you a safe voyage, and will see you when you return," the small orthodox Jew said without hesitation.

He was dressed in an immaculately clean black coat, white shirt with no tie, black shoes, and a characteristic broad brimmed hat favored by those of his religion. Piet was familiar with them and had had many profitable business ventures with the Jewish merchants of Amsterdam. He was grateful for Mr. Goldstein having made his purchases easy and sparing him embarrassment. The same courtesies were afforded by the managers and shop keepers in the Gentleman's Place and at the Outfitters. He was off to a good start.

# The History:
## The alum trade

By the late 16th and early 17th centuries, alum ranked among the more precious cargoes that were traded across Europe, valuable enough for English privateers to seize ships carrying it and taking it to home ports, where it was sold to the growing cloth industry in Britain. In the two hundred years preceding the Golden Age of the Netherlands, Genoa, Italy became the premier mover of the precious metal. It's principle competitor and enemy was Venice which similarly turned to piracy to ensure its continuing supply.

The Genoa to Flanders route was massive and controlled by the brilliantly efficient and ambitious Genoese. From thirteen hundred to the mid-seventeen hundreds, the alum shipments to Flanders contributed greatly to the flowering of the low countries and the Netherlands and made a place for such otherwise unwelcome people as Jews, Arabs, and Protestants, to thrive. In 1346, the militant merchants of Genoa captured the Greek island of Chios, situated in the northern Aegean Sea eight kilometers from the coast of Turkey across the Chios Strait. The importance of the island was that it was composed of volcanic ash and limestone, a rich source of alunite. It also produced a significant percentage of the world's gum mastic and a minor but thriving industry producing a pleasant wine and marble. The port was a convenient entrée into the Mediterranean.

Mastic was collected from a wild shrub that grows in the south of Chios; it provided the flavoring for *mastíkha*, a Greek liqueur and was used to make an early popular fad, chewing gum. Mastic was also so popular that it became a must for making incense which facilitated meditation for people along the trade routes. It was the perfume of the Geminis. Mastic gum was widely touted as a natural remedy for a wide range of gastrointestinal conditions. In addition, an aromatic oil found in mastic gum was known throughout Asia Minor and Europe to help fight bad breath. Chio had a thriving tanning industry, and the Genoese took it all over and turned the trade into a seemingly never-ending source of wealth.

The Genoese used the island as an intermediary center of trade and transshipment, collecting the yield of alunite from all the mines of Asia Minor—a closely guarded monopoly. This assured a constant supply of adequate quantities of alum to fill the holds of twenty vast specialized ships, the largest wooden ships ever built before or afterward. Ships of the Genoese alum fleet plied regularly between Chios and Bruges–year around–stopping en route at Cadiz to take on water and other supplies. That trade evolved into a unique public and private domestic trade settlement system, a coherent, mobile, and economically flexible, marvel of the age. The Genoese had branches—*comuni*, sovereign city-states–all over the world for the express purpose of importing and exporting alum early on and later for the discovery of sources, mining, importing and exporting, and manufacturing, aluminum products.

The Genoese defended and maintained their *comuni* as a near monopoly for trading alum on the Atlantic and Mediterranean coasts. They established a presence on the northern Atlantic coast of the Iberian Peninsula at Santiago de Compostela, on the Atlantic coast of Morocco, thereby gaining control of the whole western Mediterranean basin. In every area, they built and maintained a system of fortifications. The Genoese settlements around the shores of the Mediterranean and the Black Sea were of incredibly high importance because of their urban planning, architecture, and landscaping, reflective of their highly successful expansionistic-mercantile approach.

Genoa's competitors and enemies were the Venetians: The Venetian empire's period of maximum splendor–between the 12th century and the end of the 16th century–was marked by a significant expansion of the territorial possessions she had won and which she then defended militarily as fully integrated, active parts of the Venetian state. The "Gulf of Venice" in the mind of the ambitious Venetians was the entire Adriatic. Wars were fought; pirates thrived; and a world centered on alum provided an uneasy but highly profitable and useful life. In this trade the Dutch *fluyts* with no real security protections could not participate. The Dutch–like all traders—had to turn to heavily armed combat ready ships of the line to be able to exist and persist.

The value and created need for alum—aluminum—was enormous. That created a complex and major industrial and trading complex. For example, the chemical was used in the production of high quality wove papers. Wove papers were robust and lasting; it has been demonstrated that papers made during the 18th century which were never exposed to a hostile environment remained beautiful and intact for two hundred fifty years. Historical evidence indicates active use of alum for millennia before the Genoese became involved. It was used for mordanting [A mordant–dye fixative–is a substance used to set or bind dyes on fabrics, which then attaches to the fabric or tissue as in tanning]; for tanning and softening leather; for presumptive medicinal and cosmetic properties; and as an auxiliary agent in miscellaneous metal and glass finishes.]

Alum occurs in small quantities naturally; otherwise it has to be manufactured from two principal sources, alunite [alum rock or alum stone] and alum shale [alum ore or alum schist]. Small quantities of natural alum could be found–as clearly recognizable crystals–even anciently in the Egyptian deserts–south-west of the Oasis, El Khârga. It was carried by Bedouin camel trains then shipped down the Nile to Alexandria. Yemen was another ancient source. This source was crude aluminum sulphate and needed skilled treatment to convert it into ammonium alum. The process required the addition of urine. The solution then boiled, and the alum allowed to crystallize out of it on cooling. Sources of this kind were clearly limited and highly valued.

Alunite–as such–was only found not only in Asia Minor. However, all over Italy–close to sites of recent volcanic activity, Piombino, Volterra, Pozzuoli near Naples, Elba, and the Aeolian islands–large quantities of trachyte were found in formations of igneous rocks mainly composed of aluminium silicates. Processes evolved to convert the raw igneous rocks into alunite using locally available sulphurous fumes or acid. That acidified product required separating excess alumina by roasting and lixiviating [leaching]—a process of extracting substances from a solid by dissolving them in a liquid. Roasting often made the alum rock porous, facilitating the extraction of the alum, which could then be further purified by boiling and recrystallization. The sources of alunite, however, were limited to areas of active or extinct volcanic extrusion and were the sole property of Italians, especially the Genoese. The ability to extract aluminum from alum shales provided the means to create large quantities. Apart from accessibility and other economic factors, the main criteria for success in working them depended on the presence of aluminum salts, pyrites and carbonaceous material, such as oil, in the schists, as well as the availability of fuel, usually coal, for boiling and evaporating the extracts. All of these were abundantly present in and around Genoa; the Genoese had the shipping and the contractual relationships in Asia Minor and the Middle East; and, as a result, they had virtual control of the commerce in the valuable material for two centuries.

The City States of northern Italy were transformed and widened the changing market. They included, initially, the Venetian Republic, Genoa and Pisa. Pisa, however, soon succumbed to the expanding power of Florence. Genoa soon built up lasting trade links with north-western Europe, e.g. with important centers such as the Duchy of Burgundy and the extensive markets of the Hanseatic League in the Baltic, and it came to accept a lucrative role as a middleman. Raw alum or alum ore was brought to Alexandria by caravan from Lake Chad, Castile, and Greece.

The Genoese fleet brought its sources of alum from Alexandria and Bejaïa—later, Algeria–back to the home city-state. Genoa also expanded its sources of supply and recipients into the Black Sea and off the eastern coast of Asia Minor selling finished goods to Sicily, The Netherlands, Egypt, and the Levant.

Venice became Genoa's greatest and most ruthless competitor. Early on, Venice was not a manufacturing city, but she served as a sea and land transporter of goods–including alum–to other parts of Europe. Later, she developed her own industries, some of which required alum. Venice remained throughout the centuries of the alum trade as a merchant-state primarily. She maintained mercantile relations with both the Christian and Muslim worlds. Genoa and Venice fought enough battles with each other to warrant the title of them being in a state of war over commercial interests. After the fall of Constantinople, major problems for Europe arose regarding supplies of alum to meet the ever-increasing demand. For example, most of the prime qualities of English cloth were made from wool dyed before weaving. Once the Levant came under the control of the Turks, Western Europe faced an increasingly difficult situation—that of obtaining a reliable supply of alum.

Genoa, Venice, and other countries around the globe, including Europe, North and South America, and the Mediterranean, came to realize the importance of having a domestic supply of alum. Necessity has always been the mother of invention; so, the rising demands led to further expansion of the shale alum industry. That led to further exploitation of deposits of alum shale, including in France, central Europe, extending to Scandinavia, the Rhineland, and other parts of Germany. Genoa, especially, strove to provide the transportation needs and manufacturing expertise for the expanding market in competition with Venice. Harsh rule under the Turks led to a highly increased effort to manufacture alum everywhere in Europe. Although trade links continued for a time between the West and the Levant, the fall of Constantinople and the Eastern Church, eventually brought about the migration of skilled laborers and technicians, especially Jews, to the west. The Netherlands with its policies and preferences for tolerance reaped the benefits opening the scope for entrepreneurs, prospectors, and shipping companies.

The Dutch turned their attention to a small town about twenty-five miles north or Rome [within the Papal States] called Tolfa where a large deposit of Alunite was discovered. They followed the lead of Genoa, Florence, and Venice. The Popes regarded the deposits at Tolfa as a divine gift and wanted profits to be devoted to the defense of Christendom with a further crusade against the Turks. The stage was set for a fateful showdown.

## CHAPTER SIX

# A YOUNG MAN IS INTRODUCED TO ADVENTURES AT SEA

IN THE YEAR OF OUR LORD, 1640, THE MONTH OF JUNE

The *Z-Louisa Hendrika* set sail three days later on calm seas, for which Piet was grateful. They were officially bound for Alexandria, Bejaïa, and Algeria; but First Mate Van der Antwerpen took Piet aside to tell him of Capt. Corren's secret plans.

"We're headed fer Asia Minor all right, but we're gonna make a little lay over in Italy."

"Genoa?"

"Maybe, but only if the Cap'n thinks we can hold a bit more alum. Throw out the passenger's trunks or whatever it takes."

Piet laughed.

"So, what's the big secret, really?"

"We're goin' across to Rome area, a little town called Tolfa."

"What's in Tolfa that's worth a big diversion?"

"Alum. The Pope's alum, matter-o'-fac. Seems the Pope's got hisself a big deposit of Alunite and is willin' to have a little negotiation about it."

"Does the Pope want more than it's worth, Ephraim?"

"Apparently, like most of them religious folk, he wants somethin' on the strange side. Don' know what; but I'm considerable curious; and so's the Cap'n."

"And you've got my inquisitiveness way up, too, First Mate. How long before we get there?"

"Well, Laddie, it's somethin' like 234 leagues from Bruges—with a good wind we'll be there in a week if we can stay downwind like we are now. Maybe more, maybe less, dependin' on the winds and the Good Lord's pleasure."

"I'll have to learn patience, First Mate. I don't think it's in my nature."

They hit a short period of squalls midway which cost them a day. On the eighth day, they entered Civitavecchia, the Port of Rome.

"Incredible!" Piet exclaimed as they passed into the harbor amidst a forest of masts and a beehive of shipboard activity greater than he had ever seen.

"Aye, that it is." Ephraim responded. "This port came to look like this nearly two hundred years ago when the fortress was handed over to Cardinal Vitelleschi. The Papal army assumed control and took charge of the defenses. Civitavecchia again the most important port of Rome—this time not controlled by the old Roman government but by the Papal authority. That was the best thing that could happen for seagoing commerce. It was the start of international commerce and prosperity for the Papal city state. They have built and replaced a good many buildings, renovated the walls, rebuilt the aqueduct, and made the harbor free of silt and open to all traffic…for a price."

"What price?"

"A Papal tax to support the next crusade."

"Seriously, Ephraim, does the pope really plan another fool's errand to the Holy Land?"

"That's what I hear. There's no understandin' the ways of the papist, I always say."

"Apparently not."

"I'm guessing that there's likely a tax on alum since it is so valuable and so plentiful hereabouts."

"You'd be guessin' right, Second Mate. I figger we'll soon be seein' a tax too high for us to make a profit. Maybe, we'll have to do battle."

"I had never dreamed that ordinary commerce could be so complicated, expensive, and troublesome as Alexandria and Bejaïa, Ephraim."

"I can truthfully say that you have not seen the tip of the iceberg yet, My Boy. Wait'll we start doin' business with those pagans."

The two shipmates made their way along the quays of the harbor towards the Papal Customs House. Along the way Ephraim pointed out the ruins of old medieval city of Centumcellae located in the hills between Allumiere and Tarquinia. Over the decades the name changed into Cincelle and later Cencelle.

The customs house was a dour sort of place, a Catholic stronghold. The customs agents were all black robed priests. There were no women, and no smiles. There was a high order of efficiency bespeaking the importance of the port and especially of the alum trade to the Papacy. Over the years, the port of Civitavecchia had become the most important locus for the export of alum to the other ports around the Mediterranean Sea and in Europe. The export of alum made up seventy percent of the total income of the pope; so, therefore, it was considered holy.

To protect this export, Pope Julius II built the Fortress Michelangelo between 1508 and 1535. It remained a grim reminder that smuggling, attempts to ship alum without a customs stamp, or employing non papal workmen was a sure way to see the inside of one of the Fortress's dungeons.

"Good morrow, Brother," Ephraim greeted the stern agent at the entryway into the customs house."

The priest nodded, "State your business."

"Alum from Tolfa, then shipping to points east and west."

"Which ports?"

"All around the Med, Sir, and thence to Alexandria and Bejaïa."

He did not even hint at there being a secret plan on the part of the captain.

"What ship?"

"The good ship *Z-Louisa Hendrika*."

"Captain?"

"Cap'n Corren, Sir. Captain Jans Fokkenzoon Corren."

"From?"

"Bruges, Sir."

"I must correct you before we go further. I am not "Sir"; I am Father or Padre, and it is best that you address me in that fashion."

"Yes, Father."

The priest made quick calculations on his abacus.

"You are required to use Papal wagons, muleteers, and at the port, Papal stevedores. Understood?"

"Yes, Father."

"Good. The customs total is therefore the cost of twenty-four days of an ancient legionnaire's wages: One denarius or 18 Pound Sterling per day. Because of the antagonism shown by the Dutch rebels towards God's holy church, the price for the heathens is double. Take it or leave it."

Piet made hasty calculations: 24 denarius = 120 guilders. It was a staggering sum. He considered it to be akin to armed robbery or blackmail, but he kept his opinion to himself.

"That is very steep, Father. Almost twice the fee when we last did business here," Ephraim said as politely as he could manage.

"Come back into the fold of the true church, and we will be able to negotiate. Now, if you are not able to pay the custom, we cannot do business, and you cannot obtain alum. Come, you are wasting my time. Yes or no?"

Ephraim gritted his teeth and said quietly, "*Certo*."

He had to look away to conceal his fury and disgust.

"Gold," the priest said.

"We have sufficient," Ephraim said.

"Then, I will summon the notary, and our transaction will be completed. Have the young man fetch the gold, then I will issue the stamp."

He looked away and said to the man waiting behind the two mates of the *Z-Louisa Hendrika*, "Next."

They stepped away. Piet ran from the building all the way to the ship, found the captain and told him about the transaction. Capt. Corren growled and uttered several oaths, but finally ordered two men to haul a chest of golden guilders to the customs house.

From beginning to end, the transaction took four hours and put Ephraim into a foul mood that only a large cup of grog would dissipate.

"Ya need nae ta forget this day and its lessons, My Boy. We'll be back one day, and we'll see those shavelings beg for mercy. Ye mark my words. One day, yea'll be lordin' it over those practioners of popery. Just you wait."

## The History:
## The Northern Invasion

The Dutch, English and French, moved in robust numbers and enthusiastic force into the Mediterranean Sea as a result of their superior sailing ships. During the last decades of the sixteenth century, merchants from those northern European states entered in sufficiently large numbers to eliminate the previous Italian monopoly and ultimately to ruin Italian trade with the Near East by the early seventeenth century. They seized majority control of the sea's commercial, financial, and maritime, life. One historian described the period as being when "The Dutch swarmed into the Mediterranean like so many heavy insects crashing against the window panes–for their entry was neither gentle nor discreet."

Because there was no state strong enough to impose order and predictability over the marketplace of the Mediterranean, the Italian city states—particularly Genoa and Venice–lost their position of dominance. The strength of the Venetian merchant marine was cut in half between 1550 and 1590, a harbinger of the diminution of dominance to come. The result was that with state sovereignty over the marketplace so fragmented and largely unasserted, piracy—Christian, Muslim, and entrepreneurial–soared to new heights making for commerce the necessity of being on such a constant war footing that almost all ships converted to combat ready construction. Sailors became—of necessity—combatants which changed the complexion of trade itself into a militarily combatant enterprise.

There was an exception: not all Mediterranean commerce fell under putative northern control. The lucrative and extensive short haul coastal carrying trade of the Mediterranean remained highly competitive and contested even throughout the seventeenth century. The lack of all over control led to an increase in smuggling on a small scale and to an increase in piracy. In the 1620s, the Venetians regained control of several trades and trade routes that had previously been lost to the Dutch, such as the export of cotton goods from Egypt and Cyprus to Germany. On the large scale a Dutch convoy sailed to the Levant twice a year. On the smaller scale, the small swift and poorly armed ships of Marseilles found a lucrative economic niche by transporting small quantities of goods on behalf of merchants operating from and between Mediterranean ports. The carrying trade operating between Ottoman port towns constituted another example of such services rendered on a small scale for individual customers. In aggregate, such commerce was very significant and regularly challenged by the members of the northern invasion. The seventeenth century was a very dynamic era.

Throughout the century both Barbary and the Maltese corsairs had insisted on the right of *visita*, the practice of boarding ships to check whether passengers or cargo belonging to the wrong religion–according to the rules of the corso–were on board. This was a practice detested by all merchant captains, including the merchants of Marseilles who–in their determined pursuit of the coastal trade in the Ottoman

Empire–naturally carried both. Passengers on those ships traveled at their peril. There was at least a de facto corso war that carried on throughout the latter half of the sixteenth and throughout the seventeenth century.

Between the eras of decline of the Italian, Portuguese, and Spanish, navies and the rise of the maritime powers of Holland, France, and England—the so-called northern invasion, there was an interregnum which profited the myriads of Mediterranean people who lived off plunder. In the Caribbean Antilles it became the golden age of the buccaneers while in the Mediterranean it was that for the Barbary chieftains.

At its core–besides privateering and outright theft–the corso wars were driven by the Mediterranean slave trade that was at least the equal to the more well-known Atlantic triangular slave trade among England, Africa, and the Americas or the Sugar Trade Triangle. White Gold–as British colonists dubbed it–was the engine of the slave trade that brought millions of Africans to the Americas, especially to the Caribbean beginning in the early 16th century. The history of every nation in the Caribbean, much of South America, and parts of the Southern United States, was forever shaped by sugar cane plantations started as cash crops and involved negro slaves as property bought and sold by European superpowers.

# CHAPTER SEVEN

# ALUM COMMERCE, AND THE SEDUCTION OF PROFIT

IN THE YEAR OF OUR LORD, 1640, THE MONTH OF JUNE

The officers and crew of the *Z-Louisa Hendrika*, slogged the twenty-five miles from Port of Civitavecchia to the alum mines in Tolfa. They took fourteen four-wheel carts pulled by six mules or horses once each day, seven days a week for three weeks over the execrable rutted roads to the village. The carts were empty going up to the village and returned full of extremely heavy powdery alunite on the way back. Each day they made the trip up and the trip back, an exhausting and loathsome journey.

Capt. Corren and First Mate Ephraim Van der Antwerpen were on the edge of needing commitment to a sanitarium for the insane as they tried to get a semblance of efficiency and effort from dilapidated carts which broke down two or three times each way, every trip; balky animals, which had a nasty habit of dying while in harness; elitist and privileged stevedores, miners, haulers, and agents—many agents in an over bloated bureaucracy. The sailors and stevedores suffered spells of coughing which advanced to hemoptosis, and exhaustion to the point of necessitating the implementation of mere eight-hour workdays. Even beer and whiskey were inadequate to deal with the lung maladies. Men coughed themselves to death; several members of the crew and of the Papal stevedores gave up the ghost and died during their efforts to make a living. The workmen were generally stoical, happy to have a job, which was less odious than starving and watching their families dwindle and die in a hard world.

Very early on, Piet determined that the dry dust that emanated from the mines, the wagons, and the ship holds, was highly deleterious to the health of his lungs. Many of his shipmates made fun of him when he swathed his mouth and nose with tightly woven cloth and scrupulously washed the cloth at the end of each workday. However, he had the quiet satisfaction of being one of the few men who could still blow out a candle or hold his breath to swim under water at the end of the alum collection job.

Piet's quick mind took in the village and mines at Tolfa. He observed that cheap labor abounded, that there was little evidence of a security force, and several routes to the seaside. He took a little time each day to scout out the benefits and risks of the several land routes he discovered. An idea germinated in his fertile mind that suggested seductively that this was a place where a bold and enterprising young man with adequate banking could take over and become rich before the Papal soldiers got wind of his efforts.

The ship's holds were filled to the brim with the noxious but highly valuable alunite after five days of labor that bordered on galley slave conditions. Finally, they were done and ready to stand on the deck of a full and profitable ship and to breath good clean sea air.

The *Z-Louisa Hendrika*, turned north towards the Baltic ports. As they stopped in each harbor, they offloaded alunite in exchange for luxury items made of silk, furs, wool, cotton, and various metals worth double what the alunite cost in Tolfa. Capt. Corren was determined to turn over a significant profit early in the voyage in order to have funds enough to return home to Bruges with a full cargo hold to sell just before winter and the violence of the north-sea settled in. Their first stop was the Port of Le Havre on the west coast of France. The port was immense in comparison to what Piet had seen thus far. The Port of Le Havre was the second-largest commercial port in France in terms of overall tonnage, and the largest container port. Making use of the Port of Le Havre was not cheap. In order to bring the *Z-Louisa Hendrika* to quay side, required the services of an expensive pilot ship to tow the larger vessel safely through the forest of ships safely.

Le Havre bustled with controlled and efficient activity. Before noon the *Z-Louisa Hendrika*'s cargo holds were a quarter emptied of their alunite and refilled with fine hard anthracite coal. Piet took careful notes about how the workmen went about their duties for future reference. He made good pen and ink drawings of the arrangement of the port and its harbor facilities—especially its series of canal-like docks–while he and the crew waited for the French stevedores to finish their work. He spent two hours sitting on a comfortable bench in the Grand Port Maritime du Havre–a public institution responsible for administrative public service tasks and missions of industrial and commercial public service. Each function had its own small office and sufficient employees to keep the business humming. Piet made note that–if he one day were to be the administrator of such a facility—he would make it look just like this one.

For the next three months, the *Z-Louisa Hendrika* made its way north to Dunkerque, Anvers, Rotterdam, Amsterdam, Bremerhaven, Hamburg, and to its farthest north port, Stockholm, on the Baltic Sea. Piet became increasingly impressed with the business acumen and efficiency of Capt. Corren as he negotiated offloading and acquiring new cargoes at each port. Piet kept accurate notes and became increasingly ambitious as he began to acquire the knowledge that an ambitious young man needed to strike off on his own. The Ports of Stockholm were located in the largest city–and capital–of Sweden. It was located on an arm of the Baltic Sea where the Salt Bay meets Lake Mala. The Swedish port was another of the old, beautiful, and very active, major shipping ports seen on the voyage. It was one of the best natural harbors of entire world. The port was actually multiple berthing locations built on many islands and the mainland, the Ports of Stockholm were located in one of the world's most beautiful cities. Stockholm—more accurately, Gamla stan–the Stockholm Old Town—was the most beautiful city Piet had seen thus far.

It was the center of culture, politics, shipping, and economy, in Sweden and a keen rival of the Copenhagen port, which was difficult to work with. Sailing into the harbor, Piet had an opportunity to admire ancient churches including the still handsome Finnish and German parish chapels—the still walled city being over four hundred years old by 1641 when the *Z-Louisa Hendrika* arrived–Three Crown Castle, colorful historic 12th century German Hanseatic league merchant houses lining the quay streets, and a magnificent view of Sweden's fjords and harbors. The most impressive sight for Piet was the large number of 60 and 70 cannon bearing ships moored along the eastern quay next to the grand royal castle.

Fortunately for the crew, the restocking—mostly of bar iron–took three days which gave them a chance to walk about in the clean, well maintained, and remarkably colorful, city. Capt. Corren left the First Mate Ephraim Van der Antwerpen in charge of the ship and crew while he went to the southern corner of the city to conduct the ship's business. Import and export was administered largely by German merchants living by the squares *Kornhamnstorg* [Grain Harbor] and *Järntorget* [Iron]. For the first time in his life, Piet–as first mate ashore–was given the privilege to stay in one of Stockholm's finest hotels—the Gambla Stan, on Skeppsbron, overlooking Lake Mälaren, 800 feet from the Royal Palace. It was built in 1600, only 41 years ago. He reveled in the sights and sounds of the winding cobbled streets with their clattering horse hooves, carriage wheels, and the shouts of frolicking children, happy housewives, and barking Jämthund Swedish Elkhounds, the national dog; after the months of ship's food, he was captivated by the smells of roasted almonds, hot chocolate, smoky local wines, rosemary flavored Blackthorn beer, and carvers' cafés. He strolled around Riddarholmen islet and took in the sights of the palaces there. To find out if his Dutch Reformed Church religion was much different, he visited the Riddarholm Church and found it to be quite similar, making Stockholm not so much different from Amsterdam for him.

Capt. Corren turned the *Z-Louisa Hendrika* to the east for the next ports of call, and the start of real adventures for Piet van Brakel, some of which he was happy to survive. The captain decided to bypass London in the next part of the voyage, but with the intention of returning there as the last stop before making home port in Bruges.

The captain assembled the officers in his cabin to convey the planned remainder of the voyage, and to explain the reasons why he elected to make a long arm of the passage without stopping in ports of call.

"Gentlemen, while in Stockholm, I received a message from the owners, including the second mate's father, Cornelius van Brakel. It seems that the Greeks and the Turks are edging rapidly towards war again, and that has created a very profitable opportunity for us. The Greeks are in serious need of iron to manufacture weapons and are willing to pay a handsome premium for us to get a cargo to them in time to arm themselves against the heathen Turks who threaten invasion. As you know, it just so happens that we have a full cargo of bar iron which fits the bill perfectly. Our port of call is Chania in western Crete. There will be bonuses all around when we collect."

"Beggin' your pardon, Cap'n, but why don't they get what they need from Venice or even the Englanders or the French?" asked Ephraim.

"A good and fair question, First Mate. The reason is that the Turks have set up an embargo enforced by a blockade against shipping to Crete or any other Greek Island. The Venetians have too much invested in the long-term trade with the Turks and the other Muslim countries like Egypt to risk their lasting enmity. The Englanders and the rest of Europe are not keen on having a conflict with the Muslim countries; and, besides, they have too little iron at present to be able to share. The owners were contacted by Duke Regglioso–Venetian head of the *Regno di Candia* [Duchy of Candia] as they call Crete—to provide what they believe will save the Venetian hold on the island, and possibly even of Greece itself. They are willing to pay a serious—once-in-a-lifetime—premium, and we are happy to oblige."

"I presume we might encounter determined Turks as we pass into Cretan waters, Sir. Are our defenses enough?" Piet asked.

"Another good question and well put, Second Mate. The Turks have only two kinds of sailing vessels: large and lumbering cargo ships, and galley war ships. The cargo vessels are no threat, and we can move farther and faster than the galleys. Their slaves will wear out before they can ram us, and they have very little in the way of deck gunnery."

"We will need to do some training for hand-to-hand fighting, I presume, Captain."

"Glad you brought that up, Second Mate. I am aware of your exercises with the crew. Begin this very day to introduce those strange eastern fighting methods and get the men up to snuff with cutlasses. First Mate,

I will leave it to you to bring our cannoneers to readiness. That is all, men. Back to your posts."

The voyage was blessed. The weather was all fair winds and following seas with only three stops to let off a few passengers. Despite the well-known Christian and Muslim pirates that infested the seas, the *Z-Louisa Hendrika* sailed into the Mediterranean Sea all the way to the passage between Tunis and Sicily without sighting a brigand vessel.

"Too good to last, I suppose," the captain said to the officers at evening mess on the twenty-eighth day of the voyage."

"Best not to jinx it with positive projections, Sir," the First Mate said—ever the pessimist or superstitious sailor.

Ephraim was prophetic. Halfway into the morning watch, the lookout called down from the crow's nest,

"Ships ho! Look abaft and to the portside. A pair of corsairs comin' hard for us."

## THE HISTORY:
## THE RISE OF IMPORTANCE OF PORTS AND HARBORS

A harbor (haven) is a body of water where ships of all sizes and types can seek shelter, access to land venues, and storage, during periods when they are not in use. Ports are located in harbors and provide access to docking and transference of people and cargo.

Ports, historically, were usually built near natural harbors. More recently, they have also been located hundreds of miles up rivers or lakes in response to need. They are intermodal facilities—places where ship, and other transport methods converge. Ports have always played a key role in moving products both to interior sections of a country and to other countries, and therefore factored into the history of the country and the world.

Major provisions of ports include efficient management of customs regulations, record keeping, attracting and assisting clients, coordinating traffic and distribution of imports and exports, policing traffic, security for vessels and land facilities and bases for interdiction of smugglers, pirates, and invaders. History indicates that ports and harbors were crucial for military applications. A large percentage of military goods have been transported by ship, especially before the development of useful highways for trucking, railways, airways.

Historically, ports were constructed in geographically favorable locations to expedite the transfer of goods. Over time, active dockside communities emerged and thrived as waterborne trade developed and flourished. Coastal land changed as need progressed. Landside facilities development became acceptable even though some landowners protested but seldom threw up successful obstacles because expansion was inextricably linked to economic prosperity. History saw the development of landside facilities capable of accommodating ever larger and more numerous cargo ships. Such growth required longer berths, better roads, and better land conveyances. Eventually this led to large cranes, railway, and highway access. Such demands required acqui-sition of adjacent land which led to expansion of cities and of the importance of the more significant ports. Costs had to be shared, and the costs resulted in driving poorer landowners further to the interior and to less desirable locations. The costs included navigation planning such as providing and maintaining the width and depth of channels and harbors, keeping up with shipping and navigation technologies, and providing terminal facilities. Provisions had to be made for climate, seasonal, current, and tidal variations. Those and physical limitations of a waterway–including bottom conditions—over time determined the success, persistence, or failure, of a port or city. Many came and went with the demands of commerce.

From earliest history–whenever a civilization engaged in maritime trade–it recog-nized the need to develop seaports. One of the world's oldest known artificial harbors is at Wadi al-Jarf on the Red Sea. Other ancient ports include Guangzhou during Qin

Dynasty China, and Canopus, the principal Egyptian port for Greek trade before the foundation of Alexandria. In ancient Greece, Athens' port of Piraeus was the base for the Athenian fleet which played a crucial role in the Battle of Salamis against the Persians in 480 BCE which allowed the concept of individual worth to flourish. In ancient India from 3700 BCE, Lothal was a prominent city of the Indus valley civilization in what is now the modern state of Gujarāt. Ostia Antica was the original port of ancient Rome with Portus established by Claudius and enlarged by Trajan to supplement the nearby port of Ostia. In Japan–during the Edo period–the island of Dejima was the only port open for trade with Europe and received only a single Dutch ship per year. Osaka was the largest Japanese domestic port and the main trade hub for rice. Late Medieval and Renaissance ports were situated within the Mediterranean basin and grew with the advance of commerce.

A port city was recognizable because ports had harbors that were the center of the movement of people and products; they had particular buildings or spaces that dominated the city, such as dockyards, warehouses, customs houses, open markets, inns and pubs; finally, ports were recognizable because of the particular socio-economic groups that they sheltered. Generally, ports attracted a large number of merchants, bankers, bookkeepers, shopkeepers, shipbuilders, foreigners, pickpockets, pilferers, and prostitutes.

Port towns were centers for consumption and commercialization of products coming from the surrounding countryside, and they provided services. In addition to commercial trade, many of them—even in early history—served all related activities of shipbuilding, bookkeeping, notarial registration, credit, banking, ships' and crews' insurance, outfitting, and later, some came to organize specialized stock exchanges and chartered companies. Netherlands and Flemish port cities were especially successful at the stock and real estate business as it pertained to ships and the sea. Most ports were more-or-less tolerant environments for the exchange of unorthodox religious ideas, political concepts, or technological developments. The first areas to see the value of tolerance were the Dutch, and the last were the Catholic cities.

An unfortunate result of the overcrowding and transit of people from areas of endemic illness, and because most cities lacked public health regulations, facilities, or personnel or controlled access, disease—including plagues and epidemics–suffered devastation periodically. Ancient, Medieval, and Early Modern ports, and even Modern ports, fell victim to serious epidemics that threatened the livelihood and prosperity of their populations and also endangered their existence *per se*. The most dangerous threat came from the sea. The continuous arrival of foreign ships–usually seasonally bound–led to hectic periods around the docks, where surveillance was often reduced, very weak, or most often non-existent. Sick crews and contaminated products arrived in healthy ports. The ships' crews–often unaware of their health status–remained as long as was needed for their business transactions. They left for the next port trailing sickness and pestilence that quickly spread throughout the city, compounded by the overcrowding and filthy conditions within the urban setting.

For the people that lived in plague towns, the obvious choice when plague or disease broke out was to abandon the city for a place in the countryside–the traditional hinterland. Only the wealthy and healthy people had the strength and wherewithal to be able to abandon the town and to save themselves. Better educated populations of Western Europe became aware of the set of Roman Laws as regulative measures in the case of ships that had been hit by the plague or coming from areas where the plague was reported. Those enlightened cities–by Late Medieval times–turned away the plague ships and sent them back to their ports of origin. This seemed unduly harsh to the already sick sailors–but by doing so–the port cities avoided the mayhem, havoc, human, and economic, losses provoked by the spread of diseases they scarcely understood.

Smaller cities and regional ports began to develop partnerships by the Medieval period. The successful partnerships depended the partners having good hinterland and regional connections. The partnership arrangements and growth began in Northern Europe, and that gave them a distinct commercial advantage. Starting with Antwerp, Amsterdam, Hamburg, and the Baltic ports, and London, the selection process for partnerships followed the brilliant conclusion to adapt by the northerners following the waves of piecemeal political intricacies and diplomatic agreements that resulted in a great many failures. In order to have a chance to engage with a major southern European partner, most northern European ports had to fight their regional competitors in order to prevail as the main candidates for partnership. Antwerp eventually surpassed Bruges and Amsterdam and those two cities left Middleburg, Flushing, Hoorn, and Enkhuizen, behind. Southern port cities either failed or learned the hard way how to catch up.

Some of the port cities that lasted and still function well today include:

- The Medieval Flemish port city of Bruges (or Brugge), West Flanders, Belgium's history began in the 9th century CE when it was founded by Vikings. The name of the town and its port came from the old-Scandinavian word *Brygga* meaning "harbor" or "mooring place". The river Zwin linked the settlement to the North Sea, and it very quickly became an important international trading port. For a time during its history, Bruges was known as the world's chief commercial city. Today, it is one of Belgium's most important ports.
- Amsterdam: its port was first used in the late 13th century. Throughout the 16th and 17th centuries its port contributed greatly to the Golden Age of the Netherlands. Today, it is the fourth busiest port in Europe by metric tons of cargo.
- Dubrovnik: The shipping port of Dubrovnik was founded about 614 CE as Rausa, or Ragusium in what is now southern Croatia, by Roman refugees fleeing the Slav and Avar sack of Epidaurus. The prosperity of the city was historically based on maritime trade; as the capital of the maritime Republic of Ragusa, it achieved a high level of development, particularly during the 15th and 16th centuries, when it became notable for its wealth and skillful diplomacy. The city successfully balanced its sovereignty between the interests of Venice and the Ottoman Empire for centuries. The republic abolished the slave trade early in the 15th century and valued liberty highly. In its glory days the fleet of Dubrovnik equaled the fleet of Venice but was incomparably weaker than the fleet of the Netherlands. Gruz–the shipping port of

Dubrovnik on the Adriatic Sea Coast—is now one of the world's busiest cruise ports.

- Venice was founded in 421 CE by a Celtic people called the Veneti who lived along the coast of what is now Northeast Italy. Since 49 BCE they had been Roman citizens, but in 453 Attila the Hun invaded Italy. In terror, some Veneti fled to islands in the lagoon and built a village and port there. Venice was—for a time—the pre-eminent Mediterranean port. It declined drastically, but subsequently it unprecedentedly became one of most popular Mediterranean ports in all maritime history. Venice lives on as a beautiful city with its gothic architecture, Byzantine, and Arab influences and artworks, and its frenetically busy port.

- Lisbon, Portugal: the original settlement of the Port of Lisbon took place around 1200 BCE when it was a trading post for the Phoenicians. Rome ruled the Port from 205 BCE until 409 CE. Julius Caesar made it a municipality. The alpha city of Portugal is now one of the preeminent marine ports of Europe and is recognized for its rich culture in arts, education, media, entertainment, international trade, finance, commerce, and tourism.

- Istanbul, Turkey: The city today known as Istanbul has been the site of human settlement for approximately three thousand years. The original city was Lygos, and its ports were founded by Thracian tribes between the 13th and 11th centuries BCE. It is therefore one of the oldest ports in maritime history. As the new capital of the Roman Empire during late antiquity, the city rose to be the largest of the western world. Historically known as Byzantium and Constantinople, Istanbul is today the largest city and the cultural, economic, and financial center, in Turkey, and one of the major shipping ports since the Sea of Marmara, the Golden Horn, Black sea, and the Bosphorus, surround the city on all sides.

- Athens, Greece: The port of Piraeus has been inhabited since the 26th century BCE. In ancient Greece, Piraeus assumed its importance with its three busy deep water harbors located seven miles from the sea. Today, the 3,400-year-old city is the heart of cultural, political, economic, financial, and industrial life in Greece. Aside from its cultural treasures, Athens and the port of Piraeus remain vibrantly successful.

- Stockholm, Sweden: Stockholm is the capital of the Lake Mälaren Region, and as such can trace its origin back to at least two much older cities: Birka (c. 790–975 CE) and Sigtuna, which still exists but dominated the region c. 1000–1240. Stockholm received a state granted monopoly for most of the lands surrounding the Gulf of Bothnia which formed part of the city's trade territory. It was one of the best natural harbors of the era; and throughout the 17th century, countless foreign visitors marveled at the sight of large ships in the port at any one time. Today, Stockholm is a major shipping port, the capital of Sweden, and the center of media, culture, politics, and economy, in Sweden. The Stockholm marine port has nine berths and a mooring buoy which can accommodate up to ten cruise ships all at a time.

- Kuşadası is located on the central Aegean Sea coast of present-day Turkey south of Izmir. Early settlements and establishment of the port of Kuşadası were by the Lelegians and Carians who moved from the central Anatolia around the year 3000 BCE. In the 10th century BCE, the 12 cities of the Ionian League, including Samos, Miletos, Priene, Ephesus, and Smyrna, were established and were known as the most developed cities of the age; Kuşadası served their seaport. Over ensuing centuries, the city was invaded and dominated by Persians, the Roman Empire, the Byzantines, and–after disastrous earthquakes–was forced to rebuild as *Scala Nuova* serving the major Turkish cities. In the middle ages the port came under the domination of the Venetian and Genoese sailors and traders who established consulates here. Kuşadası is now a major tourist and cruise ship destination for the ancient Greek and Roman city of Ephesus.

- Alexandria, Egypt: The ports in the vicinity of Alexandria pre-date the establishment of the city itself by Alexander the Great in 331 BCE as the marine base for his fleet. Large port cities existed east of modern Alexandria along the western edge of what is now Abu Qir Bay as early as 1900 BCE. The Canopic—westernmost–branch of the Nile Delta still existed at that time and was widely used for shipping. In the period of Roman Egypt, grain was exported in large quantities from the city's Western Harbor, earning it the name "Portus Magnus". At the height of the Roman Empire, Alexandria shipped 83,000 tons of grain per year to Rome. By the time of the late Empire, the city shipped 220,000 tons of grain per year to Constantinople (now Istanbul). Today, Egypt has a total of 15 commercial ports along the Mediterranean and Red Sea coasts. The Alexandria Port Authority is the country's largest, and it handles 55% of Egypt's international trade. Overall, Alexandria's various harbors handle over 75% of Egypt's foreign trade. 80% of the country's imports and exports pass through the city.

- Bizerte, Tunisia: Phoenicians from Tyre founded the Port of Bizerte in about 1100 BCE. The port was taken over by Carthage during the Punic Wars; and finally, the Romans occupied the city and its port, which became the classical Hippo. The Turks took it in 1574 CE, and the city then became a corsair harbor and struggled against the French and the Venetians. Now, the port remains important since the region Bizerte's economy is very diverse: manufacturing–textile, auto parts, cookware–fishing, fruits, vegetables, and wheat. There are several military bases and year-round tourism. The port is being developed into a significant Mediterranean yachting marina.

# CHAPTER EIGHT

# Pirates, Corsairs, and Opportunity

In the year of our Lord, 1641, the month of October

The captain stood on the afterdeck squinting at the swiftly oncoming ships through his glass. As mobile as the *Z-Louisa Hendrika* was, Capt. Corren knew she was no match for the sleek corsairs' ships flying at them at full mast. He faced an existential dilemma: try and run, fail and fight an inevitable battle, or yield without a struggle and hope that he and his crew might survive and avoid impressment into slavery. If the ships were of Muslim origin, the specter of slavery and a short miserable life was highly likely and the loss of the ship and its valuable cargo a certainty. There was little time to deliberate. Capt. Corren chose a compromise.

"General quarters, all hands-on deck. Man the guns and stand ready," he ordered. "All sails aloft and full speed ahead."

The *Z-Louisa Hendrika* was able to stay just ahead of the corsairs almost until they came due west of Malta. By then, the corsairs pulled to either side of the Hendrika and were hailed in English by the captains of the two ships.

"Prepare to be boarded. Resistance is futile. Have ship's papers at the ready," came the preemptory orders.

Capt. Corren called out through the ship's bullhorn, "Send one emissary from each ship, no more. We are a Christian ship, and we will fight to the last man of our ship and yours before we will submit. We wish you now harm, but we will stand for none upon ourselves."

"Aye, aye," came the crisp reply.

Each corsair put down a dingy manned by an officer and a marine, all in battle dress.

Capt. Corren deemed that to be a good sign, but he knew all too well that both Christian and Muslim pirates would not hesitate to destroy them despite the general enmity between the two religions and the partiality for ships of their own kind.

"Men," he said quietly to the officers, "be prepared for treachery. Have your pistols and cutlasses at the ready but let us proceed as if this is a peaceful encounter."

The two skiffs drew alongside the port and starboard hulls. Roped ladders were dropped to the sailors. They affixed their skiffs to the hulls of the *Z-Louisa Hendrika* by an iron bolt protruding from the hulls for that purpose. The officers and noncoms climbed up the swaying rope ladders and were piped aboard.

Capt. Corren and his officers greeted the uniformed corsair officers with affable smiles to show that they entered Maltese waters in peace. The attire worn by the officers and noncoms boarding the *Hendrika* were regulation Maltese Knight uniforms—the papal garments: blood red jerkins emblazoned with large white Maltese crosses over white doublets, white britches, and heavy cuffed gloves, brilliantly polished knee-high cavalry boots, and a black plumed tricorn hat. The swords they wore were beautiful ceremonial long swords, worthless in a battle.

"Gentlemen, I am *Gonfanier* Philippe Villiers de L'Isle-Caracciolo. May I see the crew and officers' papers, Captain?" the lead officer asked politely. "I trust that each man is identified as to his religion."

Capt. Corren handed the pile of documents and said, "Every man here is a Christian as attested to in his papers. No Muslims."

The officer looked over each document that certified the religion of the sailor then handed them back to Capt. Corren.

"Thank you, Captain. These are dangerous waters, and one cannot be too careful. On behalf of the Sovereign Military Hospitaller Order of the Malta Knights Templar, I welcome you to our jurisdiction and offer our protection."

"Thank you, Sir. Your offer is most welcome. Should we expect much in the way of problems from here to our destination, Crete?"

"Unfortunately, the answer is an emphatic, 'yes'. You are no doubt well aware of the running corso war between Muslim and Christian corsairs. Those devils, the Barbary Pirates—or corsairs as they fancy themselves—are age-old enemies of the true faith. And that includes the denizens of the pirate states of Sicily, portions of Malta, and Sardinia. It is our duty as men of honor and faith to follow the rules of engagement in these waters; the heathens have no such honor. We all recognize Jews as fair targets, and we know that Muslims and their accursed religion are righteous targets. While we honor the right of *visita*, they target everyone indiscriminately. More often than not, they either murder all of the crews and passengers or sell them into slavery, which is a fiendish calamity for a good Christian."

"It is evident that you have served the cause of Christianity, *Gonfanier* [Banner bearer=major]. We salute you."

His reference was to the prominent medals on the *Gonfanier*'s chest: Gold Medal with Swords pro Merito Melitensi, Merit medals for the Lourdes Pilgrimages, and Orders under protection of the Holy See—the Order of the Holy Sepulcher. The major gave a politely humble little bow to the Dutch captain for having taken note of his awards.

"It is my strong advice to you, Captain, that you and your ship come to our port in Malta—Valleta–rest, do some trading–if the opportunity presents itself–and that you not carry on towards the Greek Islands. We cannot guarantee your safety if you decide to proceed to Crete, unfortunately."

"*Gonfanier*, we respect your information about your area and the wisdom of your advice. We accept your invitation to visit Valleta. We will make our final decision about whether to go on after further investigation in your jurisdiction. Thank you for your courtesy and hospitality, Sir."

"Follow my ship into port, Captain. My crew will see to your comfort and needs while you are with us."

The captain nodded his assent, and *Gonfanier* de L'Isle-Caracciolo made a smart about-face and left the *Z-Louisa Hendrika*.

The *Z-Louisa Hendrika* dutifully followed the larger man-of-war corsair vessel—the *Guardian of Valleta*—as closely as possible towards the port city but could not keep up with the sleeker and lighter warship. The *Guardian* had to wait an hour at the mouth of the harbor until the *Hendrika* could come along side.

As they sailed from open ocean towards the port, Capt. Corren summoned his officers to his cabin.

"Despite what was said between me and the *Gonfanier*, Gentlemen, I have no intention of abandoning our determination to complete our mission of doing business on Crete. I believe in you, in our stalwart crew, and in our fine ship. The prize we seek is worth risk. Can I count on each of you to obey my orders and to do what is necessary to land in Crete safely, even if we have to do battle with Turkish galleys?"

There was a unanimous "Aye, aye" from the officers, and they left the captain's cabin to mingle with the crew to develop an enthusiasm from them for the project.

The *Z-Louisa Hendrika* was towed by a pilot boat the last thirty meters to where it could be berthed close to the wharf. Its fore and aft anchors were dropped to good holding ground on the deep solid ocean floor where the anchor flukes could dig in securely. The heavy chain hung in a half-Catenary to the bottom. The chain attachment to the anchor was horizontal to keep the force on the anchor horizontal, a relatively new security technology for Dutch ships. The crew attached the ship's heavy ropes from the series of bollards on the deck to harbor buoys. By convention on the ship, mooring hitch knots fixed the ship to the dock and slipped buntlines were used for the buoys. They are equally good temporary knots which are released quickly with a tug on the free end. A sturdy—and necessarily long—oaken gangplank courtesy of the port authority provided an exit way from the ship's deck to the wharf.

The crew was given the freedom of Valleta after stern warnings to behave themselves or feel the lash. The officers were met on the wharf by Giovanni Paolo Lascaris, the Magnus Magister of the Sovereign Military Hospitaller Order of the Malta Knights Templar and his retinue. The man—officially classed as a prince–was tall, lean, and had the tough look of a seasoned fighter—every bit a crusader on his way to expiation.

His beard was long, salt-and-pepper, and neatly trimmed. The Magister's uniform was resplendent with color and pageantry—the papal garments: blood red jerkins emblazoned with a large white Latin cross over his white doublet, white britches, heavy cuffed gloves, brilliantly polished knee-high cavalry boots, and a crown indicating his status as a prince of state as well as the commander-in-chief of an army. He wore an ornate ceremonial sword festooned with gold trimming. His chest showed his battle medals—no religious insignias, since he was not a professed clergyman like many of his retinue.

The Magnus Magister stood stiff and stoical, the grand representation of a papal order of knights that had evolved into a fearsome military machine and the putative rulers of a small island nation state in the middle of the Mediterranean Sea. The island sat in a strategic location midway between Sicily, Tripoli, and Tunis, as a protector of the northern expanse of the Mediterranean, and of the 528 km wide Strait of Sicily between Tunisia and Sicily. They accepted and defended the responsibility to protect—for Christianity—the entrance into the Tyrrhenian Sea. After the fall of Jerusalem in 1187 at the hands of Saladin, The Great, the knights turned Malta into a fortress against the Ottoman horde at the Vatican's request. Malta cemented its position and reputation most famously when it held out against the full might of Suleiman the Magnificent in 1565. Educated Western European observers were awed by the Ottomans; they—not the Ottomans—gave Suleiman the epithet "the Magnificent" rather than the Ottomans, who named him "the Lawgiver" For that, the knights were credited for having saved Christian Europe.

Magnus Magister Lascaris was flanked by twelve knights and dames of the order in service uniform. For other than very formal occasions, the knights dressed in their work attire to convey the message that they were not just a military order protecting a religious enclave; but that they defended a sovereign nation—a claim disputed by much of the world at the time and for centuries into the future. The ceremonial rank and file retinue wore black, military-style jackets with epaulets and Order of Malta patch on their left shoulders, black shirts emblazoned with the eight-pointed Maltese crosses on a white field. They had black trousers tucked into knee-high polished black boots, an order of Malta patch on their left shoulders, and a corsairs steel helmet. The knights and dames alternated in a fan flanking the Magnus Magister and each held a sharp pointed spear staff at rigid right angles to the ground. Professed knights–unlike their Magister–wore a long silver rosary around their necks.

In addition–standing near the magister–were four standard bearers. One held a banner with the order's motto in white on a red background: *Tuitio fidei et obsequium pauperum* [Latin–defense of the faith and assistance to the poor]. A second held a red rectangular flag with a white square Latin cross—the order of Malta's Works—under a statement of the Order's fealty to the Virgin Mary as its patroness–with the title of Our Lady of Mount Philermos. A third held the personal flag of the Grand Master—an eight-pointed white cross on a red background encircled by a beaded collar and surmounted by a crown. The eight-pointed Maltese cross stemmed from its ancient links with the Republic of Amalfi. The fourth standard bearer held a heavy staff bearing the coat of arms of the Magnus Magister. The thick wooden standard was brightly colored; its gold framing gleamed in the late afternoon sun.

The centuries-old arms of Grand Master Fra' Giacomo Dalla Torre del Tempio di Sanguinetto were divided into quarters alongside those of the Order. The quarters displayed a Gules cross Argent–for Saint John—an azure, on a mount vert a square tower in perspective, the ports Sable, surmounted by a Latin cross between two mullets of six Argent. Behind the shield was a Maltese cross with the Arms surrounded by the papal Collar–symbol of the Grand Master–within a princely mantle and surmounted by a closed crown.

*Gonfanier* de L'Isle-Caracciolo stood at attention before the Magnus Magister, saluted sharply then bowed. He introduced the officers of the *Z-Louisa Hendrika* to the Grand Master.

The Grand Master—speaking in formal Italian with a translator—welcomed the officers, "Gentlemen, welcome to our country. We are happy to have been of service to you fellow-Christians and wish you to know that you are always welcome here, and you—as Christians—will always come under the protection of our corsairs. Enjoy your stay in Valleta; profit from commerce with us; and return again to feel our friendship."

Capt. Corren, in his full dress ship's captain uniform, replied formally, "Magnus Magister Lascaris, Knights and Dames of the order of the Knights Templar of Malta, I convey the sincere thanks of the good Christian ship *Z-Louisa Hendrika*, its captain and crew, for deliverance from the menace of the Muslim pirates, and for your welcoming spirit. We plan to return for trade in peace many times in the future and to further the prosperity of our Flemish nation and of yours."

The captain and the Grand Master saluted each other and shook hands.

"Fare well on your upcoming voyage. May you be safe and find profit."

"And, we wish you and your people success as you strive to protect the Christian waterways."

Piet took note of the cargo hold and began to feel a growing dread. Muslim slaves carried cargo ashore to trade with the merchants' guild and carried back onto the ship a replacement cargo of linens and sheep skins. It was a nonprofitable bargain recognized as a payment for protection by the Maltese corsairs.

The hold was divided into a third holding the cargo of baled linens and sheep skins, and the other two-thirds were bare. A chill pervaded the young Dutch first mate when his eyes adjusted to the dark, and he could begin to see row upon row of iron shackles fixed to the deck at intervals barely large enough to hold two men lying next to each other touching shoulders. As darkness fell, he watched tall stern knights pushing men in Muslim garb into the emptiness of their quarters for a voyage—a harbinger of their lives to come.

# The History:
## Pirates and Slavery in the 16th and 17th Centuries

The history and horrors of slavery in the triangle-shaped route that went through the Atlantic, linking Europe, Africa, and the Americas—the so-called Atlantic Triangle–are fairly well known to most Americans. Much less well known is the history of slavery in the Mediterranean. The 16th and 17th centuries were the zenith of that odious industry of human trafficking.

Throughout the sixteenth and seventeenth centuries, slavery in the Mediterranean region was pursued on a massive scale by both Christian and Muslim powers. Central of this, was the struggle between two empires: the Habsburgs, who controlled Spain, the Holy Roman Empire, and The Dutch Low Countries, versus the Ottoman Empire which controlled Greece, Turkey, the Levant, Egypt, and also projected their power on the Barbary Coast. Religion was central in the struggle between these two powers; so, it was acceptable to capture people from the other faith and subject them into slavery. The slavery pursued by both Christians and Muslims within the Mediterranean is therefore sometimes called 'faith slavery', which was fiercest within the Mediterranean because it was there where Christianity and Islam collided. It can be debated if faith slavery was truly pursued in the name of God primarily, or as an excuse for pursuing the trade or if it was also a lucrative business-undertaking as a secondary role. Although the debate has never been fully concluded, it is certain that at least some of the Knights of Malta truly believed in their religious cause for capturing heathens, as indicated by their writings. The *Qur'an* and The Prophet's writings and actions clearly sanction the enslavement of nonbelievers, especially women who can be sold into sexual slavery with impunity and with full scriptural authorization.

The Ottomans and other Muslim powers also relied upon the doctrine of Jihad, which conceived the struggle within the Mediterranean as holy in defense of the one true religion. The religious character of the slave-trade in the Mediterranean was publicly advertised and made abundantly apparent. However–given the immense profits gained by both factions–the economic motive of the powers dealing with slavery cannot be objectively disregarded. Just as in the Atlantic Triangle slave trade, slaves were a cheap labor force and were often forced to do difficult and hard work that paid employees refused. It was not lost on the corsairs of either religion and their land-based overlords that slave kidnappings deprived enemy of manpower and work force, thereby impairing the enemy's economic and military strength. Further, enslaving people of any importance to a nation and its religion provided a highly profitable source of ransom income.

Sultan Suleiman–known as the Magnificent in the West and Lawgiver among the Muslims–changed the Ottoman focus from the mainland to the sea for the very reasons described above. Besides being a remarkable military leader, Suleiman was a savvy businessman with an eye to capturing Christian slaves and booty. He besieged

Vienna in 1529, but this stretched his resources to the limit and consequently eventually caused him to withdraw from Europe.

Suleiman ordered Barbarossa—Muslim ruler of Algiers, and noted corsair, pirate, and slaver–to appear before him in Istanbul. After some parlaying, Suleiman convinced Barbarossa to join him and gave him the title of *Kapudan Pasha* [admiral-in-chief] tasking him to increase Ottoman naval power, which he did with considerable success. In 1534, Barbarossa set out with a fleet which disrupted mercantile trade, but also carried out raids in Sicily and against the Knights of Malta. Charles V (1500-1558), the Holy Roman Emperor and king of Spain–also known as Charles I of Spain—quickly recognized the danger posed by the Barbary Pirates and their commander Barbarossa on his South-Italian and Sicilian possessions. He actively tried to work against Ottoman ambitions within the Mediterranean. Thus, the Mediterranean Sea evolved into a lethal contest between dueling powers, fueling the practice of slavery within the entirety of the Mediterranean; and the practices hardened as matters of faith, economy, and politics, collided.

The Muslim slavery network consisted of Algiers, Tripoli, Tunis, Istanbul, and Cairo, as major ports, with numerous smaller ports in between. The Christian one included Lisbon, Valetta [Malta], Livorno, and Marseilles, as the major hubs. Dutch ships were active early on with the Christian network, but later in the 17th century, they served select Muslim ports and venues.

Between 1580-1680 the number of slaves within Algiers was 20,000-40,000. Other ports on the Barbary Coast generally were not as large as Algiers and as continuously profitable. Tunis had around 6000 slaves and Tripoli around 2,000. On average there were a total of about 35,000 slaves on the Barbary Coast. Slaves were treated abominably; therefore, there was a high attrition rate. To keep a stable population of slaves on the Barbary Coast, many replacements were needed. A quarter of the slave-population within North-Africa had to be replaced, as the attrition rate on the Barbary Coast was around 20-25%. This had to do not only with the wretchedly bad conditions that the slaves endured day to day, but also the general hygiene standard within the Barbary Coast which led to multiple plague outbreaks. Some 8,500 replacements were needed a year.

Taking into account the Reconquista, and enslavement of Moors, and Transatlantic slave trade, it is accurate to think that the numbers in Spain exceeded a million. Valetta, Malta—became the bastion of Christendom in the Mediterranean; so, it played an important role in acquiring these slaves. The slave market of Valetta in its prime competed in numbers with the expansive markets in Istanbul and Algiers, which numbered around 20,000-30,000 slaves. The Knights Hospitaller were one of the most important players within the slave-trade. The slave and pirate trades were interlinked; so, the knights became significant corsair pirates, often not particularly careful about distinguishing the religions of the captives of their piracy. In fact, both Muslim and Christian pirates preyed on their own as well as the other religion.

For the most part, well-armed English, French, and Dutch, ships tried to protect both Muslim and Christian travelers. French consuls in the Arab world issued safe-conduct to Arab Christians to protect them from western—Christian—pirates and also to protect Muslims from Muslim pirates. Neither of the protective documents were particularly successful: Muslim travelers on western ships and Christian travelers on Muslim ships were not always or even regularly secure on such ships.

In the sixteenth and early seventeenth centuries, the result was eventually a fairly egalitarian but also anarchic commercial world, including in the slave trade. The seventeenth century was chaotic; the pursuit of profit meant–first and foremost–a search for adequate protection followed by a quest for profit. This resulted in some rather remarkable relationships of convenience given the intensity of religion in the countries around the Mediterranean. Later in the 17th century, Muslim naval powers protected Christian shipping against Muslim piracy, and Muslim merchants invoked Christian protection against Maltese attacks on their shipping. Corsairing, too, was less and less structured along the lines of the eternal war between Christianity and Islam. In that era, Christian pirates—including Maltese knights–were just as willing to attack other Christians as they were to attack Muslims.

For centuries, the normal occupation of thousands of men in the Mediterranean was to set sail from their home ports in order to attack the shipping or the coastal regions of the area. Their victims were slaughtered or sold into slavery; their goods plundered and sold as prizes. The definition of the corsairs' enemies on either side was that they worshipped a different God. As the seventeenth century passed, there was a progressive exclusion of Muslims from the commercial and maritime life of the sea. In the evolution of Mediterranean commerce, there was a continuing significance of religion in the pursuit of profit. On both sides of the religious divide, corsairs came to see themselves—and were seen by others–as participants in an exalted battle against an age-old enemy of the faith. As men of honor and faith, they were obliged to follow certain rules of engagement. The most fundamental rule concerned the identity of the enemy. For the Christians, all Muslims and all Jews were fair targets. For the Muslim corsairs, the same applied to the Christians.

There was a definite inability of any one power to dominate the carrying trade in the first half of the seventeenth century, plus high levels of piracy. The last quarter of the sixteenth and first half of the seventeenth centuries was indeed a most difficult period for the policing of the seas: Turkey had now withdrawn to the eastern Mediterranean; the navies of the Italian states had declined; French naval power had been exhausted during the Wars of Religion; and the Spanish navy had been exhausted by the Dutch and Elizabethan wars. International anarchy and the exhaustion of the Mediterranean naval powers proved a fertile soil for piracy to come into its own in the hazardous waters of the central Mediterranean.

As early as Byzantine times, the Maniots –one of Greece's toughest populations– were well known as pirates. The Maniots considered piracy as a legitimate response to the fact that their land was poor, and it became their main source of income. The main victims of Maniot pirates were the Ottomans, but the Maniots also targeted ships of European countries. The Haida and Tlingit tribes, who lived along the coast of southern Alaska and on islands in northwest British Columbia, were traditionally known as fierce warriors, pirates, and slave-traders, raiding as far as California. Between 1 and 1.25 million Europeans were captured by Barbary pirates and sold as slaves in North

Africa and the Ottoman Empire during those centuries of the golden age of piracy. The most famous corsairs were the Ottoman Hayreddin and his older brother Oruç Reis [Redbeard], Turgut Reis [known as Dragut in the West, Kurtoğlu [known as Curtogoli in the West], Kemal Reis, Salih Reis and Koca Murat Reis. A few Barbary pirates, such as the Dutch Jan Janszoon and the English John Ward [Yusuf Reis], were renegade European privateers who had converted to Islam. By the end of the 17th and into the 18th centuries, once pirates were caught, justice was meted out in a summary fashion; and many ended their lives by "dancing the hempen jig".

It took two 19th century wars for the nascent U.S. Navy to stop the Barbary Pirates from exacting tribute from American ships and enslaving its sailors. Emory University has digitized records of 36,000 slaving voyages and detailed records of 91,491 Africans liberated by U.S. naval courts.

# CHAPTER NINE

# DANGEROUS COMMERCE

IN THE YEAR OF OUR LORD, 1642, THE MONTH OF FEBRUARY

Captain Corren kept to his cabin for most the voyage to Chania in western Crete. He avoided the passengers entirely and spoke to the ship's officers only when necessary. First Mate Ephraim Van der Antwerpen assumed most of Capt. Corren's shipboard duties on the tedious mid-Mediterranean trip. The Maltese corsair ship the *Guardian of Valleta* flanked the *Z-Louisa Hendrika* on its starboard side, and a second man-of-war, the *Pride of Malta*, flanked the merchant ship on its port side. Capt. Corren refused even to look at the two ostensibly defensive partners in the quest for a peaceful voyage to Crete. Piet could only wonder and surmise about the presence of the two Maltese ships and could not get the idea out of his mind that they were related to the slaves below decks.

Both Piet and Ephraim were happy to have the corsairs flanking them. The nearer they got to Crete, the more often they saw Muslim pirate ships. Those Muslim corsairs made no effort to hide their piratical intent, certainly would have attacked had the Maltese corsairs not been there making a prominent statement.

Capt. Corren emerged from his cabin at the 2-2-2 pattern of the morning watch bells shortly after the crewman in the crow's nest called out, "Land ho!" as the first indication that they were nearing Crete. Piet still had to sneak a peek at his hourglass and at the sun's position to reassure himself that it was seven o'clock in the morning. He still needed to shed some of his land lubber thinking before he could be a fully nautical oriented seaman.

He invited the three mates to a working breakfast after the bos'n's mate told the captain that they were probably no more than two days out from the port of Chania.

"I have not been hospitable since we left Malta, and I want you to know that I am sorry for that. I had a well-deserved personal torment which I did not want to share with anyone. However, it is now critical that you know of the decisions made by your captain and how they will affect you.

"You know that I was obligated to have a private meeting with Giovanni Paolo Lascaris, the Magnus Magister of the knights. You also are well aware that we took on a cargo of Muslim slaves. What you don't know is that I had to make a pact with the devil. In order to have safe passage to Crete, and to be permitted to take our alum cargo there for a profit, I had to agree to ship slaves. I am deeply personally opposed to slavery and the trafficking in human beings for any purpose. The reality is that we will never be able to trade in this part of the Mediterranean if we fail to do the bidding of the Knights of Malta.

"It is worse than just taking this dreadful cargo, I have to admit to you. At the minimum, we must also transport a cargo of Christian slaves to the accursed Turks from Crete. To fail to agree to all of that, we would all have been dead men before being allowed to sail from Malta. The Magnus Magister dangled a carrot on a stick to me that few men would be able to resist, even without the threats. Since I had to agree to this slaving voyage and all the profits we will turn after Malta gets its profit, it was only sensible for me to agree to make three yearly trips between Malta and Crete and from Crete to Laiazzo on the Turkish coast."

"Shipping slaves?!" Piet exclaimed, his face red.

He was working to control his mounting anger with difficulty.

Ephraim put it more bluntly, "I am a Christian man. I did not sign on to do slavin'"

"Is that your last word, First Mate?"

"On the subject of slavin' and with you I'll not bend, Sir."

"You are relieved of your duties as first mate as of this instant, Mr. Van der Antwerpen," Captain Corren said calmly, quietly, and with finality.

"Confine yourself to your quarters. You may join the crew in a fight if you want, but otherwise have nothing to do with the men. Ephraim, you may serve the ship as you wish, but you will obey my orders as we enter peril. Do not even contemplate sabotage or mutiny. I will not hesitate to order the punishments according to the law of the sea. Are we understanding each other? Should you speak to any man to arouse him to defy his captain, or should you be such a fool as to take arms against me, you will be dealt with as the law of the sea requires. Do I need to expand any further?"

"Nay, Sir. I'll not give you an excuse to stretch my neck. Ye'll have no trouble from me. Just pay me my due and release me in Flanders when... or if...we ever get back there."

"Then we are understood. I am a man of my word. Keep yours, and you will even get a recommendation as a man of conscience from me when you apply for the crew of your next ship. You will receive a pro-rated share of the ship's profits as the first officer to this point of time, but all you can expect hereafter is a share of the daily rations and a place to sleep. Do not try my patience again."

A pall fell over the room. Ephraim turned and left without further comment or looking back.

Captain Corren broke the chilly silence, "Mr. Van Brakel, do you accept the obligations, responsibilities, and privileges of first officer, including the requirement to obey my orders, even those related to the slaves?"

Capt. Corren asked pointedly, looking the young man directly in the eyes.

Piet took a moment to ponder his moral crisis before answering. He took care with his thinking and what he would say. His career at sea might well hinge on his next utterance.

"Aye, aye, Sir. I am no less opposed to slavery than Mr. Van der Antwerpen, but I am committed to obedience the law of the sea and to following orders. Captain, I do not think of myself as a religious man, although I come from a religious family. They would not approve, but they are practical people of commerce. They understand profit better than they do angels and demons and such. I think much the same way. Personally, I abhor slavery of any people, Muslims or Christians; but I am hardly the earth's judge, nor have I been appointed to determine how trade is conducted. I am just the second mate, and I obey the captain's orders. I will serve you and this ship, Sir, especially now as we head into dangerous waters."

"Good man. Now, Piet, I am sure you are aware that we are likely to face stern opposition from pirates and maybe even governments. How is your combat training going with the men?"

"Quite good. I think they will be energized by the approach of danger and will work the harder for it. I have faith I them and promise that they will be as ready as possible when the need arises."

"Need I go over the duties of first mate?"

"No, Sir. I have paid good attention to how Mr. Van der Antwerpen conducted his business aboard the ship, and he was kind enough to teach me considerable during the long days at sea. I will certainly ask if I need information."

"Well said, Lad. As of today, you are First Mate."

"I will give it my level best, Sir."

"Now, First Mate," said Capt. Corren, "we have some planning and work to do. Just be aware that you are the first officer and not the crewmens' friend. The safety of the men, the ship, and of the cargo, are your first responsibility as it is mine, Will the men accept you?"

"Aye, they do. They fear the pirates and are moved to work hard at the drilling. We will be ready for what comes."

The young boy whose job it was "to assist the bosun's mate", was sitting dreamily in the crow's nest just as the pre-dawn glow began to rise on the eastern horizon. He squinted to the west, took a moment to be sure of what he was seeing, then called out to the deck below.

"Land ho, to starboard east. Looks to be an island."

The officer of the day took note and decided that it was not necessary to rouse the officers or the crew yet. It was only two bells of the morning watch. Another hour and a half of sleep would always be appreciated.

Immediately after the ringing of the seven o'clock bells—2 bells, pause, 2 bells, pause, 2 bells—the third mate's assistant, Ensign Braunfel, knocked softly on Piet's cabin door and told him of the sighting.

Piet quickly shook off the torpor of his morning dreams and turned out of his bunk. Before informing Capt. Corren, he confirmed the sighting and checked against the navigation map: Crete. They were close enough to begin to make out some images of the harbor and port of Chania. He also took note of the continued presence of the two flanking Maltese corsairs.

The captain was already up and stirring about in his cabin when Piet knocked softly on his door.

"Enter."

"Captain, Sir, the watch has sighted Crete. No opposition in sight."

"What is your estimate of landfall?"

"Two hours—maybe at about two bells of the forenoon watch."

"Get the men moving. I want a tidy ship when we enter port. Ready the lines and anchors so as not to waste time. We need to get our business done as quickly as possible and then to be quit of Crete."

"Aye, aye, Sir," said Piet and left to bring the ship to life.

For once, Piet was glad for the *Z-Louisa Hendrika* to be flanked by its two Maltese corsairs. It comforted his anxiety about entering a famous port, one with the reputation of being unfriendly due to its proximity to Muslim pirates and their ships. He ignored his trepidations and moved about the ship assigning sailors to positions seeing that their weapons were at the ready, and that they were well versed in their assignments. He had more difficulty driving thoughts about the slaves in the hold below than he did in dealing with his own or the ship's issues.

As the ship's crew drew closer to Crete, it was difficult to tell for sure how large the island was. Visual images of Crete on approach from the west indicated a fairly large piece of land, but Piet knew that Crete was a lengthy slender oblong stretching farther from north to south than it did with its east-west span. Its size was amplified in a sailor's mind by the number of surrounding islands and islets. Their goal was to approach at a distance and to cruise around the north end of the island and travel in a hemi-circle around to the mid-east coast. The large port of Chania sat inside the old Venetian harbor and was known for its formidable array of Venetian fortresses.

The northern boundary of Crete forms the southern border of the Aegean Sea. The captain and crew were all on edge as they began to round the northern boundary. They could see Gramvousa, named in honor of Vousa, the wife of a famous and murderous pirate chieftain. All appeared to be quiet until they passed opposite Gramvousa Peninsula and the Balo Lagoon, between the island and the coast of Crete.

Capt. Corren stepped up beside Piet as the first mate manned the wheel.

"First Mate, pay very close attention to any movement in the lagoon. Pirates are known to launch against unsuspecting ships from there. I'll see to it that the men are well aware."

"Aye, Sir. Their blades are sharp; the powder's dry; and the men are cold sober."

The captain smiled his approval of his choice for first mate. Having been forewarned by Ephraim, Piet kept his weather eye peeled for anything moving from the area of the small inlet—part of a peninsula—which formed a segment of a low mountainous mass called Cape Tigani [Greek: Frying Pan]. The peninsula created a visual obstruction to passing ships. And—true to prediction—four small sleek sailing ships began to move towards the *Z-Louisa Hendrika* and its accompanying Maltese corsairs.

"Loft full sails," Piet ordered, "all hands on deck including cooks and medical officers with weapons at the ready. Make ready to prime the deck guns. Be smart about it."

Men ran from everywhere and to everywhere in what appeared to the inexperienced eye to be chaos. However, Piet had drilled the men endlessly; and they performed with alacrity and precision.

Shortly, the new second mate climbed the ladder to the quarterdeck and reported to Piet and the captain, "Men and ship ready for combat and await orders from the quarterdeck, Sirs."

"Well done, Second Mate. Go back and supervise the gunners. The captain will man the wheel, and I will lead the security forces if that becomes necessary. That is all."

Moving to the full sail complement increased the *Z-Louisa Hendrika's* speed through the slightly choppy light blue seas by seven knots, and she began to outdistance the oncoming pirate vessels. The Maltese corsairs dropped back and began to menace the pirates. As the flotilla from Malta rounded to the east coast of the island, their pursuers lost their enthusiasm, accepted flight as the better part of valor, and faded back to the lagoon.

"I was ready for a good fight, Sir," said the second mate, "seems a shame to have to lose the chance to teach the filthy swine a memorable lesson."

"Not a man of ours or a single bit of cargo was lost, Fredrick. Count that as a victory. The voyage is not over yet."

The three ships passed through the north entrance of the harbor between the lighthouse and the Firkas Fortress [known also as *Revellino del Porto*] still being built by the Venetians to protect the harbor entrance. The rocky eastern edge of Chania facing the Aegean and Turkey—Tabakaria—was rugged country lined with leather processing houses. Entering the harbor proper from its west side, the first thing that impressed Piet about the harbor was the Venetian guard house on the south and on the opposite—northside of the mount of the harbor—the prominent lighthouse.

The harbor was built by the Venetians during their colonization of Crete—especially between 1320 and 1356. It served the Venetian navy, and the harbor was dotted with an impressive and daunting number of tall masted military and trade sailing ships. Chania Harbor was—as well as its naval importance—one of the most important commercial ports of the Eastern Mediterranean Sea—controlled by the Venetians for four hundred years.

The *Z-Louisa Hendrika* made its way towards the south end of the harbor to where its designated mooring site awaited. Piet was impressed with how busy and prosperous the quay appeared. The closer they got to the dock yards, the more impressive Chania seemed to be as a trading center. Liberally mixed in with the tall ships like the *Hendricka* and the corsairs were an assortment of small boats and yachts–the toys of the rich. The three ships pulled up to the wharf, and harbor workers and slaves secured them with stout ropes. The ships' huge fore-and-aft anchors found secure ground on the bottom of the harbor. Captain Corren, Piet, and the captains of the two corsairs, walked briskly to the old customs building standing next to the Grand Arsenal building on its south side. Further to the south and closer to the harbor proper was a complex of Venetian docks—a single multiplex of seventeen dockyards.

Unlike the Malta customs house run by the Catholics, the Chania building was an attractive red brick edifice dedicated to getting the job done with no nonsense and with a hard eye fixed on profit all the time. It was of mutual interest to get the papers inspected, stamped, and archived; so, the wheels and sails of prosperity could remain productive.

The relevant documents were pre-signed by the supreme Venetian governor of Crete *Duca di Candia* Bernardo Morosini, and the harbor master, Giovanni di Castro-Villanova. The cargo to be loaded was listed as: assorted Cretan wine-100 barrels, olive oil-2000 liter bottles, Messara Valley cheese—200 rounds, Messara Valley wheat-1,000 bags, 6,000, animal hides-300 bales, bottles of Tarra glass for spirits-200 boxes, 12 bottles to the box, ingots pure Kantanos copper, Kydonia gold, lead, Argyroupolis silver, and Sklavopoula of Selino iron-500 each, best Cretan honey-2,000 liter jars, white slaves-300, Markos Mousotiros Aldine printing press Greek authored books-1000.

Piet was ill-at-ease when the subject of the slaves came up, and Captain Corren handled the entire matter. Piet kept a straight face as the lives and futures of those fellow human beings were determined with no more concern that if a cargo of furniture were being bought, sold, and transported.

Piet was amazed and chagrined that part of the commercial transaction included the transport of nearly three hundred Christians to the tender mercies of *esirs* [Turkish slave auctions] and eventual short lives and futures in industrial factories—working twelve hours a day, six days a week—in the blazing sun of open fields—with men, women, and children, doing back-breaking work twelve hours a day, six days a week, as agricultural laborers in sugar, rice, and cotton, fields, clearing land, planting, tending, and harvesting, or in curing or boiling sheds. The worst fate was to be dragged to toil in Turkish silver, copper, and lead, mines and smelters like the sugar cane slaves in the West Indies of the Caribbean. Mine workers seldom lived more than five years in their bondage.

Constantinople was the administrative and political center of the Ottoman Empire—about a fifth of the population consisted of slaves in the 16th and 17th centuries. Customs statistics indicate that Constantinople's additional slave importation from the Black Sea totaled around 2.5 million from 1500 to 1700. Slavery—whatever Piet Van Brakel might have thought about it—was an accepted norm. White slaves—as Christian slaves were dubbed—were favorite purchases of Catholic monks. Slavery—including sexual slavery of both males and females—was a legal and a significant part of the Ottoman Empire's economy and society.

As Captain Corren told Piet, "It's just business," but nevertheless, Piet was very glad to get out of the customs house and to be quit of the slavery business, at least for a short time.

"Piet," the captain said, "I know you are unhappy about our white slavery and even the black ivory trade and hold ne responsible for unchristian ideas and methods. I want you to know that I hate it as much as you do, but I'm trapped. Without the Maltese Knights, we could never have traveled in the Med. In fact, the Magnus Magister threatened the whole crew with execution or slavery if I did not give in. What was I to do?"

"I understand your predicament and I know things are not getting any better the farther east we go. I will support you and will use all the influence I have to keep the crew in line. But, I will never agree with slavery. It is not a personal thing between you and me."

"I hope not, My Boy. I like you, as I think you know. One day you will be the master of this ship and probably the owner. I would like for us to be friends; so, I can teach you all I know about seafaring and the business of trade on the high seas. Right now, I'm hungry. Would you care to get a bite and a little drink with me, away from the rest of the crew? And, please, call me Jans when we're not around the crew."

"I would, Sir…Jans; I'd be grateful."

The tour was short; the island was only one kilometer long. The harbor of Chania was a wonderful and colorful maze. They paused at Chania's Jewish community centered in the Old Jewish Quarter for centuries, known as Zudecca. In 1492, Jews expelled from Spain settled on Kondylaki, a small lane leading to the Etz Hayyim Synagogue which was the core of Jewish life. The building dated to the 14th century, and it was once destroyed during a pirate attack led by Barbarossa in 1538. The district streets included Zambeliou and Evraiki, which were narrow like most of the city's passages. Kondylaki Street was wider and busier since it was specially built to allow donkey carts to transport goods from the harbor.

Halfway to the mouth of the harbor, on *Akti* [street] Kountourioti, Jans found the taverna he remembered. It had no name, but the façade was memorable. Above the entrance was a large wood carving of an Italian fisherman being watched over by the Virgin Mary of Nicopeia, the Bringer of Victory and the Palladium of the Venetian Republic.

"I'm starving. It'll be fine even if the food's bad."

The owner—who was also the head waiter, cook, dish washer, and sommelier—greeted Jans exuberantly, "*Capitano* Corren, my old friend. I am so happy to have you return. How can we [apparently, the imperial, 'we'] be of service?"

"Food and grog for me and my first mate, Luigi. Bring on your best."

"Allow me to choose the drinks," Luigi said with a big-toothed grin. "Of course, it can't be the water. Even the goats won't drink the polluted stuff, and besides, we men are aware that it is likely to rust yer pipes. Nay, I've got an assortment of decent ales, mead, and cider, to wet yer whistles. For the meal, I'll bring ye some excellent Cretan wine."

The solid meal was everyday fare for the middling classes, but of excellent quality and well prepared. The first course was a platter of *cicchetti* [tapas], dolmades, and cavier, followed shortly by lamb, pork, and pigeon, served baked in separate small pies along with an assortment of fruit. Fresh vegetables were a rarity at that time of year. Small portions of wild local turbot—the succulent variety the Venetians called "*chiodato*" or "nailed" because of its bony, nailhead-like protrusions—were prepared in a variety of ways: roasted, fried, baked, and boiled. Fruits were cooked both separately and with meats. The *frutti di mare* were octopodi, calamaria, lobster, and sea urchins, on the grill. The Chelan wine was local, deep red, sweet, and seemed to come from a bottomless barrel. Piet and Jans were seeing double and weaving by the time they exited the taverna for the unsteady walk back to the ship.

The street along the wharf was a kaleidoscope of color from the highly painted and colorful waterfront buildings of the Topanas neighborhood and the red brick building at the harbor entrance by the fort which housed the Venetian naval guard, and the local artists' wares—the Cretan School or Post-Byzantine Art School which included handsome Venetian arches all along the way. The two men paused briefly to admire the protective architecture around the Venetian dockyards. The *Megalo Arsenali's* dockyards were built by the Venetians in order to construct and repair their ships. On the south edge of the Grand Arsenal lay the Neoria—protected areas for the repair of ships during winter. The fortifications included the bastion of St. Nicholas and the walls on Kasteli Hill beyond the tavernas.

Moreover—if it was necessary–a thick chain Byzantine was attached to the fortress bastion and to the base of the lighthouse on the opposite side of the harbor entrance. It could be lifted to close off the entrance to invaders.

Back at the Enoseos Coast before boarding the *Z-Louisa Hendrika,* they took a last look at the three shipyards of Moro which were named for the Venetian governor who proposed their construction on an artificial peninsula created by the citizens. Southeast–next to the docks–was located the Koum Kapi seaside area [Sand Gate] and the Sabbionara bastion, entirely built over the sea. They were the southern Venetian ramparts of the Cretan city walls. The crewman on board the ship assisted the two senior officers who they feared would topple off the gangplank and into the waiting maw of the harbor waters. Neither man remembered hitting his bed. It was only six in the evening.

After a deep and dreamless sleep, Piet and Jans were awakened by the cabin orderly who announced that it was eight bells of the morning watch. They had slept through the almost deafening 2-2-2-2 clanging of the bells. Without the intercession of the orderly, they would not have made to the quarterdeck as the *Z-Louisa Hendrika* set sail per Captain Corren's orders of the previous day. The two officers had pounding headaches which were aggravated by the abrupt 0400 awakening and the nauseating thought of breakfast.

It was half an hour before they cleared the east entrance of the harbor, and another half an hour before they began to feel the choppy waves of the Aegean Sea. That morning, the ship had taken on over 300 Christian slaves, and had added an extra 100 barrels of sweet Chelan wine to the cargo hold intended for sale in ports distant from the Muslim world. An interpreter for the Turkish language and a *console di Levanti* were required to guarantee absence of piracy on the merchant vessel and to facilitate trading links around the Aegean. Traffic was heavy in the nearby islands of the archipelago which amounted to two-thirds of the shipping to and out of the Chania harbor.

It is 574 nautical miles from Crete to the port of Laiazzo on the southwest cost of Turkey. The *Z-Louisa Hendrika* had fair winds at its back, following seas, and smooth sailing until they made it to the

300-mile point where they were well within sight of the southern edge of Turkey. Then, a severe squall hit the from the west. At first, it seemed as if the Good Lord was smiling on them because their speed increased by twelve knots. Shortly—however—it appeared to Captain Corren and Piet that the sails were going to be ripped to shreds and even the masts would fracture.

"Haul in all sails down to the top gallants on the foremasts and royal sheet on the mizzen. Hold fast," Piet ordered, staining his voice in an effort to be heard over the shrieking wind.

The ship shuddered against the seventy-knot wind but slowed down by seven knots. It was not enough; so, the captain ordered Piet to have the men furl every sail and allow the ship to drift.

"Can't be helped, but these lads are as good as monkeys up there. Give them credit… and do it now!"

Piet obeyed. The ship slowed to a safe twelve knot speed; no men were lost. However, the *Z-Louisa Hendrika* floundered adrift. The compass needle spun about crazily.

Then, as suddenly as the freak storm descended on the ship, it lifted and then began to peak out. They found themselves in sight enough of land mass—undoubtedly Cyprus.

Then, the unlucky lad whose turn it was to return to the crow's nest, called out as loud as he could, "Galleys, ho! Lots of 'em comin' fast. Look to be hostile!"

Piet and the captain confirmed the sighting. At least a dozen pirate galleys were pounding their way towards the *Z-Louisa Hendrika*. They were clogging the mouths of the Ceyhan and Karataş Rivers into the Iskenderun Bay in their haste to get into open water in time to trap the commercial vessel between the northern border of Cyprus and the southern border of Turkey.

"All hands on deck! Man battle stations!" Piet shouted. "This is not a drill. Pirates coming at us from the north and west!"

Manning of the battle stations and heavy cannons went as smoothly as if it had been a drill. Piet smiled at this small success and verification of all the hard training he had exacted of the men for the past several months.

The water had calmed, which worked in favor of both the pirate galleys and the heavy combat rigged commercial vessel.

Piet and the captain listened closely to the thump…thump…thump of the drum-beats of the coxswains of the galley slaves [Greek: *keleustes*]. They were holding steady and not at maximum speed at that point. The opposing ships were too far apart.

The main force of the galleys and the *Z-Louisa Hendrika* were near the exact center of the strait between the mainland and the island, and about twenty knots apart. The separation was closing at an uncomfortable rate. There was wiggle room, but not enough to evade two dozen rapidly moving galleys.

Piet and the captain conferred, then Piet shouted orders.

"Now hear this. First order: make ready all portside guns to fire at once on my command. When the cannonade is complete, attend to the second order: every man lash himself to a mast or hull with a sturdy rope. Use a slip knot because we will change course abruptly to the starboard. Expect further orders then."

It was a very strange set of commands, but Piet's men trusted him completely and so did Captain Corren. The large ship headed straight at the first group of galleys at full speed ahead. Upon ramping up the *Z-Louisa Hendrika*'s speed, the lookouts on the galleys sent down word to the *kelekustes*. On the *Hendrika*, Piet caught the change in the drumming first.

Thump, thump, thump, thump…

"They're at ram speed."

"Hard to port," Piet shouted and put all his strength to turning the large ship's wheel to the left.

He and the captain and more than a few crewmen feared that the ship at full sail would tip over and lay on its port side like a stricken animal of prey waiting for the hunter to arrive and deliver the *coup de grâce*.

# HISTORY:

## HISTORY OF CRETE: PREHISTORY TO THE OTTOMAN EMPIRE

Prehistory

Paleontologists have uncovered evidence including fossil footprints left by ancient human relatives dating back 5.6 MYA [Million Years Ago]. Excavations in South Crete in revealed stone tools at least 130,000 years old. A Neolithic clay figurine of a goddess dated at 5300–3000 BCE. The discovery was sensational for archeologists, paleon-tologists, and evolutionistss, since the previously accepted earliest sea crossing in the Mediterranean was thought to occur around 12,000 BCE. Stone tools found in the *Plakias* region of Crete included Acheulean type quartz hand axes. It is believed that pre-Homo sapiens hominids from Africa crossed to Crete on rafts.

The Neolithic period–the final division of the Stone Age–began about 12 TYA when the first developments of farming appeared in the Near East, and later in other parts of the world. The division lasted until the transitional period of the Chalcolithic from about 6,500 years ago. The significant shift that marked the change of periods was the development of metallurgy, leading up to the Bronze and Iron Ages. In North-ern Europe, the Neolithic lasted until about 1700 BCE, while in China it extended until 1200 BCE. Other parts of the world remained broadly in the Neolithic stage of development until European contact. Some of the early influences on the development of Cretan culture arose from the Cyclades and from Egypt. Sometime in that period cultural records were written in an as yet undeciphered script known as "Linear A". Early Neolithic settlements in Crete include the magnificent cities of Knossos and Trapeza. The archaeological record of Crete in the Neolithic period includes superb palaces, houses, roads, paintings, and sculptures.

Because of a lack of written records, estimates of Cretan chronology are necessarily based on well-established Aegean and Ancient Near Eastern pottery styles, so that Cre-tan timelines have been made by linking Cretan artifacts traded with other civilizations, including the Egyptians–a well-established scientific practice. The evidence is convinc-ing that Crete was involved in international seagoing commerce in the stone age.

The history of Crete as a continuing sophisticated society is based on radiocarbon dating traceable as far back as the 7th millennium BCE, preceding the well-known ancient Minoan civilization by more than four millennia. The Minoan civilization was the first civilization in Europe and the first–in Europe–to build a palace. The sparse animal bones include the domestic species as well as deer, badger, marten, and mouse: the extinction of the local megafauna had left little wild game behind. The first settlers introduced cattle, sheep, goats, pigs, and dogs, as well as domesticated cereals and leg-umes. The city of Chania was a Minoan city known by the ancient Greeks as Kydonia.

High quality Neolithic pottery is known from Knossos, Lera Cave, and Gerani Cave, and has been found in abundance and preserved by archeologists. The Late Neolithic era was a flourishing age with a proliferation of inhabited sites, pointing to a population increase. In the late Neolithic, the donkey and the rabbit were introduced to the island; deer and agrimi were hunted. The Kri-kri–a feral goat–preserves traits of the early domesticates. Horse, fallow deer, and hedgehog, were exotics introduced from Minoan times onwards.

Crete became the center of Europe's most ancient civilization, the Minoans. Tablets inscribed in Linear A have been found in numerous sites in Crete, and a few in the Aegean islands. The Minoans established themselves in many islands besides Ancient Crete: There are clearly identified Minoan off-Crete sites including Kea, Kythera, Milos, Rhodes, and above all, Thera—today's Santorini.

In the period before building palaces—3,000-1,900 BCE–the characteristic Minoan settlement was a gathering of people into villages and small towns by the sea, mainly in the east. Prior to that time, the population was widely dispersed with habitation in caves and shelters. In the 3,000-1,900 BCE era, houses came into use and as time progressed, had more rooms and better construction. The development of art was remarkable during this era for its sophistication and beauty. The pottery was handmade, fired, painted, and decorated, with various geometric shapes or animal icons—many of which have survived to the present day. In the early part of the era, tools and weapons were made from stone, later by bronze—the flowering of the Minoan era was largely during the bronze age. Those art objects preserved by paleontologists were of superior quality.

Early in the pre-palace era, Minoan dead were buried in caves, as in the earlier Neolithic period; but later in the pre-palace Minoan era the first formally constructed tombs appeared. Some were built with square stones and others with a circular domed shape. A cemetery was discovered in north-east Crete where two graves were unearthed with a treasure trove of grave goods 5,000 years old–the period when the important Minoan civilization was developing. It is believed that it was the graveyard for powerful families because of the quality and quantity of funerary objects.

In the first pit, the archeological team unearthed a male, probably a warrior of some note because he was buried with a short bronze sword. With him were ivory seals for making impressions on wax. In a secondary burial, the skeleton of a woman was revealed who had a great number of finely crafted beads, some made of gold, silver, and semi-precious stones. It appears that the man and the woman were a married couple. That burial site was dated approximately to the proto-Minoan period. This burial contained several dozen gold beads with a unique spiral design and an even greater number of tiny one-millimeter beads made from silver and gold, that at one time had been sewn on the clothes of the deceased.

The same team more recently discovered a small and unique burial at the same antiquarian site consisting of a tomb made from stone slabs, placed together to make a box-like structure. There, the excavators found the remains of two children, believed to be under ten and two finely crafted gold bracelets, demonstrating the skills of Minoan artisans and the remarkable and rapidly growing Minoan civilization.

In another Cretan site (beneath a farmer's olive garden), sometime between 1,400 and 1,200 BCE, two Minoan men were laid to rest in an underground enclosure carved out of the soft limestone native to southeast Crete. Both were entombed within *larnakes*—intricately embossed clay coffins popular in Bronze Age Minoan society—and surrounded by fourteen colorful ritual [amphorae] Greek jars, a bowl, and funerary vases, that hinted at their owners' high status. Eventually, the burial site was sealed with stone masonry and left forgotten and unseen for 3,400 years.

Late in the pre-palatial era, large towns are founded and the first big palaces–Knossos, Festos, and Malia, were built. Each of those palaces was built around a central open court surrounded with buildings of multiple floors. The palaces had large rooms for social functions, private rooms for the authorities, houses for workers, workshops, storerooms, theatres, baths, and sewage facilities. At Knossos, the queen had an elaborate flushing toilet system. The palace had running water for consumption and for cooking purposes. Large sanctuaries were built in caves in the palaces and on the tops of nearby mountains.

Many votive object collections included a corpulent squatting Mother Earth Goddess made from several different materials. The goddess was adored; she was one of the first gods created in the world; and she persisted through some 4,000 years and the creation and loss of writing twice. Her symbol was a double axe. Pottery of that later period developed and improved by introduction of the potter's wheel. Burial sites dating to the Late Minoan period featured more elaborate beehive-style tombs.

Genuine masterpieces such as thin-walled egg-shell ware, and multicolored *Kamares* style vases, were made and exported around the known world. The trade of goldsmithing reached the level of art and achieved technical perfection with intricate jewelry of various designs and rich decoration. Fresco pictures such as the large image of the sport of bull leaping–which included a dark-skinned figure of an agile man and the two light skinned figures of women–were uncovered by careful archeologists. Another famous fresco that has survived is of large tuna fish swimming in an Aegean blue sea. These magnificent works of art were placed on palace walls and survived for millennia despite war and earthquakes.

The Minoans apparently ruled the sea trade and did not have an army, even a defensive one. The prosperity of the civilization and the political power of Minoan Crete was a remarkably temperate time. The island became united, with its capital in Knossos and its power expanding, with trading relations with Minor Asia, Egypt and Cyprus, with strong influences on the mainland of Greece, the Cycladic islands, Rhodes and Kos islands, and colonies on the islands of Kea, Milos, and Santorini–Akrotiri site–and to some degree in Sicily. Unlike most of the course of history thereafter, those colonies were achieved not by wars, but with merchant stations. Minoan protection of the colonies from the pirates and other enemies was ensured by the Minoan naval influence without significant conflict.

It was a nearly idyllic period of history, at least for the Greeks. The city-states tended to think of themselves as Greeks first and—for Greeks—were relatively peaceful. All of that came to an abrupt and cataclysmic end sometime in the mid-second millennium BCE [somewhere between 1,645 BCE to 1,500 BCE] when Thera—present day Santorini–erupted, the single-most powerful explosive event ever witnessed. with a force dwarfing—by a factor of five–that which took place on Krakatoa, Indonesia, in 1883. The Thera explosion killed upwards of 40,000 people within a few hours, produced colossal tsunamis 40 feet tall which inundated Crete, spewed volcanic ash across Asia, spawned huge earthquakes, caused a drop in global temperatures as recorded by historians of the period, and created strangely colored sunsets for three years. The blast itself was heard 3,000 miles away. Modern geologists estimate that the force of that explosion was the equivalent of having several hundred atomic bombs explode in a fraction of a second.

Minoan culture–the dominant civilization in the Mediterranean at the time– crumbled as a result of the eruption, historians believe, changing the political land-scape of the ancient world indefinitely. Environmental effects were felt across the globe, as far away as China.

Based on the nearby island of Crete, the powerful pre-palatial Minoan civilization declined suddenly soon after Thera blew its top. Tsunamis spawned by the eruption presumably swamped its naval fleet and coastal villages. A drop in temperatures caused by the massive amounts of sulfur dioxide spouted into the atmosphere then led to several years of cold, wet summers in the region, ruining harvests. The lethal combination overran every mighty Minoan stronghold in less than 50 years. The legend of Atlantis as written by Plato and the story of the Biblical plagues and subsequent exodus from Egypt have also been connected to the epic catastrophe.

However, during the Neopalatial Period from 1,700-1,450 BCE, Minoan civilization came back. Despite the destruction from the eruption of Thera, the palaces were restored and rebuilt on a larger scale and–by the start of the Neopalatial period– the economy began to thrive again. The population increased with new settlements becoming established all over Crete. In fact, this period became the historical height by the Minoan civilization. The palaces again became the centers of economic, social, and religious, life. Around them, a rich variety of other buildings including merchants' villas, mansions for high officials and priests, workshops, storage rooms, shops, cafes, and dwellings for more lowly citizens developed. The evidence to show how people lived their daily lives comes from the large amount of archaeological finds that have been excavated. Citizens of urban settlements again became employed in trade and the import and export of wine, oil, and perfumes.

A small minority of local people worked as potters, weavers, and farmers. The most important commercial centers were located at Phaestos, Agia Triada, Agioi Theodori, Malia, and the Port of Amnissos. The society was strictly hierarchical with the King at the apex–who was worshipped as a High Priest–and the merchant class, manufacturers, and priests, commanding respect after him. This rich and thriving Minoan civilization again came to impress and influence the colonies and mainland Greece.

Around 1450 BCE, the neopalatial Minoan culture and civilization experienced another catastrophic change. The cities and palaces were once more destroyed due to a further eruption of the Thera volcano with consequent tsunami, earthquakes, and extensive fires, which demolished nearly everything that had built up. The palaces, residences, and trading centers, were destroyed together with the living quarters in Knossos. However, the palace at Knossos itself survived–remaining largely intact— until the present day. The dynasty was weakened and unable to resist takeover by Mycenaean Greeks.

Mycenaean civilization was the last phase of the Bronze Age in Ancient Greece, spanning the period from approximately 1,600–1,100 BCE. By 1,450 this warrior elite aggressive society overran and supplanted the Minoan civilization on Crete and elsewhere and ushered in the era of warring Greek city-states.

Classical and Greco-Roman Crete:

During the dark age of Greek history—800 BCE-69 CE–Crete became largely a backwater of Greek, then Roman civilization. Living in such remote and inhospitable areas was difficult and rudimentary. Over the ensuing few centuries, even the once grand Mycenaean settlements on Crete declined and largely disappeared. In 36 BCE, Mark Antony gave the island to Cleopatra as a gift. With the succession of Augustus, Crete was officially incorporated into the Roman empire. Crete again became a major cultural center in Roman times when it was a province within the Roman empire. In the Roman period Cretan piracy was still rife. The famed Cretan archers became an important fixture in the Roman army across the empire. Cretan cities were composed of various classes of peoples including slaves and foreigners and was made into a center of early Christianity.

The Advent of Christianity:

The next major change for Crete was the advent of Christianity. During his journey to Rome, Paul the Apostle stopped in Crete, preached, and proselytized, for the new religion. The brand of Pauline Christianity that came out of his visit re-ignited a centuries-old ascetic tradition, which began to flourish and to dominate Cretan life. Hermitages and monastic centers in the Asterousia mountain range were established as a consequence of Paul's and St. John Xenos' visit, and some of them still exist. Those in the Akrotiri Cape at Chania were present during the time of Piet Van Brakel's visit, and still retain their monastic character.

The island became an important Christian center, as reflected in the hundreds of religious monuments, which are scattered everywhere. The old Greek and Roman temples of Twelve Olympians were transformed into imposing basilicas and cavernous churches. The 3rd century CE saw several infamous persecutions of Christians including ten martyrs during a wild animal hunt in Gortyn's amphitheater in 249 CE. When the Roman Empire split into two, Crete was made part of the Eastern empire although the Christian church was under the jurisdiction of the Pope at Thessaloniki. Crete continued to be part of the Eastern Roman or Byzantine Empire–a quiet cultural backwater–until it fell into the hands of Iberian Muslims under Abu Hafs in the 820s, who established a piratical emirate on the island. The archbishop Cyril of Gortyn was killed and the city so thoroughly devastated it was never reoccupied. Candia–a city built by the Iberian Muslims–was made capital of the island after the destruction of Gortyn.

Venetian Crete, 1204-1669:

The Crusades were the force that brought the next of Crete's rulers. Turning their might on Byzantium, the Crusaders sacked and burned Constantinople; and the Empire was divided up. Crete was sold to the Venetian Republic for a paltry sum.

At the end of the fourth century, the Roman Empire was split in two, and Crete was attached to Byzantium (later, Constantinople, and then Istanbul). International/transMediterranean trade began to flourish when Venice added Crete to her colonies. Among other things, slave trade became very important for the economy of Crete during the 14th and 15th centuries. Cretan merchants mainly partnered with other Jewish and Venetian merchants in the early centuries. In 1589, Cretans traveled around the Mediterranean Sea, and through Syria, Alexandria, Constantinople, the Aegean, and other areas in Asia Minor, using all kinds of ships and boats. When a child was born in those seagoing days, it was said that "a sailor was being born".

From the 16th century on, the apparent threat from the Ottoman Empire forced the Venetians to reach out to the local Orthodox Cretans. They implemented policies that gave equal rights and opportunities to Cretans, thereby attaining a peaceful coexistence between the Catholics and the Orthodox Christians. With that, Crete became–not a mere trading port–but an integral part of the Venetian state. These rights were given in order to foster unity amongst the population anticipating the Ottoman invasion.

The social and economic conditions in Crete were similar to the ones in the Western European regions since they both had evolved after the Renaissance. As a part of Venice, the Cretan bourgeoisie started joining the cultural revolution that was happening in the West. Cretans–by combining the rich Byzantine culture with the European cultural influences–assimilated them, giving rise to the Cretan culture. This led to a renewal of Cretan arts and philosophy and a flowering of intertwined Venetian and Cretan society.

Venetian Crete was hardly free of troubles. Venice took firm control in 1,204 and did not relinquish her hold for four centuries. Crete was a great prize for the Venetians. Control of trade routes was extremely valuable to this already powerful merchant republic. Crete also had rich agricultural and natural resources which the Venetians exploited to the fullest. Venice treated Crete as a subject colony; and soon after assuming control they implemented a strict feudal system. The earth was taken from the people and was given to Venetian knights, with the former owners becoming slaves. Taxes and labor obligations made a hard life approach unbearable. The Venetian occupation could not be accepted by the Cretan people and their independent character. The continuous revolts for many years brought a hard repression and tortures.

High taxes and the allocation of land to Venetian colonists alienated the people and led to numerous revolts. In 1363–indigenous Cretans and Venetian settlers exasperated by the hard tax policy exercised by Venice–overthrew official Venetian authorities in the Revolt of St. Titus and declared an independent Cretan Republic. Throughout this period of oppression Cretan links with Constantinople were cemented by a common language and the doctrines of eastern Christendom. The revolt took Venice five years to quell. As a result of plagues of the Black Death, many Cretans migrated overseas during difficult periods on the island, some acquiring great fortunes abroad.

Despite that, the Venetians built beautiful buildings; and science and the arts flourished. Byzantine methods combined with the Italian Renaissance to produce outstanding achievements in painting and literature. El Greco–Greece's most famous painter–was born on Crete in 1541.

From the beginning of the 15<sup>th</sup> century an ongoing threat loomed. Constantinople fell, and the victorious Turks also took nearby Cyprus. In response, the Venetians strengthened the fortresses around the Island in readiness for a Turkish attack. The fortresses at Gramvousa, Spinalonga, and Souda, were fortified at great and worrisome expense. This expense was met by levying even heavier taxes on the already struggling and now resentful Cretan population.

By the time the Turks arrived in 1645, the true Cretans welcomed them as a means of driving out the hated Venetians. The siege of Heraklion—near Chania–made history and changed the control of Crete once again. For 21 years, the Turks attempted to gain control. As the last outpost of Christianity in the eastern Mediterranean, Heraklion received support from the rest of Europe and managed to hold off the Turks. Finally, however, in 1669—well after Piet and his Flemish sailors left the island—Venice was unable to hold on to Crete any longer. They surrendered and left Crete to the Ottoman Empire.

# CHAPTER TEN

# BETWEEN THE DEVIL AND
# THE DEEP BLUE SEA

IN THE YEAR OF OUR LORD, 1642, LATE FEBRUARY

The ship heaved at such an acute angle of turn to port that the starboard section of the deck lifted above the port by 45°, but somehow managed not fall on its side. It was coming about to face the oncoming pirate galley fleet at a 60° angle, then at 70° and still stayed right side up in the water. Piet could see that the *Z-Louisa Hendricka* would not be able to sustain the perilous strain unless he did something quickly and effectively.

It was a day of taking chances.

"All hands push everything movable to the starboard side and stand by the rails. If you are so inclined, you might offer up a prayer," Piet shouted above the din.

The crew was happy to have something to do to save themselves and the ship, and they shifted the deck weight to an almost complete placement of the weight on the right. When the ship had made 80° of its turn to face the galleys broadside, the deck began to flatten out. Now the differential between right and left was only 25° and lessening with every yard of forward travel.

The praying men took a moment of pause from crossing themselves and shouting prayers and began to cheer hosannas to God for His deliverance. Finally, the *Z-Louisa Hendricka* was at 90° broadside to the galleys and had an even keel safe deck on which the men could work.

"Prime the guns, light the tapers," Piet ordered. "Listen for my command to fire, then fire all starboard guns at one time and at four feet above the level of the sea.  Immediately after that, shift all empty guns away from the starboard gun ports and move the port guns into to the open ports and fire all of them into the remaining galleys. Await further orders."

Because of the complexity of his order and because the order violated several rules of common sense in sea battles, Piet repeated his orders twice more.

A deafening cannonade commenced almost as if one gigantic cannon had fired. He knew the galleys were within the range of his guns, and he also knew that the pirates were headed straight for him at ram speed. A cordite fog of smoke covered the deck; so, Piet could not see if his plan was working. The crewmen moved with amazing alacrity and efficiency to switch guns even though they were all deaf for the time being. The second cannonade fired again as one gun and caused the ship to jump in the water.

Before good visibility returned, Piet barked two more orders, "All hands—including officers—move all guns to the port side and get ready to repeat the previous firing orders. Hold fast; we are going to come about in another hard turn, this time to the starboard. Await my orders to fire."

It was a massive strain on the men and the ship to make another acute angle turn which included hauling the heavy guns uphill across the deck. The men now understood the reason for the strange set of orders and proceeded with a will that sent a thrill of admiration and gratitude through Piet's chest. They pulled away from the dense smoke enough to see that two rows of galleys were on fire and were in the process of nosediving into the merciless Aegean. The men hollered their defiance at the dreaded galleys; and, this time, Piet and the captain joined them.

This turn was even more dangerous than the first even though Piet made it somewhat more obtuse angle to lessen the list of the ship. The problem on the starboard turn was that the *Z-Louisa Hendricka* appeared for all the world as if she was going to ram the rear rows of galleys, a suicidal maneuver. Again, many a prayer was mumbled and signs of the cross made by the men. There was not an atheist left among them at that moment.

For all the stresses they were enduring, the men managed to reload and prime the first set of guns. Everyone but the hands required actually to light the fuse cords moved back to load and set about to prime the second set of guns

God or someone was on their side. As the *Z-Louisa Hendricka's* port side pulled into a right angle facing of the galleys, the first two rows of destroyed galleys disappeared into the azure depths and out of the way. The ship and the next rows of galleys were now less than ten yards apart. The row of galleys was now eight across as their crews and the hapless galley slaves endeavored to scatter away from the oncoming juggernaut posed by the large ship.

"Commence firing!" Piet shouted, and covered his ears.

An immense clap of thunder and lightening erupted from the *Hendricka's* guns; and, again, the ship was lost in the dense cordite cloud. The second cannonade compounded all the noise, loss of visibility, and collective deafness. The *Z-Louisa Hendricka* was moving at speed at right angles away from the advancing galleys. Two of them raced at ram speed harmlessly past the ship's stern. In the distance, Piet could see the seven or eight remaining galleys racing away to join the flight of the rear guard headed back towards the mouths of the Ceyhan and Karataş Rivers.

Capt'n Corren turned to Piet and said, "Well done, Piet. This time we won, and the devil and the deep blue sea lost."

While the captain manned the wheel, Piet left the quarter deck to assist the exhausted crew to put the deck and its guns back in order and in readiness for any further action that might present itself. He had the cooks and orderlies bring a round of grog to the grateful crew.

They were not further molested by pirates as they readjusted their line of travel towards the Turkish port of Laiazzo. Piet suggested that their attackers had sent word to the south that their ship was too dangerous to attack. Cap'n Corren just shrugged and raised an eyebrow.

They reckoned that there was less than 100 knots to go before making the Turkish port; so, after the men rested and ate, a clean-up was instituted. The men grumbled, but they were so glad to be alive that the mopping and varnishing was a comforting distraction.

The *Z-Louisa Hendricka* came within sight of land—the island of Cyprus—at dawn the following morning during a light drizzling rain. The sky was partially cloudy and crepuscular shafts of sunlight broke through, creating a sense of welcoming for the men.

"God's rays," said Cap'n Corren. "Good omen."

"Let us hope so," responded Piet.

From his interest in history, Piet knew that what they were seeing was the same view of the busy port of Laiazzo that greeted Marco Polo when he visited it in 1271. A substantial fortification stood on the tip of a small peninsula and was surrounded by the old town. There was a thick, high seaward wall that appeared to be in rather poor state of repair. The land castle had a curving wall which closed tip of the peninsula. The castle was made up of three round towers, a polygonal bastion, casemates with loopholes [shooting ports], and several embrasured windows. The basic plan of the fortress was laid in late antiquity, according to Jans Corren.

There was also a sea castle located on an island 400 meters east of the shore. The castle was made up of a tight cluster of five chambers encased inside a massive irregular bastion. A circuit wall was attached to the castle and surrounded most of the island. The sea castle did not serve as a defense structure to any significant degree. Rather, the vaulted rooms and enclosures served as storage areas for merchandise destined for Europe. The peculiar masonry and construction techniques such as dovetail sockets of the sea castle were built during the Armenian Kingdom of Cilicia era, dating from the re-fortification of the harbor in 1282 CE.

There was a prominent watchtower located 1.5 km west of the land castle built by Suleiman the Magnificent with spolia from the nearby late antique city. The lower two floors of the castle were covered with stone vaults. Near the quay, there was a lifelike statue of two young men, twin brothers—physicians—who practiced their art in the original Aegeae, as Laiazzo was known in the time of the Greeks, Romans, and Cilicians. They were Christian martyrs, killed by Emperor Diocetian. The name of the town was changed by the Venetians to rid the taint of anything associated with the terrible Roman tormentor of Christians.

Laiazzo gradually became a more important port following the fall of Acre and the natural silting up of the harbor of Tarsus. Its prominence was enhanced by the advantage of the province's good roads eastward. Laiazzo became the principal center of trade in southwestern Turkey and controlled most of the commerce between West and East. The prominence of Genoa and Venice came when the Armenian kings granted various trade privileges to them. Marco Polo wrote of the place in his journal as he was about to begin his trip to China in 1271; his records described it as a "city good for good trade," and that "all spices, silk, gold, and wool, from inland were carried to the port city."

While the crew and the local wharf workers and slaves started to unload the cargo–including the woebegone Christian slaves–the two senior ship's officers joined the captains and first mates of the two Maltese corsairs. It was the first opportunity for Piet and Jans to say thank you to the Maltese Knights, and to take them out for a sumptuous dinner.

There were no customs' problems for the Flemish sailors, but all the officers of the three ships were in for a rude surprise which directly affected the Maltese Knights.

"Your country has declared war on Cyprus and Turkey by attacking our ships in the pursuit of their duties. We regard you as pirates; and as such, we are well within our legal rights to imprison you and to hold you and your crews for ransom. Since the declaration only came to our attention yesterday morning, we shall be lenient this one time. Leave on the afternoon's tide and never return, and you will be accorded the courtesies of the city. If you are captured during a pirate raid by you, both of you will be brought back to Laiazzo and suffer beheading. Now, go."

Without even allowing the knights a single word of protest or defense, they were escorted away under guard to their ships and sailed west on the evening tide.

Piet was dismayed to have to sign to deliver slaves to Turkey shores in order to be able to leave Cyprus Island in peace. Because of their association with the corsairs, the Flemish sailors were forbidden forever to return to Cyprus.

Piet asked Jans for his take on what had just happened.

"Not entirely sure, but it is politics. Everything is politics. I understand that the Turks are negotiating some kind of trade agreement with the heads of Europe. Part of it is that those governments—those Christian governments—have to appear to be more righteous than Caesar's wife, never mind what they are actually doing. It has to do with slavery, I surmise. The corsairs of Malta claim to be on the side of God by only enslaving the heathen Muslims, and then only for the purpose of introducing them to the true religion."

Piet raised an eyebrow.

"Just like the Muslims who only enslave Christians," Jans replied to the eyebrow.

"And good Catholic castration factories in Spain with the work being done by those worthy Christians to produce eunuchs for the sultans' harems, is because their religion forbids castration."

"And only ten percent of the little boys survive; so, the good Christians have to see to it that they are buried within 24 hours as the good Muslims require," added Jans.

"How are we supposed to live in a world we don't understand?"

"'Go along to get along', some wise international trader once told me. I guess in the end that's what we must do."

They were to learn that afternoon just how true the wisdom of that statement was. A small squad of janissaries arrived at the ship early that evening.

The *boluk-bashi* [head of a small squad of janissaries] stood straight and stiff and delivered the message: "By order of the janissary agha, you and your ship shall leave this port tonight. You will deliver one large cargo of White Slaves to Laiazzo along with your usual products for sale. The port authority will inspect and see to the loading of that cargo. You are to see to the care and keeping of the cargo. Excess deaths are considered to be unacceptable. While in Laiazzo, you will receive a different cargo. When you leave Turkey, you will have a very rich cargo bound for Venice. I am authorized to tell you that this cargo is to be delivered to the doge himself and to no one else. Do you understand?".

Piet did not understand, not fully; but he was not about to say so.

Jans answered for the ship and its officers, "We understand, and we will comply, *boluk-bashi*."

"Finally, I am ordered to tell you that henceforth you must understand that you are *persona non grata*. Do not come back this way again."

It was Piet's unpleasant duty to supervise the loading of the cargo as the representative of the ship. It was impressive how young, how white, how female, and how docile, the cargo was. There were 150 girls from Eastern Europe, Russia, Scandinavia, and Greece. Each was a designated and guaranteed piece of cargo, carrying a small brand of "cv" above her left breast. Piet was sure the "c" was for Christian and could guess the meaning of the "v". Although these girls were given relatively clean and comfortable mats and decent food by slave standards, he was dismayed to the point of nausea about what he imagined the fate awaiting these innocent girls, some of whom were children.

Per orders from Jans, Piet selected crewmen in groups of four to oversee and to protect the girls throughout the voyage.

He informed them of their duties, ending with the admonition, "Do not touch any girl ever for any reason. The punishment for doing so is castration. Any questions?"

## THE HISTORY:
## HISTORY OF VENICE—600 C.E.-1797 C.E.

The history of Venice is not particularly long in comparison to many eastern and Mediterranean cities and countries, such as Crete. The commonly told history dates from the sixth century of the common era, but no surviving historical records deal directly with the founding of Venice. Such evidence as is available includes late Roman sources which reveal the existence of fishermen–on the islands in the original marshy lagoons–who were referred to as *incolae lacunae* [lagoon dwellers]. Those early Venetians lived much like sea birds, their land secured only by osier and wattle. Other evidence leads several historians to agree that the original population of Venice as an organized city consisted of refugees—from nearby Roman cities such as Padua, Aquileia, Treviso, Altino, and Concordia (modern Portogruaro), as well as from the undefended countryside as a consequence of the barbarians' invasion from northern and eastern Europe following the Roman Empire decline. The foundation of the town was the result of a flight of the people living in the Veneto *terra firma*; they escaped towards the nearby archipelago.

The newly arriving citizens fled successive waves of Germanic and Hun invasions. The Lombard hordes–whose incursions into northern Italy began in 568 C.E.–drove great numbers of mainlanders [*Veneto terra firma*] onto the islands of the lagoon, previously the homes of itinerant fishermen and salt workers who were supplanted. With the Venetians' isolation came increasing autonomy. The Roman/Byzantine *tribuni maiores* formed the earliest central standing governing committee of the islands in the lagoon, dating from 568. The Venice Republic was the biggest power of the Mediterranean during 1300's-1500's. Its territories embraced a large area in the east Mediterranean sea, encompassing the *terra firma*–that is the current Veneto and Friuli–and today's Croatian Histria and Dalmatia with their islands, plus part of the Greek islands.

Venice lies on an archipelago in the northeastern Mediterranean [aka Adriatic sea] made up of 118 flat islands well away from the Veneto coast that are separated by canals and linked by over 400 bridges. The islands are located in the shallow Venetian Lagoon, an enclosed bay that lies between the mouths of the Po and the Piave rivers. The city was not built directly on the surface of the islets, but instead supported by wooden platforms kept together by wooden piles entrenched deeply into the seabed. As a result–under the Venice lagoon–there are millions of wooden piles. A prime example is that to consolidate the ground in order to build the Santa Maria della Salute church–over a period of two years and two months–1,106,657 wooden piles were dug underwater, each of them measuring on average about 4 meters=11.2 feet long.

The traditional first doge [Latin *dux*—leader—sometimes rendered "Duke"] of Venice, Paolo Lucio Anafesto (Anafestus Paulicius), was elected in 697, according to the oldest chronicle by John, deacon of Venice in 1008 C.E. Charlemagne sought to subdue the city to his rule. He ordered the pope to expel the Venetians from the

Pentapolis along the Adriatic coast. Charlemagne's own son Pepin of Italy, king of the Lombards–under the authority of his father–embarked on a siege of Venice itself. This, however, eventually proved to be a costly failure. The siege lasted six months, with Pepin's army ravaged by the diseases of the local swamps and eventually forced to withdraw in 810. A few months later, Pepin himself died, apparently as a result of a disease contracted there. In the aftermath, an agreement between Charlemagne and the Byzantine Emperor Nicephorus in 814 recognized Venice as Byzantine territory, and granted the city full trading rights along the Adriatic coast.

From the 9th to the 12th century, Venice—owing largely to the unusual legal and political position of the small independent duchy and being situated in territorial isolation between two great empires—developed in accordance with its function as a trading intermediary. She developed into a city state [Italian: *thalassocracy* or *repubblica marinara*] along with three other cities: Genoa, Pisa, and Amalfi. Its strategic position at head of the Adriatic made Venetian naval and commercial power almost invulnerable for 300 years. Beginning in the 9th century, Venetians became brazen enough to elect their own doges. The Venetians eliminated pirates along the Dalmatian coast allowing the city to become a flourishing trade center between Western Europe and the rest of the known world—especially with the Byzantine Empire and Asia–where its navy protected commercial sea routes against piracy. Venice was a staging area for the Crusades and the history changing naval Battle of Lepanto in 1571.

The greatest threat to Venice in the 11th century was the northern invasion which threatened to cut-off Venice from its contacts in the south. The successful action taken by Doge Domenico Selvo and his successor Vitale Falier played a major role in guaranteeing Venice control of the Mediterranean. The Republic of Venice seized a number of places on the eastern shores of the Adriatic before 1,200 CE–mostly for commercial reasons–because pirates based there were a menace to trade. They were also acquired partly as a buffer against belligerent neighbors, partly to guarantee Alpine trade routes, and partly to ensure the supply of mainland wheat on which the city depended. In building its maritime commercial empire, Venice dominated the trade in salt and alunite, acquired control of most of the islands in the Aegean–including Crete, and Cyprus in the Mediterranean–and became a major power-broker in the Near East [roughly encompassing a transcontinental region comprising Western Asia, Turkey–both Anatolia and East Thrace–and the north African portion of Egypt. They established near absolute control over the rich markets of the Levant and Constantinople. Venice was the European end of the Silk Road trade route which moved goods all the way from China, and consequently was a cosmopolitan city, a true melting pot.

Venice remained closely associated with Constantinople, being twice granted trading privileges in the Eastern Roman Empire, through the so-called golden bulls [or "chrysobulls"], in return for aiding the Eastern Empire to resist Norman and Turkish incursions. In the first chrysobull, Venice acknowledged its homage to the empire; but not in the second, reflecting the decline of Byzantium and the rise of Venice's power. As a result of being located on the Adriatic Sea, from the beginning Venice always traded extensively with the Byzantine Empire and the Muslim world. By the late

13th century, Venice was the most prosperous city in all of Europe. At the peak of its power and wealth, Venice had 36,000 sailors operating 3,300 ships, dominating Mediterranean commerce.

Although the people of Venice generally remained orthodox Roman Catholics, the state of Venice was notable for its freedom from religious fanaticism, and executed nobody for religious heresy during the Counter-Reformation. This apparent lack of zeal contributed to Venice's frequent conflicts with the papacy.

The Black Death devastated Venice in 1348, and once again between 1575 and 1577. In three years, the plague killed some 50,000 people. In 1630, the Italian plague of 1629–31 killed a third of Venice's 150,000 citizens.

Venice began to lose its position as a center of international trade during the latter part of the Renaissance [15th and 16th centuries] as Portugal prevailed to become Europe's principal intermediary in the trade with the East, striking at the very foundation of Venice's great wealth. At the same time, France and Spain fought for hegemony over Italy in the Italian Wars, thereby marginalizing its political influence. Venice's long decline started fairly abruptly in the 15th century, when it first made an unsuccessful attempt to hold Thessalonica against the Ottomans between 1423 and 1430. She also sent ships to help defend Constantinople against the besieging Turks in 1453. After Constantinople fell to Sultan Mehmet II, he declared the first of a series of Ottoman-Venetian wars that cost Venice much of its eastern Mediterranean possessions.

Even more decisive than the Columbian exchange and the beginning of Atlantic trade following Christopher Columbus's voyage of 1492 was Vasco da Gama's first voyage of 1497–99, which opened a sea route to India around the Cape of Good Hope and destroyed Venice's monopoly. France, England, and the Dutch Republic, quickly followed Spain and Portugal, with their swift and sturdy ships. But Venice's oared galleys were at a disadvantage when it came to traversing the great oceans. Therefore, Venice was outdistanced in the race for establishment of colonies. The Venetian empire did, however, remain a major exporter of agricultural products, and until the mid-18th century, a significant manufacturing center.

The final fall of the Republic of Venice occurred in 1797 CE, when the Serenissima yielded to the military campaigns of Napoleon in Italy. With the Campoformio Treaty, Venice and the Veneto, plus Histria and Dalmatia, were relinquished to the Austrian Empire, which ruled over them for about 60 years.

Probably, the most famous Venetian historical figure was Marco Polo, (b. 1254, d. 1324 CE, Venice), Venetian merchant and adventurer, who traveled from Europe to Asia in 1271–1295 CE following the Silk Road. He remained in China for 17 of those 24 years during which he had dealings with Emperor Kublai Khan in Cathay and traveled 24,000 km. Upon his return, he wrote *Il Milione* [*The Million,* published in 1300] best known in English as *Book of the Marvels of the World* and *The Travels of Marco Polo.* He was not the first European to explore China—in fact, his father and uncle [Niccolò Polo and his brother Maffeo] among others, had already been there. He became famous and is remembered for his travels because of his popular book, which remains a classic of travel literature. In 1298 Marco served as a gentleman-commander of a galley in the Venetian navy. In September 1298, he was captured and imprisoned in Genoa. His fame as an adventurer had preceded him, and he was treated with courtesy and leniency and was released within a year. He co-authored *Il Milione* with a cell-mate, Rustichello da Pisa, an Italian Romance writer, while languishing in the Genoese prison.

The book described for the first time the then mysterious culture and intricate inner workings of the complex and fascinating Eastern world, including the wealth and massive size of China, its territories [including the important capital of Peking—today's Beijing–Japan, India, Mongolia, Persia, and other Asian cities and countries, His book inspired Christopher Columbus, and influenced European cartography.

# CHAPTER ELEVEN
## OVERLAND TO ANTIOCH

IN THE YEAR OF OUR LORD, 1642, LATE APRIL

Janissarsies patrolled the wharf area; and–along with agents of Turkish customs–met every incoming ship and inspected every outgoing vessel. Such scrutiny was unusual and recent, according to the sailors Piet and Jans met along the waterfront.

"What is the cause?" Jans asked.

The nervous customs officials looked around to be sure they were not being observed by government spies, but sailors answered promptly and with certainty. In the end, the answer was the same from whoever was answering.

"Slavery."

Those disposed to elaborate—a very few of those involved in trade—told the Flemish sailors that negotiations were under way among Mediterranean trading countries to make commerce easier and safer. The issue of piracy was paramount; and several nations–especially Venice– were proposing a naval policing force directed by Venice or even an international one, if enough countries could agree. The second sticking point–and one which particularly stuck in the craw of the Muslim countries was slavery, since it was legal, and approved by the religion and its book. Other–less open nations—were dragging their feet, while, at the same time, protesting their innocence with the trade despite actively participating in it. It was a conundrum. For the time being, the holier-than-thou posturing was greatly interfering with the slave trade and would continue to do so until actual customs and trade treaties were signed.

"Is the slave trade under heavy criticism here?" Jans asked one corpulent and successful international trader. "It would appear that the officials of this Islamic country are very actively clamping down on the slave trade."

Do not believe anything you hear and less than half of what you see, *Sadiq* [friend]," the knowledgeable merchant replied. "This remains Islam, and our traditions hallowed by the Prophet, may Allah bless him and his holy family, will be here when you and I are gone. You have only to travel to Constantinople to witness the auctions today, next year, a hundred years from now. The specter of the slave trade and discussions of it with *kaffirs* brings about…what we might say…a certain duplicity. It is a common saying among us when we see such a conversation beginning such a subject, 'Yesterday, I saw a man upon a stair, the little man who wasn't there. I saw him again today. I wish, I wish, that he would go away'."

"Well said, My Friend. I think that makes it clear. We just happened to come at a time when outsiders were trying to keep the little man who isn't there away…for the time being."

Temporary or not, even the very appearance of slavery was anathema during the days that the *Z-Louisa Hendrika* was in port. Their cargo—now euphemistically labelled as "Pure Cotton"–was unloaded at night and into a convoy of covered wagons without windows bound for the Topkapi Palace in Constantinople. Since the sultan, himself, was to be the recipient of the cargo, it was not worth one's life to insist on an inspection of the contents, even if the contents were emitting girlish laughter from time to time.

With the "Pure Cotton" cargo stopped for a rest overnight at a caravanserai immediately outside the lawfully appointed limits in influence of the port authority of Laiazzo, there was time for the rotund Turkish entrepreneur to revisit his conversation with Captain Jans Corren and the first mate, whose name could not remember.

It was late, and a very dark night when Aslan Polat, shook the tent flaps of the night rental where Jans and Piet were sleeping.

The two men took up their swords, held them behind their backs and inquired, "Who seeks admittance?"

"*Sadiqs* [friends], it is I, one Aslan Polat. We met on the wharf this very day and discussed the disposition of your cargo. I have a business venture to offer."

Piet peeked through the small cleft in the flap and was relieved to see the eager trader.

"Enter, *Sadiq*," he beckoned.

Polat opened the tent flaps and entered, holding an unopened bottle of English/Irish whiskey made of good quality grains in England, then sent to Ireland to make an excellent blended Scotch and Irish whiskey.

"Campbell's Malt Whiskey," Piet said, reading the label.

"Nay, *Sadiqs*," said Polat, "'Tis but aquavite. Would a good Muslim, like myself, be about plying good visitors with evil spirits?" he said with an infectious laugh.

Piet and Jans shared the laugh. So, Muslim Turks were not above sharing a little Demon Spirits with friends to lubricate discussion of a business potential deal.

Once the process of lubrication was well under way, Polat yawned and began the slow and careful presentation of his proffer.

"Brothers," he said, "I am sure if you are aware of the final destination of your most precious cargo. Yes, I know about the chests of gold and treasure in the front of your ship's hold bound for the Doge of Venice."

In fact, Piet and Jans were not aware of the contents of the chests. It was apparent that Aslan Polat, had serious sources for his information. They listened intently now.

"No, the "Pure Cotton" is the most valuable of your cargoes, and even the Sultan is aware that you have not been paid. I would venture that this bit of commerce will open previously closed doors for you, as well as provide you with enough profit to make the challenging land trip to Constantinople well worth your while."

The two Flemish seamen were now fully attentive.

"But, there is something of a snag…"

Piet—more than Jans—had expected there would be something to cast a shadow on the heretofore glowing souk owner's pitch, and his natural cynicism began to take over.

Seeing a certain diminution in the sailors' enthusiasm, Aslan gave them one of his most winning smiles.

"Nothing we can't get around…by working together."

*"Ah, ha,"* thought Piet, *"here comes the rub."*

Polat's servants and slaves brought in a fine meal to keep the interest of the Flemish sailors. They served salad to Piet and Jan's plates from the community bowl.

Polat instructed as a Cretan might tell them, "You are strange. Just use your fork and eat right out of the bowl. It is the polite way."

The salad bowls were removed, and platters of sweet and savory *figolli* were served. *Figolli* are flat cakes that have an assortment of fillings such as rabbit, lamb, and hearts. The sweet ones were filled with a layer of marzipan and decorated with icing or chocolate and a small egg. Dessert was *loukoumades*–dough balls fried in olive oil and topped with honey, cinnamon, and finely ground bits of sesame seeds and nuts. The next desserts were *bugatsa*–pastry filled with cream and cheese, and sprinkled with powdered sugar, *Qaghaq ta ghazel* [honey rings], and Maltese almond cake. With every course, Polat unapologetically served them *raki* [essentially Italian *grappa*, made from the pits and skins of grapes after the wine has been distilled off].

Piet and Jans were comfortably satiated and mildly tipsy when the last dishes and glasses were carried away.

Polat began his pitch, "The real profits lie in trade on land. The seagoing commerce has largely fixed or contract costs and therefore fixed profits. With me–an experienced Ottoman versed in negotiations—along, the maximum profits can be obtained. Remember, we go to places where there are shortages. It is an old rule: limitations and scarcity breeds higher costs and profits. The more scarcity, the greater the profits."

"And the costs," ventured Piet.

"Well said, and true. However, with me along running the caravan, the costs will be kept at a minimum. I know people all along the way. Not to suggest that you are not good judges of character and of the real value of merchandise, but my experience is greater in this very lucrative marketplace called Turkey."

"That remains to be seen," said Jans. "What is your proposal about what each of us would contribute, and what kind of merchandise?"

"Another good point. You Europeans do not know the Arab or Turkish way of negotiating...of haggling. It is a subtle way and time consuming. Your buyer will not do business without proper consideration of the niceties."

"Nevertheless, the point has been raised and is pertinent."

"Indeed. I can contribute very beautiful hand knotted carpets from the islands and from the north. I buy in large lots and therefore obtain discounts from my old friends. Because of the low prices I pay, I can sell at lower prices than the buyers would have to pay in Izmir or Istanbul. They, in turn, can profit by selling to their local markets. Everyone benefits."

"Do you bring any other products to the caravan?"

"You mean besides providing the camels, the tents, and the cameleers and camp workers?"

"I do mean that."

"Is our bargaining still friendly, Jans?"

"It is. But, I have been in commerce for decades. I have learned that everyone in a business must contribute actual products with real value and must stand to lose along with everyone else if the business does not proper. That is why I ask the question. It is not a matter of distrusting you, or to take advantage. Piet and I have come ready to make a substantial monetary contribution to match your part."

"It is not that you and Piet just escaped from the vegetable cargo hold and want to try your luck in the hard world of commerce. I fully understand that. So...I can also contribute a good dozen or maybe fifteen camel loads of brass wear—samovars, cups, plates, utensils, lamp sconces, and some art pieces. Again, I know some vendors."

"We do have cargo remaining on the ship. I think we can contribute a like number of camel loads of such things as..."

Piet handed the captain the list he had prepared.

"Assorted Cretan wines, liter bottles of olive oil, Messara Valley cheese in large rounds, Messara Valley wheat, 6,000 board feet of Sfakia forest cypress wood ship planking, high quality animal hides, bottles of Tarra glass made to hold spirits, ingots of pure Kantanos copper, Kydonia gold, lead, Argyroupolis silver, and Sklavopoula of Selino iron, best Cretan honey, Markos Mousotiros Aldine printing press Greek authored books, and many bales of the best British and Irish woolen cloth, a scarcity item here in the east."

"In goodly quantities?"

"Yes, more than thirty camels can carry, I should imagine."

"My provision of camels and men comes at a steep cost. I must make expenses, and I must receive a profit equal to the time it has cost me."

"What kind of a split of costs do you propose, Aslan?"

"70-30, with the lower amount provided by me. You will make up in actual money for the difference in the products we each provide. Our caravan will be right around 200 camels; I can load the ones you cannot with your ship's cargo. I think that's fair, don't you?"

Jans and Piet allowed a moment of pause to pass.

Piet made the Flemish offer, "65-35, with the lower amount supplied by us."

Aslan's face fell. His expression indicated that the bargaining would fail if such an outrageous split were being made seriously.

He chuckled quietly.

"Oh, you Europeans, ever the jokers. I know you do not mean that. In the continuing spirit of friendliness, I suppose I could accept a 62-38 split, but the deal could not be done with any higher outlay by me...it is only fair, but I am sure you know that, *Sadiqs*."

There was another pause; this one longer, and more serious.

"Piet broke the impasse, "Perhaps we should discuss profit splits before we make a final decision on shared costs. I propose a profit split of 62-38 with us taking the lower amount, using your own numbers. This time I do feel that breakdown is not only fair but generous."

Aslan considered strongly holding out for a better split on one or the other of the loss/profit sides of the bargain but thought better of it. He knew this was going to be a long, arduous journey; and good will in a defense against bandits would be worth more.

He smiled broadly, showing a wide gap between his large, stained teeth, "Let us drink to it then," he said, spreading his large arms as if to embrace his new true *sadiqs*.

Apparently, it was not a hard and fast rule for him to avoid alcohol as his religion required, but millennia of traditions of haggling prevailed in the post bargaining courtesies. He toasted Jans and Piet with a dark purple juice that was very sweet, and thick enough that it was almost chewable.

Two days later, an 1,100 camel caravan with an additional 100 horses and 150 sturdy mules started the first steps onto the old silk road. Because Aslan knew men in Antioch who seldom saw traders coming their way nowadays and would be hungry for goods and generous about paying, they set out on a less used track towards the south, 144 leagues away.

# THE HISTORY:
# THE SILK ROAD—138 BCE TO THE 18ᵀᴴ CENTURY CE

The silk road was more a network than a road. It was an ancient trading network which started about the time of the Han Dynasty, when Emperor Wu ruled. The ancient network of trading routes spanned from the Yellow Sea to the Korean Peninsula stretching more than 15,000 kilometers [more than 4,000 miles] from Japan, the Korean Peninsula through today's Central Asia, the Caucasus and Anatolia to the Mediterranean Sea. The system was connected by the ring of the large-scale network included the Cangarusina and the African continent. The silk road's Eastern end was in present day China [all the way to the east end of the Asiatic Continent]. Its main Western end–by several roads–was Antioch in Turkey. It was in continuous use for 1,000 years.

The global domain of the cultural exchange through the ancient world has been partially investigated by modern archeologists. For example, the various kinds of archaeological materials excavated from the ancient tombs in Gyeongju–the capital of the Korean Silla Kingdom [57 B.C. ~ 935 CE]–indicate that there was frequent exchange between Silla and other worlds. Roman-style glass ware is one of the concrete archaeological objects which show the exchange and trade between Silla and the Western world. Many kinds of glass ware were excavated from the ancient tombs–dated 5ᵗʰ ~ 6ᵗʰ century–of the Silla Kingdom. Those pieces of glass ware are thought to have been produced along the Mediterranean coast in 4ᵗʰ ~ 5ᵗʰ century and supplied by the merchants of the countries bordering on Western China through both the land and the maritime routes to Silla.

Ancient jewels–made in Tashkent and Samarkand–were traded by the same group of merchants. Flavoring, herbs, and spices, from the west; and Chinese silk, fine dishware, ornaments, jewelry, jade, cast-iron products, and decorative boxes, were also important products imported to Silla. Goods traveled from the faraway Arabian Peninsula, the Western world, and Persian carpets and the rugs hand-knotted of wool in Hereke, Turkey, were also introduced to Silla people via the silk roads. It is, therefore, evident that the cultural exchange of the Silla Kingdom was not limited to Asia but was expanded as far as Islamic and European areas via the silk road system. Historians say that it would only take one month or so for the Buddhist monks of Silla to obtain Buddhist scriptures newly introduced in or via China. According to academic research, it would not take more than six months for the hairpin as commercial goods, which ladies in Constantinople [today's Istanbul] of Turkey used, to reach the capital Gyeongju of Silla Kingdom for sale.

The routes were based on strings of oases served by caravanserais which linked China and Europe. Iraqi people went to the Korean Peninsula and lived there. Old Korean books of history tell of Islamic people who lived in in Gaeseong – the capital of the Goryeo Dynasty (918 ~ 1392 CE). Commerce over the silk roads depended on making use of areas of intense agriculture and the routes they served, to which they were linked, and those they controlled. The name came into general use because it was dependent in large part by the movement of silk from China to ancient Rome [known to the Chinese as Da Qin]—the first three centuries of the existence of the network–which was the principle terminus.

Gan Ying: in 97 CE–in order to establish trade relations with Rome directly–was dispatched by Ban Chao to Da Qin (the old name of the Roman Empire), which was the farthest westbound travel and exploration. He set out on his difficult and danger-ous journey from Qiuci [today's Kuche or Kuqa]. He crossed mountains, traversed desolate deserts and the Gobi, went over high plateaus, and finally reached the Persian Gulf by way of Tiaozhi [present day Iraq] and the Anxi Empire [Parthia]. At that time, Anxi was a key transit station on the silk road. The merchants of Anxi monopolized the trade between China and Rome; they made great profits by selling Chinese silk to Romans at very high prices. From the $4^{th}$ century onwards, the "Rome" to which all roads led in the Mediterranean world was "Eastern Rome" of Constantinople—today's Istanbul. Numerous foreign cultures were introduced through the oasis routes of Cen-tral Asia desert area and the steppe routes of southern Siberia.

Even during its long centuries of decline ending in its conquest by the Ottoman Turks in 1453, the wealth of Constantinople was legendary. Its location ensured it a very important role in the trade with the East. Following its conquest, the Ottoman Sultan, Mehmed II, immediately set out to rebuild the city and to re-establish its eco-nomic and social vivacity under the Turks. The sultan built the Grand Bazaar in the city's marketplace which served the people of the known world at the time and is still important as a commercial center in its place in Istanbul.

The last Emperor died on the walls and the Patriarch–head of the Byzantine Church–was taken captive. Many of its churches were converted to mosques. Con-stantinople eventually resurged as the capital of the great Ottoman empire and again played a central role in east-west cultural and economic exchange by the succeed-ing sultans' support and improvement of the silk road system. Ottoman control over much of Asia and the Near East facilitated the exchange of not only goods but also ideas, crafts, skills, and customs, along the trade routes that passed through Constan-tinople, bringing new influences and cultures together and promoting innovation in the Ottoman arts of ceramics, calligraphy, and stained glass.

Many traditional trade alliances were re-established. Constantinople would also become renowned for its spectacular Islamic art and architecture, particularly under the reign of Suleiman the Magnificent (1520-1566), who ordered the construction of many beautiful bridges, palaces, and mosques, including the impressive Süleymaniye mosque, built between 1550 and 1557. Of the sultans, Süleymaniye was particularly interested in building and sharing the magnificent Ottoman culture. The passage of merchants, travelers, artists, and craftsmen, from East and West who docked at the city's harbors was a vital component of the city's history and identity and ensured that Constantinople remained a center of trade and exchange along the several silk roads. However, the greatest legacy of the silk road was the exchange of ideas and beliefs: cul-ture, art, religion, philosophy, technology, language, science, and architecture. It left an indelible mark on famous travelers, philosophers and warriors: from Marco Polo [during the Yuan Dynasty (1206-1368)], to Genghis Khan, and the Sufi poet Rumi.

During the Han Dynasty (206 BCE–220 CE] and Tang Dynasty (618-907 CE), the Chinese aristocracy made intermarriages with Hun [China's northern enemy], Wusun, and Tibet, which further consolidated the stable environment along the Silk Road and expanded it. Many princesses left their familiar hometowns and reached to the remote states on diplomatic missions. Wang Zhaojun—reputedly, one of the four most beautiful women in Chinese history–and Princess Wen Cheng—who married the King of Tibet–made important contributions to the smooth flow of the silk road. Xuanzang traveled to India to study Indian sutras along the silk road and wrote a book, *Pilgrim to the West in Tang Dynasty.*

Since the silk road was so long, most merchants along it were involved in relay trade rather than outfitting an expedition to take them all the way from China to Europe or North Africa. The first merchant might purchase a quantity of silk in China and then travel westwards with it until he reached a market spot along the silk road– usually an important oasis–where he could sell it. He would then return to the east to make a new purchase, while the new owner of the silk would take the cargo farther west before selling it to still another merchant. As a result, textiles, animals, birds, and other goods, changed hands numerous times before reaching the final buyer; and several notable market spots grew along the silk road.

The Sogdians were a Persian people from the strategically located Transoxiana region of Central Asia [today's Uzbekistan and Tajikistan]. The heart of the Sogdian lands was the famous silk road city, Samarkand. They were among the most prominent traders of the silk road, and the Sogdian language became the *lingua franca* for the silk road trading stations. Sogdians frequently functioned as middle-men between traders from various cultures and countries.

The silk road spanned numerous countries and cultures; and because of the necessary relay trading, most merchants found themselves in a situation where the currency they accepted when selling the goods was no longer a currency that they could use to make a new purchase of goods. Because of this, currency exchange trading became a necessity. Currency trading was relatively easy since most coins' value was dictated by the weight of the precious metals in the coin. The most sought-after coins were those attractive standard Roman *aurei* gold pieces minted in the Roman Empire. Two other major currencies used along the Silk Road were the silver *drachm* of the Sasanian Empire [Neo-Persian Sasanian empire—224 to 651 CE] and the gold *solidus,* and bronze coins of the Eastern Roman Empire. Towards the end of the empire, the general decline of Byzantium meant that no golden solidus coins were issued – only silver coins called *stavraton* and some minor copper coins. Since they were made from precious metals, coins were ideal for international trade. However, a gold or silver coin of a certain weight would have the same value everywhere along the line; and a currency trader could exchange one coin for other coins of the same weight no matter which country issued the coin without having to worry overmuch about exchange rates.

Coins have been found for thirty-two different Sasanian rulers, and the coins' strong similarity across the Persian empire indicate that the striking of Sasanian coins was always under the control of a centralized authority. During the first part of the empire, the coin dies were mostly produced by the local mints themselves; but from the mid-5th century CE, they were almost always centrally manufactured and then transported to the various local mints along the silk road. From 878 CE and onward, the mint in Constantinople was the only source of Byzantine gold and silver coinage until the late 11th century when provincial mints were created again.

Also, items that were frequently traded along the silk road could turn into almost a type of currency in themselves, since the peoples living along the silk road knew that there was a reliable liquid market for them. If one accepted payment for his services in the form of Indian sandalwood, spices, fine cotton goods, pearls, and ivory; Chinese silk, or Indonesian pepper, the merchant knew that it would be fairly easy to barter it for other goods and services as needed.

The western end of the trade routes developed earlier as western empires started trading with India. The Greek language and mythology as well as sculpture were blended with the culture in the Indian kingdoms. Nathu La is a mountain pass in the Himalayas which connects the Indian state of Sikkim with Tibet. The pass forms a significant offshoot of the ancient western silk road. Nathu means "listening ears" and La means "pass" in Tibetan. The Nabateans controlled the trade on the spice route between their capital Petra and the Gazan seaports on the Mediterranean. Nomadic tribes ruled the Negev largely independently and with a relative lack of interference for the next thousand years. What is known of trade during that time is largely derived from oral histories and folk tales of tribes from the Wadi Musa and Petra areas in present-day Jordan. The Bedouins of the Negev historically survived chiefly on sheep and goat husbandry. Scarcity of water and of permanent pastoral land required them a nomadic life, but they established trade routes that linked to the silk road.

The eastern end took longer to form because of the warring tribes in China. In 125 BCE, Zhang Qian—considered by many historians to be the father of the silk route—became interested in further commerce with the west because of his need for larger stronger horses developed in the west. He opened the future astronomically lucrative trade routes with the west.

The Great Wall of China was built to defend against the northern states invading the southern states. When the Silk Road was regularly traveled by traders carrying precious stones, jade, gold, ivory, and glass, bandits started attacking. To protect their interests the Great Wall was continued along the Gansu Corridor. Sections of this Han dynasty wall can still be seen as far as Yumen Guan well beyond the established beginning of the Great Wall. The northern route went west along the northern foot of Tianshan Mountains, taking merchants westwards to Hami (Kumul), Urumqi, and Yining, and then reached the areas near the Black Sea, the Caspian Sea, and the Mediterranean Sea, which contributed both land and sea routes for bi-directional trade. The northern route started at Chang'an [today's Xi'an] the capital of the ancient Chinese Kingdom. The Later Han moved that capital further east to Luoyang. The route was defined about the 1st Century BCE as Han Wudi. Its contribution was to put an end to harassment by nomadic tribes.

The northern route travels northwest through the Chinese province of Gansu from Shaanxi Province, and splits into three further routes, two of them following the mountain ranges to the north and south of the Taklimakan Desert to rejoin at Kashgar; and the other going north of the Tian Shan mountains through Turpan, Talgar and Almaty (in what is now southeast Kazakhstan). The routes split west of Kashgar, with one branch heading down the Alai Valley towards Termez and Balkh, while the other traveled through Kokand in the Fergana Valley, and then west across the Karakum Desert towards Merv, joining the southern route briefly. One advantage of the northern route was that the oases were closer together.

One of the branch routes turned northwest to the north of the Aral and Caspian seas then and on to the Black Sea. Yet another route started at Xi'an, passed through the Western corridor beyond the Yellow Rivers, Xinjiang, Fergana (in present-day eastern Uzbekistan), Persia, and Iraq, before joining the western boundary of the Roman Empire. A route for caravans, the northern silk road brought to China many items, such as dates, saffron powder, and pistachio nuts from Persia; frankincense, aloes, and myrrh, from Somalia; sandalwood from India; glass bottles, perfumes, and cosmetics from Egypt; and other expensive and desirable goods from other parts of the world. In exchange, the caravans sent back goods such as silk brocade, lacquer ware, and porcelain.

The silk road commercial routes passed through the Iranian empire of Persia that controlled most of the Middle East and cultural and religious influences spread. During antiquity some of the main traders along the Silk Road were the Chinese, Arabs, Somalis, Syrians, Jewish People, Persians, Greeks, and Romans.

The southern route so helped enhance trade between the ancient Roman Empire and the Indian subcontinent, that Roman politicians and historians are on record decrying the loss of silver and gold to buy silk to pamper Roman wives, and the southern route grew to eclipse and then totally supplant the overland trade route.

Two of the most important issues for the ancient Mediterranean area and the function of the silk roads were territorial claims and control of trade routes between east and west. Two eastern imports were of particular importance in the Mediterranean world: silk from China and spices from India and Southeast Asia. The traffic in these commodities became very extensive and Roman legislative enactments reveal a continuing concern to protect it from interference. Because of this trade, the Romans and Byzantine world was in touch with the civilizations of further Asia, with China, and with India. In the early decades, there were no regular relations, and very few recorded exchanges of visitors.

There were, however, imports from both, for which the Romans; and after them, the Byzantines, seem to have paid principally in gold coin. There was little if anything that the Mediterranean world could offer as barter in exchange for Chinese silk or Indian spices. Gold—especially gold coins–however, was always acceptable; and great quantities of Roman gold coins were sent to eastern Asia to pay for the imports that came to the Mediterranean Basin. There was also a huge outpouring of gold to eastern Asia, since the Persians made substantial profits as middlemen in the silk trade for China. This was especially true when the Persians were able to extend their rule eastward into Central Asia and thus to dominate the silk trade at its point of departure.

There were occasional complaints in the Roman Senate of the drain of bullion to the East; but on the whole, the Roman world seems to have survived this drain surprisingly well; and the enlivening and profitable commerce over the silk roads continued largely undiminished.

The most direct route from the Mediterranean lands to those further east lay through the territories ruled or dominated by Persia. Consequently, there were obvious advantages–both economic and strategic–in developing routes beyond the reach of dominant Persian armed forces. The choices were the northern overland route from China through the Turkish lands in the Eurasian steppe towards the Black Sea and Byzantine territory, or the southern sea routes through the Indian Ocean. These led either to the Persian Gulf and Arabia or to the Red Sea, with overland connections through Egypt and the isthmus of Suez, or through the caravan routes of western Arabia from Yemen to the borders of Syria.

The Roman and Byzantine interest was to establish and preserve these external commercial links with China and with India, thus bypassing the Persian-dominated center. The Persian Empire tried to use its position athwart the transit routes to control Byzantine trade, so as to exploit it in times of peace, or to stop it in times of war. This meant a recurring struggle for influence between the two imperial powers in the countries' struggle for influence beyond the imperial borders of both of them. The effect of these interventions—commercial, diplomatic, and on rare occasions, military—was considerable in all those areas. Those primarily affected were the Turkish tribes and principalities in the north, and the Arab tribes and principalities in the south.

The most important commodities of the luxury trade were silk and silk brocade which were very useful for travel since they were light, of high cost, and of great and lasting value. In late Roman. Byzantine, Persian, and early Islamic times silk was of considerable political as well as commercial importance. However, by the 1070s, the Seljuk Turks defeated the Imperial Ottoman army and seized much of Anatolia. Not long after, a new force appeared from the Mediterranean. The Venetians gained a strangle-hold on the Empire's trade. Relations with Venice and the West generally and steadily deteriorated.

The Fourth Crusade's sack of Byzantine Constantinople occurred in 1204 and altered the dominance of the trade routes. The conquering crusaders were thunderstruck by the booty they removed from the city. A historian reported:

> *"It was so rich, and there were so many rich vessels of gold and silver and cloth of gold and so many rich jewels, that it was a fair marvel...Not since the world was made, was there ever seen or won so great a treasure or so noble or so rich, not in the time of Alexander nor in the time of Charlemagne...Nor do I think...that in the forty richest cities of the world there had been so much wealth as was found in Constantinople."*

Even in this period when Mongol power was in fact beginning to disintegrate, the route to China was safe and the silk road was flourishing, Constantinople being one of its main points of trade in the West. The political history of the city would change radically when—in May 1453—Constantinople fell to the Ottoman Turks. The city became once again one of the world's most important cities, this time as the capital of the Ottoman Empire. Mehmet II resettled people from across the Ottoman Empire in the capital. Although trade had fallen and the population had been depleted at the time of the conquest, it then picked up.

According to the great 14th century traveler, trade—beginning around 300 CE—was conducted by caravans of camels. According to Ibn Battuta—the explorer who accompanied one of the caravans—the average size per caravan was 1,000 camels; some caravans were as large as 12,000.

Nomads along the silk road provided fresh horses and camels and acted as guides across the mountain passes and through the sand dunes. However, nomads were also known for their military prowess, and as a result the Great Wall had been built to protect China from nomad invasions. Many nomads were horse-riding nomadic pastoralists; others were dangerous roving bandits. The Mongols, in what is now Mongolia, Russia, and China, and the Tatars or Turkic people of Eastern Europe and Central Asia, were nomadic peoples who practiced seasonal movement of livestock on the harsh Asian steppes. The herded livestock included cows, buffalos, yaks, llamas, sheep, goats, reindeer, horses, donkeys or camels, and contributed to the complexity and flourishing of silk road commerce.

# CHAPTER TWELVE

# OVERLAND TO ANTIOCH ON THE SILK ROAD

IN THE YEAR OF OUR LORD, 1642, LATE MAY

With the convoy stopped for a rest at a lush caravanserai along the old silk road just outside the provincial limits of Laiazzo on the first day of travel towards Antioch, the Bactrian camels were fed and began to settle down. Piet was sure he would never get used to the noisy brutes: moaning and groaning, high-pitched bleating, loud bellows and roars, rumbling growls—"nuz, nuz", which the cameleers called nuzzling, and frequent grunts—"nuuuuurrrrr, nuuuuurrrrr." Aslan and the Muslim cameleers told the Flemish sailors that they found the low-grade cacophony rather soothing; so much so, some of them asserted, that they were unable to sleep without it.

Piet and Jans shared a tent made of camel skins and lined with valuable Chinese silk brocade. Shortly before midnight, howling from several dozen invading men rent the air of the quiet night.

"*Allah Akbar*!!, *Allah Akbar*!! *Allah Akbar*!!, over and over and closer and closer in an increasingly threatening and thundering pitch.

Still closer, "*Qatal*!, *Qatal*!, *Qatal*!" [Arabic. Kill, Kill, Kill], and *Öldür*!, *Öldür*!, *Öldür*!" [Turkish. Kill, Kill, Kill].

Then came the unmistakable sounds of clashing swords, screams of the injured, grunting of the dying. A quick peak out of the tent opening revealed the chaos of the battle but no indication of which side was gaining the ground—caravan guards or bandits.

A few minutes after the battle seemed to have reached its zenith, there came an entirely different phrase in Turkish, this time in a crescendo and quickly diminishing loudness—the sound of men fleeing.

The bandits were shouting over and over to each other in harsh and frightened Turkish, "The Janissaries are coming! the Janissaries are coming!"

For over four centuries, that cry of alarm struck fear in the hearts of every European who heard it, from the lowest to the highest, particularly in Constantinople, Greece, the Balkans, and the Mediterranean area.

As the surprised and terrified bandits ran farther away, the chilling sentence diminished in volume. Piet stood with Jans and Aslan smiling as they watched the disciplined Janissaries put the bandits and thieves to rout. The Janissaries' *yatagan* swords—the signature weapon of the disciplined soldier slaves of the sultan—gleamed and flashed in the light of the campfires. In less than fifteen minutes, the shouting faded away. Ten minutes after that, the Janissaries marched back into camp, every tenth man holding the severed head of one of the dreaded Muslim bandits.

The Janissary sergeants presented themselves to Aslan, Jans, and Piet, and held their right hands out, palm upwards.

"Bring the chest of gold coins, you two." Aslan said emphatically. "The Janissaries do not fight for honor, God, country, king, family, or their religion. They do it for money and expect to be paid very promptly."

Piet and Jans fetched the trunks full of gold coins and watched as Aslan and the senior Janissary sergeant haggled over the price. Finally, it was decided that each *nefer* [private soldier] was to be given two Byzantine gold *solidus*, each Janissary *onbaşı* [sergeant] four, and the officers—only two Janissary *ocak aghas* [~ lieutenants]–received five even though they had not participated in the fighting.

The senior Janissary *onbaşı* nodded his head as acceptance of the payment and gave assurance that that particular gang of motley bandits would not be seen again. He, Aslan, Piet, and Jans, shared a soothing soak in a perfumed bath after all their anxiety.

For the next week, the caravan traveled ever further into the desert, ever further away from civilization, and traveled through what the cameleers called the "trails of bones" for certain of the passes which they pushed their way through which were particularly difficult and dangerous for the men and animals of the caravan. The survival of a caravan was precarious and would rely on careful coordination. Runners were sent ahead to oases so that water could be delivered to the caravan when it was still several days away, as the caravans could not easily carry enough with them to make the full journey. Piet Van Brakel longed for the cooling breezes and clean air of his ship. After eight days of fighting the scourges of the desert traveler—flies, scorpions, dust storms, thirst, polluted water, shimmering mirages, attacks and feints by bandits, and the incessant whining of the camels and stubbornness of the donkeys and mules—the caravan began to see down into the valley where the city of Antioch was supposed to be.

A single road—to use the term loosely—led from the Euphratean ford at Thapsacus and skirted the fringe of the Syrian steppe. In the higher elevations, the participants in the hot, dry, and dusty, caravan caught sight of the outlying buildings of Antioch as they proceeded south in the Orontes valley.

Antioch on the Orontes—referred to as Antakya by the Turks—lies 144 leagues [694 km] away from Laiazzo following the remnants of the silk road. The area of Antioch has been occupied by humans since the Calcolithic era [6th millennium BCE], as revealed by archeological excavations of the mound of Tell-Açana. The city was founded near the end of the fourth century BCE by Seleucus I Nicator, one of Alexander the Great's generals. The city's geographical, military, and economic, location benefited its occupants, featuring the spice trade, the silk road, and the Royal Road. It eventually rivaled Alexandria in Egypt as the chief city of the Near East.

The city was the capital of the Seleucid Empire until 63 BCE when the Romans took control, making it the seat of the governor of the province of Syria. From the early 4th century, the city was the seat of the Count of the Orient, head of the regional administration of sixteen provinces. It was also the main center of Hellenistic Judaism at the end of the Second Temple period. Antioch was one of the most important cities in the eastern Mediterranean of Rome's dominions.

Antioch was—at one time–called "the cradle of Christianity" as a result of its longevity and the pivotal role that it played in the emergence of both Hellenistic Judaism and early Christianity. The Christian New Testament asserts that the name "Christian" first emerged in Antioch. It was one of the four cities of the Syrian tetrapolis [Seleucia, Apamea, Laodicea, and Antiochia], and its residents were known as *Antiochenes*.

The city was a metropolis of a quarter million people during the times of Caesar Augustus, but it declined to relative insignificance during the Middle Ages because of warfare, repeated earthquakes, and especially due to a change in trade routes. They no longer passed through Antioch from the far east following the Mongol invasions and conquests. The silk road itself was scarcely a track; it was a dusty trail intermittently identified as such by the absence of plants in the winding track. The desert there was so dry a man's track can last a century on the dust of the little used silk road or the royal road.

The city was built in 300 BCE on the eastern side of the Orontes River by Alexander's generals after his death. In the Orontes, north of the city, lay a large island where Seleucus II Callinicus began a third walled city, which was finished by Antiochus III. A fourth and last quarter was added by Antiochus IV Epiphanes (175–164 BCE); from then until its ultimate decline, Antioch was known as *Tetrapolis*. From west to east the whole metropolitan area was about six kilometers in diameter and a little less from north to south. This area once included many large gardens, the paradise of Daphne, a park of woods and waters; and in the center of that verdant greenery rose a great temple to the Pythian Apollo. By the time Piet and Jans sat on their swaying camels and looked on what was left, it not much more than a weed strewn ruin.

In the Roman Empire and in the Byzantium and it was a key city for the early years of Christianity, the Syriac Orthodox Church, and the Antiochian Orthodox Church. From the 7th century CE with the rise of Islam, and after the 10th century CE with the Crusades, Antioch was at its zenith.

In 1268 it fell to the Egyptian Mamluk Sultan Baibars after a lengthy siege. Baibars proceeded to massacre the Christian population. In addition to suffering the ravages of war, the city lost its commercial importance because trade routes to the Far East moved north following the 13th century Mongol conquests. Antioch never recovered as a major city, with much of its former role falling to the port city of Alexandretta [later İskenderun].

By 1300, the Muslims had expelled the last of the Christian crusaders from the Holy Land. The end of the Crusades brought peace to the eastern Mediterranean, which greatly stimulated commerce and allowed individuals like Ibn Battuta to travel freely through the area. However–by that time– Antioch had lost any significance as a commercial hub; its name remained only to identify the ruins. The city had been a metropolis of a quarter million people during the administration of Caesar Augustus, but it declined to relative insignificance during the Middle Ages before the 17$^{th}$ century because of warfare, repeated earthquakes, and a change in trade routes.

By 1432 there were only about 300 inhabited houses within its walls, mostly occupied by Turcomans; and in 1642, there were less than a hundred occupied dwellings, and no apparent governmental buildings. Caravans no longer passed through Antioch from the far east following the Mongol invasions and conquests. Piet and Jans found farmers, hunters, and craftsman, who had gathered from all around the region for the visit of the caravan waiting anxiously to greet them. There had been a long drought of trading, and everyone was determined to make the best of this singular opportunity.

"We proud *Antiochenes* welcome you to our once grand city. With the coming of your caravan, we look to a time when the old silk road will once again be discovered in this area, and Antioch will be recognized for its excellent location and for its fine craftsmen. Allow me to introduce you to my townsmen. I am Abdullah ibn Muhammad ibn Abu Bakr."

"And I am Aslan Polat–leader of the caravan–at your service. We would be grateful to have pasture for our animals, a place to pitch our tents, and your spreading the word around about what we have to offer. My colleagues—Jans Corren, Piet Van Brakel—and I, would be more than happy to give a committee of your fellow-citizens an opportunity to view our wares. Perhaps, we can find special bargains for those of you who came to meet us."

"The word is already spreading. Now let me introduce my friends."

There were ten of them—farmers, herders, tanners, carpet makers, pottery makers, and artists. Aslan was good with names, and shortly, he was able to remember each name and to begin the process of buying and selling. There was half a day of good-natured haggling, followed by a fine meal—the best the women of Antioch could prepare.

The host complied strictly with old style Turkish table etiquette. Abdullah ibn Abu Bakr took his place at the head of the table, with the Aslan Polat–the honored guest–seated next to him. Aslan was seated on the side of the table farthest from the door, a custom that made no sense to Piet and Jans. The headmen of the valley sat in the middle, flanked on either side in descending order by their aides, with the least important people sitting at the ends of the table farthest from the middle, and closest to the door. The arrangement was mirrored on the opposite side. Men and women were seated in separate areas and spend the entire evening separated from each other.

Boys served the men, and girls served the women. The dinner began with tea served in small curved glasses held not by the stem, but by the lip. It would have been a gross faux pas to add milk. However, for the tender mouths of Piet and Jans, they were permitted to cold add water both to cool and to dilute it. The tea they were being served was still steeping.

Aslan quietly leaned to whisper to Piet on his right, and Jans on his left, "You need to understand that coffee in this backwater is not approved and—away from the larger centers—it is not generally available. Since it is offered all the time and everywhere, it is a gesture of hospitality and you must always take the tea, even if you do not care for it. At least put it to your lips or better, take a few sips. The Turkish rule of courtesy requires that your cup always be refilled if it is less than half full. And, you must never pour your own drink. So, pay attention to those around you.

Always be alert throughout the meal as to whether your neighbor's cup or glass needs refilling. If it is less than half full, it needs refilling—that's the rule; and your table mates will be watching. Of course, if yours is less than half full, your neighbor is obliged to refill it. He or she may not be aware, but you must not refill it yourself. You may even make an enemy because if the neighbor does not do his or her duty, it will be considered a slight to you, even if accidental. That will cause him or her to lose face.

"So, won't it be pretty obvious if we blurt out that our cup needs filling, Aslan?"

"Here is where the finesse of Turkish manners comes in. Do not speak; instead, diplomatically indicate your need by pouring a little more tea into your neighbor's glass, even if it doesn't really need it. It is a universal signal."

"How do Turks or their guests learn about all of those rules which seem to be impossibly complex?" Piet asked, concerned about making a serious faux pas.

"It is not much different from the religious mysteries of the Roman Catholics, especially, watching the mass from a distance and not being familiar. All that standing, kneeling, crossing, head bowing, and murmuring. One day, you will be part of a Japanese tea ceremony performed by a geisha girl. It is complex and incomprehensible. All of those sorts of things are learned, and so is the Turkish way."

Piet rolled his eyes in a gesture of defeat.

"Now, listen carefully, young Europeans. This matters; and there is very little time for me to teach you. First, I will tell you; and then try and do as I do. These are the rules, and I hope I don't fail to remember the most important ones: The host—presumably Muhammad—will make a toast, often a flowery and religious semi-sermon. If you are selected to be the honored guest instead of me, you do not have to speak in that same way; but, if you are the honored guest—and here I am talking especially to you, Captain—you will be expected to make a toast, usually soon after the host does. If someone else stands up and begins to talk immediately, wait for your toast until the end of the meal, just before everyone leaves. Think about your little speech now, Jans; so, you will come across as educated in the courtesies and that you are showing proper respect.

"Here, away from civilization as we all know it, utensils are rarely ever used, especially knives, which could seem to be a threat. I doubt that any utensils will be put on the table unless you make a special request, and that would be very gauche. Eating with the fingers is definitely polite. Be sure you make a show of washing your hands thoroughly. Never touch food with your left hand, even if you have the misfortune to be left-handed."

Piet raised an eyebrow.

Jans said, "I'll explain later."

Aslan continued, "Almost every man smokes a hookah at every gathering. Do not refuse the offer. Many men smoke between courses during our rather lengthy dinners.

"Unlike what you would expect, the honored guest is always served first, then the oldest man, then the rest of the men, then children, and finally women, in the separate room. The host often waits until the very last person is served before allowing himself to receive a full plate. Do not start to eat until the host either makes a toast or begins to eat.

"The host sits at the head of the table, with the honored guest seated next to him. Do not begin to eat or drink until the oldest man at the table has been served and has begun. You may want to ask your host when it is appropriate to begin. Do not expect him to talk with his mouth full.

"For some odd reason that even I, a Turk, cannot understand; the guest's chair is on the side of the table farthest from the door; but, there, you have it. At business meetings such as this, the key people sit in the middle, flanked on either side in descending order by their aides, with the least important people sitting at the ends of the table farthest from the middle, and closest to the door; the arrangement is mirrored on the other side. Men dine first.

"Always remember at the end of the meal, to thank the host for a wonderful meal. Ask the host if it is appropriate to thank his wife. If you do, avoid standing too close or to try and shake her hand or to pat her on the shoulder.

"Do not make an effort to start or to force conversation: act as if you are seated at a private table, and a abide by the rule of 'don't speak unless spoken to'. Waitstaff may be summoned by making eye contact. Do not call attention to yourself. For the sake of Allah's blessing, do not wave or call out to the waiters. This is considered to be the height of discourtesy. Since this is a business meal, it is considered disrespectful to discuss business or to share business decisions. The personal relationship you are developing is deemed to be much more important. Take your cue from the host: if he brings up business, then it's appropriate to discuss it, but wait to take your lead from his conversation.

"Water or fruit juice will not be served until after the meal is over. Here in the outskirts of civilization, many believe that drinking while eating is not healthy.

"At this table where trade is paramount, resist the impulse to sit down, and wait until your host gives you the indicated signal, often a small nod of his head. In most such gatherings, such a signal will likely come after either the host or oldest man is seated. Be certain not to wear shoes in the room where the table is set. Better to take them off before entering the house. As you move from room to room, be sure to allow the more senior members of your party to enter the room ahead of you.

"Remember to say *"s olsun"* [May what you eat bring well-being] before or after eating, and then to say *"Elinize sağlik"* [a compliment to the hostess, meaning "Bless your hand"] after the meal if the host permits such conversation. Many of the very strict Islamists forbid any and all contact with their wives, even if the man has more than one."

Jans asked Aslan if he and Piet were dressed appropriately since the other guests were in fine–even though not princely–attire.

"I have enquired of Muhammad about that. He asked if you were people of the book, and he was reassured. Your clothing is not overly outstanding, but it is better than the simple bodily coverings required of the poor people. Do not worry about that, my friends."

The handsome youths entered the open area bearing platters of food. Their manner of dress was that required by the great sultan, Suleiman the Magnificent and his successors. Elsewhere–and in the palace and its court–the royal family and its courtiers dressed very lavishly, taking full advantage of the treasures afforded them via the silk road. The Ottoman administrators enacted sumptuary laws regulating clothing. The clothing of Muslims, Christians, Jewish communities, clergy, tradesmen, and state and military officials, were particularly strictly regulated.

The boys were over dressed for the temperature, but the evening was cooling down as usual; and it would soon be chilly. They wore outer items with dun and other earth tone colors. This included a *mintan, zıbın, şal-var, kuşak, potur, entari, kalpak, sarık* [on their heads], *çarık, çizme, çedik,* and *Yemeni* [on their feet]. To demonstrate their middle-class status, the boys wore a *cübbe* and a *hırka*.

Unlike the requirements for women in many of the Islamic areas, heavy cloaking garments were not worn by the girls and women of Antioch or generally in Turkey at that time. Women's wear for such an occasion such as this dinner included: *şalvar,* a *gömlek,* a *zıbın,* and a colorful sash. Because it was–for the *Antiochenes*–a formal occasion, the woman guests and the serving girls added an *entari*. The *zibin* was buttoned to the waist, leaving the skirts open in front. The girls' *zibins* had buttons all the way to the throat, but most had buttoned their *zibins* only to the underside of their ample Mediterranean breasts, leaving the garments to gape open; even the Turks were aware of the adage that 'it can't hurt to advertise a bit'. All the girls' clothes were brightly colored and patterned even though the girls' families were of relatively modest means.

Piet and Jans took note that the clothing styles had remained stagnant for two centuries and—unlike their Netherlander compatriots—there was no chaos reflected in dress in Turkey like that which followed the political crises of the 17th century in Holland and the Netherlands. The excessive compulsion and showing off during the Tulip Era and even during the deprivations of the great tulip bust lasted until the 19th century. It was not until the 1830s, that Sultan Mahmud II attempted modest modernization in dress for Turks. Even then, changes took place only in the palace and state government sector.

The meal was modest by palace standards, but it was a grand production for the *Antiochenes*. The first platters held a wide assortment of the best produce the Antioch region could boast served as *mezzes*: olives and olive oil, pitas, honey, sesame seeds, dates, sumac, chickpeas, mint, rice, and parsley, served by girls. Boys carried dolmas–stuffed vegetables [dolma is the Turkish word for "stuffed"]. The *Antiochene* women had spent days stuffing grape leaves, chard, and cabbage, with several varieties of rice [baldo, osmancik, Chinese fragrant, wild, and also orzo pasta and bulgar wheat], ground meat, pine nuts, and a heavy dollup of spices [including turmeric, cumin, and garlic from India; and cloves, peppercorns and allspice from the Spice Islands. The stuffed creations were then stewed in oil and tomato.

Other dolmas were made with stuffings of mixed squash, onion, tomato, eggplant, peppers, and carrots—considered a particular delicacy. Those creations were stewed or baked. There were other small dishes holding cheeses, pickles, melons, nuts, salads and dips, such as tabbouleh, hummus, and mutabbal. And these were only the appetizers. The Europeans wisely took only small tastes of the great variety to conserve gastric space for the heavier dishes to come.

That was wise planning, because as soon as the little plates emptied; and the guests pushed the ceramic dishes aside, the boys and girls swiftly swept in with the heavier dishes—what Piet and Jans called the entrees—kebabs, falafel, yogurt, doner kebab, shawarma and *mulukhiyah* [a bitter leaf akin to okra shipped in from Africa] which the Europeans decided was definitely going to be a learned taste, if they were ever faced with it again. There were delicious dumplings, a holdover from the Mongol invaders. Before they threw their hands up in defeat, the men had a chance to try couscous, freekeh, and burghul—cereal dishes that they would request in that future day when *mulukhiyah* was foisted upon them. Lamb and goat were the only stand-alone meats, and they were grilled with Indonesian spices.

"If that lamb were the last thing I tasted before going to paradise, I would die happy," said Aslan.

They made a studious effort to leave just enough room for baklava, the walnut dessert which other travelers they met along the way touted highly. Before it could be served, however, a calamity occurred.

Piet's purse hung diagonally across his chest supported by a strong leather thong. It contained his ship's papers, his Laiazzo customs document, and coins–*kai-yuans* [round bronze metal discs with square holes which originated in the Tang Dynasty–and paper currency from six different countries, including Roman promissory notes, Mongol Empire hand-signed notes, Japanese washi paper bank notes, and Italian *notas di banco*. Turkey did not yet have paper money, and China reverted back to metal "cash" after a severe devaluation of its paper money in 1455. Europe did not use actual paper money until late in the 17th century.

He had developed an almost nervous tic of slipping his right hand over the full purse every few minutes or so.

At first there was a sensation of a tug on the purse. He instinctively put his right palm over the money bag. It was still there. Then, there was an unmistakable powerful pull on the purse. Piet whirled to his right, in the direction of the pulling. He looked into the wan face of an obviously very poor adolescent who was still clutching onto Piet's property. Self-preservation took over, and Piet threw a vicious punch with his strong arm and work-hardened fist. It connected squarely on the boy's chin, and the boy toppled to the ground unconscious. Less than two seconds had elapsed from the sensation of the tugging to the men around him looking at the fallen boy.

"*Hirsiz*!!!" yelled a man sitting close to Piet.

In a matter of seconds, a crowd of violently angry men descended on the unconscious thief and rendered him bloody.

Muhammad–on whose property the outrage occurred—called a halt to the beating.

"We will judge him like rational men of Allah, not inflamed beasts," he said.

Someone found iced water and splashed the boy's swollen face soaking his dirty, once white, yelek and cotton pantaloons. His scrawny lower legs and filthy feet were bare like his bony bare chest under the open collarless and sleeveless yelek which probably had never been washed.

Once the boy awakened and became aware of his surroundings, he was tied to a tree; and the sharia trial began, despite the absence of a mullah.

Eighteen witnesses testified against the boy; there were no defense witnesses. Muhammad pronounced the cringing young man guilty of being a *hirsiz*, a thief. The crime was so blatant, so indefensible, and so simple, that Muhammad needed no more time to determine the penalty than a few seconds.

"From the Holy *Qur'an*, 5:38, we read, 'As to the thief, Male or female, cut off his or her hands: a punishment by way of example, from Allah, for their crime: and Allah is Exalted in power.' Place the *hirsiz* face down with his arm stretched over a barrel. Rifat, fetch my *kilij* sword."

Rifat had already fetched the sword and ropes to tie down the young man's forearm.

Muhammad gripped the handle of the razor-sharp *kilij* and showed it to the miscreant thief.

Piet quickly took Jans and Aslan aside and whispered.

"I thought the *Qur'an* or sharia law or somewhere has a clause that says that the victim of a crime can publicly forgive and spare the thief. Isn't that so?"

"Doesn't matter a tinker's damn. If it is true and you forgive him, you will appear weak. We will not be able to do business here or anyplace in

Turkey. The word will spread. I will not let you do it, Piet. Don't fight me. In time, you will realize the justice of Allah and come to have peace with it. For now, we cannot destroy ourselves by appearing to be against the law of the Almighty," Aslan said very gravely.

Piet gritted his teeth.

Muhammad looked at Piet. The look on his face was a query, "Do you spare this scum?"

Piet gulped and shook his head.

The boy's arm was fixed to the barrel leaving a space for the sword cut. Four strong men held the struggling and crying boy down. Not a word was spoken.

The sword swung by Muhammad fell hard and true. The boy's hand was cleanly severed at the wrist and thrown to the dogs; so, he would not be able to be buried with the amputated appendage and would live through eternity without it. Two skilled women bound the furiously bleeding stump with clean linen; so, he would not bleed to death. He was dragged to the periphery of Muhammad's property and banished from Antioch for the rest of his life.

Piet's education in the ways of the Muslims was evolving; he had seen their piracy and slavery, and now he understood their justice.

# The History:
## Constantinople until Istanbul

Istanbul's beginnings were Greek, followed by Rome, then by victorious Christians, then by Muslims, who supplanted the Christians and made a truly new city.

According to Pliny the Elder in the *Natural History*, the first known name of a settlement on the site of Constantinople was *Lygos*, which was a settlement of Thracian origin founded between the 13th and 11th centuries BCE. As early as the 7th century BCE, Greek colonists occupied the tip of a peninsula on the western shore of the Bosporus Strait where the current was favorable; and–of greatest importance—the Greeks recognized there a wonderful natural harbor, known even today as the Golden Horn. It was in the ideal location to control the trade from the Black Sea into the Aegean, which was so important for supplying Ancient Greece.

About 657 BCE, Greeks from Magara, a settlement on the east side of the Bosporus Strait left that town and moved to the opposite side—what is now the European side—and created a new colony, apparently because it was better farm land. They were led by a ruler named Byzas, and the city they founded took his name. The historian Tacitus stated that the colonists moved on the order of the "god of Delphi". That god ordered them to leave the region of the Chalcedonians which the god (or the historian) considered to be the "land of the blind." The new colonists, who termed themselves "the Byzantines" founded an important port city—Byzantium–that prospered there.

The people of the new city took with them the alphabet, calendar, and cults, of the Magara; but otherwise little is known of the Greek history of the place, including its founding. The Greek settlement was not only placed in a fertile agricultural area, but it was also of strategic importance because it stood at the entrance to the huge Black Sea—the only entrance—and also protected the Straits of Bosporus  and its passage to the Mediterranean from attacks from the east and west. In addition, the city that grew up there, lay above a deep inlet known as the Golden Horn. It was defensible, because it could only be attacked from the west. Water protected the inhabitants from eastern threats. It had easy access to the Danube or the Euphrates frontiers. Byzantium was never a major influential city-state like that of Athens, Corinth, or Sparta; but the city enjoyed relatively prolonged peace and steady growth as a prosperous trading city as a consequence of its remarkable position. It was always too valuable a settlement to abandon.

Throughout their history, the people of Byzantium continued to refer to themselves as "Romans" and most of them spoke Greek until the fall of Constantinople in 1453. The golden age of the empire came during the reign of Justinian [527-565 CE] during which the empire's territories extended as far as Western Europe, and the emperor's builders constructed the Hagia Sophia, a great cathedral that still stands today. It had to be rebuilt after rabid politicians burned it to the ground during the

Nika Rebellion in 532. The rededication of the city's foremost church [cathedral/basilica] took place on December 26, 537 in the presence of the emperor, who exclaimed, "O Solomon, I have outdone thee!" The egos of public figures do not seem to have changed over the course of history.

Byzantium took on the name of *Kōnstantinoupolis* [city of Constantine—Constantinople] after its refoundation under Roman emperor Constantine I, who transferred the capital of the Roman Empire to Byzantium in 330 and designated his new capital officially as *Néa Pώμη* [*Nova Roma'*/New Rome]. In 324, ancient Byzantium officially became the new capital of the Roman Empire by decree from Emperor Constantine the Great whose courtiers had frequently suggested that the capital be relocated. Constantine determined to retain Constantinople as the capital, since it had been the capital of the state for over a thousand years by the time he conquered it. Constantinople was built over six years and consecrated on May 11, 330 CE.

Constantine laid out a new square at the center of old Byzantium, which he called the Augustaeum. The new Curia [senate-house] was housed in a large basilica on the east side. On the south side of the Augustaeum, he erected the Great Palace of the Emperor with its imposing entrance–the Chalke–and its ceremonial suite known as the Palace of Daphne. Nearby, he commissioned construction of a vast Hippodrome for chariot-races and raucous politics. It could seat over 80,000 spectators and the famed Baths of Zeuxippus. At the western entrance to the Augustaeum was the Milion, a vaulted monument from which distances were measured across the Eastern Roman Empire.

From the Augustaeum led a great street, the *Mese* [lit. Middle [Street], lined with beautiful colonnades. As the colonnade descended the First Hill of the city and climbed the Second, it passed on the left the Praetorium [law-court]. Then it passed through the oval Forum of Constantine which held a second Senate-house and a high column with a statue of Constantine himself. He had himself deified in the guise of Helios, crowned with a halo of seven rays, and looking toward the rising sun. From there, the *Mese* passed on and through the Forum Tauri and then the Forum Bovis, and finally up the *Xerolophus* [Seventh Hill] and through to the Golden Gate in the Constantinian Wall.

After the construction of the Theodosian Walls in the early 5th century, the Constantinian Wall was extended to the new Golden Gate, extending the length to seven Roman miles. After the construction of the Theodosian Walls, Constantinople consisted of an area approximately the size of Old Rome within the Aurelian walls.

The emperor Valens built the Palace of Hebdomon on the shore of the Propontis near the Golden Gate for use when reviewing troops. Theodosius I founded the Church of John the Baptist to house the skull of the saint—which is today preserved in the Topkapı Palace, put up a memorial pillar to himself in the Forum of Taurus, and turned the ruined temple of Aphrodite into a coach house for the Praetorian Prefect. Arcadius built a new forum named after himself on the *Mese*, near the walls of Constantine. Theodosius II built 18-meter tall triple-wall fortifications, which were not to be breached until the coming of gunpowder.

The turning point in the city's history occurred when Emperor Constantine I dedicated it as the capital of the Roman Empire in 330 CE. He began to rebuild an opulent city to mark his conversion to Christianity and a break from the 'old Rome' with its pagan gods. The city grew exponentially, in importance, wealth, and size, becoming one of the largest cities anywhere in the world. By the 5th century, it held around 300,000 inhabitants, by the middle of the 6th, some half a million citizens. In the 9th and 10th centuries, Constantinople had a population approaching 800,000. Obtaining a food supply was one of the principal concerns of city government and required that large quantities of grain be imported. Moreover, a city of that size and importance became a commercial center, with high demand for expensive luxuries; and it served as one of the main transit points for goods being sent to Western Europe from the East and thus a hub of commerce and exchange.

The city became famous for its architectural masterpieces, such as Hagia Sophia— which cost 20,000 pounds of gold to build–the cathedral of the Eastern Orthodox Church, which served as the seat of the Ecumenical Patriarchate, the sacred Imperial Palace where the Emperors lived, the Galata Tower, the Hippodrome, the Golden Gate of the Land Walls, and the opulent aristocratic palaces lining the arcaded avenues and squares.

The city was briefly renamed *Augusta Antonina* in the early 3rd century CE by the Emperor Septimius Severus (193–211 CE), who razed the city to the ground in 196 for supporting a rival contender in the civil war and had it rebuilt in honor of his son Marcus Aurelius Antoninus–who succeeded him as Emperor–popularly known as Caracalla.

Christian architecture and imagery was at the heart of the development of this new city, symbolized in the construction of the great Cathedral of the Hagia Sophia [The Holy Wisdom], erected under Emperor Justinian I in the sixth century. It was with good reason that a delegation from Kiev in the 10th century is said to have reported that on entering the church they *"knew not whether they were in Heaven or on earth."* The Ecumenical Patriarch of Constantinople and–as the guardian of Christendom's holiest relics such as the Crown of thorns and the True Cross–held sway in the great cathedral.

Constantinople was famed for its massive and complex defenses which accumulated over decades and centuries. The first wall of the city was erected by Constantine I. It surrounded the city on both land and sea fronts. In the 5th century CE, the Praetorian prefect Anthemius–under the child emperor Theodosius II–undertook the construction of the Theodosian Walls, a double wall lying about two kilometers west of the first wall and a moat with palisades in front. This formidable complex of defenses was one of the most sophisticated of antiquity. The city was built intentionally to rival Rome and the formidable complex of defenses was one of the most sophisticated of all antiquity. The new Romans claimed that the several elevations within its walls matched the 'seven hills' of Rome. Because it was located between the Golden Horn and the Sea of Marmara, the land area requiring defensive walls was reduced but remained an impregnable fortress enclosing magnificent palaces, domes, and towers, the result of the prosperity it achieved from being the gateway between the two continents–Europe and Asia–and two seas–the Mediterranean and the Black Sea. Although besieged on numerous occasions by various armies, the defenses of Constantinople proved impregnable for nearly nine hundred years.

After the barbarians overran the Western Roman Empire, Constantinople became the indisputable capital city of the Roman Empire. Emperors were no longer virtual itinerants traveling between various court capitals and palaces. They remained in their palace in the Great City and sent generals to command their armies. The wealth of the eastern Mediterranean and western Asia flowed undivided into Constantinople. The emperor Justinian I [527–565 CE] set out from Constantinople for the reconquest of the former Diocese of Africa.

After the victory, in 534, the Temple treasure of Jerusalem–previously looted by the Romans [70 CE], and later taken to Carthage by the Vandals after their sack of Rome in 455] was brought to Constantinople and deposited for a time, perhaps in the Church of St. Polyeuctus. That temple treasure was returned to Jerusalem to either the Church of the Resurrection or the New Church. During Justinian I's reign, the city's population reached about 500,000 people. However, the social fabric of Constantinople was gravely damaged by the onset of the Plague of Justinian between 541–542 CE which killed forty percent of the city's inhabitants.

With the restoration of firm central government during the reign of Comnenian dynasty [1081–1185], the empire became fabulously wealthy. The population rose rapidly, and towns and cities throughout the realm flourished. With the increase in trade and population, the volume of money in circulation dramatically increased. This was reflected in Constantinople by the construction of the Blachernae palace, the creation of brilliant new works of art, and general prosperity.

Venetians and others were active traders in Constantinople, making a living out of shipping goods between the Crusader Kingdoms of Outremer and the West, while also trading extensively with Byzantium and Egypt. The Venetians had factories on the north side of the Golden Horn, and large numbers of westerners were present in the city throughout the 12th century. Princes of Kiev, Venetian doges, abbots of Monte Cassino, merchants of Amalfi, and the kings of Sicily, all looked to Byzantium/Constantinople for artists or works of art. Such was the influence of Byzantine art in the twelfth century, that Russia, Venice, southern Italy, and Sicily all virtually became provincial centers dedicated to its production.

The destruction wrought by a fire great fire in 1197 paled in comparison with that brought to the city by the Crusaders in the name of their religion. In the course of a plot between Philip of Swabia, Boniface of Montferrat, and the Doge of Venice, the Fourth Crusade was–despite papal excommunication–diverted in 1203 against Constantinople. The Crusaders occupied Galata, broke the defensive chain protecting the Golden Horn, and entered the harbor. On July 27, they breached the sea walls: Alexius III fled. But the newly created puppet emperor, Alexius IV, found the Treasury inadequate, and he was unable to make good the rewards he had promised to his western allies who largely abandoned him. Tension between the citizens and the Latin soldiers increased exponentially. In January, 1204, the *citizens* provoked a riot to intimidate Alexius IV, but the only result was the destruction of the great statue of Athena, the work of Phidias, which stood in the principal forum facing west.

In February 1204, the people rose again; Alexius IV was imprisoned and executed; and the new emperor, Alexius V, made some attempt to repair the walls and organize the citizenry; but there had been no opportunity to bring in troops from the provinces; and the Latin guards were demoralized by the revolution. Crusaders made two attacks. The second from the Golden Horn on April 12 succeeded, and the invaders poured in. Alexius V fled. The Senate met in Hagia Sophia and offered the crown to Theodore Lascaris, who had married into the Angelid family, but it was too late. The emperor came out with the Patriarch to try and mollify the citizens but failed, then slipped away with many of the nobility and embarked for Asia. The next day, the Doge and the leading Franks were installed in the Great Palace, and the city was given over to pillage for three days, an action of rape, destruction, and thievery, almost unparalleled in history.

Sir Steven Runciman, historian of the Crusades, described the desecration:

*"For nine centuries…the great city had been the capital of Christian civilization. It was filled with works of art that had survived from ancient Greece and with the masterpieces of its own exquisite craftsmen. The Venetians…seized treasures and carried them off to adorn… their town. But the Frenchmen and Flemings were filled with a lust for destruction. They rushed in a howling mob down the streets and through the houses, snatching up everything that glittered and destroying whatever they could not carry, pausing only to murder or to rape, or to break open the wine-cellars… Neither monasteries nor churches nor libraries were spared. In Hagia Sophia itself, drunken soldiers could be seen tearing down the silken hangings and pulling the great silver iconostasis to pieces, while sacred books and icons were trampled under foot. While they drank merrily from the altar-vessels a prostitute set herself on the Patriarch's throne and began to sing a ribald French song. Nuns were ravished in their convents. Palaces and hovels alike were entered and wrecked. Wounded women and children lay dying in the streets. For three days the ghastly scenes…continued, till the huge and beautiful city was a shambles…When…order was restored…citizens were tortured to make them reveal the goods that they had contrived to hide."*

Of an estimated population in Constantinople of 400,000 inhabitants after the destruction wrought by the Crusaders on the city, about one third were homeless; and numerous courtiers, nobility, and higher clergy, followed various leading personages into exile. As a result, Constantinople became seriously depopulated; and for decades the hapless citizens of the once great city lived under cruel Latin misrule.

Although Constantinople was retaken by Michael VIII Palaiologos in 1261, the Empire had lost many of its key economic resources, and struggled to survive. When Michael VIII captured the city, its population was 35,000 people; but–by the end of his reign–he had succeeded in increasing the population only to about 70,000 people. To achieve even that meager increase, the Emperor had to summon former residents who had fled the city when the crusaders captured it, and to relocate Greeks from the recently reconquered Peloponnese to the capital. In 1347, the Black Death spread to Constantinople reducing the population to 50,000.

With the advent of the Ottoman Empire in 1299, the Byzantine Empire began to lose territories, and the city began to lose population. By the early 15th century, the Byzantine Empire was reduced to just Constantinople and its environs–along with Morea in Greece–making it a mere enclave inside the Ottoman Empire. After a 53-day siege, the city eventually fell to the Ottomans who were led by Sultan Mehmed II. That day–May 29, 1453—is a day which lives in infamy throughout Christendom but in glory throughout the people and nations of Islam. After Mehmed conquered Bizantium, he replaced Edirne [Adrianople] with Constantinople as the new capital of the Ottoman Empire.

As the largest and wealthiest city in Europe during the 4th-13th centuries and a center of culture and education of the Mediterranean basin, Constantinople came to be known by prestigious titles including *Basileuousa* [Queen of Cities] and *Megalopolis* [the Great City]. The local Constantinopolitans and provincial Byzantines referred to their beloved city simply as *Polis* [the City]. In Arabic, the city was called *Rūmiyyat al-Kubra* [Great City of the Romans] and in Persian as *Takht-e Rum* [Throne of the Romans]. The Russians called it *sargrad* [City of the Caesar/Tzar- Emperor].

In summary, Byzantium was the capital city of the pagan Greek Thraco-Illyrians, who ruled it from (657 BCE-33 CE), Roman Empire (33–395 CE), of the Eastern Roman—Byzantine–Empire (395–1204 and 1261–1453 CE), of the brief Crusader state known as the Latin Empire (1204–1261 CE) and of the Ottoman Empire (1453–1923 CE). In 1923 the capital of Turkey–the successor state of the Ottoman Empire–was moved to Ankara and the name Constantinople was officially changed to Istanbul.

In 1650, Constantinople–not yet Istanbul—when Piet and Jans visited the city, the population was 700,000–far greater than any city in Europe at that time.

# CHAPTER THIRTEEN

# UP THE TURKISH WEST COAST
# ON THE SILK ROAD

IN THE YEAR OF OUR LORD, 1642, EARLY JUNE

It took until noon the following day to complete the details of trading, packing the mules and camels, and tying the horses to each other in two strings. The horses became available because a Greek ship carrying a large cargo of sturdy big Greek horses—*haguenee preuse* [trusty hackney steeds]. Hackneys were riding horses, known for a comfortable seat and great endurance. The Greek vessel was blown off course in a storm and ran aground in a small sandy cove. The horses were off-loaded and taken to Antioch where the Greek captain sold them at a severe discount in exchange for help in getting his ship afloat again. The *Antiochenes* paid for the horses from their communal treasury of gold coins because they were sure that the caravan leaving that day would be willing to pay a retail price for them. After all, the Antiochenes knew full well the value of the horses in Constantinople, so far away from Greek suppliers.

Piet took charge of securing the horses. Jans supervised the loading of the string of pack camels with bales of tanned skins, leather belts and boots, camel tackle, boots, lacquer ware, and porcelain. Muhammad and his men and women packed fresh vegetables and fruit, dried fruit leather, dried figs, apricots, and grapes [called 'raisins' by the Greeks and *Antiochenes*], cinnamon sticks, cloves, almonds, ground spices of cinnamon, nutmeg, coriander, and peppercorns, jerked cows tongue and brisket, a variety of dried meats and dried and salted meats, calamari, and sardines. Aslan directed the Turks to control herded livestock including cows, buffalo, sheep, goats, horses, donkeys, and camels.

The Venetian and Flemish sailors arranged the remaining still packed liter bottles of olive oil, Messara Valley cheese in large rounds, Messara Valley wheat, 6,000 board feet of Sfakia forest cypress wood ship planking, high quality animal hides, bottles of Tarra glass made to hold spirits, ingots of pure Kantanos copper, Kydonia gold and lead, Argyroupolis silver, and Sklavopoula of Selino iron, tubs of the best Cretan honey, Markos Mousotiros Aldine printing press Greek authored books, and many bales of the best British and Irish woolen cloth, a scarcity item in the east. They added sheep skins, goat skins, and raw wool, woolen cloaks, and blankets. The *Antiochenes* traded wool dyes, hand-made cotton and wood pulp paper—a skill learned from Japanese and passed on generation to generation of *Antiocenes*–highly valued by the Ottoman court for formal documents. In return they received scarce gold and silver coins and several bolts of embroidered silk.

By noon, the caravan was once again full of trade goods and ready to move north on the silk road towards Constantinople. During the short stay in Antioch, real friendships were made; and three of the sailors married girls from the region. They proved to be good uncomplaining workers and added worth to the work force, including an ability to cook that was far better than the caravan had enjoyed during the trip from Laiazzo to Antioch. After the midday meal, the ponderous train began to make its desultory way into the desert like a huge serpentine reptile.

When they reached the west road that led to Laiazzo, they stopped for a day's encampment and rest. Jans and Piet took two of the better horses and road back into the port city of Laiazzo over the same heavily traveled dust track they had used at the beginning of their trek to Antioch.

While the two Flemish ship's officers met with the garrison sailors protecting the good ship Z-*Louisa Hendrika*, the caravanners took on a large wagon load of fresh Cypriot food: vegetables from the vegetable market in Nicosia, Halloumi cheese, mint, pita bread, vermicelli pasta, dried red chilis and onions, salted herrings, vinegar and yeast. Piet and Jans were pleased with how well the sailors had gotten along, and how ship-shape the *Hendrika* looked. They shared some of the gold and silver coins as a reward and took the entire crew out to a lavish lunch. The crew had grown by three—new Laiazzo wives and two children of the new wives, whose former husbands had perished in ocean accidents.

"When do we expect to see you next, Captain?" asked the sailor who was now in charge of the ship and its crew.

"Very difficult to say, Hendrick," Jans said, "the caravan journeys are unpredictable and ours is a long one. I think it could be as little as four months or as long as a year. I expect you to continue your excellent service to the ship and the crew. You will be rewarded the same as the rest of us from the proceeds of the caravan."

"Aye, aye, Captain. You can expect to return to a ship ready for the next voyage, Sir."

The caravan trudged on up the western Turkish coast on lengths of the silk road that varied considerably in quality. Sometimes, the road itself became hardly even a track, but it was easy to keep their bearings by noting the Mediterranean Sea on their left. They were never more than ten leagues from the beach or cliffs of the coastline. They made good time, and they encountered no bandits or greedy customs agents. The view to the south from where they had traveled gave them a moment to pause and to give thanks to God and the saints for their escape.

The hills appeared to grow up from the ground, it seemed to Piet and Jans.

Piet called out to Aslan, "What is happening, my friend? Is this a sign from God?"

"Ah, my friends of The Book, all things are from God. You know our frequently used expression, '*Inshalah*?'"

"How could we not?" Jans asked.

Aslan gave him an understanding smile, "One cannot but acknowledge the hand of Allah the magnificent, the merciful, my friends, now could one? But this event has a clear physical origin and can be explained by known things that are known. The wise can make such conclusions from all of life's events, even odd things. In the present case, take note that it would appear that the mountains are becoming larger than mountains are and that it is happening very quickly. Is that a mountain that we see, or a mirage?"

"I'm not sure," said Piet, "but I think neither. It is the wrong color, and it is on land or else I would think we are seeing the coming of a very bad storm."

"You would be at least partly right, my young friend. "It is tan brown in color. What in this desert land is that color, I ask you?"

"The dirt," said Jans, who was beginning to realize what they were looking at.

"Indeed…more exactly, it is sand."

"A sand storm?" asked Piet with incredulity.

"Ah, Allah has given us a sand-storm. It appears that it will be a large and dangerous one for the people of Laiazzo and Antioch. I do not envy them this day. It is God's mercy to us that we left when we did. In our long journey, however, we will likely see one. That I prophesy," said Aslan with a sly grin spreading over his face.

The huge wall of sand now stood higher than a minaret in Constantinople and moved towards the west enshrouding everything in its path. At the periphery of the storm, the watching men could just make out sightings of fleeing camels and burros.

"Will it overtake us, Aslan? Will we perish with the rest of the men and animals in its path?"

"I can give you several 'no's to your questions. First, no, it will not reach us. Second, no, it will not kill everything in its path; we are used to such storms; and the final, no, is that it will not keep growing until it reaches us and places to its north. It will stop at the sea. Tomorrow morning, we will look back; and it will be as if it never happened."

"I will believe that when I see it," Piet said nervously.

Aslan gave him a knowing shrug.

The next morning was a clear and sweet-smelling day. The sky seemed clearer, and the land was quiet. The insects and animals had returned to their burrows, and the birds had come to rest in their nests and in the small hollows they called home in the cliffsides.

Jans hurried to ask Aslan, "How is it that such a huge storm—one that reaches the very skies—can disappear so quickly and so completely?

Have we seen an act of your God, Allah, which only occurs in your Muslim countries?"

"Sometimes the storm and its after-affects last days or even weeks, if the conditions of the earth and skies are right or if Allah's people have not been mindful of His commands. Sometimes they are just strange storms without explanation. This I know: almost always there is a great crashing storm—what you call a thunderstorm—followed by a heavy rain in a drought ridden area. That causes a wind—often a swirling wind—that lifts the soft layers of sand, of dust, from the hard pack below and sets the dust to flying into the sky. At times, it goes so high that there is no end to that mountain of dust cloud. Sometimes, even a soft wind can start the process in a desert area with long term drought conditions. God's wind is able to lift the top layer of sand from the ground and push it in every imaginable direction if the area of the wind is large enough."

"It cannot be good for either man or beast," Piet said.

"It is often very bad, indeed, my friends. Sometimes a caravan such as ours can be so blinded by the storm and for so long that it becomes lost on the trackless desert and all perish. The grains of God's sand are like tiny knives and can destroy a man's or a camel's eyes and turn them into useless scars. Sometimes men or camels drink in too much of the sand, and the air bags in their chests are ruined. Many such cough themselves to death for months or years and become useless to their families. I do not know how God does it or why, but I have seen men get a brain fever which kills them in days. They develop terrible headaches, fevers, blood blisters on their skin, and unimaginable neck stiffness and pain. It is God's way to punish sinners to give them a dreadful way to die as an example to other members of the *ummah*. At times, it is not found what the sin of such a person is, but who knows the secrets evil men hide?"

He shuddered at the telling. "

"How is it that a good person could suffer so from God? Maybe it is better to ask, 'why does a good God allow such terrible things to happen to the good and faithful'?"

*"Allah bilir!"* Aslan said with a knowing shrug.

"I am not familiar with that phrase, Aslan. Please translate," Piet asked.

"In my language—Turkish–as it is for the entire world and all the universe… 'only God knows'."

On the twelfth day of travel, they came into sight of their second major city on their itinerary—Adana–one of the major commercial cities of southern Turkey. They had been told to look for landmarks, the ancient Taurus Mountains. The city would be seen to the southeast. The old city—first populated in 6,000 BCE–was situated in Anatolia on the Seyhan River–the northeastern edge and 35 km inland from the Mediterranean Sea near Tarsus.

Aslan held a tutorial of sorts to tell his men and the Men of the Book about Adana and its history.

"It is considered to be the oldest city of our Çukurova region. We learn of it in our great book, the *Epic of Gilgamesh.* The history of Adana is closely linked to the history of Tarsus—which Isia told of in your Book—I think about your Saint Paul. The city seems nearly to be the same as Tarsus at times, changing over centuries when the nearby Seyhan River changed its position. It grew to be great—and like Cilicia–became the most developed and important trade centers of southwestern Turkey in the old days. It has seen hard times and is now slowly returning to its time of importance. Now is a good time for us to arrive in the city, much as it was propitious for us to go to Antioch when we did. Rather like the bypass of Antioch, the Silk Road travelers became less interested in Adana after the great earthquake in the 13th century. While it was part of the Armenian Kingdom of Cilicia in the early 14th century and then after the Mamluk slave army of the Egyptians obtained the city from Emperor Constantine III, Adana lapsed into the relative obscurity of farming and handicraft making. Many of my fellow Turks have settled here; so, I know how to communicate with them. They prefer their own kind.

"It is for these reasons that I believe Allah has brought us to this place at this time. They should be ready to begin to return to their previous high status as a commercial center. The goods we are bringing in should go for inflated prices because they are scarcity items in the region. I also believe that we will benefit from their need to sell to us at discounts in order to get rid of their excess which will trade the same as the other. *Alhamd lilah.*"

"Thanks be to God," Piet said quietly, proud to have remembered at least that common Arabic phrase.

He was rewarded by a faint nod of Aslan's head.

The caravan stayed eleven days in Adana and would have stayed longer but for an unfortunate incident which will be described at the time it happened. They set up what would appear to be a semi-permanent Yörük settlement. Aslan struck a good bargain with a clan of about 200 nomadic Anatolians and Rumelians who had tired of such a settled life. The heavy Yörük tents were too cumbersome for the planned long circuit of travel they intended. Aslan had wisely packed great bundles of heavy British ship's canvas which he convinced the nomads was perfect for their needs. Not only that, but the wily Turkish entrepreneur obtained four chests of gold coins in trade for four bales of embroidered Vietnamese silk. The deal was sweetened by Aslan, Piet, and Jans, as an act of faith and trust. They rounded up almost three-quarters of their best horses that the nomads needed to be able to gather their several tribes for the great trek. Without the horses, communication from western Anatolia would be too slow to be able to gather the many nomads in time to reach the high country before winter

The nomads promised to have the horses back and in good condition in ten days. Piet was doubtful, but Aslan was very trustful of his people; and Jans was to become a convert. The nomadic horsemen raced out of their camp; and, over the next nine days, almost 200,000 nomads came into the flat fertile Çukurova region from south and western Anatolia and from Denizli and Izmir. In addition, they brought in a massive trade surplus that needed to be unloaded before the great trek, and the Adanites profited more in that ten days than they had in ten years. They gave credit to Aslan and his Men of the Book friends. They graciously accepted the accolades. That greased the skids for a landslide of profit for the caravan. It also confirmed to Piet and Jans that they had made a wise choice to team up with Aslan for the caravan journey.

A veritable mountain of cargo goods was accumulating in an open hard pack sandy area opposite to where the camels, oxen, and horses, were pastured. Aslan's keen eye was constantly measuring the goods to be sure that the animals could be loaded with the valuable merchandise and that none of it would be wasted. Special attention was paid to the fine local handicrafts: wood and copper artefacts and utensils, kilims, and woven fabrics, from the nomads who lived on the Taurus mountain plateaus. The mayor assured Aslan that there was a great demand for such well-made and creative goods—each a unique piece of art.

After nine days spent in Adana, Aslan called a halt to any further accumulation of goods.

"Tomorrow, we begin packing the animals. Every hand will have to be on hand, even if you don't think you have enough education or experience to load a pack horse or camel safely and to get the best from the animal that it can give," Aslan announced, "but tonight, we celebrate. We will have a party to end all parties. I know that many of you have taken up with women here; so, feel free to bring them. However, do not let this make trouble for us."

The packing, repacking, and careful overseers' final approval, was completed by late afternoon. The men took a brief and well-deserved nap, then were freed up to wash and put on their best finery. That took Piet and Jans less than half an hour to complete; so, they took a short tour of Adana to soak up some of its rich history.

Eighteen civilizations had ruled the city with each leaving their imprint—buildings, monuments, inscriptions, and history specialists, who had memorized the history as it was passed down from generation to generation. They were great story-tellers although much of the content of their histories was suspect but never lacking in exciting interest. The two men mounted sturdy horses for a quick tour of Adana. An older man–well versed in the local lore–served as their guide, and took copious notes of the activities of the people, the buildings, monuments, shrines, and ruins.

His name was Eymen Selçuk, and he appeared to be a throwback to the age of the Medieval Sultana Scheherazade and the *Tales of a Thousand and One Nights*. His time worn clothing consisted of what an 11th or 12th century Seljuk warrior might well have worn during the time of the crusades: *baccae*-loose trousers ending below his knobby knees and tied there; a chemise, *kirtle*, long tunic of pleated fine linen with long sleeves tightly fitted at the wrists; a frayed but immaculately clean outer tunic of pale blue embroidered silk *chauses* [heavy wool hose oppressive ambient heat]; *houseaux* [tall leather thick-soled knee-high boots]; a wide heavy leather girdle belt from which a Jambiya-Khanjar dagger with a fine Damascus blade hung; a long, straight sword in an ornate leather scabbard; a tubular papyrus container for general necessaries; and a razor sharp hatchet hung. He carried a circular shaped, brilliantly decorated hard wood shield on his left arm. His head cover was a conical shaped maroon felt hat with a corona of thick muslin.

Eymen still sported a heavy waxed mustache and a well-trimmed under jaw beard which went up his chin to his lower lip, similar to the Van Dyck style popular in the Netherlands at the time. His thick hair hung to his mid-back and had two braids on each side. The entirety of his visible hair was snow white contrasting with his sun-bronzed skin. He had a flat face suggestive of some distant Mongol heritage. Their horseback tour, mostly at a gallop–with Eymen's running commentary–took the three men to a panoply of recent and ancient buildings and monuments:

- *Varda (Alman) Koprusu*—was a grand, tall and amazing, bridge in a verdant valley of the Taurus mountains, The *"Alman Köprüsü"* or *"Koca Köprü"* [Varda Viaduct] was situated at Hacıkırı village in the Karaisalı district.
- *Adana Merkez Camii*—was a mosque located in a huge park next to the Seyhan River in Adana. The mosque was an impressive building from the outside and beautiful on the inside. The mosque was surrounded by lush green parks.
- *Tas Kopru*—was a beautiful bridge built by Architect Auxentus during the time of the Roman emperor Hadrian in 384 CE. It spanned the Seyhan River and served as an important symbol of the Roman underpinnings of Adana.
- Buyuk Saat—was the great clock tower located at the end of a long, straight cobbled street flanked on both sides by Islamic arches set against well preserved yellow brick walls.

- *Ulu Cami ve Kulliyesi*—was a mosque close to the Buyuk Saat. Its walls, domes, and minaret were constructed of handsome dun colored limestone.
- Anavarza Ruins—what remained of the extensive walls of what was once a large Roman city, the seat of the IV legion.
- *Yağ Camii*—was originally a crusader church and monastery school, then later, a mosque, one of the most beautiful mosques in Turkey. It was located in the central city of Adana.
- *Yilankale*—a ruined castle which required a sweaty climb up a rocky trail. The view of the Adana valley was breathtaking.
- *Kozan Kalesi*—an impressive castle reached via an excellently preserved cobbled road. The top of the mountain afforded a fine view of the Cilician plain.
- *Kemeralti Camii*—a well-preserved mosque located in the center of Adana. It was built in 1599 and had avoided ruin over the time until 1642 when Piet and Jans had their tour.
- *Hoskadem Camii*—a beautiful, well-preserved, simple stone, mosque reminiscent of the architectural style nearer the capital city. It had a single minaret, unlike most of the Adana mosques.
- *Coban Dede Turbesi Ve ParkI*—a beautiful natural park full of greenery and natural waterfalls. The city fathers decided that it should belong to a saint; so, they built a tower-tomb for Shepherd Dede.
- *Tarihi Roma Koprusu*—a beautiful natural park with an impressive waterfall located in Kozan. Impressive and charming with its abundant nature, a partially ruined castle, and several historical sites and culture. It was founded on Kozan stream. They marveled at the very well preserved and sturdy historical bridge of the Roman period. It was built in 325 CE and has eight different eyes. The bridge connects Kozan from east to west direction and from the distant past to 1643 present. It is the oldest bridge of the Roman period in Çukurova. A street vendor inveigled the three men into trying Kozan's liver skewer with turnips—which was tempting, but they only took a taste since they had a feast awaiting them back at the encampment of the caravan.

- *Kurtkulagi Kervansarayi*—A silk road travelers' rest area which was built on the Adana-Aleppo caravan route–one of the oldest trade routes–in the village of Kurtkulağı. The Kervansarayi [caravanserai] was built to be a very strong fortress for defense purposes. Piet, Jens, and Eymen explored escape tunnels in the lower compartments, and marveled at how well hidden they were and how defensible.

- *Kurucesme Ciftligi*—an attractive clean goat milk, yogurt, and cheese farm. Kid goats ran free and gave the three men a chance to frolic with the energetic and playful small goats. They took their fill of the excellent yogurt and cheese before riding back to the caravan encampment site to enjoy the final feasting with the Adanites and the caravanners before leaving for Izmir early the next day.

The three men were more energized than tired from their hard day's ride. They arrived back at the encampment while the sun was still up, and it was warm and balmy with a mild sea breeze. The happy city notables wanted to impress the caravanners one last time; so, they volunteered to make the feast and to make it memorable. The caravanners were served by eager Adana youths whose enthusiasm was infective. Adana had a long and well-earned reputation as a Mecca for spicy food lovers. The meal was grand beyond anyone's expectations:

- *Adana kebab* [aka *Adana kebabı* and colloquially known as *Kıyma kebabı*]– a long, hand-minced spicy meat kebab mounted on a wide iron skewer and grilled on an open mangal filled with burning charcoal. The meat came exclusively from a young lamb — less than a year old — fed on the local succulent greens. The cleaned meat and fat were hand-kneaded with a generous sprinkling of pepper and salt. After reaching a homogenous consistency, the meat was impaled on iron skewers and cooked over oak wood coals. Flatbread was pressed on the meat to absorb melting fat while warming the bread for serving. This foot-long belt of meat was served on a *porsiyn* [plate] or wrapped in *dürüm* [flatbread]. Julienned onions, diced tomatoes, salt, cumin and sumac, topped the meat. The kebab was served with side dishes–grilled tomatoes, green peppers, pickled ornamental peppers, and *ezme* salad [a paste-like mixture of tomatoes and hot peppers].

- *Shalgam*–a drink made from dark turnips
- *Shıra*–a special type of sweet dark grape juice.
- *Ayran*—was Turkey's national beverage. It was made with yogurt, water, and a little salt, and is served chilled, with grilled kebab and rice. Ayran was an ancient beverage which existed since the Gokturks diluted yogurt with water to cut the bitter taste. The ayran was served in a copper bowl with a frothy foam as was the classic way.
- Bulgar–local rough, cracked, dark, wheat tanned by Çukurova's sun. Red pepper, spices and tahini, seasoned the accompanying local greens and peppers. Lamb, beef, chicken, pigeon, and turkey were featured in hot, spicy, fatty, and traditional dishes. Thyme from the Taurus Mountains was used with the meat and to thicken the milk.
- *Lahmacun*–A Turkish classic flatbread served with meat and spices. Although similar in appearance, *lahmacun* has no cheese, a spicy taste and features ground meat. Around Turkey, the preparation of *lahmacun* varied widely all over the country. Adana's specialty was a midsize, circular, and spicy thin fat bread. The bread was topped with spices—including sumac and garlic–minced meat, onions, and tomatoes, then cooked in a stone oven. It was garnished with lemon and parsley, *then* rolled up and eaten by hand.
- *Yüksük çorbası* [thimble soup], was a popular wedding dish usually prepared—as for this occasion–the day before the wedding. While the other dishes were being consumed, the soup boiled in cauldrons over fire pits. Turkish ravioli and chickpeas in a spicy broth comprise this hearty, main-dish soup. The name for the soup came from the thimble shape of the dumplings.
- *Şirdan* [aka Shirdan]—was considered to be Turkey's strange (bizarre) dish. It was served in a hot dish using tongs. The meat dish was plopped on a piece of heavy brown wrapping paper. The

locals and the caravanners all laughed self-consciously at the meat which looked too much like a body part—one that was not talked about in polite mixed society. But, everyone in the feast was in on the national joke; and everyone shared the small guilty secret. Not so small really; it was a little over twelve inches long. Each party goer dealt with the very intimate eatery in his or her own way. As scripted, they first removed the string that kept the stuffing inside during cooking, then helped themselves to seasoning, which was arranged on the table in large glass bowls and which included coarsely ground salt mixed with cumin, red pepper flakes, and pickled peppers. As far as appearance was concerned, it seemed— at first acquaintance–that the idea of eating it might be repulsive. However, the locals—and shortly—the caravanners, recognized the good news that the pudendal shaped meat was actually made out of a sheep's intestine sheathing around the meat.

Desserts:
- *Karakush*—was a crispy dough filled with seven spices with cinnamon as the main spice, accompanied by allspice, nutmeg, ginger, and cloves. It was a specialty of Adana and Mersina [aka İçel], a city and seaport which lay along the Mediterranean Sea at the extreme western end of the Cilician Plain 65 km west-southwest of Adana. It was located near the site of an unidentified ancient settlement.

Every person in attendance at the going-away dinner was surfeit and approaching a state of stupefiedness from their excessive consumption. They found resting places wherever they could and were easing into a post prandial lassitude and sleep. Piet was the first to hear the approach of the donkey cart and the moans and wailing of the people inside it. He forced himself to sit up and take notice. The rude split log cart with large wooden wheels bumped along at a snail's pace. The six people in the cart were filthy, coughing, and heaving. As they approached the encampment, Piet saw the most dreadful sight that a man of his era could behold.

The unfortunate wretches in the cart were crying, holding their heads in their hands, coughing up blood; and worst of all, they had wide areas of blackened swollen skin on their extremities and their noses. Blood drizzled from several noses. All of them displayed swollen, tender, and painful lymph nodes—buboes—on their necks, in their armpits and groins. It was a loathsome sight; but worse, Piet recognized the import of what he was seeing: Bubonic Plague—the Black Death.

He cautiously approached the cart and signaled for them to stop. The exhausted donkeys slumped to their knees when the driver pulled on the reins.

"You have the Black Death!" Piet said, "I have seen it before. You will kill us all if you get near. Move into the trees to your left. We will bring you food, drink, bandages, and quilts, to lie on. We will post guards to protect you from mobs and to protect us from your infection. Do you understand me?"

He delivered his grim message in Dutch, Turkish, Arabic, and English and repeated it slowly because of his lack of confidence in his facility with the three non-Dutch languages. The dying people appeared to understand. They moved the cart a distance of about a kilometer and got out and lay on the ground. True to his word, Piet arranged humane care and got Jans to arrange a rapid departure from the area by the caravanners and a return to Adana's center by the hosts of the festivities.

# THE HISTORY:
# THE BLACK PLAGUE

Throughout history—as far back as pre-Biblical and Biblical times, there have been a great many pandemics and epidemics with varying etiologies: Yersina pestis, malaria, leprosy, and cholera, for example. Plagues were a curse on human society described in the Hebrew Bible and in the Christian New Testament.

Scriptures of several ancient religions contain many accounts of pestilence and epidemics, usually told of in language and religious import of catastrophe. The occurrences that became scripture were—in fact—events that swept through populations, killing many innocents. They often occurred in historically significant times of social disorder, population displacement, or environmental adversity. The scriptural accounts indicated that these scourges were a form of divine punishment for moral or devotional failure. Apocalypticism–so characteristic of the thinking of early Christianity–readily interpreted social disaster and institutional collapse associated with these pestilential events as a battle that had been duly lost against the Power of the Lord. Interestingly, such disasters were almost never considered to be the work of the devil. The element of divine displeasure is also characteristic of the ancient accounts of pestilence in the Sumerian epic of Gilgamesh, in the Indian Mahabharata, and in Oedipus's Greek city-state of Thebes.

Hebrews, Christians, and Muslims, are more familiar with the many references to epidemic outbreaks of infectious disease in the Hebrew Scriptures [*Old Testament* of the *Christian Bible*]. The plagues of Egypt during Israel's bondage that occurred late in the Egyptian Middle Kingdom were described in exquisite and frightening detail, for example, "sores that break into pustules on man and beast." The *Book of Deuteronomy* recorded that after the Israelites escaped from Egypt–aided by the parting of the Red Sea–the prophet Moses received divine instruction on Mount Sinai to exact a ransom *to God* from each of the newly liberated Israelites in order "to avert plague."

The Hebrew *First Book of Samuel* describes how–in the seventh century BCE–the Lord smote the neighboring Philistines for their violent seizure of the Israelites' Ark of the Covenant. It is recorded that "after they [the Philistines] had carried it about, the hand of the Lord was against the city with a very great destruction. And He smote the men of the city, both small and great, and they had *emerods* in their secret parts." Over 5,000 men were smitten "with a great slaughter." Historians have long been tantalized by these embarrassingly located *emerods*. The word refers to tumors—highly suggestive of the swollen lymph nodes in the groin so characteristic of bubonic plague.

Contemporary historians not associated with scriptures recorded in detail firsthand accounts of such pestilential events as [The Antonine Plague—First Pandemic Plague–of 165 to 180 AD, also known as the Plague of Galen [from the name of the Greek physician living in the Roman Empire who described it]. This plague, which might have been either measles or small pox, killed millions of people all over the empire.]; The Plague of Justinian [541–542 AD] was a pandemic that afflicted the Byzantine–Eastern Roman–Empire and especially its capital, Constantinople, as well as the Sasanian Empire, and port cities around the entire Mediterranean Sea.

The cause was related to merchant ships which harbored rats that carried fleas infected with plague. It killed a third of the population of Constantinople and a quarter of the human population of the entire eastern Mediterranean, and there was The Plague of China or possibly in southwestern China or the steppes of Central Asia. In 1331 an outbreak erupted in the Yuan Empire which have hastened the end of Mongol rule over China. Three years later, the disease killed over 90 percent of the Hebei Province's population with deaths totaling over 5 million people; The Third Pandemic Plague in Medieval Europe [1360–1500)]; Plague in the Islamic World [1360–1500]; a new chapter of the Third Pandemic Plague in Britain [1500–1647]; Plague of Athens [1500–1850]; Great London Plague [1665–1666)]; Another plague pandemic originated in China in the 1860s and spread quickly. An estimated 12 million people died, mainly in India and China. That pandemic affected every continent on the globe except Antarctica.

The San Francisco Plague of [1900–1904] was an epidemic of bubonic plague centered on San Francisco's Chinatown. The effect was significantly worsened by Governor Henry Gage–whose denial was based on business reasons–to protect the reputations of San Francisco and California and to prevent the loss of revenue due to quarantine. It was the first plague epidemic in the continental United States; Contemporary World Plague in the Islamic World [1900–1905]; and the Pneumonic Plague in Surat, Gujarat, India and Oceana [1994].

In the seventeenth century, great fear remained from the pandemic known as the Black Death. Technically speaking, The Black Death—or Second Pandemic of Plague–was one huge plague pandemic event in history and is accurately known as one of the deadliest and most widespread pandemics in the history of the world. The epidemic of 1347–1352 likely began from one of these, spreading as a result of Mongol traders opening new trade routes. Chroniclers describe outbreaks of disease among the Mongols or "Tatars" in the early 1340s which spread rapidly along the Silk Road. Ten years later, it arrived with rats on ships coming to the ports of Genoa, Messina, and Sicily. By 1346 outbreaks had occurred in the region of Europe. It peaked in Europe between 1348 and 1350 with one-third to two-thirds of the population of the earth dying. The most recent modern estimations are that the Black Death killed 50 million people in the 14th century, or 60 per cent of Europe's entire population. It is presumed to have been a bubonic plague outbreak caused by Yersina pestis, a bacterium. Approximate overall mortality estimates among those infected range between 45 and 60 percent across the affected areas.

Underlying causes include poor sanitation, crowding, no money, medical supplies, or objective science to stop or slow down pandemics, and promiscuity. Historically, infected rats and their fleas traveled easily in trade caravans and ships' holds. Modern historians and scientists have concluded that the Black Death spread at a rate of at least a mile a day, but many accounts have measured it in places to have averaged as far as eight miles a day. The pandemic ravaged communities across Europe, changing forever their social and economic fabric. The Black Death represented a turning point in history with late medieval Christian communities struggling to manage plague-time chaos on all levels and to make sense of their lives in the aftermath of the rapidly spreading disease periods.

The Black Death was–and like prior and subsequent pandemics still is–a horrible and painful disease that strikes suddenly and kills rapidly. A person could be healthy in the morning and dead by nightfall. Descriptions of symptoms and signs most often included some sort of swellings–also referred to as tumors, boils, or *apostemes* [abscesses filled with pus]–in the groin or armpit, which were exquisitely painful; and the contents of which–when lanced open–were foul smelling. Ancient and medieval writers described a disease with pustules, blisters, or black spots, coughing or spitting of blood, and a high fever, followed by great thirst and delirium or prostration. Because the disease spread quickly among family members or households, many blamed the contaminated breath of the sick for spreading the disease. This particular outbreak–which spread across Europe, the Levant, and North Africa, between 1347 and 1352–brought bubonic plague into Europe from the Asiatic steppes where it had long been endemic.

Following this epidemic, Europeans experienced recurrent outbreaks of plague over the next four centuries. As a result of the many effects of the plague on society and culture, many historians consider this half-decade a turning point in European history. Although the term "Black Death" came into common use only in the nineteenth century, it has remained a popular descriptive term for this epidemic. Many accounts of the Black Death offer an explanation for the term based on physical symptoms, but it actually comes from a misunderstanding or mistranslation of the Latin *atra mors*, which means either "terrible death" or "black death." Those living through this epidemic did not give it a specific name, but used general terms including pest, pestilence, plague, and mortality.

The Black Death was one of the most significant events of the late medieval world and spawned numerous changes, most visibly in the drastic reduction of population in those areas affected. Precise estimates of the overall mortality from the Black Death are difficult to obtain, as none of these areas kept accurate or consistent census or burial records. The historical record of the Black Death is extensive, as there are numerous first-hand accounts of the epidemic from Europe, North Africa, and the Near East. As an example, an Italian chronicler described the transfer of disease from besieging Mongol troops to besieged residents of the Black Sea port of Caffa [*Kaffa*, modern Feodosiya] by catapulting infective corpses over the city's walls.

The Black Death itself caused between one-third and two-thirds of the population in Europe and the Middle East to die over five-year period. It was described as the end of the world when people died by the hundreds each day. The plague presented itself to Europe in 1348 and to Muslim lands during 1348 and 1349. This lethal contagion epidemic caused its victims to die within three days with symptoms including discrete swelling beneath armpits and the spitting of blood. The population of Europe was 78.7 million in 1300. It dropped to 70 million in 1350.

Although the victims suffered from the same terrible–often fatal disease–the responses of Christians and Muslims were quite different. Muslims and Christians responded in a different way because of their differing ways of thinking and the consequent actions to the epidemic. Both the Muslims and Christians thought God caused the plague. However, Muslims acted as if it was a blessing from God and that prayer was negative. Christians thought that it was the punishment of their sins and blamed God. They needed a scapegoat, and Jews were always available to serve the purpose. Muslims were quite consistent in their acceptance of the plague as their due because of sin. The Christians looked at the plague in an assortment of ways across all levels of society. Christians reacted with conflicting responses. The medieval author, Giovanni Boccaccio, described in the *Decameron* a group of Christians who–believing there was little that mankind could do in the face of such a scourge–abandoned morality in favor of hedonistic pleasures. Others turned to extreme piety and prayer in an effort to appease an angry God.

In parts of Europe–especially Germany–the flagellant movement flourished for a time. Groups of pilgrims moved about from town to town holding displays of public piety in which they offered bodily penance in the form of whippings as a supplement to traditional prayers. Communities across Europe organized a variety of public processions, pilgrimages to shrines, and other forms of communal piety in addition to the whippings.

The Christians not only blamed God, they also accused the Jews specifically of poisoning their wells. In response to that spurious accusation, Christians brutally burned Jews to death; in some cities not a single Jew was left alive. Despite the efforts of many civil and ecclesiastical authorities–including the papacy–to protect Jewish residents, thousands were rounded up and executed in Spain, in southern France, and across central Europe. In San Francisco, California, the arrival of plague from Honolulu in 1900 created public panic. Because most of the early victims were Chinese immigrants, a harsh quarantine and other restrictions were quickly and irrationally imposed on all residents of Chinatown.

The Muslims did not blame the Jews, but instead they realized that the Jew were fellow and equal victims. They held strictly to their accusation that God brought the plague onto them as Muslims. Jews and Muslims prayed together and worked together to curb the epidemic and to treat the sufferers regardless of the victims' religions.

Hewing to their superstitions–including astrology–the Christians attributed the Black Death to the conjunction of planets and excessive clothing. They placed waxed cloth over their windows, refused to sleep on their backs, breathed in latrine vapors, filled their houses with fragrant flowers, and practiced flagellation.

Muslims thought the plague was to an overabundance of shooting stars, warm ovens, and demons. Muslims stayed indoors, avoided sad talk, practiced letter magic, ate pumpkin seeds and pickled onions, and drank sour juices. They viewed plague as a disaster to be endured, one which offered a martyr's death to its victims. Both groups of religious adherents believed that the plague was caused by impure air. In that, there was some truth, since pneumonic plague was present along with the bubonic type and was caused by transmission through air.

As a result of their different mindsets, Muslims carried their holy books around and prayed fervently, thanking God for His mercy upon them. Christians reacted to the pestilences, the severe poverty, and the corruption of their church, by rebelling against

God and turned in large numbers to unfeeling greed, desecration of churches and icons, and an assortment of decidedly nonChristian practices. Throughout the church, it was well-known that King Philip of France–established in Avignon, France–a pope named Clement V. Inconveniently, there was also a pope in Rome named Boniface. There were then two rival popes–a pope and an anti-pope–and a very corrupt relationship between kings, the aristocracy, and the papacy. A significant portion of the church members believed that this angered God, and he sent the plague as punishment.

Muslims and Christians alike reacted negatively towards public gatherings. Public venues such as markets, churches, mosques, or public squares, were increasingly avoided, and care for the sick often fell to either the very pious—those willing to place themselves in danger— or the very poor, who may have sought to profit however they could. Burials–which could no longer be carried out individually as a result of the excessive number of corpses accumulating–were likewise left in the hands of the charitable or the desperate. The accumulation of bodies faster than they could be buried led to a variety of psychological reactions—guilt, fear, anger, sorrow, which affected survivors for generations to come.

Doctors and others learned in health care had no better understanding of the causes or cures of the Black Plague. Prescriptions for prevention of plague included the burning of aromatic herbs–often carried out in public squares–to cleanse the air as well as the regulation of diet to maintain humoral balance. Other plague treatises advocated keeping one's mouth covered with a handkerchief or the use of a posy of sweet-smelling herbs while in public. Some advocated ensuring a patient's eyes had been covered before entering the room, believing that the disease could be passed along from direct eye contact.

The famous physician, Avicenna 970-1037 CE, described the symptoms of plague infection as the appearance of swellings (buboes) on armpits, groin, or behind the ears. Pestilence, he said, contaminates plants, the animals that feed on them, and the people who consume these animals. He saw an increase in the number of frogs, insects, and rats, that surfaced as a sure sign of an impending epidemic, but only as a forewarning; he did not recognize the causal relationship between rats and plague. The uncertainty that dominated Islamic–as well as European–opinion about the cause of an epidemic made it very difficult for physicians to find a cure for plague. Treatment centered on ways to improve air quality or advice to flee to uncontaminated areas. Avicenna recommended bloodletting; applying Armenian clay to buboes; improving the air with aromatic fruits and herbs; cooling the patient's surroundings by spraying water and vinegar; fumigating with camphor, pomegranate peel, myrtle, and sandalwood–and, in line with previous Islamic and Greek recommendations–giving the patient a daily potion of aloes, saffron, and myrtle.

Bubonic plague remains a threat: After the San Francisco Plague of 1900, Yersina pestis spread, rapidly infecting prairie dogs and ground squirrels in the North American West and crossed the Rocky Mountains moving eastward. Plague still kills people in the developing world and in areas suffering from natural or human-made disasters. Y. pestis occurs naturally in over 200 species of rodents worldwide and at least 80 species of fleas.

# CHAPTER FOURTEEN

# Mid Turkish West Coast on the Silk Road approaching Izmir

In the year of our Lord, 1642, late June

Stifling heat blazing down from a cloudless blue sky tormented man and beast in the caravan as it tried to put serious distance between Laiazzo and its plague, Adana and its threat of plague, and Izmir—162 leagues [900 km] away to the north. The plague was like an invisible monster hurrying close on their tails. Near to Adana, every hamlet, village, town, and city, was affected—many of them now empty. The closest towns to Adana had corpses scattered in the streets and in the fields with no apparent interest in or capacity to provide decent burials. Aslan—who had seen plague cities before–told Jans that the corpses showed that there were no more living souls to bury their dead. A little further on, the corpses were stacked fairly neatly like cord wood in regular piles; otherwise, the towns were empty of living humans or animals. After traveling a distance of 58 leagues, they began to see bustling cities with active and apparently healthy people going about their business.

The caravan paused briefly in those cities to learn about the plague's progress. Many of the citizens were unaware of the existence of plague further south. Some nearby cities had emptied out of people who had heard of the encroaching pestilence and had fled to the rural hinterlands to save themselves. Jans—who had a head for figures—calculated that the plague was advancing at a speed of nearly two leagues a day. He feared

that it would catch up with them. Jans, Piet, and Aslan, drove the caravan earlier and later in the day and pushed the cameleers to move their
animals to the point of exhaustion.

At last, when the men and their animals were almost spent, they came
within sight of Izmir. Aslan sent a scout on horseback ahead to inquire
about the status of the plague in the city. He was gone two days and
returned in the company of a Franciscan friar, identified even at a distance
by his conspicuous monk's tonsure of his scalp below a prominent bald
pate. The friar was seated on a small burro.

"He speaks Dutch, Turkish, Latin, and French," the scout informed
the three caravan leaders.

"Let us hear him in Dutch and in Turkish," Aslan said. "I can receive
his speech through my able interpreter, Ali."

The Catholic friar dismounted from his burro and took a moment to
stretch his legs. He wore a tunic of rough dark brown hand dyed cotton
and a hooded capuche. Around his waist was a corded rope belt with ends
hanging to the knees, with three separate knots representing his vows of
poverty, chastity, and obedience.

The friar was weather worn and deeply tanned. His face and hands
reflected a life of hard physical labor. He spoke with an air of certainty
and authority.

"My brothers," he said, "permit me to introduce myself, I am
Bonaventure, OFM, a friar of the order of the righteous Saint Francis of
Assisi. I speak truth to you this day when I answer the question of Brother
Ahmed of the Muslim faith concerning the occurrence of the feared Black
Plague in our beautiful city of Izmir. There has not been a single case
here, by the Grace of our Lord. That I swear on my oath.

"I bring important tidings—a Papal Bull from Rome, authored by his
holiness, Pope Urban VIII. It speaks–among other things–of the plague
sent upon us from God."

Anthony unrolled a papyrus scroll and began to read–the reading
slowed somewhat by the need for translation.

URBAN VIII

Papal Bull, *In Eminenti* issued this day of Our Lord, 28 April, 1641
Named on the bulla [seal] for attestation

"Be it known by all those of the true faith, it befits the Roman Pontiff that this Papal Bull is an exceptional manifest, indeed, a law regarding serious church concerns. This Bull embraces the whole extent of the object of the infallibility inherent in the teaching Church.

"Concern the first: The Papal States are engaged in a conflict with the renegade clergy of the Germans. We support the just cause of our French clergy under Cardinal de Richelieu in what has become a very long and hurtful enterprise. The Germans involved are hereby excommunicated,

"Concern the second: Condemnation of Augustinus of Jansenius for heresy.

"Concern the third: Condemnation of the astronomer Galileo for heresy against the truth faith and knowledge of the universe not approved by the Inquisition.

"Concern the fourth: Prohibition of slavery of any kind among the Indians of our lands of Paraguay, Brazil, and the entire West Indies, now and forever.

"Concern the fifth: Appointment of the Capuchin Antonio Barberini to the office of cardinal and grand penitentiary and librarian of the Vatican.

"Concern the sixth: Appointment of Taddeo Barberini to be Prince of Palestrina and Prefect of Rome.

"Concern the seventh: God and His Angels have chosen to smite the earth with a great plague as a consequence of our disobedience. It has come to our attention that certain of our faith have rebelled against God, have turned to devilish practices including torture and murder of Jewish persons, and some have even preached abroad that God is evil—an impossibility. All those reactions are the work of the Devil and are hereby condemned in the strongest language. Cease from such wickedness; return to our holy practice of treating our neighbors as ourselves. Do that, and the reproach of the Holy Trinity will be lifted. Take an example from the heathen Muslims to heart."

Urban VIII was born Maffeo Barberini. Antonio and Taddeo mentioned in the Bull are the brother and nephew of Maffeo. His papacy coincided with the illustrious and infamous career of Cardinal Richelieu of France and also with the horrific Thirty Years War in Europe. Urban was pro-French, even militarily and openly hostile to the Roman Catholic clergy and cause in Germany. He also desired the eventual extinction of Protestantism throughout the world, but he feared Habsburg domination even more; so, he entered into an alliance with the Protestant military powers. He withheld Vatican support for the Habsburgs which destroyed their claim to be the exclusive champions of Roman Catholicism. This caused the Thirty Years' War to be a conflict of differing religious ideologies and nations. The result was millions dead, the triumph of Protestantism, and the ruination of Germany.

Aslan requested fairness for his religion, and for his cameleers. Piet and Jans concurred; so, the following day, an imam from the most prominent Izmir mosque visited the encampment of the caravan. After a very pleasant Halal supper of falafel, shawarma, flavorful kabobs, and gyros, Imam Abu Bakr ibn Muhammad addressed the combined audience of Muslims, Christians, Hindus, and animists.

"Brothers of the Book, and our fellow sufferers from all lands," he began, "Allah, the All Merciful, and All Great, has sent upon us a chastisement in the form of dreaded plague. Indeed, our sins are black as the night, and we must pay. Let us thank Him for his blessing of the plague to cleanse us and to teach us the correct way since we have taken the crooked path. We have heard that in some places, the Jews have been blamed for the plague. This has been proved to be false, and we must no longer wreak chastisement or hatred upon them. They suffer as do we. Let us comfort each other as fellow human beings. Be kind and helpful to all that live among us. Let us make our persons, our homes, our religious places, and our work-places clean of filth and terrible rats. God teaches us the value of that.

"Brothers all, join with us despite our differences to cleanse our sins and to become once again acceptable to the Lord of Worlds, Allah, the Magnificent. Thank you for allowing me to speak my mind in brotherhood to each and to all of you."

Thus lifted from their terrors about what lay ahead of them, the caravanners completed the last few leagues of the journey into Izmir [Gr. Smyrna], the caravan's third main stop on the way to Constantinople. The caravanners echoed the sentiment of almost all travelers to the area. Izmir is beautiful by any standard. They made their encampment on the outskirts of the city in the alluvial plain, and the three leaders made their way directly into the heart of the city. The main part of the city extended along the calm cyan blue-green waters of the Gulf of İzmir and inland to the north across the Gediz River delta; to the east along an alluvial plain created by several small streams; and to slightly more rugged terrain in the south.

Izmir/Smyrna has been a human settlement for 8,500 years—going back to the Neolithic period. There is clear record of more than 3,000 years of recorded urban history. Its location–set in an advantageous location at the head of a gulf in a deep indentation midway along the western Anatolian coast–has kept it one of the principal mercantile cities of the Mediterranean Sea for much of that long history. It is located near the ancient city of Ephesus; and like Ephesus, Izmir/Smyrna became a territory of the Eastern Roman Empire. It was an important religious center in the early Byzantine period, but never returned to the Roman levels of prosperity.

The Turks took control of İzmir in the 15th century. After the arrival of Sephardic Jews expelled from Spain after 1492; they made İzmir one of their principal urban centers in Ottoman lands and enjoyed far better lives there than they had at the hands of the Christians. As a result of the acceptance of diversity, Izmir developed a rich cultural heritage for Turkish, Greek, Armenian, Jewish, and Levantine, communities, and for the myriad of temporary visitors from everywhere else.

Aslan, Jans, and Piet, found Izmir to be a bustling international port city thriving on goods and services arriving and leaving from all over the known civilized world. İzmir's most remarkable growth began in the late 16th century when cotton and other products of the region brought French, English, Dutch, and Venetian, traders to the region. In 1620, privileged trading conditions were accorded to foreigners—the infamous *capitulations* that were later to cause a serious threat and setback for the Ottoman state as it began to decline. In the early to middle 17th century, İzmir became one of the foremost trade centers of the Ottoman Empire. Due to the presence and needs of the foreigners, foreign consulates moved from Chios to the city starting in the early 17th century, serving as trade centers for their nations. Each consulate had its own quay, where the ships under their flag would anchor. The twenty-two year-long campaign for the conquest of Crete also considerably enhanced İzmir's position within the Ottoman realm since the city served as a port of dispatch and supply for the troops. Because of the importance of their import and export trade in western manufactured goods, there was an entire section of Izmir made up of French, English, Dutch and Italian, merchants.

The exports of the Ottoman port of Izmir largely reserved for local merchants were almost exclusively raw materials, foodstuffs, or goods requiring no special treatment or preservation. Raw materials used in the manufacturing industries of Western Europe constituted the majority of the commerce with Izmir's local businesses. The exports included raw galls, wax, safflower, medicinal drugs, and skins. Food products, wheat and olive oil from the Archipelago, currents and other dried fruits from Izmir proper, were important. The most important imports were a number of small manufactured goods from countries with advanced technologies such as watches and clocks. By mid-century colonial products were imported, exported, and re-exported, to the Levant, especially sugar, coffee, cochenille [scarlet dye made from berries], and indigo [blue dye from the Lao Cai province of Cham and India. Its price equaled that of gold.]

There was a section of Izmir that served as a safe haven for Jews. Early in the 17th century, Jews were able to set up their own synagogues, establish their own leadership institutions, and make contact with other Jewish communities of the Ottoman Empire. In 1648, Joseph Wscapa of Salonika was appointed rabbi over all the congregations of the Ottoman

Empire. Izmir became one of the three major Jewish centers in the Ottoman world.

The Jews from Izmir came there from a wide variety of different places. Some came from the surrounding villages, but others came from farther distant places both inside and outside the Ottoman Empire, such as Istanbul, Safed, Ankara, many islands in the Aegean and Mediterranean seas, Italy, and Holland. Still others were Portuguese converts who had left the Iberian Peninsula and returned to their original Judaism. In the 1620s and 1630s, they set up their own distinct synagogue called the Portugal-Neve Shalom. Before the arrival of Aslan, Jans, and Piet, that congregation split into two: the Portugali and the Neve Shalom.

The Izmiri Jews were known in the Islamic law system as *Dhimmis*—non-Muslim citizens of a Muslim country. They paid a personal tax—the *Gizia*—in exchange for government protection and were able to enjoy their own educational establishments and court systems. The *Gizia* was not grossly excessive, and by and large, Jews lived lives with very few restrictions or infringements on their personal freedom, unlike the case in more stringently Islamic regions.

Unlike many European cities Izmir was safe for travelers and citizens alike. This was owing to the heavy presence of Janissaries and other Turkish military forces whose reason for being there was to protect the highly profitable commerce for the Turkish nation.

A troop of Janissaries directed the caravanners to the Dutch consulate, protecting them from pickpockets and scam artists—in return for a hefty financial consideration—just as they had found throughout the Mediterranean and Turkish cities they had visited thus far.

The Dutch officials were efficient, pleasant, well-organized, and expensive—another similarity. The three men went into commercial mode, seeking out interested buyers and appropriate sellers. They had no intention of spending any more time in the pleasant city than necessary. Like the Dutch officials, the city had an efficient commercial bureau which quickly directed them to the large wharf-side warehouses where a dizzying array of goods was stacked neatly and visibly in the well-guarded buildings. The merchants did not trust the Janissaries any better than did the caravanners; so, they had their own private security officials who were forbidden to ask for tips or bribes.

They were comforted by watching a unit of Janissaries march six pirates to the middle of the Konak commercial square—and with no ceremony—to hang them in such a way that the men strangled instead of breaking their necks. It was apparent that Ottoman Turkey was not a benevolent dictatorship, and the three men from the ship vowed to avoid violating Turkish laws as an almost religious oath. By now, the three Europeans were hardened to the cruel ways of the Turks and other Muslims by the dictates of their religion. They turned their backs on the pirates struggling for breath as they kicked and writhed on their gibbets.

They walked to Anafartalar Road which circled around the huge outdoor Kemeraltı [Eng—"under the arch"] Grand Bazaar. To Piet, the bazaar–built by the Ottomans in the early 17th century—was a safe haven for merchants and travelers where they could spend the night and trade. Its complexity was bewildering; it looked like a labyrinth composed of narrow pathways and streets. The complex stretched from Konak Square– in the city's center–through to the ancient Roman Agora.

Kemealti was built shortly after Piet was born. The market had many old inns and small specialty bazaars. There were blacksmiths, charcoal burners, spice shops, chocolate shops, coffee shops, herbal stores [pharmacy shops], straw markets, copper masters, fine textiles and silks, and exotic products like elephant tusks and feet, and zebra skins. Piet and Jans were treated to the opportunity to see for the first time, unusual foods like fresh uncooked penises and kidneys from China, bulls' testicles from Western America, and elephant ear fish and *nouc mam* sauce from Viet Nam.

There were shops for jewelry, Persian silk trade from Aleppo and raw silk from northern China, raw cotton from surrounding Izmir pastures and manufactured cotton goods from the city's factories bound for Marseilles. Kemealti merchants had a monopoly on mohair yarn from Ankara. It was now comfortably home to all kinds of eateries—mostly street vendors with food of questionable cleanliness. There were artisan workshops for copper, silver, leather, stone, wood, and jewelry, mosques, coffeehouses, and lovely peaceful tea gardens and ornate synagogues. The bazaar was successful enough on a day-to-day basis to enable it to continue to be the fast beating heart of Izmir's trade scene.

Aslan, Jans, and Piet somehow found their way to a small mosque in the very center of the bazaar and waited by the ablutions fountain as agreed with representatives of Izmir's major trading company. The representatives were precisely punctual and all business.

Yavaş Babaoğlu introduced himself and his entourage. He was dressed in the best Venetian gentleman's attire. His face had just been shaved, and his black hair trimmed neatly in the Western fashion and pomaded in place. He smiled—like a spitting cobra—and the smile did not reach his eyes.

Aslan whispered to Piet, "Remember to count your fingers after you shake his hand. Hold onto your purse."

Effendi Babaoğlu summoned two retainers with a flick of his first two fingers on his right hand. They slipped quietly and quickly away from the crowd and returned shortly with a handsome four wheeled, six passenger British hackney carriage drawn by four horses and holding six passengers comfortably. Aslan, Jans, and Piet clambored aboard and took seats in plush red velvet cushioned carriage seats. Yavaş Babaoğlu and his assistant, Mehmet Polat, sat facing their European counterparts. No one spoke until the coach arrived at the encampment site of the caravan.

Then, demonstrations of goods, haggling, and displays of pique and pleasure, took up the next half an hour. The ending was cordial and sealed by a sip of exceedingly sweet, deep purple, nonalcoholic, grape juice. Yavaş and Aslan did most of the talking, smiling, and frowning, and conducting of the negotiations, and did so in Turkish—a source of frustration for the Europeans. When the obligatory drinks were swallowed, Aslan explained the details of the immensely profitable exchanges he had just accomplished.

There were two things of value paramount in the mind of Babaoğlu: fine silk—worth more than its weight in gold and silver coins–and Venetian gold coins. That was fine with the Europeans; they had a surplus of each. The most important trade items for the Europeans–based on their calculation of what would be in demand in Constantinople—were fine large Greek horses to add to their already significant herd and fine art work including gold, silver, and copper statuary, finally embroidered silk cloth from China, and British white cotton button shirts, and the most finely woven business suits which were beginning to be a trending fashion among the well-to-do Turkish business executives.

Both parties to the transactions pitched in to load the pack animals with a considerable care to make the paniers on each side balanced in weight and not to overload them. Burros, donkeys, horses, and camels, will all balk and refuse to take a step if either criterion is violated. Both sets of businessmen were experts, and the loading was accomplished in just under two hours.

Yavaş and his consortium were satisfied to be able to load their warehouses in Kemeraltı Bazaar with fine silk at a discount which would increase in value nearly ten-fold when the clever and artistic young local women were put to work. They had been willing to exchange their desire for more silk to obtain the increasingly valuable foreign woolen and cotton manufactured bolts of cloth and finished apparel.

Aslan, Jans, and Piet, also traded some fine local wood and copper artefacts and utensils—handicrafts from Antioch, Laiazzo, and Adana, different from the kind available in Izmir. Next came beautiful hand knotted Syrian kilim hangings and carpets and a several years supply of Yörük tents. They would be highly desirable for nomads and caravans setting out from the international port of Izmir for long treks over the Silk Road tributaries.

In return the Europeans bartered successfully for exquisite bolts of very finely embroidered Vietnamese silk for eight full chests of gold coin that needed four men to lift. As a bonus Aslan, Jans, and Piet, gave Effendi Babaoğlu steep discounts on bales of heavy British ship's canvas, heavy and finely woven hangings and carpets from the mountain nomads of the Taurus Mountains, leather goods from Morocco and Antioch, and unusual Chinese and Vietnamese black lacquer ware.

For a large herd of young healthy Izmiri horses, the Turks were willing to take a fairly large number of herd livestock—cows, water buffalo, sheep, pregnant Angora goat does, donkeys, and young robust camels. The consortium realized the value of the animals the caravan was herding that would enrich the blood of Izmir's stock; so, they had a long-term value and would fetch a fine profit. Aslan knew what Babaoğlu and his consortium knew about the herd animals; so, with quiet persuasion, he convinced Babaoğlu to part with two more chests of gold coins.

Babaoğlu–aware of the scarcity of good construction wood—was happy to receive the 6,000 board feet load of Sfakia forest cypress wood ship planking. The consortium knew they would easily be able to sell the many bales of the best British and Irish woolen cloth, a scarcity item in the east. They accepted sheep skins, goat skins, and raw wool, woolen cloaks, and blankets. The *Antiochenes* had traded wool dyes, hand-made cotton and wood pulp paper—a skill learned from Japanese and passed on generation to generation of *Antiocenes*–highly valued by the Ottoman court for formal documents. The consortium was willing to pay more dearly for those items and parted with another chest full of gold coins.

The Europeans loaded their pack animals with newly acquired chests of gold and silver coins, men's boots, European landscape paintings that would not violate the proscription against showing human or even animal forms regarded as "graven images" by the Muslims. They packed additional fresh vegetables and fruit, dried fruit leather, dried figs, apricots, and grapes–called by the Greeks and *Antiochenes*, 'raisins'–cinnamon sticks, cloves, almonds, powdered spices of cinnamon, nutmeg, coriander, and peppercorns, jerked cows tongue and brisket, a variety of dried meats and dried and salted meats, calamari, and sardines. They traded some more animal skins in good condition to increase their supply of edibles in return. Yavaş Babaoğlu, assured Aslan that would be in high demand in Constantinople if the caravan could reach the capital city before the food stuffs deteriorated. They loaded down fifty of the strongest camels with clean clear fresh water, the most valuable commodity in the desert.

Relying on Jans' extensive shipping experience, the Europeans held on to some goods they brought with them from the first Mediterranean port: packed liter bottles of olive oil, Messara Valley cheese in large rounds, the highest quality exotic animal hides, bottles of Tarra glass made to hold spirits, ingots of pure Kantanos copper, Kydonia gold and lead, Argyroupolis silver, and Sklavopoula of Selino iron, tubs of the best Cretan honey, Markos Mousotiros Aldine printing press Greek authored books, and a generous collection of gold and silver coins and several bolts of the very finest embroidered silk.

That evening the tired traders gathered in the Kemealti Grand Bazaar for a farewell treat from the consortium. The three leaders and the chief cameleers and caravanners were given generous cuts of baklava and were introduced to a new novelty–as yet almost unheard of in Europe—chocolate. They were served solid chunks of the dark brown material and found it to be intensely bitter. Seeing their dislike of the natural product, Yavaş Babaoğlu and his assistant, Mehmet Polat, hurried about to find a near boiling cauldron of sweetened chocolate drink which delighted the Europeans. Jans made a mental note to take a goodly supply back to the ship in order to get the popular fad going in Europe.

Next, they tried an exotic variation of the common chocolate called Trinitarios, named for the East Indies island of Trinidad. It was a hybrid made from a tropical plant originally discovered by the Olmec people. It was a great improvement over the more plentiful product from African cocoa beans. It was a delicate and delicious taste blend of sweet and rich. The vendor showed the Europeans how to mix the chocolate with flavorings such as vanilla, cinnamon, orange blossom, almond milk, Orgeat cream, coffee, allspice, chilis, *hueinacaztli* [a spicy flower from the custard apple tree], and *anchiote*. The latter spice turned Piet's mouth scarlet red and made him the laughing-stock of the crew. They were warned not to drink too many cups, or they would get what they called "Montezuma's revenge".

The vendor–who had actually been to Trinidad–explained that the Mexican Aztec had been a great ruler who was defeated by the Spanish Conquistadores. He was reputed to have drunk up to fifty cups of chocolate drink laced with the *anchiote* which made him into a great runner. They were also treated to a variety of French delicacies to keep them happy as they set out on the last leg of their silk road journey—Izmir to Constantinople.

A visiting chef from one of the larger French vessels in port agreed to show off his wonderous French sweets. He worked from *Du Fait de Cuisine*, the treatise on French cooking regarded as the "Bible" of gourmet wonders of France. Each man was served a small platter of small, exquisite pieces: *Blancmange* [four colored almond paste], almond milk flan, baked pears, *emplumeus* of apples [almond apple sauce], quinces in pastry, cooked pears, and sugared almonds, Hippocras [sweet spiced wine—an ingredient added in deep secrecy] and wafers, medlars [good fruit and jelly made from medlar fruit. The process begins with whole chopped and bletted fruit which is then stewed, strained, with the pulp turned into a curd style of fruit cheese, where the strained pulp is cooked with lemon curd with eggs, butter, and sugar.] and shelled nuts on the side, *pipefarces* [fried breaded cheese], and *Gruyau* [sweet almond-barleymeal].

The caravanners and sailors slept with full bellies and easy minds, ready for the coming adventure that would take them to the very heart of the Ottoman Empire.

THE HISTORY
THIRTY YEARS WAR [1618 -1648]

First, A Seventeenth-Century Latin Ode to the Chocolate Tree, translated by Aymenn Jawad Al-Tamimi:

A cardinal of the Catholic Church wrote a short work entitled *De Chocolatis Potu Diatribe* [*Essay Concerning The Drinking Of Chocolate*] in which he concluded that drinking chocolate did not mean breaking the fast. At the end of the essay is an ode composed by a Jesuit called Aloysius Ferronius.

The ode consists of two parts: the first in praise of the chocolate tree and the chocolate drink derived from it, the second in praise of Brancaccio and his willingness to break free of tyrannical dogmatism on the issue of drinking chocolate during fast-days.

### AD EMINENTISS. *AC REVERENDISS.*

### PRINCIPEM

# FRANCISCVM MARIAM

## CARDINALEM BRANCATIVM

### S CRIBENTEM

### DE CHOCOLATIS POTV DIATRIBE,

# ODE

### *ALOYSII SOCIET ATISJESV.*

Translation [abbreviation]

**To the most eminent and revered sire, Cardinal Franciscus Maria Brancaccio, author of the Essay Concerning the Drinking of Chocolate: An Ode, by Aloysius Ferronius of the Society of Jesus.**

Oh tree born in the furthest lands,

And glory of the Mexican shore,

Fertile with juice, in which the heavenly nectar

of Chocolate takes pride.


They say that Adam, the origin of people,
After being driven from the blessed seats carried the tree
To the Indians. Having found hospitable soil,
It made the noble seeds of life grow from its trunk.

Oh liquid sent from the stars, and renowned drink of the gods!
Adieu from afar, Castalian dews, and may this liquid flow
In a perpetual stream for the poets.

Oh glory of the shining purple,
And star of the Vatican crown of valour,
Franciscus, how much this juice owes to your ventures and reed-pen!


England might have learned the secret of Spain's favorite drink. English pirates attacked Spanish treasure fleets almost with impunity. One ship they stopped was loaded to the top of its holds with cacao beans. The ignorant pirates burned the entire cargo because they thought they were looking at sheep turds.

Now, back to the history of one of the major events of the Seventeenth Century–the Thirty Years War from 1618 to 1648. It was fought primarily in and throughout Central Europe. One of the most destructive conflicts in human history, it resulted in eight million fatalities not only from military engagements but also from violence, famine, and plague. It ravaged Europe and remains one of the longest and most brutal wars in human history. Twenty percent of the total population of Germany died during the conflict and there were losses of as much as fifty percent in a corridor between Pomerania and the Black Forest. On the ground, the conflict reduced the combatants to a level of savagery unequaled to that time and never exceeded since.

The war started as a battle among the Catholic and Protestant states that formed the Holy Roman Empire. At the outset, it appeared to be another one of the endless inter-religious wars that have plagued the world briefly and were largely lost to interest to all but the most intrepid researcher/scholars. However, as the Thirty Years' War evolved, it became less about religion and more about which group would ultimately govern Europe. The ideologies of religion and identification with nation-states turned men into bestial savages. In the end, the conflict changed the geopolitical face of Europe and the role of religion and nation-states in society.

After the Protestant Reformation, the independent states of the Hapsburg empire became divided between Catholic and Protestant rulership, giving rise to a short and limited conflict. The Peace of Augsburg [1555], signed by Charles V, Holy Roman Emperor, ended the war between German Lutherans and Catholics. The Peace established the principle *Cuius regio, eius religio* ["Whose realm, his religion"], which allowed Holy Roman Empire state princes to select either Lutheranism or Catholicism within the domains they controlled, ultimately reaffirming the independence they had over their states. Subjects, citizens, or residents–who did not wish to conform to a prince's choice–were given a period in which they were free to emigrate to different regions in which their desired religion had been accepted.

As a result of the Peace accord, a relatively uneasy sixty-year calm interim period persisted until Emperor Ferdinand II ascended to become head of state of the Holy Roman Empire in 1619. That provoked change which began to foment a renewal of religious conflict. During the evolution of the Protestant Revolution, the principle of religious freedom became so important that people were beginning to be killed over any restraints on such freedom. The Peace of Augsburg resulted in the Catholic hierarchy agreeing to allow religious freedom to certain protestants; the key tenet "whose realm, his religion," which permitted princes of states to be able to adopt Lutheranism, Calvinism, Hussite, Reform, or Catholicism..

One of Ferdinand II's first actions was to force citizens of the empire to adhere to Roman Catholicism, in contravention to the Peace. The power and control of the Holy Roman Empire was not nearly as significant as Ferdinand presumed. The Holy Roman Empire only appeared to have control over much of Europe at the time. In fact, it was essentially a collection of semi-autonomous states or fiefdoms held together as a loose federation. The emperor–from the House of Habsburg–had limited authority over their governance, making him a weak leader. This gave rise to the descriptor that, "the Holy Roman Empire is neither holy, nor Roman, nor an empire."

As a direct result of Ferdinand's decree on religion, the Bohemian nobility in what is present-day Austria and the Czech Republic rejected Ferdinand II and his authority altogether and threw his representatives out of a window at Prague Castle in 1618, which marked the beginning of the Thirty Years War. That event became known as the "Defenestration of Prague" [fenestration: the windows and doors in a building]. Although–at the time–it was not regarded as very serious, the "Defenestration" led to the beginning of open revolt in the Bohemian states. They were backed by the Protestant Swedish and Denmark-Norway governments. That set off the spark.

The first stage of the Thirty Years' War–became known as the Revolt or the Bohemian Revolt–marked the beginning of a truly continental conflict, and developed into a struggle for continental hegemony with France. Over the first decade-plus of fighting, sovereign states began to choose sides in an emotionally/religiously charged conflict. The Bohemian nobility formed alliances with the Protestant Union states of what is now Germany. Ferdinand II sought the support of his Catholic nephew, King Phillip IV of Spain.

The conflict spread quickly. Armies for both sides were soon engaged in brutal warfare on multiple fronts. Austria was involved in the west and Transylvania in the east. In Transylvania, the Ottoman Empire joined the Bohemians against the Poles, who were aligned with the Habsburgs. The Ottomans worked in exchange for yearly dues paid to their sultan. In the west, the Catholic Spanish army aligned with the

Catholic League, a collection of nation-states in the region of present-day Germany, Belgium and France, all in support of Ferdinand II.

Early on, Ferdinand II's Catholic alliance forces were successful, quelling the rebellion to the east and in northern Austria. The defeats were serious enough to bring about the dissolution of the Protestant Union. Further west, Denmark-Norway's King Christian IV, threw the support of his forces behind the Protestant states, and the war kept raging on. The army of Scotland joined the armies of Denmark-Norway. Despite that addition to the Catholic cause, the anti-Ferdinand forces were forced to capitulate to the alliance supporting Ferdinand II, and therefore the Protestant cause. Denmark/Norway/Scotland were forced to cede much of northern Europe to the Habsburg emperor.

But in 1630—twelve years into the war—Sweden–under Gustavus Adolphus–took the side of the northern Protestants and joined the fight, with its army helping to push Catholic forces back and to regain much of the lost territory lost by the Protestant Union. Gustavus Adolphus was killed in the Battle of Lutzen in 1632, and the Swedes lost much of their resolve.

Then came new military assistance of Bohemian nobleman Albrecht von Wallenstein, who provided an estimated 50,000 soldiers to Ferdinand II. This generosity came in exchange for the freedom to plunder any captured territory. The course of war turned in favor of the Catholics; and by 1635, the Swedes were vanquished and ceased to be a factor to be reckoned with for years.

Enter a new and expanded stage. The French—who titled themselves the most Catholic of Nations–were national rivals of the Habsburgs and had been for a long time. From its onset, they were opposed to provisions of the Peace of Prague. As an odd turn of the heretofore Catholic v. Protestant war, the French entered the conflict on the side of the Protestants in 1635.

Initially, the French armies were unable to make inroads against the forces of Ferdinand II, even after he died of old age in 1637. Spain—which also claimed the title of the most Catholic country in the world–joined the Protestant cause to fight for the emperor's successor and son, Ferdinand III, and later under Leopold I. They mounted counterattacks against the French armies and invaded French territory, threatening Paris itself in 1636. However, the French rallied, and fighting between the French-Protestant alliance and the forces of Spain and the Holy Roman Empire were at a stalemate for the next several years.

In 1640, the Portuguese began to revolt against their Spanish rulers, thereby weakening their military efforts on behalf of the Holy Roman Empire. Two years later, the Swedes re-entered the fray, further weakening Habsburg forces.

Now that the reader has the sides straight and understands the war, the next year, 1643, changed everything in the now decades-long conflict. Denmark-Norway took up arms again, but this time they switched alliances and began to fight on the side of the Catholic Habsburgs and the Holy Roman Empire.

At nearly the same time, French monarch Louis XIII died, leaving the throne to his 5-year-old son, Louis XIV. That created a leadership vacuum in Paris. Despite that vacuum–over the ensuing years–the French army had several notable victories, but also significant defeats–particularly at the Battle of Herbsthausen in 1645. In that same year, the Swedes attacked Vienna, but were unable to capture the city from the Holy Roman Empire.

In 1647, the Habsburg forces led by Octavio Piccolomini were able to repel the Swedes and the French from what is now Austria. The next year, in the Battle of Prague –the last significant fighting in the Thirty Years' War–the Swedes captured Prague Castle from the forces of the Holy Roman Empire and looted the priceless art collection in the castle. However, the Swedes were unable to take the bulk of the city. By this time, only the Austrian territories remained under the control of the Habsburgs. Basically, a frictional stalemate settled on the battlefield nations of the Thirty Years War.

Finally, in 1648, the various belligerent parties in the conflict signed a series of treaties eventually called the Peace of Westphalia, effectively ending the Thirty Years' War. The legacy of changes wrought by the war had significant geopolitical effects for Europe. Seriously weakened by the fighting, Spain lost its unbending grip over Portugal and the Dutch Republic. The peace accords also granted increased autonomy to the former Holy Roman Empire states in German-speaking central Europe—224 separate states–which were already making strong advances towards becoming frankly Protestant states. The Germans had sympathized with Lutheranism even before the reformer was excommunicated by Pope Leo X in 1521—a sentence that was never lifted. Given the freedom to do so, the German states eventually became a very strong Protestant enclave in Europe.

The changes in Europe directly related to the Thirty Years War included: a radical alteration in the balance of power in Europe. The diminished influence of the Roman Catholic church over political and social affairs throughout Europe resulted in the Catholic Church morphing into *one of the* Christian Churches instead of *the* Christian religion; Europe and its women had to cope with the relative absence of men in many cities and country sides. The spread of epidemic diseases–especially typhus–followed in the shadow of the armies. The war and the preceding Peace of Westphalia laid the groundwork for the formation of the modern nation-state, establishing fixed boundaries for the countries involved in the fighting and effectively decreeing that residents of a state were subject to the laws of that state and not to those of any other institution, secular or religious. This radically altered the balance of power in Europe, especially by reducing the influence over political affairs for the Catholic Church, as well as other religious groups.

The first European witch hunts began during the war, as a suspicious populace attributed the suffering throughout Europe at the time to "spiritual" causes. The war fostered a fear—a persisting xenophobia–of the "other" in communities across the European continent and caused an increased distrust among those of different ethnicities and religious faiths, including anti-Semitism–sentiments that persist to this day. In addition to the horrors of the brutal war, hundreds of thousands died as a result of famine caused by the conflict as well as an epidemic of typhus, a disease that spread rapidly in areas particularly torn apart by the violence.

Since the book in chief is directly concerned with the Netherlands in the seventeenth century, this author should discuss how the milieu of European wars acted on that select area. A segment of the Thirty Years War directly involved the Dutch and their religious controversies. In addition, they were involved in a longer and equally terrible conflict known as the Eighty Years War, also as the Netherlands War of Independence from Spain 1568-1648. Note that the end of two wars occurred in the same year—1648, and for the same reason. The result for Spain and the Netherlands was the separation of the northern and southern Netherlands from each other, to the formation of the United Provinces of the Netherlands–the Dutch Republic, and the permanent end of Catholic dominance and overlordship by the Kingdom of Spain.

The issues in both wars began as religious hatred and strife following the Protestant Reformation. The first phase of the Eighty Years War with two unsuccessful invasions of the provinces by mercenary armies under Prince William I of Orange [1568 and 1572] and foreign-based raids by the *Geuzen*–the irregular Dutch land and sea forces. William was born and reared as a Lutheran until age eleven when his uncle died, leaving him essentially the ruler of the Netherlands with the proviso that he would receive a Catholic education in the Netherlands. As a result, William became an advocate of religious tolerance and came to power in a highly divided large region of the Netherlands.

By the end of 1573, the *Geuzen* captured, converted to Calvinism, and secured against Spanish attack, the southern provinces of Holland and Zeeland. The other provinces joined in the revolt in 1576, and a general union—but a weak one–was formed. In 1579 the union was fatally weakened by the desertion of the Roman Catholic Walloon provinces. In 1588, the Spanish reconquered the southern Low Countries and stood poised for a death blow against the early and weak Dutch Republic in the north. Spain–in turn–had it's the attention diverted to a second front—the concurrent enterprises against England and France as part of the early conflicts that eventually lead to the Thirty Years War. The Protestants of the Dutch Republic in the North took advantage and began a counteroffensive. By the Twelve Years' Truce–begun in 1609– the Dutch frontiers were secured; and the Catholic and Protestant entities became distinctly separate. The south was Catholic and ruled by Spain, and the north was Protestant and ruled itself as such.

In 1571, the union was fatally weakened by the defection of the Roman Catholic Walloon provinces. By 1588, the Spanish under the Duke of Parma, reconquered the southern Low Countries and were very near to destroying the nascent Dutch Republic in the north. However, Spain's resources were spread thin by their conflicts with England and France. That provided the opportunity for the Dutch Republic to mount an effective counteroffensive. In 1609, the Twelve Year's Truce began, which resulted in the Dutch frontiers being fully secured.

In 1621, open fighting resumed as a part of the Thirty Years' War. The Dutch– under the direction of Prince Frederick Henry of Orange–succeeded in countering early Spanish successes. That led to the Franco-Dutch Alliance of 1635 that in turn resulted in the Walloon provinces joining and a sustained French drive into Flanders. The Dutch Republic and Spain, mindful of the accumulating power of France concluded a separate peace in 1648. That peace finalized the Spanish recognition of Dutch independence. The popular term, "Dutch courage" derives from the gin that was used by the English and Dutch soldiers during the Thirty Years War.

# CHAPTER FIFTEEN

# TO CONSTANTINOPLE AND TOPKAPI

IN THE YEAR OF OUR LORD, 1642, MID-JULY

Although the caravan headed by Aslan Polat, Captain Jans Fokkenzoon Corren, and First Mate Piet Corneliuszoon Van Brakel from Bruges entered Constantinople with 1,243 camels, 252 horses—most of them large sturdy Greek pack animals–287 well cared for mules, and 149 small, pugnacious, burros whose stamina and endurance for a long journey was nothing less than wondrous, it was barely average in size compared to the many other caravans entering the capital city of Constantinople at the same time. Because the caravans were so large and moved ponderously slowly, and the passageway through the Golden Gate was too narrow to permit caravans to move through even two abreast, the queued caravans stopped in the sweltering sun on bare sand pounded into powder by the millennia of commercial travel into Constantinople.

The three caravan leaders used their waiting time wisely to strike up useful acquaintances with other caravanners and local merchants. They had planned well due to Aslan's foreknowledge of the city and of the nerve wracking wait to enter any time in a twenty-four-hour period. They dispatched fifty trusted *bir havalı* [coolies] to purchase barrels of sweet water, fresh vegetables and fruits, and meat without worms. The coolies were instructed to haggle; failing to do so would be impolite and make them appear to be unknowing and boorish. But, they were to pay close attention to the passage of time. Capt. Aslan was determined to acquire the precious victuals of life before the supply ran out, even if the cost was dear.

The coolies hurried—in antipation of reward—and to avoid a hungry stay in a rich city. By the time their trade goods were being haggled over in earnest, the late comers were finding that pickings were slim and of poor quality. Many a Russian, English, Scots, German, and Venetian, scouting party came back with little of value and could only admit that life in Constantinople this season would be near starvation, and having to settle for brakish water over hearty ale or even a whiff of wine.

Eleven hours later, a small squadron of Janissaries sauntered by and gave the good news that their caravan was next to pass through the gate and into the city.

"Effendis, know that you are privileged to enter into the greatest city in all of Anatolia [the country would not be known as Turkey for another 279 years]."

Aslan bowed low and nodded to Piet an Jans to do the same.

"Great servants of the faith and protectors of the capital city of the Ottoman Empire, we humble merchants acknowledge the privilege afforded us. We intend to obey all laws and to assist in any way we can to you to preserve law and good order during the entire time we rest here under your protection."

The *chorbaji* [commander of an *orta* (regiment), corresponding to the rank of colonel in western armies], nodded his approval of Aslan's obsequius pledge, offered with bowed head.

"We will enjoy having you here. We see that you are prosperous and intend to pay mind to your security while you are here."

Aslan took note of the fact that the *chorbaji* had not spoken the important Turkish words, "You may pass through the gates with the help of God, the Magnificent and Generous. *Tanrı ile barış içinde olun.*" [Go with God in peace].

"We wish to help the good families of the Janissaries, if there is any way. We know the hardships faced by the soldiers, their wives, and their children, in the noble work of Allah to protect the cities and travelers. Can you suggest a way?"

The *chorbaji* stroked his beard for a few moments, apparently lost in thought.

"I hesitate to ask, Effendis, but our men and their families are in need of a hospital–a need that has gone unfulfilled due to a shrunken treasury resulting from costly engagements with bandits and infidels in the north."

He continued to stroke his beard thoughtfully, with his fierce dark eyes fixed on Aslan's.

Aslan quickly responded, "We are not rich men, but we do desire to be of help. Would you be able to accept a hundred Ottoman gold coins?"

"That would be a most generous gift, Effendis, from men of such power and wealth. We have so little, and the very thought of having a true hospital seems very far away."

Aslan turned and discussed the amount with Jans and Piet for five minutes.

He then hopefully offered, "We could, perhaps, find even two hundred coins; but we would have to plead with Allah, the All-Knowing, and the All Merciful, to see us through to a successful trading venture in the city to prevent us from becoming impoverished."

In the seventeenth century, twelve pence equaled a shilling, with twenty shillings to the Anatolian pound. It was difficult for visitors to Anatolia or Constantinople to be sure that they knew the value of the coins they were offering in payment. Each colony had a different coinage currency, but each kept to the pound, shilling, and pence, denominations. With the conquest of Anatolia and their expansion into Europe, the Ottoman Turks took over systems for acquiring gold that were already in place.

The Venetians, who were most deeply involved in trade, had been bringing gold to the West from the eastern Black Sea. North Africa acquired its gold by caravan over the Saharan desert. The Sudan region supplied gold through Cairo. As the Ottomans drove deeper into the Balkans, they took over gold mines there. The Mediterranean Sea and the Mediterranean World in that age saw gold come to be in short supply in Europe. The gold supply that was traditionally sold through traders in Cairo was disrupted and instead diverted to the Ottoman treasury. The Venetians were no longer able to take gold freely from the Crimean, and the mines in the Balkans were under Ottoman control. Careful oversight was undertaken to ensure that the coins were not debased. Inspectors were regularly sent to see that everything was in order and if anyone was caught committing malfeasance, they were dismissed from their positions and sent to Constantinople for punishment where they were most often executed.

In the sixteenth and seventeenth centuries, gold was produced only in Egypt, Anatolia, Greece, Transylvania, Spain, Arabia, and India. The first gold coins appeared in Lycia in the southwestern part of Anatolia. They were minted by weight of gold in denominations of *Kuruş, Qirsh, Ersh, Gersh, Grush,* and *Grosi*—different names for currency throughout the Ottoman territories. The names stem from the different languages used in the territories, including: Arabic, Amharic, Hebrew, Turkish, and Greek, and further complicated by different transcriptions into the Latin alphabet around the world. In European languages, *kuruş* were known as piastres. Paper money came slowly into use in the Ottoman empire only after 1862.

Aslan worked at appearing to be ashamed of his humble offer, but at the same time his eyes were pleading for acceptance by the great soldier.

The *chorbaji* smiled—a rare break in the stiff contours of his unfeeling and bland face–and offered his thanks and his hand, "*Tanrı ile barış içinde olun.*" he said.

The *chorbaji* and his troops moved on to inform the caravan behind Aslan's of their opportunity to contribute to the hospital fund. As soon as the janissaries were out of sight, Asland, Jans, and Piet, became a blur of movement to get their long caravan into motion before the *chorbaji* had a chance to get back and to find another excuse to extort them. All three men pondered how many more bits of banditry they would have to submit to before they could actually enter the city proper.

Constantinople was a magnificent huge and ancient city, larger than any of the westerners had every visited. The city straddled the Bosporus strait, a waterway that serves as a geographic border between Europe and Asia. The Turkish city thus lies in both continents. The city was established in 657 BCE by Greek colonists. The first Patriarch of Constantinople assumed religious power in 381 CE as the second of five

Patriarchates of the Ecumenical Councils of Constantinople–twelve hundred fifty-one years previously. Well before Aslan's caravan entered the fortified capital city, Constantinople had become famous for its architectural masterpieces. Entering via the Golden Gate of the Land Walls through which they passed, the awe-struck caravanners saw such architectural miracles as Hagia Sophia, the cathedral of the Byzantine Eastern Orthodox Church—which cost 20,000 pounds of gold to build. In its Christian era, it served as the seat of the Ecumenical Patriarchate, the sacred Imperial Palace where the Emperors lived. It burned down twice during its early life and was restored to be even more beautiful than before each time. The magnificent edifice was built by Byzantine Emperor Justinian I in 537 and served for 900 years as a church and 500 years as a mosque.

When the Ottomans conquered the city in 1453, Fatih Sultan Mehmet converted the beautiful Christian edifice into a Mosque with four minarets. It held that status for 482 years. The panels or medallions, which were hung on the columns in the nave, featured the names of Allah, the Prophet Muhammad, the first four Caliphs, and the Prophet's two grandsons—a marked difference from the original mosaics depicting Christian themes and images of Emperor Justinian and his Empress Theodora. The original mosaic on the main dome had been an image of Christ; but after the Muslims captured the city, it was covered by gold calligraphy.

What Piet and Jans could not know at their time in the beautiful religious edifice, was that the departing Christians had hurriedly put light plaster over the mosaics and paintings which were never discovered or destroyed. The Ottomans plastered over and repainted the walls with Islamic themes. Only after the Ottomans were forced out three hundred years later, did the victorious Christians discover the hidden iconic images and to remove the centuries' old coverings.

The caravanners' short passage into the inner city brought them into view of the Galata Tower, the Hippodrome, and rows of opulent aristocratic palaces lining the elegant arcaded avenues, handsome green and perfectly manicured squares. The men had to fight their covetous desire to have what the rich Ottoman's had, but they were very aware of what kind of men those Ottomans had to become and the things they had done to acquire all of that. They mutually agreed that it probably was not worth it.

Constantine laid out a new square at the center of old Byzantium, which he called the Augustaeum in the early years of the Eastern Roman Empire. Constantine's new Curia [senate-house] was a section in a large basilica on the east side. On the south side of the Augustaeum, he erected the Great Palace of the Emperor with its imposing entrance—the Chalke—and its ceremonial suite known as the Palace of Daphne. Nearby, he commissioned construction of a vast Hippodrome for chariot-races and raucous politics. It could seat over 80,000 spectators, and the famed Baths of Zeuxippus. At the western entrance to the Augustaeum was the Milion, a vaulted monument from which distances were measured across the Eastern Roman Empire.

From the Augustaeum, Aslan, Jans, and Piets' caravan were led by a hired guide along a great street, the *Mese* [lit. Middle Street], lined with beautiful colonnades. As the colonnade descended the First Hill of the city and climbed the Second, it passed on the left the Praetorium [law-court]. Then it passed through the oval Forum of Constantine which held a second Senate-house and a high column with a statue of Constantine himself. He had himself deified in the guise of Helios, crowned with a halo of seven rays, and looking toward the rising sun. From there, the *Mese* passed on and through the Forum Tauri and then the Forum Bovis, and finally up the *Xerolophus* [Seventh Hill] and through to the Golden Gate in the Constantinian Wall.

After the construction of the Theodosian Walls in the early 5th century, the Constantinian Wall was extended to the new Golden Gate, extending the length to seven Roman miles. After the construction of the Theodosian Walls, Constantinople consisted of an area approximately the size of Old Rome within the Aurelian walls and was underway to become an even greater city than Rome was at its zenith. By then, Constantinople was one of the largest cities in the world.

Later, Emperor Valens built the Palace of Hebdomon on the shore of the Propontis near the Golden Gate for use when reviewing troops. Theodosius I founded the Church of John the Baptist to house the skull of the saint—later preserved in the Topkapı Palace for the Christians of the caravan to worship, put up a memorial pillar to himself in the Forum of Taurus—the Bull–and turned the ruined pagan temple of Aphrodite into a coach house for the Praetorian Prefect. Theodosius II built 18-metre tall triple-wall fortifications, which could not be breached in the lifetime of any of the caravanners. The military nature of the sailors was impressed to the level of speechlessness by the massive walls.

By the 5th century, Constantinople was home to 300,000 inhabitants; by the middle of the 6th, there were half a million citizens. In the 9th and 10th centuries, Constantinople had a population approaching 800,000. Obtaining a food supply was one of the principal concerns of city government and required that large quantities of grain be imported. That constituted one of the reasons the population of the capital city had reduced to a fairly stable 650–700 thousand people in the 16–17th centuries, making it still the largest city in the world at the time Alsan, Jans, and Piet, first cast eyes on it.

Owing to its size and importance Constantinople became a commercial center, with high demand for expensive luxuries; and it served as one of the main transit points for goods being sent to Western Europe from the East and thus a hub of commerce and exchange. The three outsiders wisely spent much of their time in the remarkable and beautiful city cultivating trading partners, which paid life-long dividends to all three.

The importance of trade was evident all around the caravanners as they made their way deeper into the teeming city. It seemed that every person or family had something to sell or was seeking something to buy. They had seen the riches of what ancient Rome must have enjoyed, but none of them presumed that it was greater than this Muslim colossus. It was obvious that the city's economy was prospering well beyond any concept most Europeans had.

The caravanners had barely settled in for the night in their luxurious apartment for travelers, when a messenger requested a brief audience with Aslan, Jans, and Piet. The man was huge, had ebony black skin, but was soft and obese. His face was remarkable in that it had no facial hair save his eyebrows. He was dressed in a beautiful silk brocade gown, voluminous pantaloons, and silk slippers with bobbing tassels attached to their upturned tips. In his left hand, he held a well-worn silk covered box, but one that was obviously precious to him. In the right hand, he offered a red Moroccan leather bound document folder embossed with gold geometric features. No accurate images of people or animals were permitted in the empire because of the proscription against making or worshipping graven images.

"Effendis," the high squeaky voice of the messenger announced, "His Majesty, *Kayser-i Rûm* [Caesar of Rome: In the Islamic world, the Roman Empire was known primarily as *Rûm*] and *Osmanlı padişahları* [Sultan/ Emperor] Ibrahim DELİ, The Mad, The Conqueror of Crete ŞEHÎD [martyr] requests your presence tomorrow morning at ten o'clock exactly in The Second Courtyard seating area in front of the imperial kitchens. Do you understand the entire message, Effendis?"

"We do, *Teşekkür ederiz.*"

"You are most welcome."

Not entirely sure what the summons was about–but unwilling to take a chance of not responding to the summons–that might be dangerous; Aslan, Jans, and Piet, arose early, had a vigorous bath with soft aromatic soap, and ate a beautiful meal of fruit, nuts, yogurt, and Turkish delights. They walked briskly to the Imperial Gate, the main entrance into the First Courtyard. This massive gate–originally dating from 1478–was beginning to show wear. Piet thought it could do with a covering of slate or marble. Its central arch led to a high-domed passage; gilded Ottoman calligraphy adorned the structure at the top, with verses from the *Qur'an* and *tughras* of the sultans, especially the *tughras* of Mehmed II and Abdül Aziz I, who renovated the gate. When he was in residence, the sultan would enter the palace through the *Bâb-ı Hümâyûn* [Imperial Gate] located to the south of the palace.

Aside from an occasional Janissary security officer, there was little evident in the way of security, which surprised all three men. There was no one in the wooden apartment above the gate area. The sun was out in a cloudless sky, and it was beginning to warm up. They moved a little more quickly to ensure being on time. The distances were somewhat more than they had anticipated.

They walked into the *Alay Meydanı* [First Courtyard], an outer precinct which was the largest of all courtyards of Topkapi Palace. It was surrounded by high thick walls and covered with greenery—a broad lush lawn, small, well-groomed trees, and topiary. It was also known as the Court of the Janissaries or the Parade Court. Since it was some sort of official day, court officials and janissaries lined the path clothed in their dress garbs: the Solak janissaries ["Sons of the Sultan", the Red Regiment] were the archer bodyguards of the Sultan and given the privilege of wearing his color—claret red.

They each carried–their hands at the ready–a shining clean, tripod-mounted, single-barreled, flintlock, musket fitted with a multi-shot revolving cylinder. The regiment that day carried a mixture of two versions. One weapon–intended for use against Christian enemies–fired conventional round bullets, while the second variant–designed to be used against the Muslim Turks–fired square bullets, which were believed to cause more severe and painful wounds than spherical projectiles.

It was also the Red Regiment's privilege to wear a tall hat—called a *börk*. It was made of tubular white felt and covered his head before running down his back to below his belt. As a prominent symbol of their devotion to their order, *Osmanlı padişahları* [Sultan] Ibrahim DELİ's personal janissaries' hats had a holding place in front–called the "*kaşıklık*"–for a spoon. This symbolized the "*kaşık kardeşliği*", or the "brotherhood of the spoon", which reflected a sense of comradeship among the Janissaries who ate, slept, fought, and died, together.

*Zülüflü Baltacılar* [Janissaries who guarded the palace perimeter] carried long-shafted axes and halberds and were dressed in bright orange, making the scene intensely colorful and splendid—a characteristic for which the Topkapi Palace was famous.

The janissaries' uniforms—outfits—were entirely different than European dress or uniforms. The men wore outer items: a linen shirt that fell to just above the knees' *mintans,* [a vest; some wore *zibins*–a hip-length jacket], *şalvars* [baggy trousers over underwear], a *kuşak* [a brilliant matching red sash wound over the shirt and pants serving as a pocket for a money pouch and a dagger and as a *yatagan* sword holder], *çedik* [socks], *Yemeni* [satin slippers on the feet]. Over all of this was a long-sleeved overcoat that was open over the chest and was tied at the waist. No consideration was given to the stifling heat of the day.

Beyond the entrance, there were steep slopes leading towards the sea. Within the courtyard were the *Darphane-i Âmire* [Imperial Mint] and the Byzantine church of Hagia Irene [Saint Irene] and several large fountains from which flowed crystal clear clean water. The church of Hagia Irene was currently being used by the Ottomans as a storehouse and imperial armory after the Christians vacated the city. This courtyard was the way into where the sultan would hold court in the early afternoon. The European sailors and the rest of the serious looking visitors entering the palace followed the path towards the Gate of Salutation or *Orta Kapı* [Middle Gate or the Second Courtyard of the palace].

The large gate led into the palace. At the entrance into the second courtyard, the sailors were met by the same, rather odd-looking, man who had conveyed the sultan's invitation and was still carrying his timeworn box in his left hand. The courtyard was full of peacocks and gazelles, and they all scattered as he passed by them.

He spoke to them—calling them by name—and signaled for them to follow him and away from the large gathering crowds. They passed the crenellated gate with its two large, pointed, octagonal towers. The gate itself was richly decorated with *Qur'anic* inscriptions and the monograms of more than a dozen sultans.

The janissaries of the palace doors—dressed in bright green—held their spears in crossed positions to keep tight control. All visitors had to dismount and stand aside. Only the sultan was allowed to enter the Gate of Salutation on horseback. The servant led his guests away from the crowd and to be able to rest in the shade near the *Cellat Çeşmesi* [Chalke Gate] of the Topkapi Palace. Nearby was the Fountain of the Executioners where the executioner washed his hands and long sharp sword after a decapitation.

He squinted at the sun and did a small calculation in his head.

"It is time," he said.

Before the visitors even reached the palace's interior, they were first greeted by the spectacularly ornate Imperial Gate and the beautiful Rococo-style Fountain of Sultan Ahmet III in the courtyard. The portly black servant lead the way into the interior area of the palace to the Fourth Courtyard, which was the most private area of the Sultans. It consisted of several pavilions along with a tulip garden and terraces. The Fourth Courtyard was also known as the *Sofa-ı Hümâyûn* [the Imperial Sofa]. It was more of an innermost private sanctuary of the sultan and his family, and consisted of a number of pavilions, *köşk* [kiosks], gardens, and terraces. The servant had them stand quietly in front of a stone throne.

## The History
## Topkapi Palace: Late 1450s-2020

The history of Topkapi Palace is ancient. It began before Islam was invented by Muhammad—the vision in the cave in 610 CE. In 330, Roman Emperor Constantine I [the Great] moved the seat of the Empire to Byzantium, where he founded what he called the new Rome and renamed it Constantinople. The site was important and well-chosen because it was the intersection of routes between Europe and Asia and between the Mediterranean and the Black Sea. Almost immediately, he set about to plan and build The Great Palace of Constantinople [Gr. *Méga Palátion*; Latin: *Palatium Magnum*], also to be known as the Sacred Place.

The site for Constantine's Sacred Palace [Gr. *Hieròn Palátion*; Latin: *Sacrum Palatium*], was the large Imperial Byzantine palace complex chosen to be in the south-eastern end of the peninsula now known as Old Istanbul in what is modern Turkey. It served as the main royal residence of the Eastern Roman or Byzantine emperors from 330 CE to 1081CE and was the center of imperial administration for over 690 years. Only a few remnants and fragments of its foundations have survived into the present day.

When the victorious Constantine I moved the Roman capital to Constantinople in 330, he planned out a palace for himself and his heirs amidst the splendid grand city he planned. The palace was located between the Hippodrome and Hagia Sophia. It was rebuilt and expanded several times during its history. Much of the complex of the Sacred Palace was destroyed during the Nika riots of 532 and was rebuilt lavishly by the emperor Justinian I. Further extensions and alterations were commissioned by Justinian II and Basil I. However, it had fallen into disrepair by the time of Constantine VII, who ordered a major renovation.

From the early 11th century onwards, the Byzantine emperors favored the Palace of Blachernae as an imperial residence, though they continued to use the Great Palace as the primary administrative and ceremonial center of the city.

The Great Palace of Constantinople declined substantially during the 12th century when parts of the complex were demolished or filled with rubble. During the sack of Constantinople by the Fourth Crusade, the Palace was plundered by the soldiers of Boniface of Montferrat. Although the subsequent Latin emperors continued to use the Palace complex, they lacked money for its maintenance. The last Latin emperor, Baldwin II, went as far as to have the lead roofs of the palace removed and then selling them.

When the city was retaken by the forces of Michael VIII Palaiologos in 1261, the Great Palace was in terrible disrepair. The Palaiologos emperors thereafter largely abandoned it, ruling from Blachernae and using the vaults as a prison. When Sultan Mehmed II entered the city in 1453, he found the palace ruined and abandoned. As he wandered its empty halls and pavilions, he allegedly whispered a quote from the Persian poet, Saadi:

The spider is curtain-bearer in the palace of Chosroes,
The owl sounds the relief in the castle of Afrasiyab.

Much of the palace complex was demolished in the general rebuilding of Constantinople in the early years of the Ottoman era. The area was initially turned into housing with a number of small mosques before Sultan Ahmet I demolished the remnants of the Daphne and Kathisma Palaces to build the Sultan Ahmed Mosque and its adjoining buildings. Almost nothing was left of the original Byzantine Great Palace of Constantine. The site of the Great Palace began to be investigated in the late 19th century and an early 20th century fire uncovered a section of the Great Palace. On this site, prison cells, many large rooms, and some possible tombs, were found.

The original palace is considered by scholars to have been a series of pavilions, much like the Ottoman-era Topkapı Palace that succeeded it. The total surface area of the Great Palace exceeded 200,000 square feet. It stood on a steeply sloping hillside that descends nearly 108 feet [33 meters] from the Hippodrome to the shoreline, which necessitated that the original Byzantines construct large substructures and vaults. The Great Palace complex occupied six distinct terraces descending to the shore.

The main entrance to the Palace quarter was the Chalke (Bronze) gate at the Augustaion. The Augustaion was located on the south side of the Hagia Sophia, and it was there that the city's main street–the Mese [Middle Street]–began. To the east of the square lay the Senate house [Palace of Magnaura] where the University was later housed, and to the west the *Milion*–the mile marker, from which all distances in the Ottoman Empire were measured)–and the old Baths of Zeuxippus.

Immediately behind the Chalke Gate, facing southwards, were the barracks of the palace guards, the *Scholae Palatinae*. After the barracks stood the reception hall of the 19 *Accubita* [Nineteen Couches] and behind that the Palace of Daphne, which in early Byzantine times was the main imperial residence, including the Octagon, the emperor's bedchamber. From the Daphne, a passage led directly to the *kathisma* [imperial box] in the Hippodrome–an ancient Grecian stadium for horse and chariot racing. The name is derived from the Greek words *hippos* [horse] and *dromos* [course]. Modern French and other languages use the word in the same way.

The main throne room was the *Chrysotriklinos*–built by Justin II–and expanded and renovated by Basil I, with the palatine chapel of the Theotokos of the Pharos nearby. The Triconchos Palace on its north was built by the emperor Theophilos and accessible through a semicircular antechamber known as the *Sigma*. To the east of the Triconchos lay the lavishly decorated *Nea Ekklesia* [New Church], built by Basil I, with five gilded domes. The church survived until after the Ottoman conquest when it was used as a gunpowder magazine. The magazine exploded when it was struck by lightning in 1490. Between the church and the sea walls lay the polo field of the *Tzykanisterion*.

Further to the south, detached from the main complex lay the seaside palace of Bucoleon built by Theophilos, incorporating parts of the sea walls, and used extensively until the 13th century, especially during the Latin Empire [1204–1261] whose Catholic emperors from Western Europe favored the seaside palace. A seaward gate gave direct access to the imperial harbor of Bucoleon.

By the 12th century, Constantinople was the largest and wealthiest European city. The Byzantine Empire was delivered a mortal blow during the Fourth Crusade, when Constantinople was sacked in 1204; and the territories that the empire formerly governed were divided into competing Byzantine Greek and Latin realms. Despite the eventual recovery of Constantinople in 1261, the Byzantine Empire remained only one of several small rival states in the area for the final two centuries of its existence. Its remaining territories were progressively annexed by the Ottomans in the Byzantine–Ottoman wars over the 14th and 15th centuries.

Constantinople by this stage was underpopulated and dilapidated. The population of the city had collapsed so severely that it was now little more than a cluster of villages separated by fields. On April 2, 1453, Sultan Mehmed's army of 80,000 men and large numbers of irregulars laid a two month siege to the city. Despite a desperate last-ditch defense of the city by the massively outnumbered Christian forces–7,000 men, 2,000 of whom were foreign–on May 29, 1453, after an Ottoman army stormed Constantinople, Mehmed II triumphantly entered the Hagia Sophia, which would soon be converted to the city's leading mosque. The current Emperor Constantine XI died in battle that day; and the Byzantine Empire collapsed, ushering in the long reign of the Ottoman Empire. The Byzantine Empire had existed from 330 to 1453 CE with its capital founded by Constantine I, the Great.

Sultan Mehmet II began almost as soon as he and his victorious army entered the once great city, to build his magnificent capital. Because it was located between the Golden Horn and the Sea of Marmara, the land area that needed defensive walls was reduced, and this helped it to present an impregnable fortress enclosing magnificent palaces, domes, and towers, the result of the prosperity it achieved from being the great commercial gateway. Although besieged on numerous occasions by various armies, the defenses of Constantinople proved impregnable for nearly nine hundred years.

Some thirty sultans ruled from the Topkapı Palace [The cannonball gate] for nearly four centuries during the Ottoman Empire's 600 year reign, beginning with the conqueror Mehmet II. He planned early because he needed a new place in which to live and rule the empire. Mehmet hired four architects: Mimar Sinan, Sarkis Balyan, Davut Ağa, and Acem Ali.

He ordered the construction of the palace in the late 1450s. Actual construction started in 1465 and was built in Constantinople between 1466 and 1478. After the conquest of the city in 1453, Topkapi was created on top of ancient ruins from the Byzantine Emperors because the Ottomans wanted to be seen as a continuation of the glory of ancient power, not as just creators of a new one. In the late 15th century, the palace became the main residence for sultans. On April 3, 1924–after the fall of the Ottoman Empire–it was decided that the Topkapi Palace should be transformed into a museum. It was the first museum of the Republic of Turkey—formerly known as Anatolia.

Originally there were around 700-800 residents in the palace–but over the centuries–the number raised to 5,000 people. As the population of residents grew, changes and improvements were made. The latest iteration of palace has three main parts: The Old Palace, the New Palace, and Yildiz Palace. The one which is known as Topkapi is the New Palace.

The Old Palace—of the Ottoman era–was the first construction created in the newly conquered city to dominate the sacred hill where once the magnificent Palace of Constantine stood. It was built on the acropolis, a hill on a small peninsula between the Sea of Marmara, Bosphorus, and the Golden Horn–the site of the first settlement in modern Istanbul. The palace has a very good view of the Golden Horn, the Bosphorus, and the Sea of Marmara. It is surrounded by 5 km of walls and has an area of 700,000 sq. ft. It is known as *Topkapu Sarayi* or *Seraglio* in Ottoman Turkish language.

The New Palace was much more luxurious. Unlike the palaces of Europe–which were composed of one large building surrounded by gardens–the Topkapı Palace stood out with its structure that included a series of pavilions, barracks, kitchens, kiosks, sleeping quarters, and visitor chambers, dotted around a central enclosure. The site dominated the landscape and contained state buildings, pleasure pavilions, baths, workshops, kitchens, and residential quarters. All the sultan's private and political life was centered in this site. The ruler met with his advisers there, celebrated battles his soldiers won , and made strategic plans. With time, it also became a center of family life and local culture.

The palace continued to be renovated and expanded throughout the centuries, especially due to natural disasters that often took their toll on buildings–most notably, the earthquake of 1509, and the fire of 1665. It was damaged by fire in 1514 and after that most of the people went to live in the New Palace. The old one was partially restored and rebuilt, but fire destroyed it once more—owing to the presence of wooden roofs near to cooking and heating stoves and furnaces–during the reign of sultan Abdulaziz, 1861-1876. The Commander-in-Chief gate was put there in place of the palace which afterwards became part of Istanbul University. It was redecorated in the rococo style in 1774 under Sultan Mustafa III. The gate was decorated with *Qur'anic* verses above the entrance and *tuğra*s. The ceiling was partly painted and gold-leafed, with a golden ball hanging from the middle, the sides with baroque decorative elements and miniature paintings of landscapes.

The Harem

Inside the cloistered Harem [Arabic. Forbidden place] there were rooms dedicated to the mother of the sultan, wives of the sultan, his concubines, the harem slaves, Turkish baths, circumcision room, apartments of the chief black eunuch, and apartments of the sultan; in total, over 400 rooms. The harem was a home for hundreds of women and their children. It was also the place where princes lived until they were 16 years old. The women of Ottoman harems received the best education and worked to support the finances of the palace.

The center of the power in the Harem was located in the *Valide* Sultan's apartments. The *Valide* was the Queen Mother–the first lady of the Imperial Ottoman

Harem. The woman who ruled the harem could be the mother or wife of a sultan. The first great *Valide* was Hurrem Sultan, but there were many more of considerable Ottoman fame. All these women were powerful and had skills which allowed them to multiply the income generated by the harem. They proved their worth and thereby insured their right to remain in the safety and luxury of the Harem apartments. Shortly after the Prophet decreed the special status of women, the harem came into being. Originally, it was forbidden to all men except for eunuchs to enter, even the sultans.

That situation changed when a famously beautiful and intelligent woman captured the heart of Sultan Suleiman the Magnificent . She was born in the territory of The Crown of the Kingdom of Poland. Her name was Alexandra, but the sultan called her Hurrem—the cheerful one. She was a Christian and wanted to create a real relationship with the sultan, but to achieve her goals she also needed help from fate. As Andrew Colt wrote in his book:

> "When a fire did a great damage to the Old Seraglio (Old Palace), Roxelane used the opportunity to ask for permission to live in the New Palace – known to us as Topkapi – the center of political life and the sultan's court, where he also had an apartment. She brought with her a crowd of eunuchs, black and white, servants and domestics; once installed there, she stayed. The Harem and the state were no longer separate; the consequences of this were to prove deplorable."
>
> –Andrew Colt

The magnificent Topkapı *Sarayı Müzesi* Palace is one of the most popular and frequently visited museums in the world since 1924. Besides the elegance and opulence of the architecture and interiors of the palace and its gardens, the museum houses the imperial collections of the Ottoman Empire and maintains an extensive collection of books and manuscripts in its library.

# CHAPTER SIXTEEN

# THE SULTAN AND THE SLAVE

A s the three Europeans waited stiffly for the sultan to appear and to take his seat on the stone throne of the House of Felicity, the large black man who brought them to the throne room struck up a conversation.

"Sirs," he asked, "From what countries do you come?"

Aslan answered, "Anatolia."

Jans and Piet responded together, "The Netherlands...the land of the Dutch."

Piet asked the servant, "Were you born here?"

"No, Great Sirs, I am a Nubian Christian. Are you familiar with Nubia?"

"No, this is the first time I have heard of that place," Piet answered.

"It is in the south of Egypt, a good place peopled by Christians who migrated there to escape the persecutions of the Romans. There is a large population of Jews who keep watch over a holy first copy of the Torah."

"My name is Piet, and this is Jans. Are you familiar with our country?"

"I am. I have been there with the household on four occasions."

"For what purpose?" Piet asked naively.

Jans was too late to shush him.

"It is all right. We were there to seek slaves for the harem back in Constantinople. The last time was less than a year ago."

"Were you successful?" Piet asked in a voice tinged with vain hope.

"We were. Our Dutch contacts were most helpful and efficient. We obtained several truly beautiful young women. In fact, you can get a glimpse of one of them who is on the auction block tomorrow or the next day."

Piet's interest was now piqued to its highest.

Before he could ask another question, the Nubian Christian gave Jans and Piet another explanation.

"I, too, am a slave. The boys and girls of my village were all given to the sultan's soldiers as tribute when they captured our city. I have prospered here; the household considers me to be loyal and intelligent. I was schooled as a privileged boy, passed tests, and finally became the *kızlar ağası* [Ottoman Turkish: *agha* of the girls or also the *agha* of the House of Felicity]—the Chief Black Eunuch."

Without thinking about the somewhat strange physical appearance of the *kızlar ağası*, Piet blurted out a question that made Jans cringe, "Forgive my ignorance, what does eunuch mean?"

Jans opened his mouth to try and explain, but the *kizlar* put up his hand, "It is an innocent question. I take no offense. Perhaps your friend can better explain."

Jans blushed and stammered a little before answering the question directly, "Piet, do you see the small box the Chief Black Eunuch carries at all times?"

Piet nodded.

"In it he carries the remains of his manhood…considered his jewels. He and the others look for the day when Christ will restore them as whole men."

It was Piet's turn to blush, "I am sorry; it was ignorant of me. I understand, and I mourn for you."

"No need to do so, my kind Dutch friend. I was just a young boy when it happened. I did not yet have hair in those places."

"That makes him a safe man to protect the harem," Jans said. "Enough on that subject."

The *kizlar* went on to explain something of his education and his life, "Here in the palace, I was schooled in Turkish, Arabic, Persian, and the *Qur'an*, as well as history, geography, geometry, astronomy, inheritance law, and calligraphy."

The *kizlar* suddenly stiffened and gave Jans and Piet an authoritarian look which conveyed the unmistakable order for them to do likewise.

A large man with a full-face black beard and an aquiline nose swept gracefully into the House of Felicity and took his seat on the stone throne.

The man with the piercing eyes and the demeanor of a god looked closely at his visitors. He was dressed in the most elaborate clothing either Jans or Piet had ever seen—or ever would again. His kaftan [outer garment] was fitted to the neck, collarless, and open from the front. One of the most striking aspects of his attire was the V shape of the neck opening and the decoration of the seam of the outer kaftan where the arm joins the body. These seams normally had a narrow, inscribed band [*tiraz*] on it. The kaftan was worn over *şalvar* [trousers] which reached to just below his knees. They were narrow and form fitting and were secured at the waist with waistbands that were embroidered at the ends and passed through a six-inch seam stitched at the top of the trousers, gathering the top to fit. The *salvar* and kaftan were kept in place with a cummerbund. Because of the seasonal heat, he did not wear any inner robes over his Chinese silk underwear. There were multiple be-jeweled frogged bands used as fastenings.

On his feet he wore soft Persian boots with appliques of gold embroidered red leather. The most eye-catching part of his ensemble was his turban. It was gleaming white and stood two and a half feet high above his scalp. Each sultan's turban is Ottoman and an art of the sultan himself, which was a condition of the Sultanate. The main requirement to being in power was to be a *Mujahid* [warrior]. The turban represented a shroud over his head in order to remember the presence of death at all times.

The institution of the sultanate garnered vast riches from trade and war which were demonstrated as a sign of power. The economic boom filtered to all parts of the realm and to all industries. The textile industry shared in this wealth: the development of weaving reached a pinnacle with the addition of gold and silver metallic threads to silk textiles and even to leather. The Ottoman sultans—including the decadent Sultan Ibrahim–placed great importance on their garments and wore robes and kaftans woven and sewn of the most expensive and luxurious fabrics. Their taste for luxury and superior-quality materials significantly influenced the development of Ottoman textile weaving. Ibrahim's clothing that day was created in the *hassa nakkaşları* [palace workshops] by court designers. His kaftan was made of silk fabrics woven for the palace by textile artists in Bursa. The ensemble–particularly the silk fabrics–were subject to stringent control by the state. Details about the number of warp threads, their weight, length, twist, and dye, were established and communicated to the relevant artisans via municipal codes.

The brilliant red kaftan was made of *kemha* [heavy silk brocade], the cummerbund of *çatma* [brocaded velvet woven with threads of gold and silver]; and the *salvar* was made of cashmere imported from Venice. The cost of the sultan's garments was more than his father had brought in during his best year, Piet thought.

The designs for the fabrics used for court apparel and furnishings were created at special workshops in the palace by court designers known as *hassa nakkaşları*.

He quietly asked the *kizlar* to tell him about the beautiful design in the sultan's kaftan.

"The *nakkaşhane* [pattern, design]–the *Chintamani* motif, composed of three-ball and a wavy line–is reserved for the sultan and his immediate family," the *kizlar* told him. "Sultan Ibrahim," then he became barely audible, "is often called 'The Mad' outside Topkapi. We never even hint at that. He and his father and his favored sons have adopted Chinese art for clothing design as their own. You will see them as we tour; they include floral patterns like *Hatayi* [flowers in profile], lotus [spiraling branches with tiny leaves], Chinese cloud motif, celestial designs [sun, moon, and stars], and the endless knot motif. Another motif exclusively for the sultans' kaftans is the crown. We improved on the Western—Venetian—design and interpreted it to comply with Ottoman taste."

Sultan Ibrahim, The Mad, seemed to wake as from a dream and began to speak, bringing all other vocalizations to an abrupt halt.

"Greetings, men of the cloth, and welcome to our home, Topkapi. Your reputation has preceded you as told to me by my Grand Vizier Kemankeş Kara Mustafa Pasha."

The three men facing the sultan heard a slight series of coughs coming from behind the curtain at the sultan's back. The *kizlar* gave the two Europeans a slight nod.

"Over the next week, I wish you to tell me all about your European world—how people dress, what they talk about, what they think of my empire, and especially what you two men can do to further trade and understanding between my world and yours. My *kizlar* will bring you a message when I have time to have that conversation with you. For now—however–let me keep up my part of the arrangement. The *kizlar* and the Grand Vizier will show you about the palace and its grounds with nothing left out."

The *kizlar* gave his master a strongly quizzical look.

"Yes, my faithful servant, even there. Warn the guards and the ladies that they can expect visitors and that they are to be on their best behavior."

The large black servant bowed.

"Alas—that is a proper English word, is it not?—I must return to my official duties for now. I invite you, the vizier, and the *kizlar*, to dine in the palace kitchens with the servants. I am sure you will find that—like the rest of the palace tour—to be an interesting thing to tell your European friends."

With that, Sultan Ibrahim stood and began to walk out of the throne room. There was a rustling of the curtain behind him.

Piet and Jans looked at the *kizlar* to be sure they had heard correctly.

"Yes, my friends, you are being given a great privilege, one that even few citizens of the empire have ever been granted. The only other people to have had such an invitation in my recent memory is the delegation of merchants from Great Qing [Manchu], imperial Mongol dynasty of the Chintamani. They brought personal greetings from their Emperor Shunzhi who established the dynasty. Our spies informed us that many Han—the native Chinese people—were treated poorly. They were required to accept the traditions, the clothes, and the manners of the Mongols. The men were required to cut their hair in Mongolian fashion or face execution by losing their heads to swordsmen. We learned that Han scholarly people who attempted to criticize the rulers through literature were rounded up and beheaded. Han people were also relocated from the power centers of Beijing.

"Sultan Ibrahim applauded the delegation and plans to send back a letter of praise to Beijing. He will tell the great emperor that it is just the way he and the sultans before him treated the disloyal and unbelievers," the *kizlar agha* said.

"I trust that I need not caution you against speaking criticism about the sultan. He does not tolerate such talk in the least way. Remember that his palace and his empire is rife with spies. Trust no one enough to presume to speak ill of the Mad Sultan lest you get to see that side of him."

The three men were walking towards the Second Courtyard seating area in front of the imperial kitchens. The imperial harem and Divan were to the north of them and the kitchens to the south. The *kizlar agha* maintained a running patter amounting to a most knowledgeable guided tour as they neared the kitchen area. The smells coming from the many chimneys caused Jans and Piet to realize that they had not eaten all day, and they began to salivate. Their bellies began to growl, which made the *kizlar* laugh.

He said, "I am remiss. I have not given you my name; I am more than just a title; I am a person. I am *Kizlar Agha* Bezan Süleymani Agha, which includes both my title and the new Ottoman name I was given after I was captured from Nubia and enslaved."

"And I am Piet Corneliuszoon Van Brakel, *Agha*; that means that my father's name was Cornelius, and that my family comes from a town in the Netherlands called Brakel."

Jans added, "And my full name is Captain Jans Fokkenzoon Corren; my father's name is—or was—Fokken."

"Your father has gone to be with the Christ?" Bezan asked.

"Both of my parents. It surprises me that you are Christian, my friend. It must be difficult in this Muslim world."

"Not really, I have special status, much like the janissaries, who are also Christians for the most part."

Piet noticed that he and the other two men had fallen into an easy companionable conversation, and it pleased him to be so accepted. He garnered from Jans' face that he felt the same way.

"My friends call me by my first name, Piet. I would like it if you would do that, *Agha*."

"And I am known as Jans, just Jans."

"I would truly enjoy having friends. No one calls me by my given name, Bezan, here; and no one knows what I was called in that long-ago place where I lived among Christians. Please let us be friends and use given names."

So, it became Piet, Jans, and Bezan, a comfortable comradely trio.

"We are here," Bezan explained as they passed along a narrow outside hallway between two tall brick buildings on an internal street that took them between the Second Courtyard and the Marmara Sea. "On our right are the *Saray Mutfakları* [palace kitchens]—the red brick buildings with the tall white chimneys. The kitchens were built when the palace was first constructed in the 15th century and expanded during the reign of Suleyman the Lawgiver, the great conqueror. After the terrible fire of 1574–which badly damaged the kitchens—new ones were built. There are by this time two rows of twenty wide chimneys. We are about to enter the kitchen section through here."

He guided them to the right through one of the three doors in the portico of the Second Courtyard.

"We will enter through the Imperial commissariat—the lower kitchen–door, and I will take us by the imperial kitchen door and the confectionery kitchen door; so, you can see how great is the importance of food here in Topkapi. Our splendid kitchens consist of ten domed buildings. Besides the area for eating, there is the Imperial kitchen–better known to us as the palace school, then the *Harem* [women's quarters], then *Birûn*, the outer service section of the palace, which holds the kitchens for cooking, the beverages kitchen, the confectionery, the creamery, the storerooms, and finally, the rooms for the cooks. All told the palace has 800 workers who prepare food for 4,000 people every day. Needless to say, these are the largest kitchens in the Ottoman Empire, perhaps the largest kitchens in the world, do you think, my friends?"

"The kitchens are as large as any building in the city where I was born," Piet said.

"My friend, Piet, the kitchens are even larger than what you see here. The kitchen area includes dormitories, baths, and even a mosque for the employees."

Piet and Jans nodded to each other in wonderment.

"Are you hungry, my friends?"

"Very," Piet and Jans chorused.

"Good, our timing is perfect. We have an interesting tradition here that I will explain. We all eat here together, and many times even the Sultan's family joins in. We eat from a huge common cauldron. Can you guess why we have this tradition?"

Piet said, "To give such a large community a chance to know each other better?"

Jans simply shrugged.

Bezan smiled and said, "No, my friends. It is for a much more important reason. As you are no doubt aware, people of the Middle East, indeed throughout Asia, are correctly known for their facility with the use of poisons. More than one Sultan has died of poisoning by his brothers. Two things came of that fact. First, most Sultans had all but one of their sons killed by strangulation—as we call it, 'with a golden cord'. Second, it is not possible to carry out a poisoning when all members of the household eat together for obvious reasons."

Jans shook his head in disbelief.

"Ah yes, unfortunately, in recent decades it has become necessary for enemies to assassinate Sultans and their families by garrote or by the arrow."

He said it without a hint of a smile.

They sat down among the horde of other hungry workers and aristocrats. The three new friends waited their turn, then dipped ladles of stew from the large metal pot with a lid and handle cooking over a blazing open fire, into their personal bowls. The fare was chopped goat and sheep meat, a wide variety of succulent fresh vegetables, and seasoning with spices from all over the world. Bread was served by some of the over a thousand eunuchs and other slaves. It was as good as that coming out of the best bakeries in the West. They dipped their chunks of bread into the pot convivially with all the rest of the palace's inhabitants except the Sultan's immediate household. Dessert was a wonderful baklava made of almonds, walnuts, and copious amounts of honey.

No one died of poisoning.

Of all the many people who gathered for the communal evening meal, the most diverse and interesting to Piet and Jans were the men and women of the Chinese merchant group. At least they were the most interesting until Piet saw her. One of the harem slave girls was a petite, delicate, blond girl, the most beautiful human being Piet had ever seen. If there exists such a thing, it was love at first sight; but he was never able to get near her during the entire evening.

## THE HISTORY
## COMMERCIAL INTERACTION BETWEEN THE QING AND THE OTTOMAN EMPIRES, AND THE SIGNIFICANCE OF SILK

The economic history of the Ottoman Empire covers the period from 1209 to 1923. The empire's economy depended upon and was bound up with agriculture, transportation, and religion. The Ottoman Empire began to expand seriously during the 16th century. Trade was important even before the 16th century; and, as the empire expanded, it gradually gained control of important trade routes. The capture of Constantinople in 1453 was a key event in terms of control of trade. With the capture of great city, they took significant control of the Silk Road, which European countries used as their major trade routes with Asia. In practical terms, the Ottoman Empire blocked the labyrinthine Silk Road. Europeans and Asians could trade through Constantinople and other Muslim countries; but after 1453, they had to pay very high taxes. Ottomans themselves continued along the trajectory of territorial expansion, traditional monopolies, conservative landholding, and agriculture.

Silk and spices were brought overland into Constantinople from India and China, then transshipped to Venice and on further west. Constantinople's gold and silk commodities attracted a large number of traders over time. The quality of both land and sea transport was driven primarily by the efforts of the Ottoman administration. Road infrastructure depended on the interest of the Ottoman sultanate at the time. The condition of the Silk Road system roads was significantly better in the 16th century than it would be in the 18th century.

In Anatolia, the Ottomans inherited a network of caravanserai from the Selçuk Turks who preceded them. The administration and tax-gathering of the empire mandated an interest in ensuring the safety of couriers and convoys and of merchant caravans. The caravanserai network extended into the Balkans and provided safe lodgings for merchants and their animals throughout the system. The Jelali revolts of the 16th and 17th centuries disrupted the land-transport network in Anatolia to the point that the empire could no longer ensure the safety of merchants. Thereafter, the merchants had to negotiate and pay outlandish bribes for safe passage with the local leader of the area through which they were traveling.

The empire's interest in sea trade was erratic. The Muslim Ottomans were afraid that the sea trade to the south would potentially corrupt their imperial kingdom and further efforts to conquer their empire. They feared that the trade with foreign merchants would give the opportunity for Westerners to corrupt China and also the Ottoman territories. In general, the sultans and the merchants preferred a free-market system from which they could draw a reliable tax revenue. As a result, the empire stagnated as an agrarian economy–labor scarce, land rich, and capital-poor. In the mid-16th century–for a short time–the administration became actively involved in the spice trade to enhance revenues. Trade policies either pro or anti governmental involvement were often repealed by successor sultans. Foreign trade was suspect and considered a rather low-class pursuit. In general, the Muslim Ottomans were xenophobic about outsiders and their nonMuslim religions. Customs export taxes were only an indirect revenue source compared to the more than forty percent of the emperor's revenue that came from agriculture, especially wheat.

That set of attitudes and policies resulted in a nearly constant trade imbalance; Constantinople was the single exception. It ran a small import surplus. Foreign trade was a minor part of the Ottoman economy; but, in contrast to the protectionism of China, Japan, and Spain, the Ottoman Empire had a liberal trade policy, open to foreign import which attracted merchants to the empire in droves from all over the civilized world. China's silk manufacturing industry was booming and producing a huge excess of exquisite silk, and its trade routes were being usurped by other countries. For that reason, they were attracted to Constantinople and were willing to trade very liberally in favor of the Ottomans.

The main areas of maritime importation into Constantinople were: the Aegean and Eastern Mediterranean–main trade: wheat; the Red Sea and Persian Gulf–main trade: spices; the Black Sea–main trade: wheat and lumber; and the Western Mediterranean—an eclectic broad commercial variety.

Jerusalem was the center of trade, business, and religion of the Ottoman Empire. Muslims, Jews, and Christians, coexisted more or less peacefully. The Ottoman Empire controlled the trade routes to Asia from Constantinople, and they collected taxes from each passing caravan. Although the taxes were onerous, most traders shrugged and accepted them as the cost of doing business, and better than fending off bandits or engaging in warfare. The Ottomans had a monopoly. The Muslim Ottoman empire was in control of the sole trade route—the Silk Road–that existed. But they were selfish and interfered with open trading.

Constantinople was a city at the convergence of all land routes to the spice centers of the East and took advantage by levying prohibitively expensive tariffs on goods transported through the city. Trans-Saharan trade routes were based on the exchange of North African salt for West African gold. The original trade routes began from the capital in Changan, reached into the Gansu corridor, and ended in Dunhuang near the edge of Taklimakan. When overland trade routes that brought Europe its spices, silks, perfumes, and other exotic goods, were cut by the Ottomans, Europe sought to establish new trading routes to Asia.

The spice trade route, stretching from China to the United Kingdom by both land and ocean, introduced the outside world to Chinese culture, art, crafts, and cuisine. The trade–even coming from the xenophobic and insular Qing dynasty–unintentionally created a unique blend of culinary diversity. The spice trade during the 16th and 17th centuries brought black pepper, cinnamon, cardamom, ginger, turmeric, nutmeg, and cloves, from Asia via the ocean Spice Trade route. Merchants took advantage of the security of Mongol trade routes while moving from the Black Sea into Central Asia. This assisted the Chinese to increase its Middle-Eastern commerce. That led smoothly to an increase in Chinese-Ottoman trade because the Ottoman administration was directly involved in the spice trade with the aim of increasing revenue. The availability of Chinese and other Asian goods spurred the wealthy Ottomans to seek ever increasing possession of exotic and luxury goods. Because of the value added taxes and tolls exacted by the Ottomans, merchants from all corners of the world sought alternative trade routes to China. While trying to find a trade route to China by sailing West from Europe, Columbus discovered America for the Europeans.

The Silk Road routes were complex and difficult. They stretched from China through India, Asia Minor, up throughout Mesopotamia, to Egypt, the African continent, Greece, Rome, the Netherlands, and Britain. Increasing efforts to circumvent the Ottoman restrictions lead to increased opportunities for the Chinese to bring their products closer to Constantinople and Persia. When the Mongol Empire expanded across Eurasia in the 13$^{th}$ century, it not only established a new political order but also unified the trade networks that spread across northern Eurasia, connecting China, Central Asia, the Middle East, and the Slavs in Eastern Europe, within one system. The introduction of paper money in China in the 13$^{th}$ century allowed the export of silver and its equivalents to Central Asia via the caravan trade, supporting the Mongol economic boom of the 14$^{th}$ century.

The Russian government banned imports of tobacco from being sold anywhere. They had not reckoned with the extreme popularity of the addicting drug. Demand soared throughout the world. It was cheap to grow—especially with slave labor—easy to transport by sea, and convenient to convey finished products overland. China and India had no such prejudices, and their merchants benefitted considerably from Russia's intransigence. Tobacco from China became a luxury item which made commerce between China and the Ottomans even more profitable.

In the 17$^{th}$ and 18$^{th}$ centuries, Western countries were extremely eager to reach the profitable Chinese market and to bypass the greedy Ottomans due in large part to China's privileged geological location. Although China had traded their riches with Europe along the Silk Road for centuries, several Chinese governments were reluctant to aid the Europeans to travel to their country. That changed, when—in the 16$^{th}$ century—Europeans were first introduced to an exotic drink from China: tea. Once introduced, the drink became so popular that its price skyrocketed, and the China reluctantly gave in to the profit and progress that tea provided. The Ottomans were quick to buy into the new craze.

The Ottomans had access to Chinese porcelains from the mid-fifteenth century onward. The quality and durability of Chinese ceramics was so great that Topkapi purchased a collection of 10,700 pieces of blue and white Chinese porcelain during the 15$^{th}$, 16$^{th}$, 17$^{th}$, and into the 18$^{th}$ centuries making it one of the finest porcelain collections in the world. By the 18$^{th}$ century the palace collection had 16,566 pieces. The collection ranged from the late Song Dynasty, the Yuan Dynasty, the Ming Dynasty, and the Qing Dynasty. The pieces in the palace included many nearly priceless celadons—otherwise, most expensive Chinese celadons were exported to Eurasia. The exquisite celadons added great ascetic value to the blue and white porcelain which was used as crockery. Many Chinese manufacturers of export porcelain included a wide range of Chinese porcelain made almost exclusively for export to the Ottomans. The bulk export wares in the later years were typically tea wares and dinner services, often blue and white decorated with pagodas, trees, lakes, and pastoral scenes, which became popularly known as the willow style.

The great Qing expansion over their two centuries of power nearly tripled the land area under the control of a single dynasty, and it created permanent domination of the eastern portion of Central Eurasia. It laid the basis for the economic boom, population growth, migration of peoples, and geopolitical claims to hegemony that still underlie the modern Chinese nation-state. Trade between the Qing Dynasty and the Ottoman empire enriched both.

The great traded goods of antiquity continued to be commonly shipped in the Byzantine Empire of the medieval period and throughout the rule of the Seljuks and Ottomans: olive oil, wine, wheat, honey, and fish sauce. Terracotta amphorae were traded at the end of voyages to Constantinople and remained the storage vessel of choice in the Muslim capital. Other goods which were traded between regions of China and the Ottoman Empire included cattle, horses, sheep, pigs, bacon, vegetables, fruit, pepper and other spices, medicines, incense, perfumes, soap, wax, timber, metals, worked gemstones–lapis lazuli, from India and Afghanistan—ornate glass, ivory—raw and carved from India and Africa, worked bone—including disarticulated wrist bones for superstitious predictions and games–flax, wool, textiles, Bulgarian linen, Russian fur, Chinese silver plate and enamels, Baltic amber, bronze, and brass goods–including vessels, statuary, and urns. The brass goods included especially valued buckets and decorated door panels destined for Italy. The slave trade–with slaves supplied from Arab territories and Russia–remained a staple industry.

The Chinese, Greeks, and Portuguese, contributed coarse pottery tableware. The Ottomans favored slipped red-bodied ceramics with stamped or applied decoration in the early years and then slowly replaced them with finer Chinese wares which were lead-glazed, white-bodied, and still later, red-bodied. Decoration for the less fine ceramic ware was impressed, incised, or painted. Constantinople became a major production center and exporter for white-bodied ceramics, and Corinth produced a large quantity of red-wares beginning in the 11th century. Oddly enough, there was considerable overland export traffic of the less valuable ceramic ware towards the Chinese major cities. Russian merchants came to Constantinople via Black Sea ports with their many varied goods. They brought with them caviar, fish, honey, fur, leather goods, and wax, as well as their own textile manufactures.

Silk was the great driving force of commerce from antiquity onward. Best evidence indicates that the history of silk dates to about 3,300 BCE. However, a silk cocoon cut by a sharp knife and primitive loom fragments found in Yangshao culture archeological digs in the Hemudu culture site may push that date back to 4,000 BCE. Bombyx mori–the caterpillar of the domesticated silk moth—was the greatest secret in the history of Chinese commerce. Silk was first introduced from China and trafficked as raw silk, but imported raw silk was eventually replaced by silk produced on mulberry farms [the only food of silkworms] in Phoenicia and then Constantinople from 568 CE.

Silk remained confined to China and treated as a state secret until the Silk Road opened at some point during the latter half of the 1st millennium BCE. The penalty for divulging the secret about the silk-worms or actually carrying a worm and some mulberry leaves out of China was decapitation. Allusions to the fabric in the Old Testament show that it was known in western Asia in biblical times. The first physical evidence of the silk trade per se was the discovery of silk in the hair of an Egyptian mummy of the 21$^{st}$ dynasty, c. 1070 BCE. Scholars believe that starting in the 2$^{nd}$ century BCE, the Chinese established a commercial network aimed at exporting silk to the West

China maintained its virtual monopoly over silk production for another thousand years after that. In fact, China became widely known around the world as the "Kingdom of Clothing and Dresses". After the Tang dynasty, silk spread gradually throughout Chinese culture and finally into commercial trade. Silk and Chinese culture travelled first to the Koreans who were both geographically and socially close to the Chinese. Later, it moved on to the Indians, Malaysia, Vietnam, and to most regions of Asia, as a result of industrial espionage.

By 522 CE, the Byzantines had managed to obtain a significant supply of silkworm eggs and were well enough informed to begin their own sericulture. The silk factory at the Byzantine capital was under imperial control, and the five silk guilds were under the auspices of the Imperial Prefect of the city. Other notable silk-producing sites within the empire included southern Italy, Greek Thebes, and Corinth. The Arabs also began to manufacture silk at the same time. By then, silk was produced in such quantities that it was cheaper that hemp, and its use was no longer only limited to the manufacturing of clothing. Archer's ropes, fishing lines, side filling, and tight bowls for the transport of the water, became other popular functions.

Once the silk trade–and especially after the secrets of sericulture [silk farming] became well-known—silk became an extraordinarily popular luxury fabric in every area accessible to traveling Chinese merchants. The silk road was developed in the 2$^{nd}$ century BCE because of silk, not vice versa. In the 17$^{th}$ century when the Flemish seamen, Piet Corneliuszoon Van Brakel and Captain Jans Fokkenzoon Corren, were in Constantinople; Chinese silk exports had become less important, although they still maintained dominance over the luxury silk market; and they were still highly sought after by the rich people of the Ottoman Empire. The artisans of Constantinople discovered the art and skills of sericulture and the silk brocades of the capital of the Ottoman Empire were highly sought after; and, in fact, became an export product to western Europe and even back to China. Sericulture has become an important cottage industry in countries such as Brazil, China, France, India, Italy, Japan, Korea, and Russia. Today, China and India are the two main producers, with more than 60% of the world's annual production.

# CHAPTER SEVENTEEN

# THE SLAVE AND THE DISCOVERY OF LOVE

IN THE YEAR OF OUR LORD, 1642, LATE-JULY

It was hardly even light out when Bezan awakened Piet and Jans to begin their two days of touring Topkapi and the city itself. How early it was, was punctuated by the muezzin's *adhan* [call to the *Salat al-fajr–* morning prayer] which came almost immediately after the two Flemish sailors opened their eyes. By tradition, the first prayer of the day came before sunrise when the approaching daylight was just sufficient to see a stretched hair to the time when a stick or a pole, acts as an *shakhis* [indicator] is made to stand on a level ground, and its shadow falls to the west at the time the sun begins to rise in the morning; and as the sun continues to rise, the shadow cast by the indicator reduces in size towards nil.

> *"We have awoken, and all of creation has awoken, for Allah, Lord of all the Worlds. Allah, I ask You for the best the day has to offer, victory, support, light, blessings and guidance; and I seek refuge in You from the evil in it, and the evil to come after it,"* sounded the muezzin's powerful baritone voice.

The three men stood silently and respectfully for the period of time it took for the Muslims to recite their prayer for the day. None of them were Muslims, and therefore not required to pray as the Muslims do. Bezan led them out into the faintly increasing sunrise.

"It is a good time to be out and about because this is the time when God's creatures are at their most active. Listen to the music of the bird calls."

They stood silently and listened to the beautiful stains of a nightingale's song, repeated over and over. Two laughing doves cooed back and forth to each other. A Rüppell's Warbler made its call, and it was still dark enough for a Pallid Scops owl to ask "who?" accompanied by the evocative song of a Caspian Snowcock which was wintering in Constantinople. The melodious sounds of the songbirds were interrupted by the harsh call of a whooper swan and the dissident honking of a small flock of Greater White-fronted Geese. A Eurasian kingfisher had to add its noisy call. A mother tufted duck and her ducklings sailing down a canal added their quacking to the background din.

As the morning light suffused the palace and the city, and gave the first indications of what the heat of the day was going to be like, Bezan led his friends to one of his favorite areas of the palace—an aviary to which only the royal family was allowed to visit. A net covered area the size of a Venetian plaza enclosed a myriad—a museum–of live birds attended by several dozen specially trained ornithological keepers.

Bezan took pride in pointing out many of the birds flitting and swooping about. It took only a few minutes to realize that the *kizlar agha* was a veritable encyclopedia of knowledge about birds, and not just those indigenous to Turkey.

He pointed out a dizzying array of local and of highly exotic winged specimens and entertained Piet an Jans with an ongoing patter about many of them: sunbirds, herons, cranes, egrets, thrush nightingale, Eurasian scops owl, bee eater, bald eagle, golden eagle, short-toed eagle, goshawk, falcon, kites, buzzards, harriers, ducks, geese (called goats when large), flamingoes, *hasida* (Heb. In English-stork). Adding to the morning din were screeching peacocks used as guards of the *harem* [Arabic-forbidden place], black and white swans, Ring Ouzel (a Blackbird), with a tuneful song that attracts small birds which it pursues and eats.

Continuing to demonstrate his encyclopedic memory of the aviary's birds, Bezan went on naming ostrich, sparrows, rufous bush robin and White-throated Robin, blue tit, goat head (tufts on head), corvids, jays, nightjae (goat sucking blackbird), *lammergeiers* (vultures), hierax (small eagle), gulls, shearwaters, large black Mediterranean cormorants, finches, 'the Persian bird'–the Himalayan Monal (also known as the Impeyan Pheasant–a bird of the Himalayas which has iridescent plumage ranging from green, purple, blue and bronze, a striking green crest, and a tail that almost touches the ground.

Bezan was enjoying the genuine friendship and attention from his new friends and was showing off a bit for them. He talked faster and pointed out a variety of birds of paradise from Papua, New Guinea, White-breasted Kingfisher, Eurasian Kingfisher (a vividly blue-green back and a noisy call), flying foxes (large fruit-eating bats), long-eared bats, blackheaded bunting, starlings, myna birds, Chelidōn (Rumpf), Yellow Wagtail (a finch-sized bird which is beautifully colored, forages in the grass, frightening horses by imitating their voices and flying belligerently at them—lives by rivers and marshes), swifts, woodcock, partridge, francolins, pelican, wrens, flycatcher, common] whitethroat warbler, crow and hooded crow.

The most fascinating birds in the collection were tiny creatures that Piet and Jans had never seen or even heard of. Some—minuscule winged jewels that buzzed around their heads in tiny clouds—were particularly fascinating and perplexing; Piet and Jans could scarcely believe they were real.

"Those tiny birds cause one to question whether they are large insects or tiny birds. The French call them *oiseaux mouches* [bird flies], the Portuguese call them *beija-flores* [flower kissers] or *chupa-flores* [flower suckers]; and the Spanish name is *picaflores* [flower stingers]. The English have an amusing name for the amazing little creatures. Some call them humbirds, and others like the name 'hummingbird'. I like that name best as well. Listen for the buzzing of their wings. Some very tiny species in Brazil are known as called *besourinhos* [little beetles], and the people of the island of Cuba have a bee hummingbird they all the "*zunzuncito*". It is a word that comes from the sound the bird makes— the English call that an '*onomatopoeia*' [Greek: listen or sound]. The German name is *Kolibri*, and the Spanish call them *Colibri* (a bird whose body was "no larger than that of a hornet or a stag beetle), ruby throated hummingbird, weighing in at slightly over one-tenth of an ounce (barely 4 grams), was the most beautiful of all the hummingbirds.

"I see them as 'the soul in flight'," Bezan offered as an insight into his own sensitive soul.

Jans remembered an experience from his childhood related to birds, "My mother once took me to the Rijksmuseum in Amsterdam. I still remember a bird painting named, *De Jumantsubo vlakte te Susaki bij Fukagawa, Hiroshige, Utagawa* [english: The Jumantsubo plain at Susaki near Fukagawa, Hiroshige, Utagawa]."

"I have been to the museum myself, but I don't remember that painting," Piet admitted.

"I have been there on four occasions, and also to Japan where the actual scene exists," Bezan told them."

"You never cease to amaze me, My Friend," Jans said.

It was approaching mid-morning, and the heat of the day was becoming oppressive.

Bezan told Jans and Piet that it was time for them to go to the seraglio, "perhaps the most interesting place in all of Constantinople, or even Turkey."

There was so much secrecy and security surrounding the *seraglio* [women's apartments, harem] that Piet felt nervous and awkward. He was glad to be in the company of the large and politically powerful Black Eunuch. They passed a protective phalanx of Nubian eunuchs holding large, razor sharp Persian white scimitars. Once in the chambers, Jans and Piet were impressed to the point of speechlessness about three things: the opulence of the large chambers which were crowded with priceless carpets, wall hangings, couches, and draperies; the crowds of people—women and eunuchs—so numerous that there was scarcely a place to sit; and the women, ah, the women!

Piet and Jans had not been even as close to a woman as arms-length in a year. Damped down longings rushed to the surface, and the two men bit their tongues to force the feelings and responses back into the far reaches of their minds. There were beautiful women from all races, ethnicities, and lands. There tall blond Nordics, sinewy muscular blacks, short slavs, and petite, doll-like Asian girls. They universally seemed bored, and almost afraid to allow their eyes to travel to the two fascinating men in their midst. Unlike anything either man had ever seen, almost none of the women were covered from the waist up. Piet's stringent Dutch Reformed Church upbringing gripped him with a nagging sense of shame at what he was seeing. But, his healthy masculinity put up a stern resistance to his religious feelings. He knew he had to get out of there soon before his body betrayed him.

Bezan diverted his attention, "Take note, Gentlemen, every woman here—slave or free—is a wife of Sultan Ibrahim. The holy book of the Muslims allows the sultan to have as many as five wives of the imperial rank of Kadin, and an unlimited number of wives with the rank of Ikbal. Of those women, he has two hundred."

Jans and Piet struggled not to gasp in disbelief. But, they were standing among a huge number of gorgeous women, maybe as many as a hundred.

"*No man can manage that many women,*" Piet thought. "*He would wither away to nothing in a month.*"

He held that thought and changed to, "*what a terrible, boring, unfulfilling, life this must be. Knowing women, it must be a den of infighting, scheming, and manipulating.*"

Piet would have been shocked to know just how accurate his thinking was.

He was jolted back to full attention when he looked towards one of the exits. The beautiful angelic Dutch girl he had seen the previous day was standing with three other young women—more accurately, girls. She was weeping silently and appeared to be completely disconsolate in comparison to the woman lounging on couches without a care or interest in the world.

The reason for the sorrow pouring out of the girl became evident in less than a minute. Two of the eunuchs walked up to her, placed a metal neck band and wrist and ankle shackles on her delicate skin. The ankle shackles allowed her to make slow short steps. She was wearing an embarrassingly sheer middle-class *cübbe* [mid-length robe with a diagonal opening down the front]. Despite her efforts to keep herself covered, the lack of a sash or cummerbund made that nearly impossible with her shackles in place.

Piet could not bear what he was seeing. He moved his body in preparation for a dash across the room to help the girl. Bezan anticipated the move and knocked him to the ground.

"You will be slashed to pieces if you take even one step in that direction. Fortunately for you, no one has noticed you yet."

Piet gnashed his teeth, but remained still, his blood boiling.

The girl and her three companions were dragged out of the room. Piet felt like weeping.

He controlled himself in time to be able to be introduced to a regal woman who walked away from the slaves and over to where the Europeans and the Black Eunuch were standing.

Bezan made the introductions, "Great Valide Sultana, may I present the two Flemish sailors of whom your magnificent husband, the sultan, spoke. This is Piet Corneliuszoon Van Brakel, and this man is Jans Fookenzoon Corren. Gentlemen, I have the honor to present Valide Kösem Sultan, who is Sultan Ibrahim's greatly esteemed mother and the utmost authority in the Imperial Harem who rules over all other women in the household.

"*Hanimefendi* [Madam]," Bezan became fully formal by using the title given to the imperial consort of the Sultan of the Ottoman Empire. "You do us honor by allowing us to enter the forbidden area, but even more so to deign to speak to such as us."

The valide sultana looked the men over with eyes that missed nothing.

"Young man, I saw your reaction to the three slaves who were going away to be sold at the Constantinople auction. They are odalisques—female slaves or concubines, whose lives are decreed to take place in a harem, especially odalisques in the seraglio of the Sultan of Turkey. Be cautious and do not be dismayed; it is our way; and nothing you feel or do can change it. However, Mr. Van Brakel, you may have the privilege to purchase a slave because you are a Man of the Book—but more importantly—because I give you permission. No one will challenge you."

The auction was scheduled to begin at the stroke of one o'clock in the afternoon, a little over an hour from that moment. Piet again had to exercise control, this time to keep from dashing out of the seraglio and towards the center of the city.

Bezan waited until the three men were once again away from the cloistered and stifling harem apartments.

"Piet," he said, "It is fitting that I tell you that the valide sultana is of slave origin herself, and she maintains a soft place in her heart for girls who find themselves to be nothing more than chattel. We are headed in the direction of the slave auction. There is no need to hurry; it would be unseemly. We will get there in time, I assure you."

Bezan led his new friends past what was once the Byzantine Column of Arcadius. After the Ottoman conquest and the changes that remodeled Constantinople, it was located in what became known as *Avrat Pazarı* [Women's Market]. Bezan called it one of the many talismans of the city. There was an ancient a fairy-cheeked female figure on its summit, which brought birds to the area and that subsequently fell to the earth and provided the city with food according to legend. Next to the throne stood a life-sized golden tree—the object of the visit by the three sightseers. On its metal branches perched dozens of gilded man-made birds, each somehow singing the song of its particular species. The mouths of those birds were opened by some kind of mechanical device, and the song filled the air as if by magic.

As they made their way through the labyrinthine streets of Constantinople, Bezan continued to play his role of professor.

"I am sure you are familiar with the lore surrounding birds, My Friends. If not, let me refresh your memories about birds' eggs: He who eats an owl's eggs will always be shrieking. He who eats a dove's egg will be followed by ill luck. The egg of any bird with yellow plumage will cause a fever. Any person who eats a mockingbird's eggs will never keep a secret. Any person who robs a kissdeer's nest and eats its eggs will certainly break an arm. Eat a bird's egg of one with blue plumage will be restless so long as he or she lives; no place will have the power to hold you long."

Piet and Jans each raised an eyebrow, but Bezan appeared to be serious; so, it was the better part of politics not to react more than that.

As they passed Blue Mosque, Bezan pointed to an exquisitely authentic appearing tree made of bronze. Its delicate branches were filled with filled with birds–crafted of bronze and gilded over. When they were close enough, the two sailors were dumbfounded to hear that those gilded birds emitted cries appropriate to their different species. Bezan could not tell them how that was accomplished.

They took a rest, got a drink of water from the underground Basilica Cistern—located 150 meters southwest of the Hagia Sophia—and waited for the vizier to arrive. He had been requested by the valide sultan to make Piet's way easier at the slave auction.

Piet and Jans were too absorbed in their admiration of the remarkable cistern to be aware when the vizier slipped up beside them.

Bezan saw him immediately and nudged the two sailors.

"Gentlemen, I have the honor to present, the Grand Vizier Kemankeş Kara Mustafa Pasha."

Almost reflexively, Piet and Jans gave a polite bow. The grand vizier nodded to them and called each man by name in heavily accented Dutch. They acknowledged his effort and rewarded the second most powerful man in the Ottoman Empire with an appreciative smile.

The grand vizier switched to English, "Gentlemen, Kizlar agha, the time is nearly upon us when the auction will commence. The valide sultan would scold me sharply if I did not get us there on time. There is a bit of business to which I must attend before you nonbelievers are permitted even to be present. A little baksheesh will have to change hands to allow you to make a purchase."

They hurried to the *Yesirf bezestan* [covered market] in silence. There, they met an *ajamee* [apprentice slave dealer] who had been prearranged by the valide sultan to escort the four men to the *esir pazan* [special market] for the Wednesday weekly auction. The *ajamee* swept past the guards with his entourage in tow and to the *esir ham* [the self-contained slave market building unique to Constantinople]. The apprentice slave dealer stopped at small office immediately outside the gate to the *esir pazan* building. A sign in Turkish on the office door read, "Bazaar for the sale of female slaves". The *ajamee* stepped aside to allow the grand vizier to speak to the director of the *esir pazan* and the weekly auctions.

The deference shown the grand vizier was no less than groveling. The director bowed so low that his forehead nearly touched the floor.

"How can such a humble one as I serve the grand vizier of the sultanate?"

The grand vizier maintained the haughty facial expression of a stone statue, and said simply, "My associates wish to observe the auction and to make purchases if they find a worthy choice."

The director asked the pro forma question, "Are they Believers or Men of the Book, oh great one?"

"They are my friends, Director," the grand vizier replied in an obvious *non sequitur.*

"Do you see any issue with the sultan's edict, Great Sir?"

The edict forbad attendance at the slave auctions by nonMuslims to prevent European tourists and sex-slave traders from being present and absolutely prohibited nonMuslims from purchasing or transporting slaves from Constantinople. It dictated that all members of the slave dealers guild must be Muslims and approved by the government. Slave dealers were thereby prohibited from applying either white face paint or rouge to slave girls to disguise negresses and are enjoined not to cover the girls up with excessive clothing. For anyone else, that would have been a serious quandary; but the grand vizier was not "anyone else". He was, in fact, the author of the edict.

"This is a special case, Director, a legal exception."

It was said with such finality, that the director ceased speaking. The grand vizier passed a velvet bag full of ducats as baksheesh, thereby ending the negotiations.

"For the *pencik*", the grand vizier said as he and his guests left the office and headed for a privileged front row seat in the auction area.

There were various taxes to be paid on the importation and selling of slaves for the benefit of the empire and its sultan. One of them was the "*pençik*" [literally "one fifth"]. This taxation was based on verses of the *Qur'an*, according to which one fifth of the spoils of war belonged to God, to the Prophet and his family, to orphans, to those in need, and to travelers.

The *esir pazan* occupied an area where the former Byzantine slave market had stood. It was a large quadrangular court, two stories high, surrounded by a portico, with a gallery above. Each story contained 300 small wooden cells similar to those in a monastery. The cells constituted the walls of the auction and spectator areas completely surrounding it.

The ground floor was for the blacks; the second floor was for the light-skinned beauties of Circassia, Georgia, and Greece. There was a large platform for display of slaves to be auctioned. Attached to one area of the wall was a rather decrepit coffeehouse and near it was a half ruined old mosque. Around the three habitable sides of the court ran an open colonnade, supported by wooden columns, and approached by steps at the angles. Under the colonnade were platforms, separated from each other by low railings and benches. As the day progressed, the railings and benches were filled with men—mostly old men—smoking, drinking coffee, and lazily haggling over prices, waiting for the show to begin.

At exactly one o'clock, a gong sounded; and a parade of slaves were marched out from a cell area and across the platform. In keeping with the edict that the slaves not be excessively covered, every person, male and female, old men and women, children—intact and castrated—was completely naked. They received a crisp blow from a club if they attempted to cover themselves. Men holding numbered cards quickly mounted the platform to make their choices. The men who wished to purchase a slave—or were just dirty old voyeurs and abusers—examined the slave's eyes, their teeth, all parts of their bodies, including their secret parts. The purpose of the nakedness was for the convenience of the purchasers so that the men could more easily determine the poor creatures' faults and imperfections.

The beautiful young blond Dutch girl was not in the first three groups of human property for sale.

"Will she be on the block today? Will she be brought out soon?" Piet asked, his anxiety beginning to interfere with his control.

The grand vizier said calmly, "She will. The valide sultan wills it."

Bezan explained, "Those who were just sold or returned to the cells, came from the middle chambers—second raters. The Dutch girl will be in the next set; notice that the guards are opening the doors to the south and east where the best quality is kept. Early in the day, the slave traders lead away the tithe of the captives which once belonged to the emperor. They are destined for domestic work in the rich houses of the empire. The rest are sent to the *Avrat* bazaar for sale. In the *Avrat*—unlike here in the *esir pazan*—one buys the mother, another the child, another a boy, another a girl. In the *Avrat*, in one place sit old men, in another young men of ripe age, in another place boys. Any of them with the day's price who to purchase a boy leads him into one of the separate rooms, strips him, inspects his limbs—and if he likes him—he buys him.

"The most expensive slaves are those between ten and thirty-five years of age. The highest prices go for European virgin girls thirteen to twenty-five years of age and teenaged boys. Circassian girls were described by the slave sellers as fair and light-skinned. They were the most expensive, reaching up to 500 Venetian ducats or Ottoman sultani gold coins. Second in popularity are Syrian girls. Turks are fascinated by their dark eyes, dark hair, and light brown skin. Their price could reach up to thirty ducats. The slave sellers advertise them as having 'good figures when young'.

"Eunuchs are a special group among the slaves. A 10-year-old child's price will be ten ducats or less in today's market, a castrated boy of the same age will easily be worth thirty. A white widow may fetch thirty-five ducats. Nubian girls—especially the dark ones like me—are housed on the bottom floor in the worst cells. They are the cheapest and least popular, fetching only twenty ducats or less."

The next set of slaves were pulled from the south and east doors and onto the platform. There were a few indiscrete cat-calls and descriptions of the attractive white women and the sweetest looking little castrated boys. Piet's Dutch girl was third in the line after a statuesque Circassian woman and two castrated boys who were sold with only minimal mauling and even less haggling over price.

The Dutch girl was next. She knew she was being ogled and was ashamed. She reached to cover her private parts and received a quick blow for her efforts. An old, rather enfeebled old man cackled out a bid for fifty ducats. The crowd of men laughed. A boy—obviously from a rich family—shouted out a seventy-five ducat offer.

Bezan and the grand vizier nodded to Piet.

"Eighty ducats," he called.

"Ninety," the boy countered.

"One hundred," Piet called out trying not to sound desperate.

"One hundred fifty," the old man croaked.

The guild slave seller challenged him, "Show me that you have 150 or more ducats, old man; or you will be arrested if you continue bidding."

He lowered his head and slunk away.

The slave seller glanced meaningfully at Bezan and the grand vizier who responded with almost imperceptible head nods.

"Sold to the fair-haired man," declaimed the slaver.

He had the Dutch girl's neck ring hack-sawed off and had her riveted-on bracelets cut off. They represented that she belonged to the Sultan's harem. Piet was expected to examine her to prove his indifference to the girl as a human being. He swallowed deeply and walked up the stairs to the platform.

As he approached the girl, she begged in Dutch, "Please do not hurt me, Sir. I am young and untouched. I will not fight you."

Piet put his jacket over her, covering her to her mid thighs.

He spoke gently and quietly in Dutch, "*Je bent nu veilig. Ik zal voor je zorgen.*" [You are safe now. I will care for you], and you will be set free as soon as we can leave Turkey."

She was astonished, and for the first time since she was kidnapped from the ship with her family, she began to cry.

Piet wiped her tears—paid the one hundred ducats—and took hold of her hand. He led her down the stairs and over to where the grand vizier, Jans, and Bezan, were standing.

"We need to leave promptly," said the grand vizier, "before anyone with any standing realizes what has just taken place."

## THE HISTORY
## HISTORY OF THE JANISSARIES 1365-1826

The Janissaries were a specialized Islamic military corps–the first full-time trained army since the fall of the Roman Empire and the first standing army in European history. Sultan Murad I [(1362–1389] founded the elite special military corps about 1365 to be the Ottoman Sultan's household troops and bodyguards. Originally, the Janissaries were made up solely of *dhimmi* [non-Muslims—usually 'men' of the book, who were granted the privilege to live in peace under Islamic law by paying a set of two taxes–the *jizya*, a poll tax, and the *kharja,* a land tax. A privilege of being a Muslim in the lands controlled by Muslims was freedom from those taxes, another was general discrimination against non-Muslims—early on a nonviolent form of second-class citizenship. For example, although *dhimmis* were allowed under Sharia law to perform their religious rituals, they were obliged to do so in a manner not conspicuous to Muslims. Display of non-Muslim religious symbols–such as crosses or icons–was prohibited on buildings and on clothing. There were serious consequences of violating the rather rigid Islamic laws related to "non-believers" in the Islamic dominated countries.

Janissaries began as slaves and became an elite corps made up of kidnapped young Christian boys who were taken away from their families and homelands. Select prisoners of war were enslaved as Janissaries as well. Some fell under Islamic rule as tribute taken from conquered Christian cities. The *jizya* tax is from the *Qur'an*–Sura 9:29— which stipulates that *jizya* be exacted from non-Muslims as a condition required for jihad to cease. Many–but not all–converted to Islam; and conversion was not always forced upon them. In fact–during some periods–they were not encouraged to do so; and at others they were forbidden to do so. While they were slaves, they were so famous for their internal cohesion cemented by strict discipline and order; that–unlike other slaves–they received regular salaries. Despite their putative slave status, their vaunted military skill and internal cohesion as a unit gave them unique power.

They were forbidden to marry or engage in trade by the sultans, who jealously guarded the special relationship between him and his guards. For receiving special privileges, their complete loyalty to the Sultan was required.

Many important Muslims became concerned and disgruntled by the arrogant bullying by the Janissaries. An occasional sultan determined to enforce limitations on the corps, but the powerful and elite unit was strong enough to resist even the sultans they served. By the seventeenth century, there was a dramatic increase in the size of the regular Ottoman standing army. To compensate and to increase their numbers, the Janissaries corps' originally stern and strict recruitment policy was relaxed. Corruption began to creep in as the corps became richer, more powerful, and less beholden to the sultans. In time, civilians were able to buy their way into the corps in order to benefit from the improved socioeconomic status it conferred to its membership.

Gradually–but not altogether slowly–the corps began to lose its military character and to become more of an enriching and vain civilian organization.

It is often forgotten that the Janissaries were part of the royal army as well as the personal guards of the sultan. They were not at all the main force of the Ottoman military. In the early years, Janissaries were only one tenth of the overall Ottoman army, while the traditional Turkish cavalry made up the rest of the main battle force. Records indicate that the number of Janissaries in the 14th century was 1,000 and increased to about 6,000 in 1475. But the number of *Timarli Sipahi* [provincial cavalry which constituted the main force of the army was 40,000 well equipped and trained men]. The Ottoman Empire used Janissaries in all its major campaigns–including the 1453 capture of Constantinople–and they became rich from their share of the spoils similar to the modern day Revolutionary Guard of Iran.

As Janissaries became aware of their own importance, they began to desire a better life. By the early 17th century Janissaries had such prestige and influence that they dominated the government despite their comparatively small numbers. They could mutiny and dictate policy and hinder efforts to modernize the army structure. They could change Sultans as they wished through palace coups. They made themselves into rich landholders and tradesmen. They also changed policy to limit the enlistment to the sons of former Janissaries who did not have to go through the original training period in the *acemi oğlan* and were allowed to avoid the exacting physical selection, thereby reducing their military value. Since the Janissaries could effectively extort money from the sultan; and since business and family life replaced the original martial fervor, their effectiveness as combat troops decreased even further. As a result, the northern borders of the Ottoman Empire slowly began to shrink southwards after the second Battle of Vienna in 1683.

In 1449 they revolted for the first time, demanding higher wages–which they obtained. The stage was set for an evolution into decadence. After 1451, every new Sultan felt obligated to pay each Janissary a reward and to raise his pay rank. Sultan Selim II gave in and allowed Janissaries permission to marry in 1566 which undermined the exclusivity of loyalty to the dynasty. By 1622, the Janissaries were deemed to be a serious threat to the stability of the empire. Through their greed, hedonism, and lack of discipline, they became—to all intents and purposes–a law unto themselves. They brought themselves to the level that–against modern European armies—they were ineffective on the battlefield as a fighting force from that time forward.

In 1622, the teenage Sultan Osman II–after an Ottoman defeat during war against Poland–determined to curb Janissary excesses. Outraged at becoming "subject to his own slaves", he tried to disband the Janissary corps, blaming it for the disaster during the Polish war. In the spring, hearing rumors that the Sultan was preparing to move against them, the Janissaries revolted and took the Sultan captive, imprisoning him in the notorious Seven Towers; he was murdered shortly afterwards.

The Janissaries were a highly formidable military unit in the early years, and generally feared as an incorruptible and merciful fighting force. As the process of becoming a more or less civilian organization, they became reactionary and more interested in their tradition, their accumulation of riches, and in accruing power for themselves rather than providing crucial service to their sultan. At the same time, Western Europe swiftly modernized its military organization, military discipline, and technology. Too preoccupied with their own concepts of self-importance, the Janissaries became a reactionary force that resisted all change. That fit the general static character of the religion of Islam; and apparently, no one was fully aware of the danger of the changes occurring around them.

Steadily the Ottoman military power became outdated. Instead of seeking to improve, to learn from their opponents, and from their own mistakes; the Janissaries reacted as threatened and frightened bullies. As the Janissaries observed that their treasured privileges were being threatened, or when outsiders offered to modernize them—usually by going to the sultan of the period–or particularly when they believed that they were at risk of the sultan deciding to supersede them by cavalrymen, they did the unthinkable. They rose in rebellion to bite the hand that fed them.

In 1807, a Janissary revolt deposed Sultan Selim III, who had tried to modernize the army along Western European lines. The rebellions became highly violent on the side of the Janissary rebels and on the side of the regular army, now the favorites of the sultans. Ever mindful of the Janissary threat, the sultan spent the next several years discreetly securing his position. The Janissaries' abuse of power, military ineffectiveness, resistance to reform, and the cost of salaries to a bloated and soft corps by then numbering 135,000 men–many of whom were not actually serving soldiers–had all become intolerable to Sultan Mahmud II.

The Janissaries were suppressed but at a serious cost to the Ottoman Empire. The cost came at the expense of the empire itself and was irreparable. It was too late for Ottoman military power to catch up with the West. By 1826, the sultan was ready to move against the Janissaries in favor of a more modern military. The sultan informed them–through a religious *fatwa*–that he was forming a new army, organized and trained along modern European lines. Predictably, they mutinied and advanced against the sultan's palace. In the ensuing fight, the Janissary barracks were set in flames by artillery fire resulting in 4,000 Janissary fatalities. The survivors were either exiled or executed; and their possessions were confiscated by the Sultan. Finally, the corps was abolished altogether by Sultan Mahmud II that year in what came to be called "the Auspicious Incident", during which more than 6,000 Janissaries were arrested and executed. The last of the Janissaries were then put to death by decapitation in what was later called the Tower of Blood, in Thessaloniki. The Janissaries were no more; and the inevitable decline of the empire brought it to its own end in 1913, during World War I.

# CHAPTER EIGHTEEN
## ANNEKE AND PIET

Piet followed the recommendations of Grand Vizier Kemankeş Kara Mustafa Pasha to the letter to protect Anneke from kidnapper/ slavers. It did not take long for him to realize that Anneke had a middle [descriptive] name and a family name of which she was very proud. In total, she was Anneke Blandina van den Voor-Hees. The middle name must have been prophetic on part of her father—Blandina, diminutive for fair-haired. Jans, Piet, and Aslan—when they were again able to reunite—had no illusions about the danger the beautiful young girl faced. The triumvirate was always fully armed and never once allowed her to be entirely out of their sight, not even when she took care of private needs. Men ogled her, postured for her, and followed her. Jans and Aslan recognized how fully smitten Piet was by her, and they became increasingly avuncular towards her. Piet and Anneke often laughed at the two older men as they vied with each other for her platonic affections.

Once the specter of her fate at the hands of slave-owners dissipated, Anneke began to come out of her protective shell and interacted with the three men as if they were family. Piet made sure that she came to look upon him as a very proper suitor; and that, in time—when she and Piet grew accustomed to each other—she would be able to see him as more than her savior or big brother, but as a possible husband. Her vivacious personality blossomed out of the shell of silence she had maintained during her time as a harem slave of Sultan Ibrahim. They learned that her birthday–her fifteenth birthday—was to occur on September 21. This caused a flurry of activity on the part of the men, and endless giggles and blushing of the girl as the new little family prepared for the celebration. She missed her fourteenth birthday while she was on a slave ship covering herself with dirt, clothing herself in old, torn, and filthy, rags to tone down her radiant beauty as much as was possible.

One of the men watched her as the other two went off through the enormous and old Grand Bazaar. It was established in 1455 and grew exponentially in the succeeding two centuries. Sultan Mehmet II had erected it as an edifice devoted to the trading of textiles and precious jewels near his palace in Constantinople. He called it the *Bezzâzistan-ı Cedîd* [New Bedesten-*Bedestan* of Gems and bazaar of the cloth sellers]. All three men surrounded Anneke anytime they even came near to the *Esir Pazarı* [the slave market]. They enjoyed a sense of freedom and excitement when they took their girl to the *Sahaflar Carsisi* [old book market]. Anneke was the treasured only daughter of a rich commercial family, and she was given an education that rivaled the best offered to the scions of the elite of Europe.

She proved to be very intelligent and inquisitive, which endeared her to the tutors her parents provided, and she developed a love for books. At home, she grew up in a Dutch speaking home; and her education in school and onboard trading vessels provided an opportunity to learn French, English, and Italian—the languages of trade. Her captivity made her fluent enough in Arabic and Turkish to understand most of them when she was spoken to. One of her loves during her life in the harem was Persian poetry which gave her a smattering of that mellifluous language.

Aslan took it to be one of his important duties to teach her to speak Turkish fluently well. Over three months, she was fluent enough to speak usefully with a Dutch accent, and during the lengthy periods spent in a caravan after they left Constantinople, her Turkish became almost accent free. By dint of her personal efforts, she was able to use a larger vocabulary than most of the workmen around her.

Asland and Anneke settled in to enjoy the musty old books, and Anneke delighted in finding a beautifully bound and well protected copy of the complete works of the founder of Persian poetry and literature,

Rudaki, a book of *hairens* [couplets with a single coherent theme] by the Armenian medieval poet, Nahapet Kuchak, and Saib Tabrizi, a Persian poet. Anneke was familiar with Tabrizi's style of classical Arabic and Persian lyric poetic *ghazals* [rhyming couplets] and could recite a few of the beautiful passages from memory. Even if the girl had not had such striking beauty, her charm and intelligence would have won over the vast majority of Europeans and Asians.

While Anneke looked with real joy in other nooks and crannies of the wonderful old bookstore, Aslan secretly purchased Rudaki's book of *hairens* for his birthday present to her. As they walked back into the bazaar to meet up with Piet and Jans, Anneke softly recited a stanza from one of Rudaki's poems, probably written when he was blind:

> *I saw a bird near the city of Sarakhs*
> *It had raised its song to the clouds*
> *I saw a colorful chador on it*
> *So many colors on its chador*

"That is beautiful, Dear Anneke," Asland said in Persian.

"*Sepaas*," [Persian-Thanks] she said. And again, "*Teşekkür ederim*," [Turkish-Thank you], which made him laugh with pleasure.

During Anneke's and Asland's absence in the bookstore, Piet and Jans had done their own haggling and shopping. Piet had asked the jeweler to find him the best that he had. After a fifteen-minute search and thirty-minutes of friendly haggling, Piet settled on a magnificent Ottoman aigrette made of gold, several good diamonds, and a rainbow of other colored gemstones. The hardened old jeweler was actually touched by the obvious love that the ardent young man had for his girl and made as little profit as his family could bear. Jans settled on an Ottoman jade and gem set *Qur'an* box. The box itself was oval shaped and made of silver, and it was studded with a variety of large precious stones. He had fancied a beautiful ruby ring from Burma but had finally decided that it would appear too much as if he were a suitor instead of an adoring uncle. Piet made the most extravagant purchase of his life after a lengthy but enjoyable ritual of haggling—a gorgeous and very large pearl ring set in almost pure gold.

They were nearing the end of their stay in Constantinople, and the caravanners needed to fill up the sturdy leather and wicker packs on their now seven thousand dromedary [Arabic] camels and two thousand tough little Moroccan ponies for the long trek to the sea. Asland and Jans stayed with Anneke while Piet returned to the Topkapi Palace to meet with the grand vizier and the Chief Black Eunuch, Bezan. The two astute men wanted to profit from their association with Aslan and the two Flemish sailors. It would be a serious matter of trust on both sides. The Constantinopolitans understood that the Europeans could simply abscond with the treasures of the caravan, and the Europeans had to trust the Topkapi officials that the value of the commodities were what they said they were and that they would not be accosted by a palace led guard unit posing as bandits.

After pleasant greetings, the Grand Vizier lead Piet and Bezan to the camp of the Chinese traders. Jans stayed behind to ensure that Anneke was safe and secure in an obscure palace room on the lower floor of one of the mid-size and obscure courtyards where she was to stay with one of the valide sultana's most trusted and valued *kalfas* [ladies-in-waiting]. Until the return of her men, Anneke was ensconced in the *kalfa's* personal apartment.

He caught up with Piet and the Grand Vizier as they drew close to the lavish Chinese encampment. They were met by the Imperial Envoy of the Chinese delegation to Constantinople, Zhuang Han Zhidi of the Eastern Han, himself. The Grand Vizier took the lead and bowed low, taking care to bow a little lower than the Chinese leader.

"Mr. Zhuang, it is once again a pleasure and an honor to meet with you. We have come from the court of Sultan Ibrahim to conduct business as we agreed three days past."

"The honor and pleasure are mine, oh, Great Vizier. May the God of Heaven shine his blessings on you and your father as well as on the sultan and his esteemed family."

"The tent in which we stand is a monument to the splendor of Qing society. May I congratulate you?"

"This is but a humble tent, but it pleases me that you enjoy a small view of our silks and carpets, metal ware, and precious gems. But, let us wait until after the serving of tea–also named "*cha dao*" [the way of tea or the art of tea]–before getting into the tedious details of business."

"As civilized men would do," said the Grand Vizier.

Mr. Zhuang struck a small gong with a padded leather mallet. In a matter of seconds, a trio of fairy-like, small, and exquisite, girls glided into the room bearing a bowl full of tea leaves, teapots, spoons, cups, and saucers. All three girls were wearing a traditional *kua*: the ensemble has two parts: a jacket and a floor-length skirt in brilliant fire red. The jacket featured a Chinese-style collar with line designs in gold thread. The jackets fit the delicate girls' beautiful figures and had widened sleeves that ended below their elbows. The jackets had buttons that opened to the front which was lined by gold thread. The gold line and flower designs covered the jackets' fronts, sleeves, and backs. The skirts fell nearly to the floor like ball gowns, giving a bold, grand, appearance.

One girl served to hold the tea and gifts on a pearl white serving plate while the other girl prepared the tea. She first asked Mr. Zhuang if he and the guests had agreed upon the ceremony time and who was to be served first.

He nodded at the guests. All proceeded in silence to follow Lu Yu's *The Classic Art of Tea*. The highly esteemed poet and former Buddhist priest had strict notions about the proper procedure for brewing, steeping, and serving tea; and his book had become the Asian world's Bible for the tea ceremony.

The third girl stood behind to ensure there was always enough warm tea to refill the small tea pot.

For the formal serving, Mr. Zhuang was the first to present the tea and to pour cups for the other men. Then, he indicated to the Grand Vizier to take his turn. Each man served to the eldest man first and on down to Piet, the youngest. For every man, there were four teacups on the tea tray. They were careful always to serve the teacups with both hands and greet the men they served by their formal title in the family. That mantra was repeated multiple times.

The serving girl said, "Father, please drink the tea," as she served him, and he repeated the ritual to the Grand Vizier, who repeated it to Aslan, and Aslan to Piet.

After drinking the tea, the host presented gifts to the guests in the form of red packets and a beautifully crafted piece of jewelry to each man.

As he gave the gifts, Mr. Zhuang said to each guest, "Esteemed and honored guest, may the God of Heaven pour out his blessings of safety and prosperity upon you."

The tea ceremony was finished when all the guests and Mr. Zhuang and the girls were served.

Piet broke the formal and reverential spell of the perfect tea ceremony, "Mr. Zhuang, never have I seen such beautiful ceremony. You and your girls should be very proud. If I could be so bold, I would like to make a request of you and your family. My friends and I have become wards of a truly lovely young woman, much the same beauty and character of your own daughters. I would be greatly appreciative if you would teach my Anneke how to perform the ceremony. She is very bright and learns quickly."

Mr. Zhuang took the request as a high compliment to his family and to his culture.

"It is only rarely done, young man. But your courtesy and plain speaking have pleased me, and it also pleases me that you did not ask for some valued treasure while I am feeling in a generous mood. That does credit to you and to your father."

"Thank you, Chief Envoy."

After a brief rest and a walk together in the growing dusk, talk of business began. Because of the peace and tranquility of the tea ceremony—the "*he*" which translates to "peace", the "*jing*" which translates as "quiet", the *yi*" which means "enjoyment", and the "*zhen*" which most closely meant "truth"; the trading proceeded without rancor or unreasonable demands from either side. During the Qing dynasty, trade had become problematical because the court and the Manchus made many rules to interfere with commerce and exchange of information with foreigners; had too much wealth and therefore no need of external wealth and its accompanying taint to the Qing culture; they had strict set of rules that people had to follow in order to trade which sharply decreased profits; and the foreign traders had to pay damaging VATs and assorted other fees.

Chief Envoy Zhuang held to a more liberal policy, and he was far away from the court in Beijing. He proposed an understanding among themselves and their countries that would allow an increase in profit for all. He knew he was taking a risk, but he was sure that the Europeans were a trustworthy pair. When he met Anneke, he was captivated and began a course beneficial to the Europeans which could have placed him in grave danger from his Mongol masters.

In the end, Piet, Jans, and Aslan, filled the majority of the caravan's camel loads with Chinese goods: Green tea: that not fermented during processing and thus retains the original color of the tea leaves. The most famous green tea was the expensive Dragon Well tea, grown on the hillsides of Hangzhou with a mild, mellow, sweet, chestnut, flavor. It thrived in high elevations with cool temperatures and had a sweeter, softer, taste than the other tea plants and thus, beneficial in herbal medicine. All tea leaves for the caravan were harvested by hand. Chinese coolies from the camp carefully loaded ponies with the precious leaves, and hundreds of camel paniers were pressed full of the most beautiful patterned silks any of the Europeans had ever seen, indicative of what the Qing dynasty had been withholding.

Skilled Chinese traveling tradesmen very carefully packed bag after bag of Yixing and porcelain teapots, heavy iron and steel tools and weapons, raw minerals and their derivative products—objects of trade that should have been classified as prestige goods; but the Chief Enjoy turned them into common-use goods with a stroke of calligraphy. There were prestige goods aplenty—gold, silver, gems, glass and asbestos, and common use goods—steel, copper, lead, and tin.

Piet was awed by a beautiful kind of translucent Chinese glassware and commented about it.

Mr. Zhang called it, "petrified ice" and believed that his description was correct.

Like the Greeks, Romans, and Italians, before them, Piet and Jans—the foreigners—were most appreciative to obtain a large list of gems in the commercial transactions: sapphires and diamonds from the West coasts of India; lapis-lazuli from Kokcha Valley of northern Afghanistan; rubies from Ceylon; Baltic amber; coral and pearls, from the Red Sea and India; and Nephite jade from Central Asia. In addition to other sources, Sri Lanka and Burma provided sapphires, rubies, and topaz, over the Silk Route;

while India was famous for its green agateso, beryls, gold, silver, white jade, and pearls. From the region called Vietnam, the Chief Envoy told his customers, came a tribe known as the shark-people who lived under the sea of Champa's coast; they were rich in pearls. From there and from the capital city of Beijing came strings of true pearls as large as a quail's egg and golden chains fit for the neck of a potentate.

And there was gold, fifty camelback loads of it.

"We have plenty," Mr. Zhang said, "We have our marvelous gold mining-ants. I, myself, have seen skins of the *myrmeces* [very large ants], which dig up our gold."

Throughout the history of China, gold was the most valuable thing in the entire world; it was immortal and never decayed.

The well-known Chief Chinese Envoy, explained that, "Because of gold's amazing ability to last through a plethora of harmful exposures and to demonstrate a magical longevity, in China it is used for medicinal purposes. The Han people have associated gold's lastingness with longevity and even eternal life. Chinese alchemists eat it and enjoy longevity; the "immortals" of our time and yours swallow gold and pearls and enjoy eternal life in heaven and on earth. But gold pieces are heavy and cannot stay long in the intestines. That is something of a drawback for traders. Gold is capable of removing all the toxins from smallpox and skin ulcers when applied to the affected skin. Our copper also has medical use for ocular diseases. When calcined, it is employed for all sorts of purposes. For example, it is used for getting rid of white spots and scars around the eyes. Mixed with milk, it is curative of the dreadful ulcers upon the eyes."

Slaves and hired labor loaded camel after camel, and horse after horse, with heavy loads of steel produced by the Chinese factories from the Han Dynasty onwards, and which was very appreciated in Rome, where the technology to make steel was unknown.

"The ancient Roman historian, Pliny, the Younger, spoke of the different kinds of iron, 'of all the different kinds of iron, the palm of excellence is awarded to that which is made by the Chinese, who send it to us with their tissues and skins'. As you can realize, my friends, Chinese culture and manufactory has a long and trusted history. Our mercury and cinnabar are also of importance, even historical importance. They have been used in China, Rome, and Hispania. There were uses in cosmetics, medicines, and poisons, of this mineral. More than in poisons, this cinnabaris of ours is extremely useful in antidotes and various medicines. Should a witch concoct a poison, our physician can use a form of it as a substitute for the other, and so employ an antidote. We are an advanced people, and I am letting you know many of our secrets. I tell you this one secret: the White Lotus Society uses this cinnabaris as a poison against the leadership of the khan's inner circle. It is feared that they will bring an end to the Qing Dynasty."

The Chinese, the Flemish sailors, and Aslan, the Turk, parted with gift giving. Mr. Zhang gave them two camel loads of scarce white tea. It is made from immature, unripened tea leaves that were still covered with a downy, silvery, fuzz tea; leaves that were picked shortly before the buds had fully opened. He told the men that it carried the reputation as the tea with the most health benefits. Because he was something of a romantic, the Chief Envoy gave Piet and Anneke an exquisite tea set used for the ceremony meant to be a meaningful keepsake for their wedding. Piet and Jans gave each of their new friends a beautiful dagger made of Sheffield steel from London, honed to a sharpness that would make them excellent shaving razors. The handles were hand crafted from ebony wood inlaid with abalone shell. The Asians knew that they were now in possession of the finest knives in the world. The value and beauty of the gifts being passed from friend to friend was emblematic of the breadth, depth, and persistence, of their friendship.

Jans made one more request of his benefactors, "Noble Chief Vizier and Noble *Kizlar Agha*, please wait a moment."

He turned and whispered to Piet, who listened intently, then his face became one great smile. He nodded victory.

Jans said to the vizier and the *kizlar*, "Please allow us to follow you back to the palace; so, we can accomplish one last, great mission."

They nodded their agreement, and in a few minutes were back in the beautiful Hall of Felicity—one more very special gift given to the Flemish men for their very special mission. Jans whispered to a slave girl, and she floated out of the room. In minutes, she returned with Anneke who—during her absence from the men—had been treated to a scented bath in a beautiful porcelain tub, then dressed in an elegant, modest, shiny white, silk gown with a three-foot long train. Anneke looked somewhat bemused when she came into the Hall of Felicity, but graced Aslan, the two Flemish sailors, the Grand Vizier, the *Kizlar Agha*, as if she were a deity incarnate, and Valide Kösem Sultan, mother of the sultan, with a radiant full-toothed smile. All returned the joyous smile, even the usually taciturn valide.

The other members of the assemblage quietly took a double step back and stood with looks of anticipation.

Piet had slipped into an adjoining dressing room and had unobtrusively returned dressed in a kaftan, turban, and slippers of the same lustrous white silk as Anneke's gown. He stepped lightly up to her and gave her a smile of pure endearment.

He knelt on one knee and extracted a small, box covered in imperial Tyrian purple silk—reserved for members of the sultan's household. All others were forbidden to have that particular color, except if the Sultan or the Sultana themselves had granted permission. He opened the lovely little box and displayed a large, perfect pearl on a wide gold band. The pearl was a near match for the white silk garments of the couple, except that it had a luster of its own which captured the ambient light in the Hall of Felicity.

"Anneke Blandina van den Voor-Hees," he said, and she shivered, near to tears.

"Yes, Piet."

"Would you do me the great honor of becoming my wife, my friend and partner through all that life may hold for us?"

Now, she did cry, silent tears of sublime joy softly coursing down her alabaster cheeks, now pink with excitement.

"Oh, my dear Piet, I am thrilled. Yes, yes, yes!" she exclaimed, and every person in the room began to applaud except for the young couple who were lost in each other.

"Let this be the day, then, my dear love."

"Can this be real? Am I in a wonderful dream?"

Even the former slave girl and now Valide Sultana, allowed soft tears to flow silently. In her heart of hearts, she was once again a girl running free in her native Sofia, Bulgaria, innocent and carefree.

Jans and the Grand Vizier came out of the dressing room dressed in the finest silk kaftans and turbans that the Topkapi Palace had set aside for such important occasions.

Jans said, "I am Captain Jans Fokkenzoon Corren, master of the good ship Z-*Louisa Hendrika*. By my authority as the captain, it will be my great pleasure to assist Grand Vizier Kemankeş Kara Mustafa Pasha in the performance of the marriage before the One God and all these assembled. Please put your right hand on the Holy Bible."

The Grand Vizier said, "Anneke, my dear, please put your left hand on the Holy *Qur'an*."

She was trembling, but she did as she was asked and rewarded the officiators with another of her room-warming smiles.

Piet was directed to place his hands over hers.

Jans looked the young man and woman directly in their eyes and said, "Dearly beloved, we have come together in the presence of God to witness and bless the joining together of this man and this woman in Holy Matrimony. The bond and covenant of marriage was established by God in creation, and our Lord Jesus Christ adorned this manner of life by His presence and first miracle at the wedding in Cana of Galilee. It signifies to us the mystery of the union between Christ and His Church, and Holy Scripture commends it to be honored among all people.

"The union of husband and wife is intended by God for their mutual joy; for the help and comfort given each other in prosperity and adversity; and, when it is God's will, for the procreation of children and their nurture in the knowledge and love of the Lord. Therefore, marriage is not to be entered into unadvisedly or lightly, but reverently, deliberately, and in accordance with the purposes for which it was instituted by God.

"Into this union Anneke and Piet now come to be joined. If any of you can show just cause why they may not be lawfully wed, speak now, or else forever hold your peace."

No one in the audience uttered a word.

"I charge you both, here in the presence of God and the witness of this company, that if either of you know any reason why you may not be married lawfully and in accordance with God's Word, do now confess it."

Piet and Anneke both shook their heads.

"Anneke, will you have this man to be your husband; to live together with him in the covenant of marriage? Will you love him, comfort him, honor and keep him, in sickness and in health; and, forsaking all others, be faithful unto him as long as you both shall live?"

"I will," she whispered looking deeply into Piet's eyes.

"Piet, will you have this woman to be your wife; to live together with her in the covenant of marriage? Will you love her, comfort her, honor and keep her, in sickness and in health; and, forsaking all others, be faithful unto her as long as you both shall live?"

"I will," Piet said. His voice boomed with determination.

Jans turned and looked at the people in the room, "Will all of you witnessing these promises do all in your power to uphold these two persons in their marriage?"

The congregation, Christian and Muslim responded, "We will."

"Who gives this woman to be married to this man?"

No one in the room dared move. The Lord of the Palace, The Sultan, stepped forward out of the shadows and said, "I, Sultan Ibrahim II, give this daughter of my house in marriage to this fine Man of the Book."

Both Piet and Anneke felt as if they were going to faint. The room fell profoundly silent. Few of the people there–though members of the household–had every actually seen the

man. The sultan then broke all protocol and smiled a beaming, joyful grin at the young couple. They bowed low.

Piet said, "Great One, on behalf of my wife and I, we thank you from the depths of our hearts. We treasure this moment above all others."

The sultan stepped to the back of the throne room.

The Grand Vizier then spoke, "Anneke, Piet, do you accept each other in the sacred bonds of marriage?"

He turned his gaze to Anneke.

"I, Anneke, offer you myself in marriage in accordance with the instructions of the Holy *Qur'an* and the Holy Prophet, peace and blessing be upon him. I pledge, in honesty and with sincerity, to be for you an obedient and faithful wife."

Piet said, simply, "I pledge, in honesty and sincerity, to be for you a faithful and helpful husband."

The Grand Vizier handed the couple a contract written in Turkish, Arabic, and Dutch. The bride and groom—as they had been tutored–demonstrated their free will by repeating the word *qabul* [I accept, in Arabic] three times. Then Piet and Anneke—the groom and his new bride–Jans, and Aslan, acting as the witnesses, signed the contract. Thus, was the simple Muslim marriage ceremony concluded, making the marriage legal according to civil and religious law.

Following the signing of the contract, Valide Kösem Sultan brought a single perfect Medjool date. Piet and Anneke shared the piece of sweet fruit, and they were man and wife.

THE HISTORY
HISTORY OF GOLD, 40,000 B.C.E. – THE 17ᵀᴴ CENTURY

Human fascination with gold is older than recorded history. It is not known for sure when the first human picked up a gold nugget and admired it. However, experts of fossil study have observed flakes of gold in Spanish caves used by the Paleolithic Man about 40,000 BCE. Most archaeological evidence shows that humans who came into contact with gold were impressed by the metal, since gold has been found all over the world; it has consistently been found by archeologists in gravesites over millennia; and it has been mentioned numerous times throughout ancient historical texts.

Gold was discovered in its most basic and natural state–in streams and in the ground of the ancient world–and gold is one of the first precious metals known to mankind. As a natural response to its beauty and rarity, gold became a symbol of royalty and glamor in nearly every culture that was able to obtain it. Throughout history, gold has been treasured for its natural beauty and radiance. For this reason, many cultures have imagined gold to represent the sun.

Egypt and Mesopotamia:
The first firm evidence we have of human interaction with gold occurred in ancient Egypt around 3,000 BCE-2,600 BCE when the ancient Mesopotamians forged some of the first gold jewelry, The ancient civilizations appear to have obtained their supplies of gold from various deposits in the Middle East. Gold objects made more than 5,000 years ago have been found in Egypt. Particularly noteworthy are the gold items discovered by Howard Carter (1874 –1939)–a British archaeologist and Egyptologist–and George Edward Stanhope Molyneux Herbert, 5th Earl of Carnarvon, in 1922 in the tomb of Tutankhamun. This young pharaoh ruled Egypt in the 14ᵗʰ century BCE. Mines in the region of the Upper Nile near the Red Sea and in the Nubian Desert area supplied much of the gold used by the Egyptian pharaohs. When these mines could no longer meet their demands, deposits elsewhere–possibly in Yemen and southern Africa–were exploited.

Artisans in Mesopotamia and Palestine probably obtained their supplies from Egypt and Arabia. Recent studies of the *Mahd adh Dhahab* [Cradle of Gold] mine–in what is now the Kingdom of Saudi Arabia–reveal that gold, silver, and copper, were recovered from this region during the reign of King Solomon (961-922 BCE). In 950 BCE, Solomon's famed temple was built using gold as a prevalent construction material, legend holds.

Gold played an important role in ancient Egyptian mythology and was prized by pharaohs and temple priests. It was so important–in fact–that the capstones on the Pyramids of Giza were made from solid gold. The Egyptians also produced the first known currency exchange ratio which mandated the correct ratio of gold to silver: one piece of gold is equal to two and a half parts of silver. This is also the first recorded measurement of the lower value of silver in comparison to gold.

Gold was among the first metals to be mined. It was first found at surface level near rivers in Asia Minor such as the Pactolus in Lydia. Gold was also mined underground from 2000 BCE by the Egyptians and later by the Romans in Africa, Portugal, and Spain. There is also evidence that the Romans smelted gold particles from ores such as iron pyrites. Archeologists have established that by 3600 BCE gold was first smelted down by Egyptian goldsmiths. The Egyptians also produced gold maps–some of which survive to the present day. These gold maps described where to find gold mines and various gold deposits around the Egyptian kingdom. As a decorative covering, gold plate and gold leaf have been used to decorate shrines, temples, tombs, sarcophagi, statues, ornamental weapons, and armor, ceramics, glassware, and jewelry, since the ancient Egyptian era. Perhaps the most famous example of gold leaf from antiquity is the death mask of King Tutankhamun.

As much as the Egyptians loved gold, they never used it as a bartering tool. Instead, most Egyptians used agricultural products like barley as a de-facto form of money. The first known civilization to use gold as a form of currency was the Kingdom of Lydia, an ancient civilization centered in western Turkey.

Concerns over the authenticity of gold led the Egyptians to devise a method to determine the purity of gold around 1500 BCE or earlier. This method is called fire assaying and involves taking a small sample of the material under test and firing it in a small crucible with a quantity of lead. The crucible was made of bone ash and absorbed the lead and any other base metals during the firing process leaving only gold and silver. The silver was removed using nitric acid and the remaining pure gold was weighed and compared to the weight before firing. Gold is such a precious material that for centuries various attempts were made to produce it through alchemy–that is the chemical transformation of base metals into gold using the philosopher's stone [*lapis philosophorum*]. First attempts were made in China in the 4th century BCE and also in ancient Greece–and although unsuccessful, nevertheless–the activity laid the foundations of modern chemistry.

Gold–with its malleability and incorruptibility–has also been used in dental work for over 3,000 years. The Etruscans in the 7th century BCE used gold wire to fix in place in humans substitute animal teeth. When drawn out as thread, gold was also woven into fabrics. Gold has also been used in medicine also. For example, Pliny in the 1st century BCE, suggested that gold should be applied to wounds as a defense against 'magic potions'.

Africa:

The first gold from Guinea or later the Gold Coast [Ghana] was carried by the Phoenicians and Carthaginians to Europe in the 6th and 5th centuries BCE via the sea. The trade connections on land from West Africa via Timbuktu [Tombouctou] in Mali, to the Mediterranean, were established by the Muslim Saracens in the early 9th century CE. This led to a continuous trade of gold from West Africa in exchange of brass, iron, and iron products [weaponry], silver, salt, cloth, and horses. In the 14th and

15th centuries BCE, the gold coinage of Portugal, Spain, and Italy, was nearly entirely minted from West African gold

But only the arrival of the Portuguese on the Gold Coast in 1471 is historically documented. They started trade in gold dust at the mouth of the river Pra at Shama after having made the passage via the ships, the *Cabo Tris Puntas* [Cape Three Points] and *Cabo Corso* [Cape Coast]. This gold trade was monopolized after a short time by the Portuguese Court and led in 1482 to the construction of the castle *Sao Jorge Da Mina* [St. George of the Mines]–later Elmina–with the aim to secure the gold trade mainly against other European competitors. Up to the end of the 17th century the activities of the other European forces were restricted to trade [barter] of gold for goods only. Likely, the Portuguese were the first Europeans who carried out gold mining on the Gold Coast besides the common gold trade. Until the end of the 16th century, Portugal remained the only power operating permanent trading posts on the Gold Coast. A large number of slaves were quite often lost through the collapse of the gold diggings. For the early part of the 16th century, the gold dust bought annually is estimated at 24,000 ounces, about 10% of the world production of gold during that era.

In 1592, the first traders from Netherlands reached the Gold Coast. They were by far better organized and prepared for all kind of trade. They established themselves with three trading posts. In 1580 Portugal was conquered by Spain and the reformed Northern Provinces [Netherlands] separated by secession from Catholic Spain in 1581. Consequently, the Dutch undertook everything possible to drive the Portuguese away from the Gold Coast–this to reduce the income of their enemy, Spain. Between 1600 and 1630, all gold used by the mints of the Netherlands came from Guinea/Gold Coast. The Dutch West Indies Trading Company was founded in 1629, and the Portuguese were forced out of their possessions on the Gold Coast between 1637 and 1642. Every African king possessed his own gold mines from which his subjects dug the gold which he traded to other black men who lived nearer to the coast. Therefore, the gold passed from hand to hand until it was sold to the Dutch.

By his special order of July 13, 1680, the Emperor Elect Frederic Wilhelm Brandenburg-Prussia sent two ships, the *Wappen of Brandenburg* [commanded by Bartelsen] and the *Morian* [commanded by Blonck] which were equipped and sent to the West African Gold Coast for trading purposes. The undertaking was rather unsuccessful because the Dutch took the *Wappen of Brandenburg* away and sequestered it and forced the *Morian* to leave the waters off the Gold Coast, this in order to defend the Dutch trade monopoly. By 1694, trade became again increasingly more difficult, due to the outbreak of war between the Dutch and the people of Commenda. Such wars always interrupted the gold supply from the hinterland. The Dutch mining attempts at Abrobi Hill in the hinterlands of Ghana led to open conflict, because this hill was held sacred by the people of Commenda since the time of the collapse of the Portuguese mine there in 1621. The mine had been closed with a fetish to pacify the gods of the earth and underground. The new mining activities were stopped by force; the miners were abducted as prisoners. The Dutch had to withdraw and were engaged over several years with this war.

Friedrich I sold the castle and trading forts for 6000 Ducats to the Dutch West Indies Company with an agreement dated, November 22, 1717. At this time, no Brandenburgers were living at Gross-Friedrichsburg. When the Dutch came to take over the castle, a civilian named Conny rebuked them and defended it until 1724. In that year, he had to withdraw in face of a united force of the Dutch and the English. From 1725 onwards, Gross-Friedrichsburg–renamed Fort Hollandia–remained under control of the Dutch but without much economic success until finally the Dutch surrendered the castle to the English in 1872 as they finally withdrew from the Gold Coast altogether.

Minoan Civilization:

The Bronze Age was the third phase in the development of material culture among the ancient peoples of Europe, Asia, and the Middle East, following the Paleolithic [Old Stone Age] and Neolithic [New Stone Age]. The term denotes the first period in which metal was used. The date at which the age began varied with regions; in Greece and China, for instance, the Bronze Age began before 3000 BCE whereas in Britain it did not start until about 1900 BCE.

The jewelry of the Minoan civilization based on Bronze Age Crete discoveries demonstrates–as with their Minoan visual art forms–not only a sophisticated technological knowledge (for the purposes of this article, metalwork) and an ingenuity of design but also a societal joy from vibrantly representing nature and a love of flowing, expressive shapes, and forms. The materials utilized in the production of Minoan jewelry included metals such as gold, silver, bronze, and gold-plated bronze. Semi-precious stones were used such as rock-crystal, carnelian, garnet, lapis lazuli, obsidian and red, green, and yellow jasper. Amethyst was also popular and was imported from Egypt where it was no longer fashionable in jewelry, a fact which illustrates the Minoan independence of mind regarding materials and design. Faience, enamel, steatite [soapstone], ivory, shell, glass-paste, and blue frit or Egyptian blue [a synthetic intermediate between faience and glass] were also at the disposal of Minoan jewelers.

Jewelry took the form of diadems, necklaces, bracelets, beads in glass, shell, semi-precious stones. In the case of gold, the art pieces often took the form of flowers such as lilies and in some cases with incised decorations or whorls added in filigree, pendants–particularly leaves, axes, and cones, but also animals and birds. They crafted armlets, headbands, clothes ornaments such as wafer thin, sheet gold circles, stars, and heart shapes, which were sown on to garments; hair pins such as crocus flower heads–and hair ornaments–usually in the form of gold leaves and flowers. An outstanding example is a large gold daisy from Mochlos. Minoan artisans made pectorals, chains–ranging from heavy gold links to very fine examples with minute rings–and earrings; solid gold bull's heads were among the finest surviving examples.

Ancient Greeks and gold:

By 550 BCE, Greeks had begun mining for gold throughout the Mediterranean and Middle Eastern regions for many years, causing gold to draw speculation from Plato and Aristotle regarding its origins. Because of being frequently located in water, gold was often thought to be a dense combination of water and sunlight, based on the limited scientific and geological understanding of both substances.

The graves of nobles at the ancient Citadel of Mycenae near Nauplion, Greece–discovered by the German, Heinrich Schliemann in 1876–yielded a great variety of gold figurines, masks, cups, diadems, and jewelry, plus hundreds of decorated beads and buttons. These elegant works of art were created by skilled craftsmen more than 3,500 years ago.

The first pure gold coins with stamped images are credited to King Croesus of Lydia [western Turkey] 561-546 BCE and a contemporary gold refinery has been excavated at the capital, Sardis. By 564 BCE, Lydia improved the refining techniques of gold and established the first international gold currency. Other Lydians claimed that the first use of gold as money began in 700 BCE, it is part of common lore to remember the kingdom of the famous fortune seeking King Croesus - circa 550 BCE.

Later in history, the ancient Greeks viewed gold as a social status symbol and as a form of glory amongst the immortal gods and demigods. Mortal humans could use gold as a sign of wealth, and gold was also a form of currency. Contrary to what many believe, the Olympics tradition of giving out gold medals to victors did not begin until the modern Olympics and has little to do with Greek tradition.

Romans:

The Romans significantly expanded on the technology and mining capabilities of the Greeks, related to the vastness and resources of the Roman Empire, and the curiosity and entrepreneurial spirit of its citizens. They built water-based mining operations, and were responsible for several of the first stream-based gold mining machinery including: mining hydraulics, sluices, Long Toms [small sluices that use less water than a regular sluice]. It is a sloping trough 12 feet long, 15 to 20 inches wide at the upper end, and flares to 24 to 30 inches at the lower end], and water wheels.

The Romans also mined underground using mostly slave and prisoner labor. Their method was further enhanced by developing a roasting technique that became a more efficient method of separating gold ores from other rock, making their gold purer and more valuable. One of the most famous gold coins in antiquity was the Roman *bezant*. First introduced in the reign of Emperor Constantine, it weighed up to 70 Troy grains and was in currency from the 4th to the 12th centuries CE.

Incas:

In the Inca civilization of Peru, gold was considered the sweat of the sun god Inti and so was used to manufacture all manner of objects of religious significance, especially masks and sun disks. In ancient Colombia, gold was similarly revered for its luster and association with the sun and in powdered form was used to cover the body of the future king in a lavish coronation ceremony which gave rise to the legend of El Dorado. Incans, Aztecs, and numerous other civilizations, also used gold prolifically throughout very early history, including it in religious ceremonies and in famous architectural designs.

The gold in the Aztec and Inca treasuries of Mexico and Peru believed to have come from Colombia, although some undoubtedly was obtained from other sources. The Conquistadores plundered the treasuries of these civilizations during their explorations of the New World, and many gold and silver objects were melted and cast into coins and bars, destroying the priceless artifacts of the Indian culture.

The Bible and gold:

Gold is also mentioned in the Bible, where Genesis 2:10-12 describes the lands of Havilah, near Eden, as a place where good gold can be found.

There is one common trend across all ancient civilizations: gold is a status symbol used to separate one class from another. From emperors to priests to the elites and upper middle class, those who held gold also tended to hold power.

Gold coins in use over centuries:

Dutch gold goldgulden (1497) with the image of a globe surmounted by cross.
Dutch gold angel (1531-1577) of Thorn with a scene of St. Michael slaying a dragon.
Dutch gold rose noble (1583) of Campen depicting a king on a ship.
Hungarian gold ducat (1598) depicting King Rudolf II in full armor.
Flemish gold rose noble of Ghent depicting a king on a ship.
French gold écu (1607) of Henry IV displaying the coat of arms of France.
Spanish gold escudo (1607) with an image of a cross.
Dutch gold 1/2 cavalier (1613) of Gelderland showing a charging knight.
Dutch gold double ducat of Zeeland depicting the king and queen of Spain.
Dutch gold 1/2 cavalier (1616) of Overijssel showing a charging knight.
Italian gold coins:

In the tradition of the early Renaissance, Italian mints continued to strike impressive gold coins with beautiful portraits and religious scenes.

Italian gold 2 doppia piece (1622-1646) of Oroardo Farnese, Duke of Parma, depicting the Virgin and child crowned by angels.

Italian gold 10 doppia piece (1628) of Ferdinand II. Duke of Tuscany, showing John the Baptist.

Italian gold 10 scudi piece (1641) of Carlo Emmanuele II, Duke of Savoy, and his regent mother Cristina.

Italian gold 2 scudi piece (1690) of Pope Alexander VIII depicting sheep with garlands on an altar.

Mughal [Mongol], India:

The 17th century was a high point for the Mughal emperors of India. Akbar [1556-1605] consolidated the subcontinent and, while he himself was illiterate; he expended great sums of money on arts and letters. Shah Jahan [1628-1658]–who erected the Taj Mahal in memory of his deceased wife Mumtaz Mahal–also required enormous amounts of gold and lesser coinage. Mughal coinage of this period is known for its distinctive Arabic script.

Rum Seljuk Turkish gold dinar [1200] of Rukn al-Din Sulayman II depicting a Turkish cavalryman.
Mughal gold mohur [1623] of Jahangir depicting the sign of Sagittarius.
Figured gold Islamic coins
Mughal gold mohur [1684] of Shah Jahan from Burhanpur, India.

The Mongol invasion of the Middle East under Genghis Khan [1155-1227] significantly affected Islamic gold coinage. Iran's Il-Khan Mongol dynasty introduced decorative frames while retaining the traditional inscriptional style. Multilingual inscriptions were used, reflecting the cultural diversity of the people ruled by the Mongols. Some powerful rulers did not claim authority in their own right but marked their coins with the names of weak overlords, e.g. the Il-Khanid gold dinar [1285] of Arghun Khan.

The Fall of Constantinople:
In 1453, the last vestiges of the Byzantine Empire–in decline since 1204–fell to the Ottoman Turks under Mehmet II "the Conqueror" [1451-1481]. The city remained the capital of the Ottoman Empire.
Genoese gold ducat of Filippo Maria Visconti, Duke of Milan [1421-1435].
Ottoman gold *sultani* [1478-1479] of Mehmet II, from Istanbul [Constantinople]. Ottoman gold coins of the period were closely linked to the standard of the Venetian *zecchino*.

Spain and the New World:
In 1492, King Ferdinand and Queen Isabella [1479-1504] financed Christopher Columbus' voyage to the New World, which was ultimately an immense source of silver and gold for the Spanish monarchy. By the mid-16th century, Spanish rulers were flooding Europe with *reales*. Also, in 1492, Ferdinand and Isabella completed the Reconquista, driving the Jews and Muslims out of Spain and into the Ottoman Empire.
Gold double ducat of Ferdinand and Isabella from Toledo, Spain.
Nasrid gold dinar of Muhammad IX [1427-1429], one of the last Muslim kings of Granada, Spain.
Ottoman gold *altun* of Sultan Bayazid II [1448-1512] from Istanbul. Bayazid invited the Jewish and Muslim refugees from Spain to settle in Ottoman territory.
Silver 8 *reales* of Philip II (1592-1597) from Potosí, Bolivia. [pieces of eight]
The Price Revolution, sometimes known as the Spanish Price Revolution, was a series of economic events that occurred between the second half of the 15th century to the first half of the 17th century. It was most specifically linked to the high rate of inflation that occurred during this period across Western Europe. Prices rose on average roughly six-fold over 150 years. This level of inflation amounted to 1–1.5% per year–a relatively low inflation rate for modern-day standards–but rather high given the monetary policy in place in the 16th century. Generally it is thought that this high inflation

was caused by the large influx of gold and silver from the Spanish treasure fleet from the New World, including Mexico, Peru, and the rest of the Spanish Empire.

The shortage of precious metals during the late 15th and early 16th centuries eased in the second half of the 16th century. The Spanish mined American gold and silver at minimal cost and flooded the European market with an abundance of valuable coinage. This influx caused a relative decrease in the value of these metals in comparison with agricultural and craft products. This deficit occurred because of Spanish demand for foreign products exceeding its exports to foreign markets. Furthermore, depopulation—especially in southern Spain–resulted in a high rate of inflation. The failure of the Spanish to control the influx of gold and the price fluctuations of gold and silver from the American mines, combined with war expenditures, led to three bankruptcies of the Spanish monarchy by the end of the 16th century.

# CHAPTER NINETEEN

# To London

IN THE YEAR OF OUR LORD, 1643, LATE JUNE

O n the last evening of the caravan's stay in Constantinople, Jans, Piet, Anneke, and Aslan, hosted a small dinner for their friends in the capital city. To ensure privacy, Aslan reserved Gorgoptulos– the entire restaurant–known for its diversity and delights from a variety of cultures ranging from the Eurasian to the Mediterranean–celebrated Constantinople as a port city bringing together two continents. The neighborhood was upscale and never busy, a basic requirement for the chosen guests. Gorgoptulos Restaurant was located on a tree lined side street next to a very well-preserved Byzantine Greek Orthodox Church with beautiful mosaics and frescoes. Aslan had to do some persuading in order to convince his partners and the high-born guests that the food was the best in the city. Secretive culinary guilds during the Ottoman era prohibited chefs from writing down recipes; one could only trust his or her experience or that of gourmand friends.

The guest list was as urbane, sophisticated, and experienced, as the restaurant: *Kizlar Agha* Bezan Süleymani Agha, the Black Eunuch, second in command in the harem and palace, Grand Vizier Kemankeş Kara Mustafa Pasha, Valide Kösem Sultan–Sultan Ibrahim's greatly esteemed mother and first lady of the Imperial Ottoman Harem, Ali Orhan Pasha, Janissary general and hero of the siege of Buda, and Zhuang Han Zhidi, Imperial Envoy of the Chinese delegation to Constantinople. It was a diplomatic tribute of the first order that these luminaries agreed to attend, and personal success that the Piet and his wife, Jans, and Aslan, had developed relationships close enough to have the evening be a dinner among friends, and future business associates.

The evening was a great success. In private, the hosts and guests relaxed and acted as themselves rather than their high titles. Their table was situated in tree-shaded courtyard appealing because it was the time of year when Constantinople had turned steamy. Over the centuries of its presence in the city, Gorgoptulos had accumulated a repertoire of hundreds of dishes.

The first course of the meal was two soups—an almond soup served with pomegranate and nutmeg; the recipe was over a century old, and cornbread and buttery chard soup—which were quintessentially Black Sea dishes. Appetizers included fried liver rissoles dunked in sweet-and-sour molasses, and *hamsi* [anchovy] pilaf, another Black Sea favorite. The main dishes were slow-cooked goose atop almond pilaf, and the perennial favorite baked fruit—melon because of the approaching summer—stuffed with savory lamb and beef, and a copper pan of glistening *muhlama* brought steaming hot to the table. *Muhlama* is another Black Sea favorite consisting of a trio of *koloti* cheese, golden cornmeal, and butter.

Aslan instructed the other hosts and the guests, "The cheese has a very high fat content. You have to eat it fast or else it sets," he said.

The *muhlama* proved to be a hit novelty to all of them, none of whom had ever eaten spaghetti. They dipped into the common bowl and twisted the stringy cheese around their forks, following Aslan's example. *Muhlama* is something like stretchy spaghetti.

Aslan explained some more, "The best ingredients from the Black Sea are in that bowl—the very best are in there—the best Trabzon butter, the most savory *koloti* cheese available in Constantinople, and the freshest cornmeal."

Despite her previous lowly station in the harem as a slave, Anneke charmed everyone and added her beauty to the splendor of the meal. The guests accepted her as a free and presumably high-born woman, perhaps because her golden hair was piled high atop her head and had several beguiling ringlets, or because she wore a form-fitting 17th century Dutch dress at its most glorious. Her formal afternoon gown was made of gold and black Dutch brocaded silk. It had a low bodice which gave more than a small hint of cleavage. The bodice and her petticoat were of equally luxurious smooth silk–a deeper gold silk. The silk was slashed between the brocaded motifs. At the center of the back of the gown's small upright collar were two holes to fasten a support for an elaborate lace collar standing high behind her head and neck.

The dinner was a resounding success for Piet and Anneke. For a girl so young, a Christian, and a former slave, Anneke had learned a great deal about how to behave in the highest strata of society. Her native intelligence and the degree of education she brought with her from the Netherlands stood her in good stead. She was able to converse in several languages with the elite of the sultanate, and to charm them with more than her stunning good looks. The best descriptor of the girl was given by the Greek ambassador to the court in an aside to Pete.

"She is the reincarnation of Diana. Her face would easily launch a thousand ships...and dare I say, her motherly form is the great Greek golden mean."

Piet was proud of her, and she of him. Their match seemed destined for great things and for great happiness.

The following day, the tide came in early, and obliged the sailors to leave on the tide before it was light—just after the *Fajr* prayer caused the city to begin to come to life. It promised to be a beautiful day on the Mediterranean, one blessed with the sailors' delight of a fair wind and a following sea. Their travel remained blessed for five days, and they made an average of twelve knots a day [The derived unit of speed being the knot, one nautical mile per hour] in the direction of London, their final destination.

Those five days were idyllic for the two honeymooners. Besides the great physical pleasure they enjoyed, Piet found his lovely new wife to be his intellectual match. They reveled in his teaching her, and he knew that it would not be long before she would outstrip him because of her superior mental capacity, agility, and curiosity.

Like Piet, the captain and the crew enjoyed trying to match wits with the versatile girl.

The former first mate sat at lunch with her, Piet, and Jans, and worked at having her develop a good measure of seamanship.

"Ah, lass," he said, "Ye must know and remember that a fathom is six feet—the length a goodly man can stretch from open arm to open arm. A sturdy rope is lowered into the water to measure depth. A cable, or cable length, is the length of a ship's cable, about 600 feet, give or take. A nautical mile is 10 cable lengths. At sea, a league is three nautical miles. And remember the size of a man's foot. That has long been a standard unit for the measurement of length by people everywhere. Use it with a jaundiced eye, though, Lass. Feet are way different—just think of your wee ones compared to that big lummox of a husband o' yours. Am I goin' too fast for ye?"

"No, Sir," she said and recited the definitions verbatim having only heard them once."

He shook his head in admiration, "Ye're nay just a pretty thing, my girl. Ye have a very good head on yer shoulders."

Piet beamed with pride. Anneke had been a very very good catch for an ambitious young and upcoming man.

Anneke had not forgotten that she had come from a family of modest means, and she treated the crew with kindness and respect. They responded by holding her in something amounting to reverence. An indication of that level of respect is that she was the only woman aboard the ship and was never referred to for her striking beauty or sumptuous form by even the saltiest of the dogs. Part of the respect was that they lowered their eyes when she passed and took genuine joy when she favored even the lowliest swabby with one of her radiant smiles.

One of the common seamen dared to presume to teach her more seamanship and found her a delightful, receptive, and quick-learning pupil.

"Ye might like to remember how visibility at sea is determined, crude a measure though it is. It begins with a person on dry land determinin' the greatest distance at which he or she can make out objects–ideally black and ideally of medium and known size–against the horizon sky with the unaided eye. At night, there is at least something of a measure: the equivalent of seeing during the day comes at dark from usin' lights of known candle strengths at already known kinds of distances determined down the ages. Ye should remember that visibility of less than 100 meters is reported as zero, and danger lurks out there in the dark. Maximum visibility is three miles to the horizon if ye are a six-footer standin' at sea level."

She nodded her head in understanding and gave him her pleasant pupil-to-teacher smile, which made his day.

Two days out from the port of Laiazzo, the second mate took it upon himself to teach Anneke a new language: the terms used for seas, and parts of ships.

"Aft and baft are the back of the ship. The front of the ship we call the bow. Knowing port and starboard a bit harder to remember. I was told once about a famous Flemish admiral who after he died was found to have a sheet of paper with directions written his own hand: 'Port is left'" which made Anneke laugh.

"Remember, port is the left side of a ship as you look at the boat from the bow, and starboard is the opposite. I mean it is the right side of the ship as you are facing the bow. Now, Lassie, recollect all of this because there's going to be a test when we're finished."

"I'll take it as a challenge, second mate. Care to make in the form of a friendly wager?"

"What do you have in mind, My Girl?"

"I clean your room for a week if I lose; and you holy stone the cables for two days, if I win."

"You drive a hard bargain. Remind me not to play at cards with ye."

Feeling tested, himself, he raised the bar for her, "Now, here's a few more terms any good sailor has to know: there's the boom. It's the horizontal pole which extends from the bottom of the mast. The way sailing ship is able to us the power of the wind power in order to move forward or backwards is by adjusting the boom towards the direction of the wind. The rudder, you probably already know is a flat piece of wood beneath the ship. It is used to steer the ship. Since ours is a pretty big vessel, we control the rudder using the big wheel up in the bow. A couple of more terms should be enough for today. There's leeward usually called the 'lee' which is the opposite of windward—meaning that it is the direction opposite to the way the wind is blowin' at the time. So, logically, windward is the other way—the way the wind *is* ablowin'. Now it makes but good sense that sailing ships like to move *with* the wind, making the windward direction probably the important sailing term to know. So, Lassie, you can slip that little tidbit into a conversation with an old salt and make him think you are smart, even for a girl."

It had been a bit of a risk to attempt such a jest, but the girl had an intelligent sense of humor to compliment her general cleverness, and they both got a good laugh. The second mate remained one of Anneke's chief admirers; his attention to her good brains took some of the pressure off his natural man tendency to admire her somewhat lower attributes.

"Maybe one last bit for you to know, so's not to muddle your pretty head. There's tacking. It means to turn the bow of the ship through the wind so that the wind changes from one side of the boat to the other side. The boom of a boat will always shift from one side to the other when performing a tack or a jibe. And there's jibing. It's the opposite of tacking, meaning is about turning the *stern* of the boat through the wind so that the wind changes from one side of the boat to the other side. The boom of a boat will always shift from one side to the other when performing a tack or a jibe. Jibing is the less common technique than tacking, since it involves turning a boat directly into the wind which might seem to be illogical.

About 8,000 people from Constantinople were engaged in Black Sea trade alone, providing the city with rice, salt, honey, butter, and leather from the ports of northern Anatolia, Crimea, and Europe. They and a vigorous trade with Spain, the Netherlands, France, Germany, Venice, Italy, and the Baltics, combined to make Laiazzo, Turkey's large south-western port an extraordinarily busy commercial center every day. Jans, Piet, Anneke, and the crew had to wait two days to take their turn to enter and to be able to make arrangements to transfer the goods from their Turkish ship to the *Z-Louisa Hendrika*.

Their fine Dutch vessel and loyal crew had remained in port keeping the ship in good repair and doing business well enough to have turned a profit nearly every month of Jan's and Piet's absence. The holds were a little over half full of cargo the portion of the crew left in Laiazzo had deemed likely to turn a handsome profit when they finally returned to Europe.

The reunion was both joyful and tinged with sadness. The joy came from the realization that the crew and its captain were reunited and largely in fit condition. The good news was added to by learning that six of the crewmen had married and started families during Jans', Piet's, and the land crew's, absence. The sad news came in two forms: four men had died. Three suffered accidents typical of seamen, and one had died during the Black Plague. The remainder of the Laiazzo-bound crew had practiced the discipline imposed by the port authority to quarantine themselves until there was not a single case of the terrible pandemic for a full three months.

Jans kept the news of the profits gained by the land crew to himself until late in the celebration of their reunion. When all the reminiscences had been shared, enough ale consumed, and stomachs filled, he provided a great surprise.

"Lads, would you get five or six stalwarts to lug some chests onto the deck of the *Hendrika*?"

He had intentionally held back the chests for effect.

The men strained and struggled to load the six very heavy chests onto wagons pulled by oxen from one ship to the other.

"Piet, would you do the honors?" Jans asked.

Piet had the six keys to the sturdy locks on the chests. He quickly undid the clasps and asked Anneke to open the covers and stepped back dramatically. Jans had placed security guards on the wharf and at the gangplank to keep out greedy-eyed interlopers.

The chests were packed so full of gold bullion and gold coins that scarcely a wafer could have been added. The gold gleamed and caught the ambient light. It was as if a group of good and faithful men had all died at once and had been escorted through the Pearly Gates over streets paved with gold to receive their just rewards. They were dumbfounded, exhilarated, and hysterically overjoyed.

Jans allowed the crew to run their fingers through the piles of coins, more money than any of them had ever seen, felt, or even dreamed of before. Once the excitement subsided, Jans spoke out to get their attention.

"Now to business, men. Land Mate Andries has done a fine yeoman's job of tallying up the profits and losses for the Hendrika during the time we land-lubbers were away. I will simplify: the profits were six hundred thousand guilders."

That drew a short gasp from the crew who had never been apprised of such arcane complexities as profit and loss before. All they were interested in was how shares would be distributed.

"Now, officers, mates, and Anneke, would you care to guess the value of this cargo of gold? Incidentally, all the gold is in the profit column, since we had to pay any debts incurred as we went."

Anneke's hand shot up.

Jans and Piet laughed.

"I am sure that Piet's clever wife has already done the figuring; so, I won't let her guess quite yet."

Anneke pouted theatrically making everyone start to laugh.

"All right, let's hear some guesses."

Since no one in the crew had the faintest idea, the guesses ranged from three-quarters of a million guilders to over fifty million.

Jans smiled as the pleasure of the guessing game warmed the morale of his fine crew.

He said, "Finally, men, I will break the suspense. Our first mate, Piet, has spent some days while we were at sea counting the treasure. I was on the watch for pirates while he was enjoying himself. His final tally after six separate countings was 186 million guilders."

There followed a nearly hysterical gasping, shouting, laughing, and even crying. Every man knew that there was sufficient money in his share to retire with his family in comfort for the rest of their lives.

When order was restored, Jans made an announcement that was a surprise because it was unusual–if not unprecedented–in maritime division of shares with crew members.

"When we make port in Amsterdam, we will cart our chests ashore and divide into shares. We will divide the total into a thousand shares. Every man gets one full share at least—a total of fifty-two shares. We will include the families of our dearly departed brothers. Every officer is to receive four shares. The captain receives eight shares, first mate six shares, second mate, five. The remainder will be banked to ensure that the good ship gets its full repairs and refurbishing, and that we can purchase the cargo for our next set of voyages. The excess left in the bank will be halved to provide a cushion for the future. One half will stay in the bank, and the other half will be doled out to any man who made this voyage and wishes to return and to serve again."

"Thankee, Capt'n," a crewman from the back said, speaking for the whole crew.

"Now, men, word of the value of our cargo is bound to leak out. We will be shadowed and harassed by pirates all the way back home. We will have to remain combat ready and ever watchful. I know I can count on every man to do his duty. As for myself, and Piet, I swear before almighty God that I will fight to the death if need be for the ship and for my crew."

The crew caught the excitement and determination.

As if they had rehearsed, the crew showed three loud "Huzzahs."

## The History:
## History of Gold from the 17<sup>th</sup> Century to the Present

Gold in the 17<sup>th</sup> Century:

In the 17<sup>th</sup> century, gold was still the metal used for large-scale international transactions. Because of the multiplicity of denominations, merchants needed to weigh coins in order to determine the proper exchange value. At the end of the 17<sup>th</sup> Century the Brandenburg Prussians had undertaken mining activities on the Gold Coast already apart from gold-trade in conflict with the dominant Dutch.

Gold in United States, 18<sup>th</sup> Century to the present:

1792 – The United States adopted a gold and silver standard.

In 1792, the United States Congress made a decision that would change the modern history of gold. Congress passed the Mint and Coinage Act. This Act established a fixed price of gold in terms of U.S. dollars. Gold and silver coins became legal tender in the United States, as did the Spanish Real [silver coin of the Spanish Empire]. At the time, gold was worth approximately 15 times more than silver. Silver was used for small denomination purchases while gold was used for large denominations. The U.S. mint was legally required to buy and sell gold and silver at a rate of 15 parts silver to 1 part gold. As a result, the market rate for gold rarely varied beyond 15.5 to 1 or 16 to 1.

That ratio changed after the Civil War. During the Civil War, the U.S. was unable to pay off all its debts using gold or silver. In 1862, paper money was declared to be legal tender, marking the first time a fiat currency [not convertible on demand at a fixed rate] was used as an official currency in the United States. Just a few years later, silver was officially removed from the U.S. Mint's fixed rate system in a bill called the Coinage act of 1873–and criticized by American citizens as the Crime of '73. This removed the silver dollar from circulation, although coins worth less than $1 still contained silver. The United States would never use silver dollars again. Throughout the late 1800s, the issue remained an important political topic. In 1900, the gold dollar was declared to be the standard unit of account in the United States and paper dollars were issued to represent the country's gold reserves.

The history of gold has long been connected with money, but gold relinquished that role in developed economies after the outbreak of the Second World War. The Gold Standard was a system under which nearly all countries fixed the value of their currencies in terms of a specified amount of gold or linked their currency to that of a country which did so. Domestic currencies were freely convertible into gold at the fixed price and there was no restriction on the import or export of gold. Gold coins circulated as domestic currency alongside coins of other metals and notes, with the composition varying by country. As each currency was fixed in terms of gold, exchange rates between participating currencies were also fixed.

THE SMITHSONIAN AGREEMENT:

In 1933 as the Great Depression loomed, President Roosevelt suspended the convertibility of gold into dollars when it was still worth only $20.67 per ounce. By Presidential proclamation, the conversion was reestablished, though at a higher rate of $35 per ounce. In 1944, the Bretton Woods Agreement fixed the global price of gold. The two World Wars wreaked havoc on the gold standard and world financial markets. It obviously did not help matters that the Great Depression occurred in between those two wars.

After decades of war and conflict, world leaders came together under the Bretton Woods Agreements. This system created a gold exchange standard where the price of gold was fixed to the U.S. dollar. This was a radical experiment that had never been done before, and it made the United States very powerful on the world's markets. The U.S. dollar was chosen for the Bretton Woods system because the United States was easily the world's strongest economy coming out of the Second World War. Unlike previously strong European nations, the United States did not have to repair infrastructure or fix towns that had been bombarded throughout the war.

The day the price of gold was pegged to the U.S. dollar is one of the most important points of U.S. history because it helped make the United States the global superpower it is today. In 1944, gold was fixed at $35 per ounce for the foreseeable future. In the early 1970s, another conflict–the Vietnam War–caused the gold exchange standard to collapse. America's budget was in ruin; and in 1971, President Nixon suddenly decided to end the Bretton Woods system with a moment known in history as the "Nixon Shock".

THE GROUP OF TEN

On August 15th of 1971, President Richard Nixon suspended the convertibility of dollars into gold, which culminated in a *purposeful defaulting on the United States debt*. Almost immediately Nixon's administration began negotiating with industrialized countries to determine a new exchange rate.

It was not until December, 1971 that the next landmark event in the American history of gold took place. During that month, members of ten countries and the central banks of England and the United States–called the Group of Ten–met at the Smithsonian Museum and signed the Smithsonian agreement that effectively adjusted the fixed exchange rates that had been previously established at the Bretton Woods conference in 1944. Between 1971 and 1976, a number of attempts were made to salvage the gold standard. However, the price of gold continued to rise beyond what any currency could sustain.

As a result, many gold pricing charts date their beginning to around 1970. Between 1970 and 1971, the price of gold was relatively flat before skyrocketing to a record high of $800+ in 1980. Gold pricing charts from the 1940s to 1970s, were a nearly flat line of $35 per ounce. As of 2014, no countries in the world use a gold standard. In short, no currency in the world is backed by gold at the present time. However, most countries in the world maintain large gold reserves in order to defend their currency against possible future emergencies.

America's gold reserves are held at Fort Knox, Kentucky. The heavily-defended location holds an unknown amount of gold; the amount is officially classified by the United States government. However, it is widely accepted that the United States holds more gold bullion than any other country in the world–approximately 1.3 times as much gold as the next leading country, Germany. As with anything labeled "classified" in the United States, there are a plethora of right-wing conspiracy theorists who argue that Fort Knox is actually empty and that the gold is held in some secret location or does not exist at all. You are on your own to decide the veracity of that.

Since the 1970s, the price of gold has steadily increased. In 1970, gold was $35 per ounce. In August 2011, that number had risen to nearly $2000 per ounce. However, the years in between were not a smooth upward slope, and gold–like any other investment–went through a number of ups and downs over the ensuing decades. The price of gold has experienced two major spikes since the 1970s: once in 1980 and the other in 2011.

Geopolitical tensions between 2003 and 2008 continued to elevate the price of gold. And in 2008, the global economic crisis increased the price of gold even further. After reaching a high of over $1,900 per troy ounce in 2011, gold has fallen to between $1,200 to $1,400 in recent years.

Reasons why the price of gold is high include:
•Properties of Gold

Gold is called a "noble" metal–an alchemistic term–because it does not oxidize under ordinary conditions. Its chemical symbol $Au$ is derived from the Latin word "*aurum*." In pure form, gold has a metallic luster and is sun yellow; but mixtures of other metals, such as silver, copper, nickel, platinum, palladium, tellurium, and iron, with gold create various color hues ranging from silver-white to green and orange-red. Gold is considered to be of great value because it commonly occurs in its native form; that is, not combined with other elements; because it is beautiful and imperishable; and because exquisite objects can be made from it and have been from before recorded history.

Sources: Gold is primarily found as the pure, native metal. Sylvanite and calaverite are gold-bearing minerals. Gold is usually found embedded in quartz veins, or placer stream gravel. It is now mined in South Africa, the U.S.A. (Nevada, Alaska), Russia, Australia, and Canada.

Pure gold is relatively soft–it has about the hardness of a penny. It is the most malleable and ductile of metals. The specific gravity or density of pure gold is 19.3 compared to 14.0 for mercury and 11.4 for lead. Impure gold–as it often occurs in deposits–has a density of 16 to 18, whereas the associated waste rock [gangue] has a density of about 2.5. The difference in density enables gold to be concentrated by gravity and permits the separation of gold from clay, silt, sand, and gravel, by various agitating and collecting devices such as the gold pan, rocker, and sluice box.

Fineness, Karats and Troy Ounces:

The degree of purity of native gold, bullion [bars or ingots of unrefined gold], and refined gold, is stated in terms of gold content. "Fineness" defines gold content in parts per thousand. For example, a gold nugget containing 885 parts of pure gold and 115 parts of other metals—such as silver and copper—would be considered 885-fine.

"Karat" indicates the *proportion of solid gold* in an alloy based on a total of 24 parts. Thus, 14-karat (14K) gold indicates a composition of 14 parts of gold and 10 parts of other metals. Incidentally, 14K gold is commonly used in jewelry manufacture because it retains the beauty and holds it shape better. "Karat" should not be confused with "carat," a unit of *weight* used for precious stones.

The basic unit of weight used in dealing with gold is the troy ounce. One troy ounce is equivalent to 20 troy pennyweights. In the jewelry industry, the common unit of measure is the pennyweight (dwt.) which is equivalent to 1.555 grams. One cubic foot of gold weighs more than half a ton.

Reasons for gold's value:
- Scarcity: Gold is difficult to find and extract in the present world. In the late 1800s, any town with a single gold nugget was instantly transformed into a gold rush town. Today, only about 2,000 tons of gold are created per year. To put that number into perspective, about 10,500 tons of steel are produced in the United States *every hour*. It is well documented that the world's holdings accumulated during all recorded history to the present is only about 120,000 metric tons.
- Suffice it to say that the total world's hoard of the shiny metal will occupy a single cube 60 feet by 60 feet by 60 feet—which is equivalent to the approximate volume of three 12-room homes. The value of that block would be approximately $1.4 TRILLION.
- Gold is relatively scarce in the earth, but it occurs in many different kinds of rocks and in many different geological environments. Though scarce, gold is concentrated by geologic processes to form commercial deposits of two principal types: lode (primary) deposits and placer (secondary) deposits.
- Physical characteristics: Gold is a chemical element with the symbol *Au* and atomic number 79, making it one of the higher atomic number elements that occur naturally. In its purest form, it is a bright, slightly reddish yellow, dense, soft, malleable, and ductile metal. Chemically, gold is a transition metal and a group 11 element. It is one of the least reactive chemical elements and is solid under standard conditions. Gold often occurs in free elemental form, as nuggets or grains, in rocks, in veins, and in alluvial deposits. It occurs in a solid solution series with the native element silver and also naturally alloyed with copper and palladium. Less commonly, it occurs in minerals as gold compounds, often with tellurium.
- Gold has some phenomenal physical characteristics—especially when used in electrical applications. Gold is an excellent conductor; furthermore, no metal is more malleable and ductile than gold. A small bit of gold can be hammered into many smaller sheets. In fact, one ounce of gold can be stretched [drawn] to form a wire that is 50 miles long. Gold plated copper wire requires only one ounce of gold to plate a 1,000-mile-long thread of copper. Gold does not corrode; and so, it became a symbol of immortality and power in many ancient cultures.

- <u>Aesthetic attributes</u>: One of the simplest reasons why gold is valuable is that it is beautiful, a fact attested to by the manufacture of fine and elegant objects for the past 40,000+ years. Over time, rulers have loved displaying gold in throne rooms, tombs, and on top of Egyptian pyramids. Its unique coloring and warm luster have fascinated humans for many millennia.

- Even in most ancient cultures, gold was popular in jewelry and art because of its value, aesthetic qualities, ductility, and malleability—the same reasons that it is popular and valued today. Electrum–the natural alloy of gold and silver–was used in jewelry by the Egyptians from 5,000 BCE. Gold jewelry was worn by both men and women in the Sumer civilization around 3000 BCE, and gold chains were first produced in the city of Ur of the Chaldees in 2,500 BCE. The Minoan civilization on Crete in the early 2nd millennium BCE is credited with producing the first cable chain jewelry, and the Minoans of Crete made a vast array of jewelry items using an extensive range of techniques. Gold jewelry took the form of necklaces, bracelets, earrings, rings, diadems, pendants, pins and brooches. Techniques and shapes included filigree (a technique known to the Egyptians from 2500 BCE where the gold was pulled into wire and twisted into different designs), beaten thin shapes, granulated [surface decoration with small, soldered granules of gold; and enhanced by embossing, chasing, inlaying, molding, and engraving.

In South America, gold was similarly worked by the Chavin civilization of Peru around 1200 BCE and gold casting was perfected by the Nazca society from 500 BCE. The Romans used gold as a setting for precious and semi-precious gemstones, a fashion continued into the Byzantine era with the use of pearls, gems, and enamels.

Discovery and development of gold products in The United States-18th and 19th centuries:

Gold was produced in the southern Appalachian region as early as 1792 and perhaps as early as 1775 in southern California. The discovery of gold at Sutter's Mill in California January 24, 1848, by carpenter/millwright James W. Marshall launched an incredible gold rush. Marshall discovered gold on banks of the South Fork of the American River while building a sawmill for John A. Sutter in the valley the Nisenan Indians knew as Cullumah. Henry Bigler and Azariah Smith–like other workers at the mill–were veterans of the famous Mormon Battalion, and wrote about their experience in their journals. Bigler recorded the actual date when gold was discovered, January 24, 1848.

That discovery sparked the gold rush of 1849-50, and hundreds of mining camps sprang to life as new deposits were discovered. Gold production increased rapidly. Deposits in the Mother Lode and Grass Valley districts in California and the Comstock Lode in Nevada, were discovered during the 1860's; and the Cripple Creek deposits in Colorado began to produce gold in 1892. By 1905, the Tonopah and Goldfield deposits in Nevada and the Alaskan placer deposits had been discovered; and United States' gold production for the first time exceeded four million troy ounces a year–a level maintained until 1917. Gold rushes occurred as early as the times of the Roman Empire, whose gold mining was described by Diodorus Siculus and Pliny the Elder, and probably further back to ancient Egypt. The following is a brief description of a few gold rushes.

1870s gold rushes:

A number of gold rushes occurred throughout the 1800s. Since a single gold nugget could make someone a millionaire, prospectors rushed to far-flung corners of the planet in search of riches. In the 19th century the wealth that resulted was distributed widely because of reduced migration costs and low barriers to entry. While gold mining itself proved unprofitable for most diggers and mine-owners, some people made large fortunes; and merchants and transportation facilities made huge profits. The resulting increase in the world's gold supply stimulated global trade and investment.

Notable gold rushes of the period included:
- North Carolina (1799): The first major gold rush in America occurred in 1799 in North Carolina, when a young boy, Conrad Reed, found a 17-pound "glittering stone" in Little Meadow Creek, on his father's farm. When assayed, it was discovered to be a massive 17-pound gold nugget.
- Thirty years later, in 1829, Frank Logan or his slave, made a find in White County, Georgia, in Dukes Creek; there are two other equally plausible anecdotal accounts–the Georgia Gold Rush in Lumpkin County near the county seat, Dahlonega, occurred and soon spread through the North Georgia mountains, following the Georgia Gold Belt. By the early 1840s, gold became difficult to find in the southern Appalachians.
- California (1848): In January, 1848, John Marshall discovered traces of gold while building a lumber mill near Sacramento for a pioneer named John Sutter. Despite Sutter's initial desire to keep the matter private and concealed, rumors spread and were confirmed by San Francisco publicist Samuel Brannan.

As word spread, Americans and immigrants alike abandoned their pursuits in favor of the Gold Country of California, eventually earning them the nickname, "Forty-Niners." The ensuing California gold rush brought a total of 300,000 people to the state. Those who did not come by sea primarily traveled from the eastern the United States by way of the California and Gila River Trails. The hardships for those traveling were substantial; and while a few people made a fortune from their findings, many were hardly able to break even and pay for their trip. This was partly due to how quickly the work necessary to obtain gold got progressively more strenuous. More fortunes were made by merchants serving the excited prospectors and later their families.

The progression of difficulty in obtaining the California gold went something like this:
1. Picking up gold off the ground.
2. Gold found in streams and riverbeds using the panning technique.
3. More sophisticated and in-depth gold mining techniques.
4. Technologically advanced systems requiring serious financing.

The longstanding effects of the Gold Rush made it a significant event in America's young history, having increased the population of San Francisco from 200 in 1846; 25,000 in 1848; to 36,000 by 1852. During that time, roads, schools, churches, and businesses were built, along with other towns, eventually leading to the establishment of California as a state in 1850. Prospectors came from across the world to San Francisco. There were so many recent migrants to San Francisco, in fact, that the massive San Francisco harbor was filled with empty ships. Nobody wanted to sail away from the bustling boomtown.

The San Francisco professional football team is famously named after the "49ers" of the gold rush of 1848/49 in California.

- Klondike (1896-1899):

Gold was discovered in the Klondike River in the Yukon Territory of Canada and in other parts of British Columbia. It became one of the last great gold rushes. Prospectors travelled to the far north and fought harsh winters to claim their fortune in the land of the midnight sun. The main goldfield was along the Klondike River near its confluence with the Yukon River. The gold rush led to the establishment of what was to become Dawson City, Canada; and it also helped open up the relatively new U.S. possession of Alaska to exploration and settlement. The Klondike Gold Rush was a migration by an estimated 100,000 prospectors to the Klondike region of the Yukon, in north-western Canada, between 1896 and 1899; only around 30,000 to 40,000 eventually made it to the gold fields.

Gold was discovered there by local miners on August 16, 1896; and, when news reached Seattle and San Francisco the following year, it triggered a stampede of prospectors. The rush began on July 15, 1897, in San Francisco and was spurred further two days later in Seattle, when the first of the early prospectors returned from the Klondike, bringing with them large amounts of gold on the ships *Excelsior* and *Portland*. The press reported that a total of $1,139,000 [equivalent to $1,000 million at 2010 prices] had been brought in by those two ships. This reporting proved to be an *underestimate*. The migration of prospectors caught so much attention that it was joined by outfitters, writers, and photographers. To reach the gold fields, most prospectors took the route through the ports of Dyea and Skagway in Southeast Alaska. There, the Klondikers could follow either the Chilkoot or the White Pass trails to the Yukon River, and sail down to the Klondike. Some Klondikers became wealthy, but the majority went in vain.

The Canadian authorities required each of them to bring a year's supply of food, in order to prevent starvation. In all, the Klondikers' equipment weighed close to a ton, which most carried themselves, in stages. Performing this task, and contending with the mountainous terrain and cold climate, meant those who persisted did not arrive until summer, 1898. Once there, they found few opportunities, and many left disappointed. To accommodate the prospectors, boom towns sprang up along the routes. At their terminus, Dawson City was founded at the confluence of the Klondike and the Yukon Rivers. From a population of 500 in 1896, the town grew to house approximately 30,000 people by summer 1898. Built of wood, isolated, and unsanitary, Dawson suffered from fires, high prices, and epidemics.

Despite this, the wealthiest prospectors spent extravagantly, gambling, and drinking, in the saloons. The Native Hän people–on the other hand–suffered from the rush; they were forcibly moved into a reserve to make way for the stampeders, and many died.

From 1898, the newspapers that had encouraged so many to travel to the Klondike lost interest in it. In the summer of 1899, gold was discovered around Nome in west Alaska, and many prospectors left the Klondike for the new goldfields, marking the end of the Klondike Rush. The boom towns declined, and the population of Dawson City fell. Gold mining production in the Klondike peaked in 1903, after heavier equipment was brought in.

• Australia (1850s onward):

Australia hosted a number of major gold rushes throughout the latter half of the 19th century. Gold was discovered in New South Wales and Victoria in the 1850s and in Western Australia in the 1890s. Gold rushes helped to populate empty areas of the Australian Outback. Towns throughout Australia owe their existence to the gold rushes of the 1800s. Various gold rushes occurred in Australia over the second half of the 19th century. [Ballarat, Bendigo, and Beechworth, Victoria; Bathurst Hill End, and Gulong, New South Wales; Canoona, Queensland; Charters Towers, Queensland; Coolgardie, Western Australia; Gympie, Queensland; Halls Creek and Kalgoorlie, Western Australia; and Queenstown, Tasmania].

The most significant of these were the New South Wales gold rush and Victorian gold rush in 1851, and the Western Australian gold rushes of the 1890s. They were highly significant to their respective colonies' political and economic development as they brought a large number of immigrants and promoted massive government spending on infrastructure to support the new arrivals who came looking for gold. While some found their fortune, those who did not, often remained in the colonies and took advantage of extremely liberal land laws to take up farming.

• Africa (1886-1896):

It was not until 1886 that the massive wealth of the Witwatersrand was uncovered although there had been rumors among indigenous Africans that gold was there. Scientific studies have pointed to the fact that the "Golden Arc" which stretches from Johannesburg to Welkom was once a massive inland lake, and that silt and gold deposits from alluvial gold settled in the area to form the gold-rich deposits for which South Africa is famous. Two earlier prospectors discovered gold in the Witwatersrand but the demand for secrecy required them to be paid off and driven from the area.

Explorer and prospector Jan Gerrit Bantjes (1840-1914) was the first and original discoverer of a Boer Witwatersrand gold reef in June 1884 having prospected the area since the early 1880s, as well as co-operating the Kromdraai Gold Mine in 1883 to the northwest of present-day Johannesburg together with his partner Johannes Stephanus Minnaar in an area known today as "The Cradle of Humankind". However, those were minor reefs, and the general consensus held that credit for the discovery of the main gold reef has been attributed to George Harrison, whose findings on the farm Langlaagte were made in July 1886, either through accident or systematic prospecting.

This was false, coming at a time when British greed led to the attempt to give credit for the discovery to the Anglo sector to justify claiming the Witwatersrand fields as British. This move was one of the factors leading to the Anglo/Boer War of 1899-1902. The Witwatersrand Gold Rush in the Transvaal of South Africa was important to that country›s history, leading to the founding of the capital, Johannesburg, and to tensions between the Boers and British settlers. South African gold production went from zero in 1886 to 23% of the total world output in 1896. At the time of the South African rush, gold production benefited from the newly discovered techniques by Scottish chemists—the MacArthur-Forrest process—of using potassium cyanide to extract gold from low-grade ore. Harrison sold his claim for less than 10 Pounds before leaving the area.

News of gold spread rapidly and reached Cecil Rhodes in Kimberley. Rhodes and his partner Robinson with a team of companions rode over 400 km to Bantjes' camp at Vogelstruisfontein and stayed with him for two nights near what would later become Roodepoort. Rhodes purchased the first batch of Witwatersrand gold from Bantjes for £3000. This purchase would be the first transaction of the newly formed company Consolidated Gold Fields of South Africa.

The world's largest gold rush ever had begun, and South Africa would never be the same. News spread around the world and prospectors from Australia to California began arriving in masses. The first lanterns of a soon to be Johannesburg began flickering along dusty streets. What was just a dusty mining village known as Ferreira's Camp quickly became a teeming city, Johannesburg. In ten years, it was the largest city in South Africa

For a number of years all went well, but then President Paul Kruger of the ZAR [South African Republic] began getting worried so many foreigners would soon outnumber the Boers, and the first of certain "measures" were put into place. Bantjes, whose father Jan Gerritze Bantjes had educated Kruger when he was a boy during the Great Trek, had discussions with Kruger regarding those "measures." One of them was to place heavy taxes on the sale of dynamite to the foreigners so as to slow the momentum.

This only agitated the miners and gave the British another reason to make a grab for the gold fields and take the lot for themselves. The disastrous Jameson Raid followed which put Cecil Rhodes in the spotlight. The Jameson Raid was supported by Rhodes and led by Sir Leander Starr Jameson. Its intent was to overthrow the Transvaal government and turn the region into a British colony. There were 500 men who took part in the uprising; 21 were killed and many arrested, tried, and sentenced. The discovery of gold, Boer resentment over the large number of *Uitlanders* [foreigners] in the Witwatersrand leading to heavy taxes, the denial of voting rights for the gold miners, and the raid, were precipitating factors not only in the gold rush, but the cause of the Second Boer War.

As a result of the rapid development of the goldfields on the Witwatersrand in the 1880s and the demand for coal by the growing industry, a concession was granted by the ZAR government to the Netherlands-South African Railway Company (NZASM) on July 20, 1888, to construct a 26 kilometer railway line from

Johannesburg to Boksburg. The already numerous Netherlanders began to be a dominant population of voters and of economic power.

South America: 1690-1815 and 1860-1906
- The Brazilian Gold Rush started in the 1690s, in the then Portuguese colony of Brazil, part of the Portuguese Empire. The gold rush opened up the major gold-producing area of *Ouro Preto* [Portuguese for *black gold*], then the aptly named *Vila Rica* [Rich Town]. Eventually, the Brazilian Gold Rush created the world's longest gold rush period and the largest gold mines in South America. The rush began when *bandeirantes* discovered large gold deposits in the mountains of *Minas Gerais*. The *bandeirantes* were adventurers who organized themselves into small groups to explore the interior of Brazil. Many *bandeirantes* were of mixed indigenous and European background who adopted the ways of the natives, which permitted them to survive in the interior rainforest. While the *bandeirantes* searched for indigenous captives, they also searched for mineral wealth, which led to the gold being discovered. More than 400,000 Portuguese and 500,000 African slaves came to the gold region to mine. Many people abandoned the sugar plantations and towns in the northeast coast to go to the gold region. By 1725, half the population of Brazil was living in southeastern Brazil.

    Officially, 850 tons of gold were sent to Portugal in the 18th century. Other gold circulated illegally, and still other gold remained in the colony to adorn churches and for other uses. The municipality of Ouro Preto became the most populous city of Latin America, amounting to about 40 thousand people in 1730 and–decades after–to 80 thousand. At that time, the population of New York was less than half of that number of inhabitants; and the population of São Paulo did not surpass eight thousand
- A gold mine at El Callao, Venezuela, started in 1871, was–for a time–one of the richest in the world; and the goldfields as a whole saw over a million ounces exported between 1860 and 1883. The gold mining was dominated by immigrants from the British Isles and the British West Indies, giving an appearance of almost creating an English colony on Venezuelan territory.
- Between 1883 and 1910, Tierra del Fuego [Spanish-Land of Fire], the southernmost region of Patagonia—Argentina and Chile–experienced a gold rush attracting a large number of Chileans, Argentines, and Europeans, to the archipelago. The gold rush begun in earnest in 1884 following discovery of gold during the rescue of the French expedition passenger ship, the steamship *Arctique,* near Cape Virgenes. During the first few years of the gold rush, mining expeditions boomed; and would-be miners flooded the area in hopes of instant riches. More than 2,000 kg of gold were collected in just three years from the Islas of Lennox and Nueva.
- The gold rush of Tierra del Fuego was never as profitable as was first hoped; and by 1885, the majority of the gold deposits were depleted. By 1910, all gold mining had ceased. During the gold rush of Tierra del Fuego, the indigenous Selk'nam people were poached in what is now known as the Selk'nam genocide.

The native population was significantly reduced and replaced with new Croatian, Chilean, and Patagonian, immigrants when the miners left.

# CHAPTER TWENTY

# SAFE RETURN AND
# TWO GIFTS IN LONDON

IN THE YEAR OF OUR LORD, 1645, LATE AUGUST

The voyage from Constantinople to London with its several diversions was consistently profitable which increased the value of the cargo by nearly half and the danger from pirates by multiples. The need for secrecy and security was central to everyone on the *Z-Louisa Hendrika*. Everyone was relieved to be back in Christian waters, even though they knew that piracy was a major industry; and the Christian pirates were no respecters of religious faith. Anneke was especially pleased to be near to European soil and the anticipation of being out of the confines of the ship and away from the continuous six degrees of motion: heave, sway, surge, roll, pitch, and yaw. Her discomfort was multiplied by the fact that she was heavy with child—well into her eighth month. She was nauseated; she felt bloated; her ankles had doubled in size; and she could not bear to look at herself in a ship's mirror because she could see only ugliness and weariness.

Piet was a worried young husband and father to be. He grew more anxious every day, fearing that his tired young wife might have to deliver her child on the ship without benefit of hospital, doctor, midwife, or nurse. The ship was dirty, and Piet feared for the safety of his wife and unborn child. He was aware of the reputation of hospitals for filthiness and danger to women in labor. But, he was sure that he and the crew could scour a hospital room to protect the two passengers who had become as precious as the cargo to them.

Anneke—with her keen luminescent blue eyes and avid curiosity—was the first to sight land. She raced to the deck master and told him. He ordered a seaman to climb aloft and observe.

In a few minutes, he yelled, "Ahoy! Ahoy! Land ho! It's Europe!"

Anneke found Piet and took his arm; so, they could see the first glimpses of something that was like home to both of them. Jans joined them and smiled as land became more certain. He sniffed the air and took a hard look at the estuary water joining the open Atlantic.

He lost his smile and said, "See the brown water? That tells us that we are nearing London. It pains me to say, but we can smell it as well."

Anneke—in the advanced stages of pregnancy—was especially sensitive to the odors and shortly began to gag. A nearby sailor—an old salt who had made the voyage into the outlet of the Thames multiple times before—was ready to help his "little gel" as he affectionately called Anneke. He produced a pristine white handkerchief made of finely woven cotton that he had saved all the long voyage to give his sweetheart—who had married another man while he was gone.

He poured a few drops of strong French perfume that he had saved for the same purpose on the pretty piece of cloth and handed it to Anneke.

"Little missy, put this ta yer wee nosie all the way up the stinkin' river. It'll help ye."

Anneke held the cloth to her offended nose, and her nausea began to abate.

"Oh, Gerald, I thank you from my heart. I know you were saving it. I will keep it clean and will wash it to be pretty again when we get away from the river. You'll find another sweetheart to give it to."

"Ach, Lassie, I think Oim a bit long in the tooth for athat any more. I'll feel better knowin' ye and the sweet baby that's acomin' will fare better for havin' it close by."

She leaned forward and gave the grizzled sea salt a peck on his cheek, and he blushed scarlet and bowed his head. Piet noticed that he was careful not to allow any dirt to reach that spot on his cheek for the rest of the slow sailing up the Thames.

Jans had been to London many times over his long maritime career. He explained something about the river and its condition.

"We're traveling from the Atlantic estuary on the west going east through the south of England to the Thames Pool. That's the harbor and wharves—the biggest and busiest in the world, I'm told. The waterway and its banks are very delicate, in a way. We are only allowed to go five miles and hour; so, we don't injure the plant life and the dirt. Look at the banks. Business thrives, and that's part of why we're here. Lucky for us that we don't have to go far up stream. After a certain point, there are no locks to control the rapids, only dams, or weirs, controlling the water's flow and providing the necessary power to mills along the banks. Boatmen navigating the river up there are forced to 'shoot the weir,' meaning they have to race through a slot opened in the dam. The dams are a sorry lot, made of turf and rotting wood, really shabby affairs. Or otherwise the poor blighters have to portage their vessels around the obstruction. It's hard life.

"I tell you now and remind you more than once. You are never to touch the river water, get it on your clothes, and keep the new baby away from it no matter what. We're here in the tidal reaches of the unfortunate river; it's just a badly managed open sewer."

He had his own perfumed handkerchief that he placed over his mouth when he breathed.

"The Thames has been that way for centuries—since before the 1000s, I'm told. The people of London and its industries have discarded their rubbish in the river, seems like forever. This awful stuff has included the waste from slaughterhouses, fish markets, and tanneries. The buildup in household cesspools all too often overflows, especially when it rains, and washed into London's streets and sewers which eventually led to the Thames and out to contaminate the very ocean. It's a deadly, diseased, sewer; and the experts say it is biologically dead—not a living thing in it, animal or plant."

"That's not all I smell," Anneke said, holding Gerald's handkerchief pressed to her nose and mouth.

"It's a surprise that you can distinguish any one bad from another bad, Anneke, my dear, there's a lot of contributors. The air itself is noxious. Besides the river being an uncovered latrine and cesspool, there's constant foul smoke emitted by burning sea coal, and backed-up chimneys that have suffocated people in their beds for centuries. Sometimes there are great stinks and great smogs that join up with 'pea-soupers' to make it all but impossible to live in the city or voyage on the river."

"What's a 'pea-souper'?" asked Anneke.

"It's a green fog so thick you cannot see your hand in front of your face. You can taste and almost chew the air."

Anneke had a little gag at the thought of it.

"I'm sorry to upset you, but there is more you need to know. Remember this; do not go anywhere alone. There are pickpockets, cut-pockets, cheats, and men who hurt women, all about. Do not drink or eat anything that either Piet or I have not approved; there are money grubbers who will serve drinks and food laced with the deadly night shade berries, Rue, Spurge, Laurel leaves, Ricin made from castor beans, hemlock—the poison that killed Socrates so long ago—strychnine made from seeds of the plant *Strychnos nux vomica*, Curare—which is a mixture of some kind of plant from South America that is used by the natives for poison arrows and blowgun darts, and, of course arsenic, which is used as a medicine to treat the 'French Disease'. I'm not entirely sure, but it seems to me that the cure is worse than the disease."

Piet interjected, "We can see the Pool from here, but the harbor looks like a forest of dense ship masts. How do we get to a mooring dock, Jans?"

"We wait. Could be a few weeks or as long as three months during busy time, and this looks to be one of those. We'll have to take a long boat to the wharf and do some investigating and put in our names and the name of the ship to get into the queue."

Anneke listened, then spoke quietly, "Piet and Jans, I think my time is coming on and probably won't be another day before we see a new little Van Brakel. I will need to go into the city with you, or you will become a midwife before you're twenty-five."

Piet looked stricken. The thought of being responsible for bringing a new baby into the world and risking his beloved wife was more than he dared imagine.

"We will get to shore and find a good hospital this very day!" he exclaimed, the primeval cry of an expectant father.

"I know just the place," Jans said. "I will send a rower ashore to see if it is still doing God's work."

It took two hours for the sailor to maneuver his way through the dense thicket of boats and ships and to get the needed information about hospitals. He reported back to Jans.

"Cap'n, Sir, it's still St. Thomas's by far. However, they're afumigatin' the place to get rid of a new plague of the cholera."

He extracted a piece of paper from his waist purse and read, "There's a sign on the wharf at Saint Katharine's Docks near the customs 'ouse sayin' '*Whereas unfounded Reports have been circulated of the prevalence of Cholera in the St. Katharine Docks, Notice is hereby given, that no such Disease exists within the Walls of the Establishment. By Order of the Board, John Hall, Secretary.*"

"Now that's a black lie, the real people along the docks tells me. One young guy showed me an alley where there were three bloated corpses alayin' there in the piles of trash."

Jans said, "Then as we go about our business, mind who you talk to and who you touch. Our first stop is at St. Thomas's Hospital. We know we'll be safe there, and our girl will be clean and safe to bring forth her first born."

Every man took a turn rowing the skiff towards the stairs on the part of the Thames between London Bridge—the bridge being the farthest reach that could be navigated by a tall-masted vessel—and Cuckold's Point, the eastern extremity of the Pool of London—located at the north-eastern tip of the Rotherhithe peninsula.

Even with her growing discomfort, Anneke took in the sights of the most congested port in the world with the animated curiosity and enthusiasm of a child.

"It looks like a forest of masts," she exclaimed as they weaved their way through the large vessels of the East India Company anchored off Blackwall.

The East India merchantmen were very large ships, full-rigged, and multi-masted, and capable of sailing great distances without making a port. Within Anneke's vision were ships of the

English navy—hulks, galleasses, and galleys. The variety of ships and boats was staggering; the congestion was so dense that Anneke and "her men" could scarcely see the water, which was a blessing.

They rowed in and out between Elizabethan pinnaces, carracks–giant three masted vessels with square sails on the fore and main masts and lateen-rigged on the mizzen. They had very high fore and aft-castles— which, at 1,200 tons, before the advent of the galleon were the largest ships afloat. They were used for trading voyages to India, China, and the Americas, by the Spanish and Portuguese. A carrack carried an immense amount of power and thus was able to fend off pirates with relative ease.

The variety in The Pool included small, lightly armed, warships called corvettes, Thames 'Gresham Merchant Ships', frigates, river barges, sloops–the single-masted sloop had a bowsprit almost as long as her hull making her one of the swiftest vessels of her day–Dutch *fleuts*–merchant ships, similar in design to a barque, which were inexpensive to build, and could carry a large cargo, factors that gave the Dutch their 17$^{th}$ century mastery of maritime commerce—small trading ships called caravals, which had morphed into eighty foot long square-masted ships used by the Spanish and Portuguese for exploration. There were scores of schooners with all the best features for a pirate ship—shallow draft permitting sailing into shallow rivers where government ships could not get them. Also, in prominent numbers were barques–small three-masted ships which were also fast ships with a shallow draft.

Jans gave Anneke a running tutorial on the ships she was encountering, "there's a brig; they're fast and maneuverable and are used as both naval warships and merchant vessels; that's a brigantine which is a sail and oar driven small warship mainly used in the Mediterranean by pirates. You're a smart girl and good with languages; so, you may be interested to learn that its name comes from the Italian word *brigantino*, meaning brigand. That one of the left, is a cutter—the smallest commissioned ships in the fleet. It gets its name from the fact that their excellent maneuverability for coastal patrol because they are good for 'cutting-out' raids. When it comes the *Z Hendrika Louisa's* turn to dock, a pilot cutter will serve as the ferry harbor pilot."

Near in towards the wharves they passed German North and Baltic Sea galliots, ketches, luggars, and *pinckes* [Eng. pink]. Piet and Jans hurriedly named off the large military vessels near the wharves: *"HMS Adventure, HMS Assurance,* the *Botik of Peter the Great,* the Dutch Ship

*Brederode, HMS Constant Warwick, HMS Dragon,* English ship *Elizabeth,* French ship *Leopold,* English ship *Nonsuch,* English ship *Phoenix,* French ship *Soleil,* English ship *Swan,* French ship *Tigre,* Dutch ships *Aemilia, Blessing of Burntisland, Blessing of the Bay, The Flying Deer, the Griffin, the Mary and John, Princess Amelia, HMS Sovereign of the Seas,* and the *HMS Unicorn.*"

That brought them to the Blackwell Stairs and the immense, famous Dock of the Pool with its customs buildings. The river was lined with nearly continuous walls of wharves running for miles along both banks. The wharves held a long line of port industries: sugar refining, edible oil processing, lead smelting, casting of brass and bronze, shipbuilding, timber, grain, cement and paper milling, and armament manufacture. The industries upon which the country depended were there: Millwall Iron Works, Thames Ironworks, Greenwich, Deptford and Woolwich dockyards. London was the major center of shipbuilding in England, including at Blackwall, London, Thames Ironworks and Shipbuilding Company, and Samuda Yards.

Massive amounts of coal were handled directly by riverside coal handling facilities, rather than the docks. There were two large piers which dealt with coal and with the transfer of coal to lighters for delivery to other users.

Nearby Blackwall Yard was small but an extremely busy body of water that was a major shipyard on the River Thames. It had been engaged in ship building repairs for over 350 years. The docks and shipyards were heavily protected by private security guards who were considerably better paid than London bobbies. Smuggling, theft, and pilferage, of cargoes, and more than their share of violent crimes, were rife on both the busy open wharves and in the crowded warehouses. The desperate poor fell into crime as a last resort despite the drastic penalties for being caught; for example, pickpocketing and counterfeiting were capital crimes; and public hangings were almost an ever day occurrence.

They moored at Blackwall Yard and got out of the dinghy. All around them were ships in various stages of completion. Fifty years ago, the HEIC [Honorable East India Company] had decided to build its own ships and leased a yard in Deptford that still prospered. Anneke looked pale and sweaty, and occasionally her face knotted with pain. She fought herself not to cry out, knowing how much that hurt the sensitivities of "her men".

Giant Able Seaman Andries Janszoon Jukes was a kind and sympathetic man for all his massive muscles and battle scars. He recognized that the climb up the Blackwell Stairs would be too much for a little girl in Anneke's delicate state. He towered over her, and she smiled. He had given her posies when he could, shares of his rations, and once somehow found a bar of perfumed soap to give her.

He leaned over and swept her into his burly muscled arms, grinned at her, and pursed his lips as if in a platonic kiss. He carried her up the stairs with no more effort than if he were toting a four-year-old. When they got to the solid platform of the wharf, he gently set her down. She rewarded him with a peck on his scarred cheek and a warm hug. He blushed and shuffled but was as pleased as he had ever been. Women were usually afraid of him, but none of them should ever have been. The little girl, Anneke, heavy with child, was forever precious to him.

The men surrounded Anneke and they half-carried and half-fast-walked Anneke as they hurried across the expansive wharf towards Saint Katherine's Docks. Piet found a foreman of a cab company and hired three hackney coaches which were primitive springless boxes on wheels pulled by one horse and a driver. He explained to the foreman,

"My wife is about to bring about new light into the world, and it is an emergency. Get us to St. Thomas's in record time, and I'll double your pay."

"Don't you worry your 'ead, Guv. We'll 'ave the lassie in the lyin' in ward before ya can say 'Jack Robinson'."

True to his word, the three hackneys rattled and crashed their way through the city, aided by helpful bobbies to Trenet Lane on the north side of St Thomas Street, Southwark. The hospital was old by any standards; it had been in service for the past three hundred years. Originally, it was named for St. Thomas a becket. After some extensive refurbishing, it was officially re-dedicated, this time for Thomas the Apostle.

Andries found a cart, and "her men" wheeled Anneke into the lying-in entrance on Borough High Street.

Her condition was evident and the first attendant to see her, asked Anneke, "How far apart are your pains, my dear"

"No more than ten minutes, Sister."

"Reg'lar are they?"

"Yes, Ma'am."

"You boys follow me. We're up to the delivery room. Move smart, now!"

They arrived at the delivery room areas and found considerable disarray. The man in charge—obviously, the head doctor–walked around the rooms fumigating them with smoke from resinous woods. Nurses and aides were giving furniture and floors strong scrubbings with lye soap followed by strong-smelling carbolic of lime. One orderly's job was to apply a solution of the carbolic of lime to the window blinds.

Piet asked the doctor, "Is there something wrong here, Doctor?"

"Not now, Son. We had a touch of the Cholera end of last week, but the patients have all passed on to their Maker, and we have cleaned the hospital top to bottom."

"Will my wife be safe to have a baby here?"

"Safest place in England, my boy. Don't fret. She's in good hands."

Just then, Anneke cried out in pain, and the sisters whisked her into the delivery suite. "Her men" watched nervously through the door as Anneke was helped onto the delivery table.

The good doctor gave each man a small medicine cup filled with a powder mixture made of Virginian snake root, bezoar stone, unicorn horn, dried toad sweetened with myrrh, cinnamon. and angelica root.

"To ward off the Cholera, boys. Nothing better for it."

For all his country bumpkin look, Andries watched the proceedings with the keenest eye. As the great doctor approached Anneke in his delivery gown, Andries strode purposefully into the room and confronted the doctor.

"What is the meaning of this?" the doctor demanded

Andries calmly–but with perfect assurance–asked, "Man, did you wash your hands with carbolic soap before coming into this room?"

"Of course, I did. I do so every morning. Now get along and let me bring this baby into the world."

"No," Andries said.

"What do you mean?"

"Wash your hands now. My mother was the midwife in our parish, and she had a near perfect record of preventing childbed fever. She told me often that it was because she washed her hands before and between every patient. She demanded clean linens. This little girl of ours will have nothing less."

There was something about looking into the eyes of a nearly seven-en-foot-tall, 380-pound giant that suggested to everyone involved that compliance with his reasonable request was easy enough to do. Everyone in the room went out and washed with the caustic soap and wiped on sterilized towels.

Anneke was small, young, and delicate; but she was a trooper. After six hours of hard labor, she delivered a ruddy, caseous cheesy covered baby boy who did not have to have his bottom spanked to announce his unwanted entrance into the harsh world. He yelled his head off and made everyone laugh with joy. The baby was placed on Anneke's bare chest, and he climbed up to her nipples and took hold.

Then, a sort of miracle happened. A second baby boy entered the world four minutes later. There was joy nearing rapture among "her men", and Piet wept in thanksgiving.

Several times during Anneke's lying-in period, "her boys" visited her. Piet usually stayed the night.

Piet and his shipmates spent the long days industriously getting the *Z-Louisa Hendrika* offloaded and the customs rigmarole taken care of. He thanked the doctor and the sisters every day for the gift of the two robust baby boys and at the end of the lyin-in, as they were about to cart Anneke and the two gifts from God out of the hospital, Piet took hold of both of Andries's hands.

"Andries, my very good friend. I am forever grateful to you. You have a place with me for as long as I live. I will be as loyal to you as you have been to me."

THE HISTORY:

HISTORY OF LONDON: PRE-HISTORY TO THE 17<sup>TH</sup> CENTURY

Because the history of London is so long and so well documented, even this limited history would fill volumes of narrative. For that reason, the author has elected to give a brief chronological list for part of the history. In addition to its brevity even as such a list, there are very considerable gaps of information, both because of limited space and due to choices made by the present author.

Pre-history:

The LBP [Last Glacial Period] encompassed the era from BCE 115,000-BCE 11,700 years ago. This "most recent glacial period" extended from about 2,588,000 years ago to the present–over time and with considerable warming–extensively removing the vast majority of glaciers around the globe with the exception of Antarctica. During the Ice Age, deep layers of chalk were deposited at the rate of about one centimeter a year in what would become the Greater London Area, which was covered with water at the time. As the ice-melt retreated north during the Pleistocene Era between 1.5 MYA and roughly 10,000 BCE, it revealed a bowl-shaped depression created by the upward movement of the Alps during the LGP. Within the bowl, there is a floor of sand and clay deposited 65 MYA (at about the time the last dinosaurs disappeared), the upper layers of soil and rock having been stripped away by glacial movement. The rims of the bowl constitute the present-day hills at Harrow and Highgate. Very large volumes of water flowed out of the bowl, covering southeast Britain with water. The flow was through what is now London via a very wide slow-moving stream, which came eventually to be known as the River Thames. At that time, the river was pure, and crystal clear, and soon filled with fish and water plant life.

As the river flowed lazily along over thousands of years, it deposited gravel at its edges creating terraced banks. Archeologists have found human made tools 500,000 years old in those banks. Over time—as the Thames narrowed–the findings of the tools were such that the more primitive tools were nearer the valley banks, and the more recent were found progressively closer to the river bank of the present era, indicative of continual living by humans in the area for a very long time, including a paleolithic hand axe. There was a Mesolithic tool manufactory and remnants of the makings of mead and beer. Most of what is the modern-day City of London lay under the water of the wider Thames. Over most of the past 50,000 years of recession of the width of the Thames, the suburb of today's Southwark was under water. The evidence is clear that people have lived in London for over 15,000 years.

Erosion from the many tributaries of the Thames over the last several hundred years created the topography of the area of Greater London and deposited a mixture of gravel, clay, and brick-earth, from which much of London has been built. The softness of the clay has created a lasting problem of failure to make solid foundations for buildings and bridges throughout the city's history.

Archeologists have discovered and catalogued a wide assortment of animals that were extant in that period: mastodons, mammoths, hippopotami, rhinoceri, hyenas, buffalo, bear, lions, reindeer, giant beavers, sharks, and mackerel. They also found tons of archeological human rubbish thousands of years old.

Early inhabitants—who left no written record—apparently made no permanent buildings but, rather, drifted about through the region. Evidence of the presence of later human involvement began when the world began to warm, and animals returned to the London area. 6,000-year-old timbers were found in what is now Vauxhall. The original people who came and stayed were linked to the Brettonic-speaking Celtic tribes from northern Europe and the west of France. Shortly before 100 BCE, south eastern Britain was invaded by north eastern Gauls—the Belgae. Unlike the Celtics, the Belgae were a fairly advanced people militarily who had learned the use of chariots and sling-stones for warfare. They built large fortresses surrounded by ditch/moats to protect themselves. They were advanced enough to have created a hierarchal society ruled by kings and nobles. Archeological evidence indicates that they settled largely in what was the rich farm country of modern-day Kent and Buckinghamshire.

During the 1$^{st}$ century BCE, Belgic Catuvellauni tribes entered the area north of the Thames in what is modern Middlesex, Hertfordshire, and Bedfordshire, and established a royal capital on the River Lea near St. Albans. Trinovantes lived to their east in present day Colchester. People of Belgic origin—eventually known as the Regnenses—occupied what became south London, Surrey, and Sussex; and the Cantiaci settled in Kent with their major settlement in Canterbury. To the west—along the upper Thames valley—a people known as the Atrebates lived.

The wide and deep Thames was an excellent waterway for travel and for fishing, but its forested hillsides constituted a difficult terrain to traverse; hence the river became a natural barrier to separate the different peoples from each other. Before the Romans came, the Belgae created a road system that permitted extensive travel and brisk trade. Those routes were very similar to the later Roman roads. Their pre-Roman minted coins were found all along those routes.

Roman Era:

| | |
|---|---|
| 54 BCE: Julius Caesar's first invasion of Britain | 1066 CE: London conquered by Wm the Conqueror |
| 43 CE: Naming of Londinium | 1123 CE: Rahere establishes St. Bartholomews |
| 41 CE: Roman invasion of Britain | 1176 CE: Stone Bridge built |
| 60 CE: Queen Boudicca burned Londinium to the ground | 1220 CE: Westminster Abbey rebuilt |
| 61-122 CE: Rebuilding Londinium | 1290 CE: Expulsion of the Jews |
| 120 CE: Hadrianic fire of London | 1326 CE: London revolution-deposition of Edward II |

190 CE: Building of the Great Wall

407 CE: Roman withdrawal from London

457 CE: Britons flee to evade the Germanic Saxons

490 CE: Saxon domination

587 CE: Augustine mission to London

604 CE: Foundation of a bishopric and St. Paul's

672 CE: 1$^{st}$ reference to Port of London

672 CE: Growth of Lundenwic

851 CE: London razed by Vikings

886 CE: London retaken and rebuilt by King Alfred

892 CE: London citizens repel Danish invasion Fleet

959 CE: Great fire. St. Paul's burned

994 CE: Unsuccessful siege by Danish Vikings

1013 CE: 2$^{nd}$ siege, London conquered by Sweyn

1016 CE: 3rd siege by Cnut, repulsed

1050 CE: Rebuilding of Westminster Abbey

1348 CE: Black Death-1/3 of population killed

1381 CE: Wat Tyler's revolt

1406 CE: Plague

1414 CE: Lollard revolt

1442 CE: Strand paved

1450 CE: Jack Cade's revolt

1476 CE: Caxton's printing press established

1484 CE: The sweating sickness

1509 CE: Henry VIII ascends to the throne

1535 CE: Execution of Thomas Moore

1535-1539: Spoilation of monasteries and churches

1608-1613: Construction of the New River

1642-1643: Construction of earthen walls and forts against the King's army

1648 CE: Execution of Charles I

1665 CE: The Great Plague

1666 CE: The Great Fire

## Medieval London

As an introduction, the author will include a short introduction to provide some backdrop to the historical fiction of this novel. First, consider the name of the city. To the Romans it was Londinium, a name which morphed over time into Londinio, Londiniensi, Londinienslum, Lundunes, Lundene, Lundone, Ludenberk, Longidinium, Kaerlud/Kaerlundein/Caer Ludd [Lud's City], Cockaigne [to the Celtics] and even to Augusta in 358 to highlight its importance as an imperial center. Ludgate Hill and Corn Hill remain from that era. Throughout its long history, and often for obvious reasons, it was nicknamed, "the Big Smoke", "The Smoke", and from time to time, "The Big Wen", a reference to a small skin cyst filled with sebaceous material, which was at times purulent. Over time its river became a huge busy port, and the city became one of the great metropolises of history.

The original Londinium was a rough Roman military camp established by Julius Caesar which the Romans abandoned in the 5th century CE. However, of the fifteen British main roads in the 2nd and 3rd centuries, seven ran to and from Londinium and modern highways have links to those past thoroughfares. The numerous streams extant in that time still exist but now run underground. An example is the Hidden River Fleet which was an important of London before there was a London, before even the Anglo-Saxons came. It is the largest of the city's hidden subterranean rivers, one that was used by the Romans as a major water thoroughfare. Like many other rivers, as London grew and its industry and population flourished in the Middle Ages, the stream became progressively more choked with rubbish and debris and polluted with tons of unmentionables. There were attempts to correct the man-made-mess, but they failed. The originally clear and productive river which became a serviceable canal ended up as an open sewer. By the beginning of the 18th century it humiliated Londoners to have a flowing putrid sludge moving through the city; so, they bricked it over, and it was forgotten for 250 years. However, it kept flowing beneath the sidewalks of London, still serving as a sewer going nowhere.

The early settlement was no more than half a square mile in area, smaller than a modern London park. In 60 or 61 CE a rebellion lead by an Iceni woman, Queen Boudica. She had a very legitimate grievance: her father, King of the Iceni, who had possibly aided his tribesmen in a failed revolt against the Romans. He died and left a will dividing his lands and wealth equally between Rome and his wife Boudica and two daughters which included the stipulation that his wife Boudica would reign as queen.

The Romans would have none of that. Roman law did not allow females to inherit and expropriated all wealth for taxes and for Roman development by businessmen. To add injury to the insult, Roman elites had their soldiers flog her, rape her and her daughters, and enslaved their kinsmen and nobles. Boudica was displeased, to say the least. She fomented a revolt which resulted in driving out the Romans from their garrison, killing of 30,000 citizens, and razing the settlement to the ground. She was subsequently defeated by a Roman legion and executed. Queen Elizabeth honored her with a statue that still stands in the city because she likened to herself as a leader. Thereafter the Roman leaders rebuilt the city, turned it into a thriving secure military encampment and commercial city.

Late in the first decade CE, Londinium's population peaked; and it was the largest city in Britannia with a population of 30,000 to 60,000. By mid 2nd century the city reached its zenith—having built stone houses, townhouses, brick public buildings, piped water, and a fairly sophisticated drainage system; but that was short-lived. Emperor Hadrian visited in 122 CE and shortly thereafter a fire destroyed the city again. The destruction razed magnificent buildings and at least temporarily destroyed the morale of the city. It shrunk in size and importance until the Antonine Plague struck between 165 and 180 CE causing the population of London to diminish by two-thirds.

Anglo-Saxon London came gradually into being after German Saxons entered the city when the legionnaires left to attend to the chaos going on in Rome as it was being sacked in 410 CE. Emperor Honorius told the citizens they had to fend for themselves before he fled west with all the valuable treasure of the city. Apparently, the Romans abandoned London for the next two hundred years, and the Saxons did not use it as a major city. Over the next hundred years, Angles, Saxons, Jutes, and Frisians, arrived in the vicinity and established small tribal areas and kingdoms. In 255, there was sufficient interest in preserving the city that the citizens built a new wall by the Thames to protect against recurring raids by Saxon pirates. That wall ran roughly where Thames Street is today which formed the shoreline.

In the 5th and 6th centuries, the area was administered as the Kingdom of the East Saxons. Germanic Anglo-Saxons subsequently established colonies in the area; and–in the seventh and eighth centuries–made use of the port which they named Lundenwic [meaning London settlement/trading town]. In 886, King Alfred the Great resettled the land inside the old walls, shored up its defenses, and called his settlement within the walls, Lundenburh [fortified town of London]. Covent Garden still existed since Roman times, but the port became Ealdwic [old settlement], modern Aldwych.

After 893, the burgers and defenses of London appeared to be enough that Vikings could no longer prevail or retaliate. The early 10th century was an era of peace. The peace was marred not by men; but in 961, there was another great fire in which St. Paul's was destroyed, followed by the plague. In 982, there was another massive fire. Then, the Vikings chose to launch many attacks, all of which were repulsed successfully because by that time, London had acquired its own army. In 1013, however, the Danes came again, this time in force, and took the city. But, something that seemed like a miracle to the citizenry of London took place. Olaf of Sweden came to London and saved the city. He was beatified as a prospective saint by the religious citizens and soon afterwards, Danes settled peacefully outside the walls and eventually assimilated.

The area around and within the walls prospered and became the religious center of Westminster. After the defeat in the Norman conquest, new citizens flocked in and used various different names for their city of refuge: Lundin, Londoun, Lunden, or Londen, finally settling on London. The square mile within the old walls has been known since that time as "The City of London", or "The City", indicating it to be a city within a city. The rest of the metropolis is generally referred to as "Greater London".

Most people consider the start of the Middle Ages in Europe to be 500 CE when Rome finally fell. It may be more accurate for Londoners, however, to date the medieval era to Christmas Day, 1066. More about that later.

Trade and commerce on land and on the river grew fairly steadily during the Middle Ages interrupted at times by conflicts, plagues, and civil unrest; and London grew rapidly as a result. In 1100 CE, London's population was only about 15,000. By 1300—two-hundred years later–it had grown to nearly 80,000. Trade in London was organized into various guilds, which effectively controlled the city, and elected the Lord Mayor of London.

The government of the city was by a Lord Mayor and council elected from the ranks of the merchant guilds. These guilds effectively ran the city and controlled commerce. Each guild had its own hall and their own coat of arms, but there was also the Guildhall (1411-1440) where representatives of the various guilds met in common

The guilds were not just competitive; the members behaved like the Montagues and the Capulets. They were violent and would attack a member of another guild for the slightest provocation with beatings with clubs, stabbing with swords and heavy knives, or anything handy. Violence was a daily occurrence in the 13th century with massacres, and street fighting. Those crimes often went unpunished for lack of witnesses but pity the poor man or woman who was sentenced to serve a term in the infamous Newgate Prison. Bodies were dumped into the Thames every day from the prison. Across the river, the Clink jail was not much better. The mean streets of London were violent, unsafe, odoriferous, dirty, and pestilential.

Medieval London was made up of narrow and twisting streets, and most of the buildings were made from combustible materials such as wood and straw, with thatch roofs as tinder which made fire a constant threat and a frequently realized one. There was a great fire in London in 1077 during the Norman rule, another in 1212, and the Great Fire of 1666 which gutted much of London within the city wall. The master of understatement would concede that sanitation in London was poor. London lost at least half of its population during the Black Death in the mid-14th century. Between 1348 and the Great Plague of 1666 there were sixteen outbreaks of plague in the city. It was a tough place to live.

London was extremely noisy and had been since Roman times. There was a certain central roar to the city. Church, convent, and guild bells, rang out the time of day, celebration festivities, calls to church services, the tinkling sound of small bells on dray horses' necks, and from the ubiquitous taverns. Even prostitutes signaled to prospective clients with hand bells. London was a city of trades and the noise of pounding hammers everywhere—blacksmiths, tanners, repair men, builders, and "Lucifers"— the match sellers who signaled their presence with continuous pounding on whatever was handy—and tinkers who banged on their pans–went about their work twelve to eighteen hours a day.

If all of the rest of the noises had somehow vanished for a moment, there would still have been the white noise formed by the sound of people clomping along on wood tile streets, and all sorts of animals pulling carts and vehicles of every description throughout the city. Farm animals were driven along the city streets, and an occasional runaway horse added to the general clamor. Countless vehicles of all sorts plied the streets contributing to the chaos and the omnipresent din: carriages, omnibuses, glass coaches, street coaches, wagons, carts, dog-carts, and funeral corteges. In addition, London was a musical city with scores of celebratory bands marching to commemorate saints, funerals, and festivals. Conversely, it was deathly silent at night when all the noisemakers went to their rest. It was described as "the city of the dead" at night. Citizens of Cheapside complained that the silence woke them up and disturbed their rest.

London was a diverse city of polyglots, trades, and ethnicity, from around the known world. The traditional costumes of a dozen different cultures could be seen on a walk on any street inside the city walls on any given day. Immigrants were mostly poor and worked at the lower end of the economic scale. They came from Italy, Turkey, Russia, Sweden, France, and Spain. Their numbers included: Americans, Irish, "hunter Indians", Malays, Chinese, Moors, and Negroes. Generally, the diversity was tolerated and appreciated because of the enhancement to commerce it brought. However, anti-Semitism was rife, discriminatory, regularly brutal, and often murderous.

London was the foremost center of England's Jewish population. Refuges flowed in from the Rouen Pogrom in 1096. The first Jewish quarter was established in 1128. They were prohibited from ordinary commerce but could be money lenders. Christian merchants were forbidden to engage in usury. Jews were hated and discriminated against for the very trade that had been imposed upon them. Extreme violence against Jews took place in 1189 in their quarter and their homes were burned. Whole families were beaten to death or burned alive. In 1190, after it was rumored that the new King had ordered their massacre because they had presented themselves at his coronation.

In 1264 during the Second Barons' War, Simon de Montfort's rebels occupied London and killed 500 Jews while attempting to seize records of debts. In 1272, many hundreds of Jews were hanged because of suspicion that they had adulterated the coinage; they were made to wear a tabula of the stone tablets to signify their race; they were subjected to Jew-baiting, which became a sport equivalent to cock-throwing, bull-baiting, dog-fighting, or pelting some poor wretch locked in the stocks. Eighteen years later, in 1290, London's entire Jewish community was forced to leave England by the expulsion by Edward I. They left for France, Holland, and further afield; their property was seized; and many suffered robbery and murder as they departed the city.

The Irish were not treated much better. They were subjected to mob violence because they worked for lower wages than the English, a situation over which they had no choice or control. Bigotry is described by Americans as being as "American as apple pie", and much the same can be said for Medieval London, perhaps substituting black pudding [blood, milk, animal fat, onions, and oatmeal] for apple pie.

In the early Middle Ages, England had no fixed capital per se; kings moved from place to place taking their court with them. The closest thing to a capital was Winchester where the royal treasury and financial records were stored. This changed from about 1200 when these were moved to Westminster. From this point on, royal government became increasingly centered upon Westminster, which steadily became the de facto capital; and Westminster Palace became the center of the feudal system of government.

Westminster was a small town upriver from the City of London. From the 13th century onwards, London grew up in two different parts. Westminster became the Royal capital and center of government, whereas the City of London became the center of commerce and trade, a distinction which is still evident in our day. The area between them became entirely urbanized by 1600. An acknowledgment of London's status as a capital was that surrounding cities sent their condemned criminals to Newgate Prison for execution. It was the City of London who elected the next king. The first theaters started there in 1576.

For all its street crime, excessive alcohol use, debauchery, and violent sports, London was famous for its religiosity and piety. London was a city of churches—more than 100 of them within the walls—monasteries, covent gardens, colleges of priests and friars, and various of them—along with the manor houses–owned a major portion of the land and had hands in many of the profitable businesses. At one point in the medieval period there were thirteen monasteries in the city. Today, these houses are remembered only by the names they gave to their area, such as Greyfriars, Whitefriars, and Blackfriars. Bells rang from steeples constantly throughout the city; there were hordes of religious hermits begging in the streets; the streets surrounding St. Paul's Cathedral were named: Pater Noster Row, Ave Maria Lane, Amen Court, and Creed Lane. Every year vast numbers of religious pilgrims visited the city to enjoy miraculous cures—chroniclers recorded hundreds. The pious added to the congestion of the city by praying in the streets. A holy well was located in Hyde Park, where sick children were immersed. There was a nod to religious tolerance, but Catholicism ruled the city for the most part. In 1170, Henry II had Thomas à Becket murdered for his disagreement with doctrine favored by the royal court. Becket was later canonized as an English saint. Medieval London was a curious mix of violence and devotion.

Attempted and actual invasions and revolts of London: Probably the most important of these was the Christmas Day in 1066 when William, Duke of Normandy, and his retinue walked along St. Giles High Street and turned south to Westminster, having only recently laid waste to Southwark and was preparing his siege of the London Wall. The war was over—for all intents and purposes–after his defeat of Anglo-Saxon king Harold Godwinson II in a decisive battle that took place in October. The English king died in the battle, leaving the way open for the easy Norman Conquest of England.

The Battle of London as anticipated never took place. By one sort of hook or crook or another, certain Saxon nobles opened Ludgate and the French walked in and headed for Cheapside and St. Paul's. They met little more than token resistance from a militia or "army" of citizens who were determined that no foreign leader would enter and conquer their city. They fought well, but it was a forgone conclusion which resulted in great mourning by the families of the fighters. On that day, William (then called the Conqueror) was crowned king in the new Westminister Abbey. Oddly, the citizens' resistance resulted in the world recognizing London as an independent and sovereign city-state which remained as such for the ensuing three hundred years.

William and his descendants realized their purpose to subject the city and to cause a number of remarkably positive things—changes in the form of government, construction of great buildings including Westminster Hall which became the Palace of Westminster, Baynard's Castle, and Montfichet›s Castle, and repaired the defensive walls. He built a castle in the southeast corner of the city to keep overly independent citizens under control. This castle was expanded by later kings until it became the complex now known as the Tower of London. During William's and his sons' and grandsons' time, the Tower acted as royal residence, a royal mint, a treasury, and housed the beginnings of a zoo. It was not until later that it became famous as a prison. He exacted riches from the city and essentially brought an unprecedented period of peace.

In 1097, William II, began construction of Westminster Hall, close to the abbey of the same name. The hall proved to be the basis of a new Palace of Westminster. Between 1176 and 1209, the most famous iteration of the London Bridge—the first stone bridge–was built on the site of several earlier wooden bridges—the first being

Roman. This bridge lasted 600 years and remained the only bridge across the River Thames until 1739. Because the passage across this one bridge was narrow and clogged with traffic, it was much quicker and easier for travelers to hire waterboatmen to row them across the river or to transport them up or down river.

The city played a pivotal role in the outcome of the struggle between Stephen and Maud between 1135 and 1154. King Stephen's reign was full of turmoil because of the conflict between him and King Henry's daughter, Empress Maud [Matilda]. Her father, Henry II had willed the throne to Matilda, but the barons opposed her. Both Stephen and Maud claimed the throne of England and tore the country apart in a nineteen-year-long cat and mouse drama of a civil war trying to get it. Maud was supported by her half-brother, Robert of Gloucester, who could not claim the throne because he was a bastard. Although the Londoners initially supported Maud, her flagrantly arrogant behavior when she occupied Westminster so angered the citizens that they revolted; and Maud was forced to flee London in disgrace and in fear for her life. However, her son, Henry III, succeeded her and perhaps is best known for having introduced the first pipes to carry waste effluvia in an underground sewage system in the thirteenth century.

It appears that nothing lasts forever. May, 1216 saw the last time that London was truly occupied by a continental armed force. It happened during the so-called First Barons' War. With the help of the citizens of the city, young Prince Louis VIII of France marched freely through the streets to St Paul's Cathedral, and while there was celebrated as the new ruler. The ease with which the "invasion" occurred was because the barons expected that Louis would free the English from the tyranny of the despised King John. Fate or the barons who had thrown their allegiance to the 29-year-old French prince were fickle. They decided to throw their support back to an English king when John died. It took several hundred years before London could shed itself of the heavy French cultural and linguistic influence which accompanied the Norman conquest. Over that time, the city was largely responsible for the development of Early Modern English.

In 1381, London was again invaded; this time during the Peasants' Revolt of 1381 led by Wat Tyler, A determined group of peasants stormed the Tower of London and executed the Lord Chancellor and the Lord Treasurer. The peasants then looted the city and set fire to numerous buildings. At the end of the "invasion" Tyler was stabbed to death by the Lord Mayor William Walworth in a confrontation at Smithfield, thus ending the revolt.

The London merchants supported Edward IV in his grab for the throne in 1461. In gratitude Edward knighted many of the merchants. In 1456–during the Wars of the Roses–there was strong support in London for the Yorkist cause. The Lancastrian Henry VI was forced to leave London for the Midlands, was later captured and kept for five years in the Tower of London. London was eventually re-captured by the Yorkist Edward IV in 1471, and Henry was executed. This gave the Yorkists the throne and ended the first phase of the Wars of the Roses.

The author fears that he has given somewhat short shrift to the spectacularly destructive fires and the horror of the pestilences that intermittently descended upon

London. We will consider one of each as examples. They occurred in 1665 and 1666 respectively in very close proximity of time.

The Great Plague of 1665-1666:

Disease was always a grim specter in filthy London with its polluted waterways. Even when cesspits and new sewers were built, the result was often not beneficial. Swamp gas [methane] generated in them often caught fire and exploded. People were trapped in their homes and were burned to death or suffocated. The cesspits and sewer tunnels were home to thousands of rats, fleas, and mountains of bacteria to foster and perpetuate disease.

London has been called "The City of the Dead" because of its many and terrible plagues. The Black Death of 1348 killed 40% of London's population. The pestilence of 1528 was so rapid and violent that thousands died in just five or six hours. In 1603, 30,000 Londoners were killed. No one ever seemed safe. During the Great Plague, thousands of corpses were hauled through the streets and dumped onto wet soil because there were not enough grave diggers to allow proper burials. More than a thousand corpses were dropped into the burial pit in Houndsditch. The carts were stacked so high with loose corpses that it was difficult to keep them from falling off. Some living people threw themselves into the burial pits out of unremitting despair. Citizens still alive cringed in fear in their homes when at night they heard the rumble of the dead cart. Some muttered that "There is no God, or God is a devil" in their despair. The burial area of Mount Mills remains waste ground to the present day.

At the height of the Great Plague, London saw almost no traffic except the dead carts. The river was deserted. Huge bonfires were set at in the main thoroughfares to create a miasmic smoke to ward off whatever it was that caused the disease and its spread. There was a constant nerve-wracking tolling of the bells for the dead. The plague persisted for so long that grass began growing in the dirt of the main thoroughfares. The infection rate abated a little during a short rainy period then returned with a vengeance. Records revealed that, on average, 18,317 died each week. As the disease began to wane, the records showed an encouraging number of only eight thousand dying each week of September. 1665

Signs went up that read, "Lord, have mercy on us." People tried to work to avoid starvation but many of them died during simple transactions in the market. Prisons were set up to quarantine victims from the relatively well. There were murders of the Watchmen tasked with finding and isolating the sick. The quarantining was so complete finally, that every house took on the character of a gaol. The London governor put out an ordinance that "all graves shall be at least six feet deep" which was roundly ignored for lack of able grave diggers. Beggars and prostitutes were driven from the city, as were conjurers, sorcerers, witches, quacks, and mountebanks. Many of the latter moved through the city selling curative "plague waters". Many ordinary Londoners went about wearing charms, philtres, pagan relics, exorcisms, amulets, zodiac signs, and the written phrase "*Abacadabra*". Street healers dispensed nutmeg and spiders wrapped in their own silk, Turkey and Rhubarb and Sulfuric Acid pills, Iron Jelloids, Zam Buk Ointment, Eno's Fruit Salt, Owbridge's Lung Tonic, Clarke's Blood Mixture, and Anderson's Scots Pills; many of the same treatments were still available as late as 1876. East side women and girls wore blue glass beads to ward away the contagion. Since London had taken on the aura of a prison, keys–as symbols against the quarantine and the pestilence–were sold in a brisk retail business.

Red crosses were placed on the doors of households in quarantine, a metaphorical reference to the idea that the disease was always smoldering. Old city records indicated that 68,596 people died during the epidemic. However, the people died faster than they could be counted, and their deaths could be recorded in either church or city records. Historians have found that the actual number of deaths almost certainly exceeded 100,000 out of a total London population of 460,000. Worldwide, it is estimated that over 100 million people out of an estimated world population of less than 600 million perished. The concept that rats or other vermin might be the vector of the disease did not come to mind until more than 100 years later.

The Great Fire of 1666:

The cause of the fire was debated from its onset to several centuries later, but the evidence was clear early on. Thomas Farriner of Pudding Lane had a contract to make ships' biscuit from unleavened bread for the navy. It was baked, sliced, and dried into hard tack, for the navy victualling office. He left his workplace for the night leaving his brick beehive oven with faggots in it still aglow to aid the next morning's baking. For the morning, he brought the faggots up to temperature—very hot as required for the type of biscuits he made. He lifted fresh faggots from the floor and placed them in the oven to add to the fire. When the temperature was right, he raked out the faggots leaving a hot oven to begin the day's baking.

An hour after midnight on Sunday, September 2, Farriner's manservant smelled smoke, found the ground floor so full of smoke that he could not breathe; but he managed to rouse the household. The situation was dire; the flames and smoke had made descending the stairs impossible; so, they all crawled out over the roof and across to the neighbor's window shouting as loud as they could to raise the alarm. The first victim of the great fire was the maidservant who was too afraid of heights to get onto the roof; so, she died in the smoke and flames. Community action was obligatory by law in London, and people poured out of their buildings to locate where the hew and cry was coming from.

There was a driving wind, and very quickly noise from the milling people, and the crackling flames which made coordinated effort difficult. Nonetheless, the aroused citizenry began throwing buckets of water on the already furious blaze. London in the early and mid 17th century was a tinder box of houses and other buildings made of old dry wood and plaster with thatched roofs that easily served as kindling and aggravated the fire spreading in the wind by jumping in large burning pieces from roof to roof. As the fire began to race downhill towards Thames Street, the Lord Mayor was summoned.

Experienced men demanded that the mayor give the order to demolish a line of houses ahead of the flames to create a fire brake, but the mayor refused because he did not have signatures of the owners.

He argued that the fire was hardly anything, and blustered, "A woman could piss it out," and left the scene to go back home to his bed.

Unfortunately for him, that sentence was recorded for eternity in the *Diary of Samuel Pepys* and would haunt him to his grave and earned him a place in history. Four hours later, 300 houses had burned to the ground and the great fire was racing down Fishstreet by London Bridge. The entire southeast quarter of the city was now under great threat, Its course along Thames Street included the old "paper" buildings on the wharves filled with barrels of pitch, tar, hemp, rosen, and flax, which produced a tower of fire. People living along the course of the wharves and the river began frantically to throw everything they had into boats. Soon there were not enough boats; so, they pitched lifetimes' sets of belongings into the fetid river.

The king was informed and fled the city along with many other privileged people. As he did, thousands of people were trapped on London Bridge and perished. The city had a plan to combat and to contain such fires. At the first outcry, people were to line up in double lines running from the river to the source of the fire. Bucket brigades were to haul water up one side and empty buckets back down for refilling on the other side. There were troubles with both the plan and its execution: there were not enough buckets; people soon became exhausted and could not continue; and besides, there were hardly any officers around to provide direction. Furthermore, although there was an improved set of fire fighting carts that were in the city, they were untried. They were set on sledskids and required twenty-eight very strong men or eight draft horses to haul the carts up the hills. There were not enough horses; the streets were too narrow, and the men were too slow and wore out before they got to the flames. The progress was excruciatingly slow and eventually the system proved to be useless.

Other devices were placed in church towers to be able to pull them down, but their use was too little and too late. Large iron scoops were available in places to throw large batches of dirt to quench the fire. Most of them were unworkable, too spread apart, and not located in strategic places; so, like the other devices, proved to be nearly useless. The city had invented large squirts—sort of large syringes—which could squirt a thin force of water some thirty feet. The mayor had used the squirts to disperse crowds as he moved through town in processions. They proved to be impractical, like spitting into the wind.

There was an aggravating human factor. Because of recent forays against and from the Dutch, mobs of people decided that the fire was a Dutch attack; and they ran about creating chaos, mob violence, looting, and impediment, to the already limited fire-fighting capacity of the beleaguered city. There was plenty of blame for humans, including for those who got rich by profiteering; but, in the end, it was decided that the strong easterly winds were the most defeating factor, "God's great bellows that fanned the flames." Samuel Pepys sat down and wept for his city. A contemporary diarist, John Evelyn, said, "I went againe to the ruins; for it was no longer a Citty."

In the end, the Great Fire destroyed the homes of 70,000 out of the 80,000 inhabitants of the city. But for all that fire, the traditional official death toll reported is extraordinarily low: just six verified deaths. To remember the fire, the city of London erected a monument. Six people have committed suicide by jumping off it, and two have fallen accidentally to their deaths—more than died in the fire itself. By the number of charred corpses later found by archeologists, the presumption is that thousands of unrecorded people perished without anyone seeing their ends.

On unfortunate result was that many ignorant Londoners clung to the idea that the fire was deliberated started by the Dutch as an act of war, one of the accumulating causes of what would become the first Anglo-Dutch war.

# CHAPTER TWENTY-ONE

# ONSET OF WAR BETWEEN THE *Z-LOUISA HENDRIKA* AND ENGLAND

IN THE YEAR OF OUR LORD, 1645, SECOND WEEK IN SEPTEMBER

Anneke and the two baby boys were blooming with good health. Their mother's abundant rich milk gave both wiggly creatures cottage rolls for legs, and round, cherubic smiling faces. The three were the pride, joy, and expectation for an abundant future, not only for their parents but for the 168 god fathers of the officers and crew. The boys now had names: Piet Pietzoon Van Brakel, and Zander Pietzoon Van Brakel, the latter for Anneke's father—which pleased her greatly. Jans and Piet were satisfied enough that the new family was secure and healthy and it was time–almost time posthumous–for them to depart from London with its diseased air and water and to move on to the execution of a long kept secret plan the captain and the first mate had been working on. The impetus for the plan was strengthened by the current spate of naval incidents occurring between the Dutch and English fleets, several of which had taken place too close to London for comfort. It had become the better part of wisdom to look like, talk like, and to act like, Londoners rather than Netherlanders; and it was time to go.

The *Z-Louisa Hendrika* was undergoing critical refurbishing to ready itself for its part in the grand plan hatched by the captain and first mate. The hull was being plated with wrought iron; the decks were reinforced with transversing heavy metal bands; and an additional row of gun ports was added to each side. The ship builders' and iron-workers' guilds were only too happy to supply additional cannon and iron ball ammunition. It took time and made the ship's officers nervous, but it did afford some time to get to know London.

First, they made tours to the richer part of the city. The prime real estate in London was the Strand, where many rich landowners built homes. Lawyers settled at the Temple and along Fleet Street. In the less affluent, but busier and more exciting parts of the city they explored among the streets which were named after the particular trade which practiced there. For example, Threadneedle Street was the tailor's district, Bread Street had bakeries, and on Milk Street cows were kept for milking. There was also a very active livestock market at Smithfield.

The post-medieval City of London was largely a place of decency, civility, and strong religious beliefs. But the post-medieval suburbs of London were another story, rife with prostitution, disease, and mass burials in Cross Bones Graveyard, which the touring seafarers took in. This south London graveyard had become known as the "single-woman's" cemetery because of its high concentration of sex worker graves. Since women of ill-repute could not be given a Christian burial, Cross Bones became an unofficial dumping ground for them and other poor people living in squalor outside of London. There was a red fence outside the graveyard densely decorated with small tributes in the form of flowers and ribbons and the names of those buried without ceremony. Most of the graves themselves were unmarked.

A group of pilgrim/knights traveled to Jerusalem in 1119 CE armed and following a strict and austere religious code of conduct which included swearing an oath of poverty, chastity, and obedience. They were not allowed to drink, gamble, swear, to kiss their mothers, or to wear pointy shoes. The knights grew in number, strength, and prestige. In 1185 the Temple Church in central London was consecrated and could be easily recognized by its unusual round nave. By the late 13th century, the Crusades were losing ground to the Saracens and were proving to be less profitable to the pope and King Philip IV of France. They turned against the order and coveted the Knights' treasures. The order was suddenly, unofficially, and forcibly, disbanded by Pope Clement V on Friday, October 13, 1307 CE on phony charges of heresy, corruption, homo-sexuality, financial corruption, devil-worshipping, fraud, spitting on the cross, and performing forbidden practices, and then officially disbanded by Pope Clement V 1312 CE.

Friday, the 13th, or Black Friday, has been an omen of bad luck until the present day.

During those years, the treasuries, buildings, and fleets of ships of the order, were plundered; the senior knights were tortured hideously to get them to confess to their crimes and to reveal their hidden treasure caches. The order's grand master Jacques de Molay was tortured every day for two years without giving in and was burned at the stake without yielding, confessing, or repenting.

In England, their lands were seized by the crown; and King Edward II used the land and buildings for law colleges that later became the Inns of Court. Piet was particularly fascinated by the dark side of London's history freely shared with the Hendrika's crew when they visited.

On Hart Street, they were escorted to the St. Olave Hart Street church. It was something of London in miniature, a layer cake of the past and present—boom piled on bust, war piled on plague, fire piled on farming. It was an obvious small hidden treasure of the city and the last resting place of a number of luminaries known to the Dutchmen (and woman). It was built on the site of the Battle of London Bridge from 1014. In the crypt they found a well where King Olaf II of Norway was said to have rallied his troops to help drive the Danish Vikings out of London permanently. The church was located next to the home of the 16th century royal spymaster, Sir Francis Walsingham, chief of Queen Elizabeth I's many spies.

Anneke wrote down the names of streets that were locations for various trades: Staining Lane (also the area for the Habardashers), Bread Street (also the place of the Salters), Clothworkers Street (earlier for both Fullers and Shearmen), Mark Lane (In the 15th century, the street was where basketmakers were allowed to 'mart' their wares), Cheapside Street (Market), Shoulder of Mutton Alley, Pudding Lane (Pudding=the entrails and organs that fall off butchers' carts as they headed from Eastcheap to the River Thames to dump their waste on barges.), Milk Street, Honey Lane, Poultry Lane, Old Fish Street, Frying Pan Alley

(Ironmongers), Booty Lane (?bootmakers, ?Viking booty), Threadneedle Street (needlemakers), and Petticoat Lane (actually meaning 'dung heap) to name enough to have made Anneke and "her men" tired.

They spent two days seeing monuments, memorials, and famous buildings, which were impressive but fairly boring. The squares in London were very many and beautiful, such as St. James, Soho, Bloomsbury, and Red Lion. Most of the rest of the city varied from tiresome to loathsome. They walked along rutted gravel roads where rubbish was thrown out of the windows onto the streets below, turds piled up on the riverbanks, street signs that advertised for prostitutes, walks up away from the docks where sweepers had to remove offal, dung, and other assorted unpleasantness, in order to make the street passable; and the smells beggared description. All the streets they walked on were atrociously covered in filth and dirty water that had been dumped from upper windows. Horse manure and human waste were also common to come across on the street.

The men were disturbed by the evidence of poverty and its effect on the city, but Anneke was dismayed. The common people were largely illiterate, ignorant, and superstitious. The majority of people during the era of Stuart Britain were poor, with a large portion living in terrible poverty. Only half the population could afford to eat meat every day. Life was simple and laborious. Many of the common people lived hand-to-mouth. The people who were employed did menial and often unsafe work as shoemakers, smithies, tailors, porters, saddlers, glovers, and chimney sweeps.

Everywhere on the streets, Anneke had to look at people selling a variety of objects–from mops to oysters to their own used clothing. She turned her head away from the sellers of human wares: gambling, tooth drawers, prostitution, and sale of pornographic drawings. However, she was intelligent; she had to recognize the "economics realities" of the 17th century in England because many women were reduced to working as prostitutes, actresses, coal miners, and jail keepers—the lowest of the low.

Vagrancy was everywhere. The poorest relied upon charity from family, neighbors, their fellow townspeople, and from begging–especially from begging. Angry and hungry soldiers—whose pay was often in arrears–were seen plundering ordinary people's stocks of food and livestock, leading to undernourishment or even starvation. Skinny wraiths roamed the streets looking for handouts to stay alive. Black slaves existed and were a hot issue during the early half of the century in London. Their labor made commodities available and cheap, but the idea of slavery being wrong was extremely prevalent; and Anneke was deeply saddened at the sight, having known slavery in her own life. No matter the protest, however, slavery continued until its abolition in 1833.

Anneke became increasingly grateful about her own situation—the equality and genuine affection in which she lived on the ship with "her men". In London, it was evident that sexual inequality was regarded as perfectly natural. Women were bound to obey their fathers and brothers, then their husbands, and then their sons. In general, women had very few rights and experienced oppression at the hands of the patriarch. The mother of the household would often have many children because not many children were able to survive early childhood. Women who were found to be too argumentative or radical could deal with cruel and humiliating public penalties.

Life expectancy during this period was generally a good deal shorter than in the present day. The child mortality rate was very high, and childbirth was a dangerous and potentially fatal event for the mother, too: if the trauma of birth didn't kill her, infection could days later. Between 10-25 women out of 1,000 perished as a result of childbirth in the Stuart period. 12-13% of children died during the first year of their lives, due complications such as diseases, physical accidents, and birth trauma. People in London died from largely preventable causes such as worms, plague, dysentery, or a rather disgusting ailment called "griping in the guts" [diarrhea combined with a terrible stomachache]. Personal hygiene was not high on the Stuart agenda and often all but impossible. Parasites such as fleas, lice, and intestinal worms, affected every social class in Stuart Britain. The average and poor families of the late 17th century England did not yet have the luxury of piped water, which created a rarity in bathing.

Anneke would never be able to erase fully from her mind the gory spectacles of blood sports including cock-fighting, dog fights, bear-baiting, and several public executions, they passed which were regarded by the jeering onlookers as popular entertainments.

One element of London that Anneke and "her men" enjoyed was to taste—for the first time—exotic foods like bananas, pineapples, and chocolate. Because of the expense, such foods were mainly for the upper class, which, apparently included the crew of the *Z-Louisa Hendrika*. Coffee and tea had become so popular that the first coffeehouses had opened. The upper classes tended to see them as veritable dens of political dissent and intrigue, but the lower and middle classes flocked in all day, every day.

Coffee was considered a man's drink, and women were not welcome in coffeehouses. Tea—on the other hand—was regarded as more of an aristocratic ladies' drink; hot chocolate—which also appeared for the first time in Britain during the 17$^{th}$ century—was a luxury enjoyed by both sexes in the upper echelons of society. Anneke—being no shrinking violet—enjoyed all three and acquired a lifelong taste for them.

The war between England and the *Z-Louisa Hendrika* began as the Dutch people began to wend their way back to the docks and their ship.

## THE HISTORY:
## FASHION IN THE 17TH CENTURY

As is the case at the present time, there were avid fashionistas in the 17th century, and London was the place to look for the latest styles and trends. It was a complex, ever-changing, and unforgiving world, especially for upper-class women. For a woman to make a serious fashion faux pas would quickly attract scorn. In those critical times you literally might even get driven out of town.

In all periods and places in recorded history there has been resistance to change and protests (often feigned, perhaps) about the changes in styles, particularly those of women. An early 17th century pamphlet, entitled, *A Treatise Against Painting and Tincturing of Men and Women*, that "once a yeere at least" an Englishwoman "would faine see London, tho' when she comes there, she have nothing to doe, but to learn a new fashion". The hostility may or may not have been warranted, but comments about women coming to the capital in order to view the latest trends were accurate. London was rapidly becoming the financial, military, commercial, and fashion center, of the Western world.

A major attraction of London was the wide and diverse range of shopping opportunities for the well-to-do. By Queen Elizabeth's reign in the second half of the 16th century, merchants were importing a wide range of different fabrics, dyes, and textiles which meant that clothes were becoming more diverse, colorful, and alluring, for shoppers. Most of the linen and lace came from Italy and the Low Countries; but by the end of the 17th century, more exotic commodities such as East Indian chintz and calicos became available.

Women had a selection of fabrics to choose from and were able to purchase a range of expensive accessories as well. These were both decorative and practical. Muffs not only kept hands warm, but functioned as substitute handbags to store handkerchiefs, money, and scent. Face masks and hoods became popular in the second and third decades of the century, and that enabled women to move around the busy city without being recognized. Many women were able to distinguish themselves from other competing women by personalizing their clothes by adding laces, ribbons, and flowers, or by embroidering designs and patterns.

Clothes could be purchased from great many different places throughout the busy populous city. Wealthy women–such as the wives of London citizens who lived in the great manors–shopped at the Royal Exchange and the New Exchange. For them and the rest of the women of the town and who came from without, there were tailors, shoemakers, embroiderers, glove-makers, lace makers, furriers, and milliners, to be found throughout the City and in neighboring Westminster.

As the clothing industry developed, more ready-to-wear clothes became available at cheaper prices for the common women of the city. Either by choice or necessity, many women continued to make their own clothes or purchased second-hand ones, often from other women who were prominent in the trade. Many of these second-hand items could have been stolen and the theft untraceable, and shoplifting by women became a growing problem in the later decades of the 17<sup>th</sup> century. Even law-abiding women did not have to purchase all the clothes they acquired. Large numbers of women worked as domestic servants and were given work clothes by their employers—often paid for out of their wages. Altruism was not a common virtue in The City. Young people gave and received clothes as gifts when courting; elderly women left items of clothing and textiles to female relatives and friends in their wills; and poor women received donations of clothes via their parish if they were eligible for poor relief. The truly poor or those of the wrong color, religion, employment status, and those lacking adequate soap or clean water wore hand-me-downs, and finally descended into rags when they hit the bottom economic strata.

London women were believed to be more fashion-conscious and better-dressed than their sisters in the provinces, and were considered to be paragons to be emulated. When visiting, they took all their best apparel with them; so, that their friends in the country, may see all their finery and be jealous. Travelers from other countries also commented favorably on the fashionable styles of London metropolitan women. In the later 16<sup>th</sup> century an Italian lady of means observed that women wore "dresses laced up to the neck, which make them appear very graceful" and a German Duke described the London ladies as "magnificently appareled". Part of the appeal to him was that some of the women he saw wore "gowns after the old German fashion". In 1662, a Dutchman walking in Hyde Park wrote that "one can see here the most beautiful ladies' dresses".

In London, especially, wearing appropriate clothes for the occasion was very important. Working women needed to have a set of practical informal clothes for everyday wear but aspired to have particularly nice outfits to wear on special occasions. In his *Diary*, Samuel Pepys wrote in 1660 that his wife, Elizabeth, even changed her clothes before she went to see her husband and their friend at The Miter, a tavern in Wood Street. Many women would refuse to go out if they believed they lacked appropriate clothes to go "a visiting". Friends and family members often pitched in to lend a hood, a scarf, or a muff, to make up for the deficit.

In London—as perhaps nowhere else to the degree Londoners did—people noticed and commented if women wore anything unusual or distinctive. Neighbors were quick to take notice if a woman stepped out in her "best apparel", and she would be questioned in a friendly way as to where she was going. Women also dressed well if they had to appear in court, the theater, or church, and endeavored to create a good competitive impression even if they had to borrow the outfit. Weddings were then—as they are now—frightfully expensive. Weddings were opportunities for celebration and extravagance, and most fathers-of-the bride knew they could not risk being seen to be a miser.

As in all places and times, one of the main reasons young single women wanted to dress well was to attract the attention of suitors and potential husbands. London was full of such desiring young women. The girl might leave from the suburbs with somewhat limited apparel and return "very well appareled"—and might even bring back with her a proper man to support her future. There was an advice book in the 1670s for the many young women who wished to apply for positions as companions of gentlewomen. The author commented that there was "a kind of privilege in youth for wearing fashionable clothes" and that dressing well would "add more beauty", and, parenthetically, a better chance for getting a good placement and a better future. Dressing well helped women to find paid employment. The women who worked in the shops in the Exchange were deemed to be well dressed, and a gentlewoman named Elizabeth James took on one young woman as a servant because she was "a pretty young wench, and handsomely "appareled".

Dress mattered to older London women too, of course since it demonstrated their status and authority. Married women wore distinctive scarves and hoods. When a 16th century sheriff's wife had her portrait painted she wore a fur-trimmed velvet gown to show off her *ascent* in London society. In 1659, Goody Marstone was given twelve shillings by the vestry of the parish of St Benet Paul's Wharf so that she could provide clothes for the orphaned daughter of her friend Goody Tessy to help the girl to get a place as a domestic servant. The vestrymen thought this to be a worthwhile investment, ensuring that in the long run there would be one less poor woman for them to provide for.

Throughout the 17th century, particular decades witnessed fashion crazes. In the 1610s women wore doublets and broad-brimmed hats, both of which were considered to be very masculine items of clothing. In the 1690s, complex top-knot hairstyles–incorporating large quantities of ribbons–were all the rage. As an eternal principle, older generations disapproved of dress, speech, and mannerisms, of the next younger genera-tion. Moralists were quick to condemn new trends. In 1619, John Williams preached a sermon before King James I on abuses of apparel. Further along, into the 1690s many ballads–the pop songs of the age–condemned the fashion for top-knots, arguing that young women would turn to prostitution in order to afford the new hairstyle.

Legal records reveal that London prostitutes at the upper end of the vice trade–the early modern equivalent of escorts–were particularly well dressed. These women were given specific outfits in order to attract clients, and many received clothes as payment in kind for their services. An Elizabethan bawd, one Mistress Hibbens, had "divers suits of apparels" including "silk gowns of several colors" which were worn by the girls who worked for her. But in practice, the clothes of noblewomen and the wives of wealthy citizens were not always significantly different from those of highclass prosti-tutes. "Dressing like a whore" constituted one of the most egregious of social faux pas. Early modern women tried to strike a balance between being fashionable and attrac-tive, but not showing too much flesh. In 1628 Catherine Baker was brought before the church courts for defaming Christian Nevell as a "button-smock whore", an insult which suggests that Catherine thought Christian's outfit was too revealing.

Oddly enough, cross-dressing was not especially unusual. Before the Restoration, male actors played the female roles; and some women chose to wear men's clothing, either to be fashionable–as a reflection of their sexuality–or because it enabled them to walk the city streets in disguise without being harassed by men. A daring new fash-ion term referred to as "Romantic negligence" arose for having one's portrait painted in *undress*, wearing a loosely fastened gown called a *nightgown* over a voluminous che-mise, with tousled curls.

# CHAPTER TWENTY-TWO

# THE FIRST BATTLE IN THE WAR BETWEEN THE *Z-LOUISA HENDRIKA* AND ENGLAND

IN THE YEAR OF OUR LORD, 1645, FOURTH WEEK IN SEPTEMBER

The officers and crew of the *Z-Louisa Hendrika* finally tired of their tour of London with all its sights, energy, and smells, and were ready to re-board the ship. The garrison security crew sent word that the ship's cargo area was empty and ready for the plan as laid out by the captain and first mate. Everyone was anxious enough to board the ship that they moved quickly down Bishopsgate Road which followed onto Grace Church Road which lead directly to the dock. They walked past an official government wall poster pasted late the night before, "*Hear ye and heed all London Citizens: Parliament has today passed an act whereby there shall be laws barring the Dutch from involvement in English sea trade.*"

As they grew close to the wharf and dock area, they began to hear raucous yelling and metal banging on metal. Jans sent an able seaman to ascertain what was going on.

Seaman Jenks reported back, "Cap'n, Sir, there's considerable fussin' on the docks. I regret to report that it is in close quarters to the *Z-Louisa Hendrika*."

"A mob, a riot?" Jans asked.

"I'd call it that."

"Soldiers or riff-raff?"

"Mix of up-town swells and slum low life."

"Weapons?"

"Nothin' serious. Pikes, a musket or two, swords, clubs, brooms, and quite a few hay rakes. No sign of bein' organized or official. No police presence neither."

Jans huddled with Piet for a few minutes, then announced, "We'll keep on. Seems things are getting ugly in the town and it's directed against us Netherlanders. Keep your powder dry and your swords loose in their scabbards."

They were more careful now but still made good time. Two men were assigned as scouts and kept Jans and Piet apprised of the fluid situation of the docks. When they got to Thames Street, Jans dispatched a third of the men to run ahead to the exact mooring dock where the ship was rocking in the gravy-like water.

The men aboard readied the anchor windlass in the forecastle on the main deck to haul the anchors in as soon as the crew came into view on the dock. One man stood by each wharf hawser to release it when the men, Anneke, and the children, were safely on deck.

The crowd sensed the activity on board and became more angry and agitated. Jans and Piet walked briskly in front of the tense sailors—eighty-four of them. Anneke and the twins walked behind giant Andries in the protected middle of the marchers. The curses, blasphemies, and insults, to and about the Dutch rose by several decibels the closer the ship's company came to the ship and to the riled crowd. Children ["mudlarks"] on the mudflats stopped their scavenging in the muck to watch the excitement.

"It's a good day for a Dutchman to die!" yelled the putative leader of the mob, a grizzled–and obviously drunk–wharf rat.

Jans decided that this was the moment to make his declaration: "You are illegals and criminals. More importantly, you are no match for my regular navy fighters, [a bit of an exaggeration], and they will fire on my command. Back away, you blackards; or you'll feel the edge a Dutch blade."

His voice was deep, conversational in loudness; and he never blinked an eye. Someone in the ragtag mob made obscene comments about Anneke and her babies and started to advance at the ranks surrounding her.

Andries said to Anneke, "You stay stock still and right here. I am goin' to go reason with the man."

He pushed through the six-deep ranks of his own men and strode purposefully until he stood directly in the blustering man's face. The mobster drew his skinning knife and made a lunge at Andries, who stood head and shoulders and 150 pounds heavier than the little man trying to be a big man.

As the knife came forward, Andries stepped deftly to the side and put his hand around the man's skinny wrist. Andries's hand around the stick narrow wrist was as big as a ham. He gave a quick jerk on the wrist, breaking it. The man howled and struggled to extract himself without Andries paying any attention to him. The giant bent forward, picked up the challenger and raised him high over his head. Then, he made a straight leap in the air and heaved the mob challenger over the heads of the first six rows of followers. The mobster landed head on into two of his fellows and bowled them over. The skinny man's neck snapped like a breaking branch; one of the men on the ground was unconscious; and the other had blood gushing from an obviously smashed nose and upper jaw. He tried to scream but just gurgled, choking on his own blood.

Andries stood stolidly before the crowd below him and gave them a look of utter disdain. He turned and walked sedately back to Anneke. After a minute of uneasy pause, the crowd began to beat swords against pikes, iron rods against metal pots, and stamping their feet. They surged forward.

Piet blew his bos'n's pipe, and every sailor turned to face the disorganized hooligans. The outermost ranks of sailors took one long step forward bringing them close enough to their noisome enemies that they could smell the halitosis of the braggarts. All of them on one accord made a single full-throated guttural Dutch battle holler.

"*Wahr di buer, die garde kumt*" [Beware, peasants, the guards are coming], stamped their feet in unison on the deck twice, dropped the muzzles of their muskets to aim at the chest of the agitators on the front row, and began a deliberate slow march directly into the mob.

Nobody in that mob had anything to gain, and everything to lose; so, what with Andries, the giant's, demonstration, and the sailors' orderly martial advance, the front ranks of the mob broke. The sailors hollered again, and suddenly the rioters dispersed in a disorderly chaos.

The ship's crew, Anneke, and the god-children, walked briskly and purposefully up the gang plank and onto the main deck in good order. The plank was raised; the fore and aft anchors came clanking onto the deck dripping filthy sea water; and the hawser lines dropped into the Thames. The sails were all unfurled, and the *Z-Louisa Hendrika* turned out towards the middle of the crowded Thames. Heedless of the outcries of the other ships courteously waiting their turn in the single-file queue, she made a new sea lane and began racing along against the current coming dangerously close to colliding at times, but guaranteeing that the other ships moved over. The Dutch ship broached no interference and cleared the estuary in record time.

Anneke's only comment, uttered with her winning smile was, "Oh, look, there are groves of green willow and hawthorn trees and fields covered with Queen Anne's lace and cow parsley. Look, see the swans, green-head mallards, and black-headed coots, paddling through the reeds!"

Her very youthful, girlish, and exuberant, exclamation caused the anxious sailors to laugh uproariously and to clap each other on the back. Her joyful outburst spoke of their successful escape and of the success awaiting on the north coast.

In half an hour they were on the open sea headed north with a welcoming clean smell of saltwater coming from the unpolluted ocean. They had a brisk nor-noreast tail wind and made good time. They kept well out to sea where the wind was good, and they had less to fear from her majesty's navy or from English privateers.

When they were north enough to be near the Cleveland coast of North Yorkshire, Jans turned hard aport and put the ship into the Rosedale Port near the middle of the North York Moors. They knew the area by making out the rows of domestic properties and individual houses on the top of the cliff. They took on perishable supplies and chatted up the locals in the pubs to ascertain if they had received any notice of raiding by Dutch ships. There had been no such news. Jans bade the mayor goodbye and a hearty thanks for the town's graciousness, and the *Z-Louisa Hendrika* left the port for Robin Hood's Bay. They moored their ship among large numbers of barges filled with heavy bags of alum powder.

The ship's officers reconnoitered the large village of Great Ayton which was located five miles south-west of Guisborough, on the banks of the River Leven in North Yorkshire. Great Ayton stood on the edge of the North York Moors. The village showed its prosperity by its paved streets and well-maintained buildings. Large numbers of men in work clothes wearing pointy, wide-brimmed capotain hats for protection from the sun labored to unload river barges packed with bags of alum into sea barges waiting in the bay.

Jans and Piet rented a skiff and two rowers for the five-mile trip upriver to Guisborough. There, they saw the early parts of preparation of alum from open pit mines in the Cleveland hills to the milling process in the middle of the city. The two men were inquisitive, pretending to be buyers from Belgium looking for a reliable source of the profitable powder. They learned all they needed to know: security was skimpy, only local boys on guard wielding clubs. There was no constabulary as such and no British military guard or ships in Robin Hood' Bay. The choices for the Dutchmen were two: attack Guisborough and force the laborers to truck or float the bagged alum to the bay, or simply gain control of Great Ayton and dragoon workers there. The choice was obvious, and the two Dutch privateers headed back to the *Z-Louisa Hendrika* with a plan.

Twelve good men stayed on the ship for security and to be able to sail out of harm's way should Jans's and Piet's plans run afoul of their hopes. Anneke and the boys were secured in the captain's quarters and locked inside over her vehement protests. The remainder of the ship's crew divided roughly into halves with one half responsible for securing each of the towns—Great Ayton and Guisborough. The Dutch sailors/privateers exited the ship stealthily at two bells of the middle watch. The sky was pitch black from overhanging clouds, and Great Ayton was devoid of all artificial light to allow the tired workers their full sleep.

Jans and his crew surrounded the town and placed armed sentries at frequent regular intervals. Piet's men purloined skiffs and rowed upstream to Guisborough and did much the same thing there. The plan was to wait until first light and the clanging of four bells that marked the start of the morning watch. The fog and clouds cleared; and it looked to be a bright warm day, a perfect setting for a large project of thievery.

The history of mutual aggression, theft, piracy, smuggling, and kidnapping, between the inhabitants of North Yorkshire and the Flemish was long and inimitable to any feelings of friendship, or expectation of security, from such predation. So, it came as no great surprise when the villagers' day started with the loud clanging of four bells from the ship and the shouting of angry Dutch voices yelling, *"Wahr di buer, die garde kumt."*

The doors of homes and strategic buildings crashed in, and the sleeping Yorkshiremen abruptly awakened to frowning armed guards having invaded their privacy and lives. The men and women were herded roughly into the towns' squares and made to stand quietly at attention. All the children were driven crying and upset into the two largest churches and held under guard as a message to their parents.

The same scenario was repeated in Guisborough. Jans and Piet and their men separated the men and strong women from the women and children. The women who did not appear to be fit enough for heavy labor were interned in the church, given food and water, and stern warnings by two heavily armed and scowling Dutch sailors who stayed with them.

The Guisborough men, strong women, and older boys began loading skiffs with large bags and sending them down river. It was exhausting work, and Jans had to devise shifts to allow periodic rests which prolonged the already quite inefficient process. At the Ayton end of the river, the impressed English men, women, and boys worked quickly to hasten the time when the accursed Flemish would be gone. The *Z-Hendrika Louisa's* holds began slowly to fill up with closely stacked sacks of precious coarse grey powder. Piet was in charge of the Ayton end. He recognized that the citizens were approaching exhaustion; so, he called a stop.

He ordered his sailors, "Get them into the shade. They are of no worth to us if they can't work. Send some women and girls for food and water."

The citizens collapsed in clumps and rapidly fell asleep. The guarding sailors saw to it that every one of them ate and drank their fill.

"Push the water," Piet ordered. "Dry, overheated workers can't keep going."

The rest period was about half an hour, and the sailors drove the impressed and unwilling workers back to their thankless task. By late afternoon after a great deal of unpleasant prodding and another rest period, the holds were nearly full. The last of the full skiffs from Guisborough tied up at the Ayton quay and were in the final loading process when the trouble started.

From what seemed to be nowhere, English long bowmen fired deadly arrows into the entirely unsuspecting Dutch sailors felling four on the Guisborough wharf before they could begin to mount a defense and to make an orderly retreat into the remaining empty skiffs and to push out into the main flow of the river. The towns people began to cheer and to throw rocks at the departing Dutchmen. Half-way down river to Great Ayton, the skiffs were ambushed from the banks of a narrow stretch of the river. Two more sailors sustained grievous wounds, but the worst injury was sustained by Jans Corren. Blood seeped from around the shaft of hardwood arrow embedded deep in his mid-chest. His breathing became uneven and coarse. One of the sailors attempted to extract the arrow, but the pain was too severe; and Jans ordered him off.

"I'm a goner, anyway. Let me die in peace. But–before I do–get Piet to come to the skiff with all the men to hear my last will and testament."

The sailors devised crude—but fairly effective—shields from pieces of wood and heavy cloth found on the bottoms of the skiffs and were successful in warding off most of the arrows, which were now being fired from a distance which was becoming out of range for the Englishmen.

Jans was gasping for breath when they tied up in Great Ayton. A sailor ran to get Piet.

"Cap'n's had a mortal wound, First Mate. His dyin' wish is to have you and the men come to hear his last words. Better get a move on; he can't last much longer.

Jans's chest wound was putting out more blood and now bubbles of air. He was coughing up a hemopneumo froth from his mouth and nostrils. He was beginning to turn grey and was in severe pain.

Piet sent five men to herd all the towns people into the church and to stay with them as additional guards. He ran hard to get to Jans. It did not take a ship's surgeon to be able to tell Piet that his captain and friend was rapidly sloughing his mortal coil.

"Can I help?..." Piet started to ask.

"Let me talk. Don't have much longer. Go to my wife in Brussels if she's still there. Give her my share. Piet–my young friend–you are now captain and owner of the *Louisa*. Save the men. Share equally..." he began to cough interfering with his ability to talk. "Give me a Christian... burial... at..."

And Captain Jans Fokkenzoon Corren was dead.

The captain was taken back to the ship, and Piet and the crew went aboard giving heed to look out for bowmen or angry citizens who might have gotten enough courage to attack.

The British had a local militia—hence the longbowmen—but no means of communicating to the Royal Navy in time to chase the Flemish pirates (or Dutch privateers, depending on who is talking). The *Z-Hendrika Louisa* was under full sail on the North Sea headed SSW towards Amsterdam. Piet halted sailing in a calm sea roughly midway to conduct a proper and undisturbed burial at sea for their departed captain.

The body was carried into his stateroom and laid out on the conference table. The ship's surgeon, Dr. Abraham Liebowitz, saw to the care and washing of Captain Corren's last remains. The sailmaker–Seaman Hendrik Jewkes–helped sew him into his bed clothes and put him on a piece of clean sail canvas. He expertly sewed the edges together, tied a fifty-pound ballast to his ankles, and closed the shroud over Jans's face. Piet was very surprised to see Seaman Jewkes take a very large needle and heavy waxed twine and run it from one side of the facial covering, through the captain's nose, out the other side and tied it with a Celtic sailor's knot to make it doubly secure.

"Why did you do that, Jewkes?" Piet asked, willing to confess his ignorance of some at-sea burial customs.

"It is an old custom, Sir," Jewkes offered, "to make sure the presumed dead man is really dead, I suppose."

"It would likely wake me from the dead," Piet said and shook his head.

It was Piet's first formal duty as captain of the *Z-Louisa Hendrika* to conduct his predecessor's Christian burial at sea.

Six men carried the shrouded corpse up from the captain's chamber and placed him reverently on a wide plank supported on the inward side by a gunpowder barrel and on the seaward side by the gunwale. The pall bearers took one step back and stood at attention.

Piet and Anneke took their places facing the prepared body in its heavy covering with the crew standing quietly, heads bowed across from them. Anneke held her boys' hands and they behaved perfectly—a remarkable feat for two children with the energy of hummingbirds.

Anneke held a Dutch *Statenbijbel* [the first translation of the *Bible* from the original Hebrew, Aramaic and Greek, languages into Dutch, ordered by the Synod of Dordrecht 1618], and Piet held an English *Book of Common Prayer*.

"My friend and shipmates, it is our sad duty to say farewell to our captain who has seen us through triumphs and trials for the past three years. Jans Fokkenzoon Corren was a good man, one of the very best. He will be mourned and remembered."

He read from John 11:25-26, Job 19: 25-26, I Timothy 6:7, and Job 1:21. Anneke offered a sincere and emotional prayer about good life and life beyond death, with an additional several scriptures included. She gave her prayer in clear, melodic Dutch.

Then, Piet quoted from the *Book of Common Prayer*, "'We therefore commit his body to the deep, to be turned into corruption, looking for the resurrection of the body, when the sea shall give up her dead, and the life of the world to come through Our Lord Jesus Christ; who at His coming, shall change our vile body, that it may be like his glorious body, according to the mighty working, whereby he is able to subdue all things to himself.'

"I am a man of the sea, and I wish my comrade, friend, and captain, 'Bon Voyage'. May he feed the whales, be meat for the fishes of the sea, and be welcomed to the deep as he settles into the best, deepest, and widest, grave in the world."

He saluted Captain Corren; Anneke said, "*Soepel zeilen en God zijn met u*" [Smooth sailing and God be with you] then the cannoneers shot off a thirty-gun salute as the pallbearers slowly lowered him into the moving waters. The entire crew watched as he sank away from sight.

As the ship made its way back towards the Flemish port city of Bruges, Piet and Anneke shared their memories of the voyage and of their dearly departed friend.

"What should our first efforts be when we arrive in port, do you think, Piet?"

"I have given it some thought, and I think our first piece of business should be to settle our debts. I have one on the wharf; and we—as the new owners of this fine ship and captains of its crew—need to find Mrs. Corren and give her the captain's share of the profits. That goes for the investor's share for my father who made it possible for me to be a part of the crew and to find you. I owe him dearly. I sorrow that your family was taken into slavery and lost to the world of decent people. I wish I could have met them, and I wish that I could share with them our good fortune, my love."

"Indeed, we must do all of that; and then, we must move into the future. I have the feeling that is our century, and our future will blossom with it. Let us leave the past in the past and toast to new beginnings, my dear husband."

## -THE END-